Acclaim for

HYBRID

"*Hybrid* takes the world and characters of *Enhanced* to a new level. Packed with higher stakes, greater depth, and a setting that lets your imagination run wild, *Hybrid* takes you on an adventure you won't easily forget."

— NOVA MCBEE, award-winning and bestselling author of the Calculated series

"Enthralling! *Hybrid* is pure adrenaline and twisting suspense that left me breathless. It was everything I wanted in a sequel and more. Kade's immersive world building, innovative technology, and gripping characters make this a story you won't forget!"

— S.F. RHOADS, award-winning author of The Colliding Line series

"*Hybrid* is a wild ride begging you to read more. Kade draws you into a lush world, filled with delectable details, cultural nuances, and plot twists that will keep you guessing until the end. I eagerly await the next chapter in Urban's journey!"

— CANDICE YAMNITZ, author of *Unbetrothed*

"Once again, we put on our XR suits and dive into Kade's world of high tech and genetic manipulation, where not everything is as it seems. With heartbreaking betrayals, plot twists that keep you guessing, and expanded worldbuilding, *Hybrid* will have you on the edge of your seat from page one. Yet sifting through all the incredible technology, Kade reminds the reader that family and friendships are what truly keeps us grounded to reality."

— AMBER KIRKPATRICK, author of *Until the Rising* and *Unleashed*

"*Gattaca* meets *Hunger Games* in this continuation of Candace Kade's action-packed story. With vivid imagery and fantastic science fiction elements, I felt like I had been transported into a high tech future. Loved *Hybrid* and can't wait for book three!"

– MORGAN L. BUSSE,
award-winning author of The Ravenwood Saga and Skyworld series

"I love it when I can hand a book to my preteens and teens and know that it will be an exciting read, yet also clean. *Hybrid* is a heart-pounding continuation of the Enhanced series, where Lee Urban's pursuit of truth amidst danger and chaos keeps readers on the edge of their seats. As she joins the elite Dragons AI team, tensions between Enhanced and Naturals escalate, threatening society's fragile balance. Urban's quest for her origins and adoption secrets adds depth to the story, making *Hybrid* a thought-provoking read that challenges beliefs and leaves a lasting impact. Don't miss this gripping addition to the Enhanced series for an unforgettable adventure!"

– TRICIA GOYER, USA Today bestselling author of 90 books, including *A Secret Courage*

"An electrifying tale of genetics and identity, where the search for family intertwines with high-stakes action. Kade weaves a thrilling story of one teen's exploration of the bonds of family in a genetically enhanced world. *Hybrid* is a gem of a story!"

– ELLEN MCGINTY, author of *Saints and Monsters*

"Slick and intelligent! Imaginative worldbuilding lays the groundwork for pulse-pounding action in *Hybrid*. Kade's real-world experience with Asian culture beautifully imbues *Hybrid* and makes for a riveting, incredible read. Hop on for this thrill ride!"

– RONIE KENDIG, award-winning author of The Droseran Saga

"*Hybrid* is a captivating second installment in Kade's science fiction trilogy. The immersive and utterly unique setting is full of rich details and fascinating technology. With plenty of mystery, thrilling action, and relatable characters, the story kept me eagerly turning pages. I will be impatiently awaiting the next book!"

– B.L. DEAN, author of the Shades of Starlight series

"On the heels of self-discovery in *Enhanced*, Lee Urban plunges into another high-stakes adventure in *Hybrid*. Brimming with imaginative yet familiar new worlds, and super-fun tech, the search for the hybrid is on. Urban's dogged determination, the support of a uniquely talented cast, and unexpected twists and turns make this book irresistible. Dive into *Hybrid* at your own risk–it's going to keep you up late!"

– E.A. HENDRYX, author of *Suspended in the Stars*

HYBRID

HYBRID

THE HYBRID SERIES | BOOK 2

CANDACE KADE

Published by Enclave Publishing, an imprint of Oasis Family Media, LLC

Carol Stream, Illinois, USA.
www.enclavepublishing.com

ISBN: 979-8-88605-102-5 (printed hardcover)
ISBN: 979-8-88605-103-2 (printed softcover)
ISBN: 979-8-88605-105-6 (ebook)

Cover design by Kirk DouPonce, www.DogEaredDesign.com
Typesetting by Jamie Foley, www.JamieFoley.com

Printed in the United States of America.

For *Baobei.*
We may have taken a while to find each other,
but you were worth the wait.

URBAN AIMED STRAIGHT FOR THE DRAGON. The creature's bulbous eyes and enormous fangs grew larger as she pulled hard on the throttle of her motorcycle.

Then the projection flickered over, engulfing her in cherry-blossom red and tangerine orange before the virtual creature passed behind. In its wake, the scent of wet animals, fresh manure, and street food became sharper, contaminating New Beijing's normally pristine air. The clash of cymbals, upbeat drums, and hum of chattering people roared around her.

Urban tuned them out, focusing on the pulsing green arrow overlaid on reality which was guiding her. She couldn't be late her first time back home.

Overhead, virtual red *hongbao* envelopes and soft snowflakes drifted down. Further up in the sky, projected fireworks boomed and flashed, illuminating the evening with a dazzling display of color.

Teeth chattering, Urban wished she had worn her smart suit. Having spent the last two weeks in the Outskirts, she didn't have hers, for fear of attracting attention from the Naturals who only had outdated models. Swerving, she narrowly avoided hitting a Super clad in ancient armor and carrying a stun club.

She accelerated again, weaving past a Flyer with glowing

neon-green wings and an Inventor surrounded by an impenetrable wall of hovering drones. The bots pulsed and formed words in the sky and drifted around the Inventor like waves of the sea.

Urban ducked to avoid them.

Flames shot skyward from a woman wearing a colorful mask, and the frigid air grew warm from the fire. The Artisan dipped her head behind her arm, and when her face reappeared, she wore a different mask. The crowd clapped.

A Camo shimmered into view out of nowhere directly in front of Urban. She slammed on the brakes, her tires skidding loudly and the scent of burning rubber assaulting her nose. The Camo, oblivious, waved at the crowd, then disappeared again.

Huffing a breath, Urban slowed her speed to a crawl as she passed an Artisan dancing on stilts, then wove her way through an Inceptor, Giver, and Aqua, completing the eight gene pools.

Year of the Horse! a virtual sign projected. Up ahead, horses came into view and the stench of fur and manure returned, stronger this time.

The watching crowd pointed. A father lifted a little girl with a tail and pink hair up onto his shoulders. A Super boy, already as tall as a full-grown man, fed the *Balikun* sugar cubes.

Mothers bounced babies while chatting with friends. Fathers handed out red *hongbaos* to elated children. Couples linked arms and leaned into each other for warmth. A lightness filled the air and joy permeated every smile.

A hollowness welled up in Urban's chest at the sight.

She activated the hands-free setting on her motorcycle and pulled her out-of-place leather jacket closer around her. *I'll never belong like them.* Her vision blurred.

In front of her, a bot with a laser poleax shocked a horse as it fought wildly against its restraints. These ones had been experimental breeds the Asian Federation deemed too dangerous for rider or environment.

They were one of a kind–the last of their kind.

An Enhanced blue *Yunnan* Aqua racer reared up, nearly shaking free the water bowl which encased its head and allowed it to stay ashore without suffocating. It snarled, displaying razored teeth.

A Tibetan horse bucked and whinnied, sending pulsing speckles across its body dancing. It stood five hands taller than the other horses and flung its mane, sparking with electricity. The crowd backed away from it, eyeing the horse, and sparks, warily.

Urban felt like these freak-show horses on display. Ever since the Games, when her sosh had skyrocketed, she'd felt even more out of place: surrounded by a sea of people, and yet utterly alone. Even in the Outskirts she hadn't fit in. Now, returning to the Metropolis, she remembered how much she stuck out here too.

I don't belong anywhere.

Belong. The word ached in her thoughts like an old wound. *Once the hybrid is found, I'll be able to live in the Metropolis without hiding. But it feels a million kilometers away.*

Urban ducked under acrobats swinging from bars, flipping in midair before locking hands and flying back to safety. They were one slip, one miscalculated swing away from plummeting to their deaths.

How similar to Urban's own precarious act she traipsed every day, pretending to be Enhanced.

As grateful as she was to her adoptive parents for taking her and her sister in, sometimes she wondered what things would have been like if they'd been adopted by a Natural family and lived in the Outskirts instead.

Urban turned down a street full of parked vehicles and free of the parade and crowds. But she couldn't free herself from her own thoughts. She made her way toward one of the tallest buildings at the Metropolis's center, mind racing faster than her electric motorcycle.

There had been news that her birth parents might still be alive. The trouble was, the lead was in the Western Federation. Her adoptive parents would never let her leave the Asian Federation to follow it. Not to mention, they'd seemed less than enthused about tracking Urban's birth parents down. Every time Urban brought it up, they redirected the conversation.

Urban's bike skidded on a patch of ice. She nearly wiped out before regaining control and focusing on the road.

Around her, this part of the Metropolis was silent and mostly empty. Bright paper lanterns dangled overhead, illuminating the streets in chili-pepper red. Jumbotrons virtually displayed the parade and a commentator's voice echoed loudly through the street.

"The 2124 Annual Lunar New Year Parade is bigger and better than ever before. With every Gene Pool Award winner represented, and over one hundred different animal species, it's no wonder that New Beijing citizens have turned out in record numbers."

It's no wonder it smells.

Urban bolted down another road. A prioritized ping notification popped in her retina display, but she blinked it away as she concentrated on her augmented maps.

". . . this year, thousands are participating in the Lunar New Year's first week tatt fast."

Urban's attention jumped back to the jumbotrons, where a New Beijing government official spoke. She recognized him as the Head Prefect from various news broadcasts she'd seen in the past.

"Join us in taking off the overlays by using the Augmented Free app. Once downloaded, your retina will automatically deactivate for the duration you set. An external display will alert others in reality to your status."

The broadcast shifted to demonstrate someone with a blinking yellow light in their eyes.

Urban's forehead wrinkled. She'd seen augment-free campaigns before, of course, but it seemed like they were happening more these days.

"Many of the top Key Opinion Leaders are participating. In addition, each Head Prefect will be awarding participants who successfully complete the challenge with a .05 sosh increase. A recent medical study shows significant mental and physical health benefits . . ."

The voice faded as Urban zoomed down into an underground garage. She swiped the golden tatt on her wrist, and her bike locked with a click.

Urban sat there a moment in the cold, harsh lighting of the garage. After weeks in the dirty, chaotic Outskirts, the pristine white walls seemed to close in around her–too bright. She had been looking forward to this moment of returning home, but now all she felt was dread. Unseen shadows seemed to lurk beyond the walls.

This was the first time she was back since the attack.

At the end of last semester, an Enhanced with an illegal, and alarming, number of enhancements had tried to kill her. The *Jingcha* had yet to find him.

Fear raked a cold, sinewy finger down Urban's spine.

He could be anywhere.

Movement at the exit of the garage quickened her pulse.

A cat darted into view, and she released a breath. But she still couldn't shake the feeling that someone watched her.

Shoving her unease away, she climbed off her motorcycle and made her way toward the elevator. She punched the 131st floor and scanned her tatt. With a jolt, she shot upward, the lift slowing as she neared the top. It stopped, and the doors opened, revealing a familiar dark marble floor. She made her way toward a set of inky black doors standing regally at the end of the hall.

Urban lifted her hand to knock.

Images flashed in her mind. Memories from the last time she'd seen her family. Worry creases around Mother's eyes. Lucas's glare. His back turned to her as she said goodbye. Her father's tired gaze.

Apart from her sister, she hadn't seen any of them in two weeks. Ever since she'd gone into hiding, contact had been minimal. Mother had sent her a few encrypted messages about logistics for the holidays, but that was it. Urban wondered if Lucas was still mad and blamed her for the attacks on their family.

She rapped on the door.

Nerves mingled with excitement in anticipation of seeing them all again. She held out a sliver of hope that maybe things would be fine. Otherwise, pretending to be a normal, functioning family over the holidays was going to be awkward.

The gargantuan doors swung open. A Natural maid with mousey features extended a warm hand towelette before motioning her inside. "Your Father's on the roof, Miss Lee, about to take off."

Ignoring the towelette, Urban stepped upon a Persian rug, tugging her levitating suitcase behind her.

Stillness cloaked the house. An unfamiliar darkness filled the usually bright interiors. The smell of Mother's Bulgarian perfume lingered faintly in the air. The scent brought a wave of nostalgia.

How things had changed since her last trip home. There was no music or laughter. No parties or guests–only silence.

Urban wondered if it was because the house was bugged. Knowing someone could be listening even now made her walk faster as she headed to a washroom to change.

Emerging in a trendy XR silk outfit, she pulled her levitating suitcase past walls with paintings, a dried-up fountain, pristine white couches, decorative fans, and then up a set of stairs.

Following the hum of engines, she came to a garden with

three idling helix-pods. Their excess wind made the surrounding plant life dance like crazed fans at a rave.

Her shoulders sagged in relief the moment she was out of the house. Somehow, being on the roof and back with her family made her feel safe–even if it was probably an illusion.

"There you are!" Mr. Lee yelled above the noise. He wore a stylish turtleneck sweater under a suit, ever the picture of a successful businessman. His perfectly parted black hair was thicker than she'd remembered. Was he using stimulants to fight back his ever-receding hairline?

But the creases in his forehead seemed deeper and his expression wary, as if he'd aged significantly in the time Urban had been away.

She knew her parents were planning on rejoining the organization fighting for advancements in genetic enhancements for all, but she hadn't heard anything about the progress. While in the Outskirts, Everest's mom had kept her abreast of the developments, but AiE re-forming in the Metropolis was dangerous business. Especially since her parents had been targeted for being involved years ago.

"Get in." Father gestured at one of the pods, interrupting Urban's thoughts.

As she did so, Urban couldn't help the disappointment that bubbled up in her chest. No, "Thanks for being on time," or "Happy New Year's Eve," or "I'm so glad you're safe!"

Mr. Lee tapped his foot against three boxes full of fruits, pastries, and other gifts for the relatives back home. "I won't be late two years in a row for the family's Lunar New Year celebration!" His voice boomed so loudly, Jiaozi–lounging next to one of the boxes–let out a startled meow.

On instinct, her sister's giant Enhanced cat vanished, though Urban noticed a guard in the other pod yelping in surprise as an invisible force landed in the seat next to him.

Urban was glad–for once, Father's anger wasn't directed at her.

Urban's sister sprinted gracefully up the stairs, two mini drones struggling under the weight of her suitcase. Her large, beautiful eyes sparkled, and she broke into a smile upon spotting Urban. With her long, white-blond hair blowing wildly in all directions, she looked like a model.

Lillian stowed her suitcase neatly into the waiting pod. Sliding into the seat next to Urban, she wrapped her in a tight embrace. Her two drones nestled up against Urban, then flew to Lillian's shoulder, where they came to rest like birds of prey.

"Good job, Peppa and Dede." Lillian stroked her drones as if they were pets. "How were the last few weeks in the Outskirts? Sorry I had to leave you there alone. You know how AiE is."

"It's mostly just me at the house. Everest is gone and his parents are rarely home."

Lillian made a sympathetic face.

Urban shrugged. "What's the update with AiE? I still don't understand what you and Trig do."

Lillian brightened at the mention of her fellow AiE operative and Urban's bodyguard. "As Finders and Protectors, we protect Naturals from harassment and danger. So basically hacking into the *Jingcha's* feeds and rescuing anyone who needs it."

Urban's eyes grew round. "Does that happen a lot?"

"Fortunately, no. Most of our time is spent looking for the genetic link between Naturals and Enhanced."

Urban leaned forward. The genetic link–or the hybrid, as she'd learned last semester–actually existed. "Any progress?"

"Actually, yes." Lillian lowered her voice. "We found a lead. Remember how Ash stabbed our attacker's wing?"

Urban nodded.

"Well, we ran some DNA tests and traced it back to the Western Federation."

The Western Federation. Just like the lead on my birth origins. Is it possible they're linked?

Urban dared to ask, "Could I be the hybrid?"

“Unfortunately, no,” Lillian sighed. “Coral and I hacked into the PKU Games last semester, that’s the only reason it broke. Other people don’t know that and may think you’re the hybrid, but we know better.”

“Are you sure?” Urban felt sheepish even asking. To be honest, she wasn’t sure if she wanted to be the hybrid. It made her a target. Then again, she already was one.

“Our adoptive paperwork came with our genomics analysis, remember?” Lillian kept her voice low. “We already know you’re a Natural. Of course, there’s always the possibility when someone hacked our paperwork, our records were altered. That’s why we’re trying to figure out who hacked them. But even then, your genomics have been analyzed since then.”

“Hurry up!” Father was shouting. “These *fagao* will have dried up by the time you all get your sorry rear ends out here!”

Lucas sauntered out of the stairwell, three suitcases in tow. “No one likes those bland cakes anyway, Dad.”

Mother followed close behind, patting down a stray wisp of hair. “Lucas, dear, why do you have so many bags?” She eyed her son’s suitcases, a perfectly penciled eyebrow raised in disapproval. “We’ll only be in New Harbin for a few days.”

“This suitcase is full of the stuff you gave me for the holidays.” Lucas gestured at one. “This is for extravagant parties.” He kicked another with his foot. “And this one is full of thermal swimwear.”

“Swimwear?” Father huffed, climbing into the pod. “The high will be minus thirteen Celsius. The water will be frozen. You’d be crazy to attempt swimming this time of year.”

“They’re smart thermal, and I’m Enhanced. I’ll be fine.” Lucas spotted Urban and muttered, “Unlike some people.”

Urban tensed, but Lucas only retreated to the back of the pod to stow his luggage.

Mother gave Urban a genial smile upon seeing her. “Urban!” She came forward as if for a hug.

Hesitating, Urban stood from her seat and met her mother at the edge of the pod. Bending down, Urban gave her an awkward embrace. It was simultaneously too tight, and yet loose in the wrong places.

"It's so good to see you again." Mother's eyes had more lines around them than usual, but her smile seemed sincere, though Urban could never be sure. She'd found out last semester just how good of a liar her mother could be.

Urban smiled politely, suddenly uncomfortable at this display of affection from her normally reserved parent.

Mother took a seat next to Father, and Lucas gave up on attempting to shove his suitcases into the storage compartment. Dragging one of them into the main cabin with Lillian and Urban, he placed the suitcase on his lap.

Urban winced. "Your suitcase is hurting my leg."

"It's barely touching you!" Lucas snapped. "You're always such a baby."

Urban shifted and turned her gaze out the window as the doors shut automatically. Being back with her family made her feel like a little girl again. Sometimes, it was as if all the ways she'd grown and changed since attending uni had never even happened.

Last semester, she'd been thrown into the Games, survived as a Natural, and even turned into a KOL with many brands requesting her as their Key Opinion Leader spokeswoman. Urban had accepted an offer from Croix, the athleisure brand. The pending crypto points would soon mean she had freedom from her parents, since she wouldn't be dependent on their allowances.

The last two weeks, especially surviving and blending in in the Outskirts, had changed her. But with her family, none of it seemed to matter.

She thought about what the next semester could look like. Her parents still didn't want her going back to school, but Urban had grown restless in the Outskirts. Several weeks of living in her ex-boyfriend's parents' apartment, and she was desperate to get out and find answers about the hybrid.

The wind outside grew louder and more violent. Natural servants and Inventor guards climbed into the other two pods, fighting against an onslaught of wind. The noise-cancelling bubble activated with a pop, surrounding the Lees in silence. With a lurch, they lifted off the ground and into the sky.

Urban's thoughts drifted back to her origins. She'd gone over it again and again, but couldn't make sense of it.

Two weeks ago, her parents had found something linking her past to the Western Federation. The adoption agency had initially accepted her from there. Which made no sense.

Urban stared at her hands. She didn't look like she was from the Western Federation. Her features were too dark and she was petite, even by Asian Federation standards. It seemed unlikely she could be from anywhere else.

On the attacker front, they had initially thought Supers Against Soups, the brutal organization started by Supers who killed Naturals attempting to mix with Enhanced, were behind the attacks. But if the attacker was from the Western Federation, could it still be SAS?

So many dead ends.

The buildings faded further below as they climbed into the sky.

"*Wo zi,*" Father swore in Federation Mandarin, as their pod joined a swarm of others. They came to a standstill mid-air. "I told *Nainai* we'd be there in time for the family reunion dinner."

Urban's mouth watered at the thought of the dinner. Last year's feast had left her in a food coma for days. She was pretty sure the New-Year-Nine kilo gain was a thing, even for the Enhanced.

"Yeah, we're definitely not gonna make it in time." Lucas stuffed several sheets of dried seaweed in his mouth. "Good thing I brought snacks."

Lillian eyed the seaweed bag with disgust. “So that’s where that smell is coming from. Can’t you wait until we’re not in a confined space to eat those?”

“I’m hungry!” Lucas protested.

Lillian made gagging noises.

As they inched their way across the skyline, Urban pulled up her pings, remembering she’d received a prioritized one earlier. It was from Dr. Gong, head of Peking University. Her nerves spiked.

[Dr. Gong: Lee Urban, I would like to be the first to congratulate you. Your spectacular and, quite frankly, baffling performance in the AI Games has warranted the attention of more than one recruiter. After consulting the team lead, and running rigorous AI analysis on your performance, the team has decided to offer you a spot on the Dragons’ team starting this coming spring semester.]

[I know there was some concern around your safety. However, I can offer you housing in our KOL dormitory. State-of-the-art security exists to ensure all of our high-profile students receive quality care and protection. Should you choose to accept this offer, you will receive free room and board in the KOL dormitory. On behalf of Peking University, we sincerely hope you will accept this opportunity. Please inform myself and the Dragons’ team leader of your decision no later than the Lunar New Year. All the best, Dr. Gong.]

URBAN LEANED BACK IN HER SEAT, DAZED.

Last semester, when the Inventors had chosen her as their gene pool representative in the AI Games, she'd thought that was the end of it. There had been ten contestants and only one spot available. The thought had never even crossed her mind that she'd actually make it onto the team. *How long do I have to make a decision?*

Lunar New Year was tomorrow.

Do I want to join them?

Soon, Lillian would be going back to school for the Spring semester. Urban's friends Coral and Ash wouldn't have time to visit, either, as they'd be busy with class. Everest, her ex-boyfriend, would be the only one left in the Outskirts, and spending time with him sounded painfully awkward.

If she was honest with herself, she actually missed uni. Even though she was constantly on her guard and stressed about grades, she liked going to classes with Coral and Ash. She even had started to enjoy her workouts at Infini-Fit with Lillian, and jiujitsu training with her skilled instructor, Orion.

As a KOL, how long can I stay hidden in the Outskirts?

Urban's mind hummed, connecting pieces.

KOLs have the world at their fingertips. Access to data and people. It's the perfect opportunity to get the answers I need to find the hybrid. Then, maybe SAS and anyone else who thinks I'm the hybrid will leave me alone.

If Dr. Gong is willing to put me in the KOL dorms, I'll be safe. Then again, what if my Natural DNA crashes the AI again? I can't afford to make that mistake twice.

"Crossing into the yellow zone. We will be accelerating in one minute." The pod interrupted her thoughts. The last helix-pod in the line before them shot off, going from zero to 5Gs in seconds. Urban watched its slick, black-and-white circular sides fade into the distance.

"Please fasten your belts and secure your belongings."

Lucas strapped on his belt and adjusted the suitcase on his lap, digging it into Urban's knees.

"Ten, nine, eight . . ."

The pod passed through the protective barrier, air filtration systems clicking on.

"Three, two, one."

The helix lurched forward. Urban slammed back against her seat as the pod accelerated, the corners of her vision turning black.

"Gonna pass out?" Lucas whispered so only she could hear. "Too bad you're not enhanced to withstand supersonic travel, like me."

Urban gritted her teeth, but said nothing. As the pod approached cruising velocity, her vision returned.

"Cruising speed reached," the helix announced. "You will arrive at your destination in thirty-two minutes."

Below, the tall, shiny Metropolis buildings, like cavernous stalagmites, gave way to dusty plots of land. Soon, overcrowded buildings, black from pollution, rose into view.

As they passed over the Outskirts, Urban wondered how Everest was celebrating the Lunar New Year. Surely not enduring lavish reunions and endless questions from relatives. What would he think of Dr. Gong's offer to join the team?

It doesn't matter what he thinks. It's my decision.

And yet, somehow, it didn't feel like it. Her parents would have an opinion. AiE, Lillian, her roommates, anyone and everyone she knew would want a say. She shut her eyes.

I still have a day to decide.

She shoved the decision, thoughts of the attacker, and AiE, all out of her mind, trying to relax. She was finally back with her family and determined to enjoy one of her favorite holidays.

The helix eventually slowed, as flaming scarlet and orange rays filled the pod. The iridescent lights of New Harbin blinked into view. The Metropolis was smaller than New Beijing, but still had an impressive number of high-rises streaking up into the darkening sky. This time of year, they all emitted a festive red glow.

The helix crossed into the white zone and they began their descent into the Metropolis. With a jolt, they touched down on a private landing strip. A winter garden in full bloom surrounded them–snow blossoms, weeping willows with genetically modified white leaves, and two songbirds that chirped cheerily in their cages.

Beyond the garden, tall buildings stood proudly, like Supers guarding the Federation's council.

The other two pods landed next to them. Natural servants and Inventor guards climbed out and helped move the Lees' luggage. Several GX100s, resembling mini tanks and costing a month's salary of an average Metropolis worker to rent, idled nearby. Urban had seen several ads for them, claiming to be the most secure rides on the market.

She stepped onto the landing and was confronted with cold, dry air. She darted toward the closest vehicle. Climbing inside, she was hit with a blast of heat, along with blaring New Year's music. Clanging symbols and children's voices carried the happy tune. Urban scooted across the warmed leather seats.

"Ugh. Not this song again." Lucas took the seat furthest from Urban. "Why do they play the same music every year?"

"I kind of like it," Lillian said. "Always gets me in a festive mood."

"Festive, shmestive." Lucas flicked at a dangling mini paper lantern.

The vehicle fell silent as they pulled away from the landing. Outside, hoverboards, autonomous vehicles, and pedestrians packed onto the road and sidewalks, a mass of migrating birds all heading home. In the sky above, lights from delivery drones, helixes, and flying vehicles flickered like a thousand twinkling stars.

"We're already an hour late," Father growled as they came to yet another standstill in the middle of New Harbin.

Mother touched up her makeup. "Maybe next year, we should take the holiday traffic into consideration when timing our arrival."

There was a noncommittal grunt from Father.

Lucas had decided it was snack time again, and a putrid scent filled the vehicle as he opened a pack of octopus ink-flavored rice balls. His fingers were already coated in black.

"Lucas! We're going to show up at our relatives' smelling like an aquarium." Lillian brushed at her dress as if to wipe the scent away.

Lucas grinned. "Excellent. You know I forgot my aquarium cologne."

"If that's real, it's absolutely disgusting." Urban's nose crinkled.

Lucas pretended not to hear. Though he made sure to chew the next bite with his mouth wide open.

An hour later, they exited New Harbin's Metropolis and zoomed across a speedway. After twisting and turning down several roads, they reached the suburbs where gnarled trees grew thicker and the traffic all but disappeared.

Their vehicle stopped in front of a towering gate. Guard sheds flanked the snow-covered path and a force field blocked their entry. A Super carrying a deactivated stun pike emerged from one of the sheds. He wore a lightweight jacket and didn't look cold in the slightest. Urban was always impressed by Supers' ability to withstand extreme temperatures.

After scanning Father's tatt, he marched back to the shed. A second later, there was the pop of the force field dissipating, and they rolled silently through. The air fell silent, snow blanketing every surface like a soundproof wall.

The Lunar New Year was always celebrated at Uncle Lee's house. This time, coming from the Outskirts, Urban couldn't help but notice the opulence.

Gold statues, hidden beneath snow, lined the road. Exotic pets roamed through a garden, lake, and miniature stone forest. Two sleeping elephants stood silent and still in the middle of a white field. Each wore a red smart vest to keep them warm. A light dusting of snow covered their heads. Red sleeves snaked up their ivory tusks, each studded with glittering diamond bells.

"Remember when the elephants were small and we used to race them?" Lillian asked with a wistful smile. "After seeing that horror flick about deranged elephants, Lucas was terrified when Auntie tried to put him on one."

Lucas scowled as the sisters shared a laugh. "Whatever. That was ages ago."

They came to a stop in a small clearing. Thick, dead foliage crowded around on all sides. A steaming fountain, lit up in glowing colors, splashed into a pool. Several valet bots took the SUVs from them.

The Lees and their entourage walked to the other side of the fountain, where a giant pagoda rose above the trees and bushes. The ancient building's wood was meshed with metal and lit up with warm colors. Industrial techno music drifted over the water, a sharp contrast to the peaceful surroundings.

A pond wrapped around the pagoda served as a moat. Giant, glowing koi, the size of a large dog, swam lazily through the water. It looked deceptively shallow, but Urban could make out the underwater cavern below. She shuddered at memories of her Aqua cousins attempting to get her to swim in it.

Father stepped up to a willow tree and flashed his tatt across its hidden security scanner. The tree beeped, and a moment later, hovering stones appeared on the top of the pond, forming a path to the pagoda.

Urban had always thought her uncle's security system to be overboard. Now, after the past few months, she was grateful. Her parents had thought it would attract too much attention to bring her Camo bodyguard, Trig, to the family reunion. Without his constant invisible presence, she felt vulnerable.

They crossed the stone pathway and reached two giant lion statues guarding the entrance to a massive doorway. Square pieces of red paper hung on either side of the door, the upside-down character for *fu*, or fortune, painted on them.

A vid recorder above the entryway scanned the party. A moment later, the sound of slippers padded across the floor.

The door flung open.

"Hello!" Uncle Lee welcomed warmly. "Come in, come in!" He ushered them inside, leaving them in the wake of his overpowering cologne.

Urban's eyes slid past him and latched on a figure lurking in the back of the hallway. There was something oddly familiar about the shock of black hair and the way he carried himself, confident and relaxed, yet with an air of authority.

Sharp eyes looked her way, and her breath caught.

Everest.

URBAN REMAINED FROZEN IN PLACE. *WHAT IS Everest doing here?*

She realized why it had taken her a second to recognize him. He'd switched out of his dated Outskirts tech and wore the latest XR suit, and his retina displays had changed his eye color to a stunning blue.

A steady yellow light blinked in the corner of his eye. Urban recognized it from the augmented-free challenge.

Smart. Using it as cover.

Urban managed to school her features as she forced her feet to step into the warm hall. She couldn't let on that she recognized Everest. And she certainly couldn't let her uncle know that Everest was a member of AiE and a Natural.

Am I supposed to know about Everest being here? Pretend to be surprised? Then again, no pretending necessary on that front.

Several pairs of minx fur slippers were already laid out, as was customary. Urban slipped out of her heavy boots and donned the silky-smooth slippers, trying to corral her wild thoughts away from the boy standing meters away.

She thought back to their last conversation, where he'd offered to give her time to think and had left an open invitation to date again.

Do I want that?

So far, she'd been too busy adjusting to the Outskirts, reeling from the attack at the Reservoir, learning about SAS bugging her family's house, and all the news from her parents about the strange events surrounding her adoption.

Turning to face the group, she feigned interest in the pleasantries exchanged, pretending not to notice Everest. Heat crept across her cheeks, and not just from the warmth of the room.

"Come in." Her uncle ushered them inside to a tastefully decorated receiving hall. Golden mirrors and framed paintings cluttered nearly every portion of the walls, and Natural maids stood at attention, forming a long row of watching eyes. One of the Naturals sat at a wicker chair playing the *erhu* and filling the room with its stringy notes. Urban barely noticed any of it. She kept sneaking glances at Everest, still lurking in the back of the hall.

Her auntie joined them. "How good to see you!"

Father handed the *fagao* and other gifts to his brother and sister-in-law.

Auntie turned and swatted at her husband. "Dear, you didn't introduce our guest!" She turned back into the hallway and dragged Everest into the circle. "Look who's already here." She beamed at Urban. "Your boyfriend!"

My what?

Lucas gave Urban the side-eye while Lillian stiffened. Only her parents seemed to keep a calm exterior, though she could tell by the muscle twitching in Father's jaw he wasn't too happy about this development.

So much for pretending not to know Everest.

How did he get in here? Then Urban remembered Everest had access to her digital key so they could communicate in private. It was the same key she used to communicate with Auntie, and showing it must have convinced them to let him in.

Her parents probably recognized him as the Outskirts lead for AiE whom she'd been staying with. But they knew nothing of her past relationship with him. What must they be thinking?

The air had gone still and Urban realized everyone was waiting for her response.

What was the right move? How long had they been "dating"? Should she embrace him like long-lost lovers? A new interest?

Her head hurt from the possibilities.

Fortunately, Everest took the lead. "Thanks for the invite, Urban. Your aunt and uncle have graciously given me the house tour." He started to move forward toward Urban but slowed at the look on her face.

Instead, he smoothly turned to face her parents. "It's so nice to finally meet you. Your daughter has told me so much about you." He extended a gift basket full of colorful fruit. "Here, this is for the family."

There was a slight pause, then Mother accepted the gift, all smiles. "You shouldn't have." She almost seemed sincere.

"Come, come, the food has already been served." Auntie ushered the Lees toward the dining hall. A long line of Naturals followed in their wake, but Urban and Everest hung back.

Urban rounded on him the moment they were alone. "What are you doing?"

Everest stepped back at the vehemence in her tone.

"Showing up at my relative's house like this?" Urban struggled to keep her voice down. "I thought you said you'd give me time to consider dating again. Why are you forcing my hand, pretending to be my boyfriend?"

Everest extended his hands in a gesture of peace. "I can explain."

Urban glared daggers, waiting.

He lowered his voice. "The Advancement in Enhancement's org wanted me to do this. It's their idea."

Urban's expression wavered.

"AiE is trying to boost my sosh," Everest continued. "They want to transfer me to the Metropolis. Also, I need to be here for tomorrow's operation."

"Operation?"

Everest glanced both ways, then stepped closer. He smelled of jasmine and smoke from the Outskirts. The familiarity of it forced the archives of Urban's brain to retrieve unwanted memories that twisted in her gut.

". . . we found the scientist," Everest was saying.

Urban blinked. "Sorry, who?"

"The scientist who invented the microneedle patch. We think he can lead us to the creator of the hybrid. The lead is here, in New Harbin."

"Here? Why didn't you tell me any of this when I was at your parents'?"

"AiE suspects we have a mole. They only told me the plan yesterday. I'll explain everything later. For now, we need to find out a way to get through the night as . . ."

"A believable couple?" Urban snorted. *This would happen to me.*

Everest's expression was apologetic.

"Do my parents know?"

"They should be getting a message from AiE."

Urban flung up a hand. "That solves one of three thousand and six problems."

Two relatives entered the greeting room, interrupting their conversation.

"Urban, dear." Aunt Song glided up to them. "So good to see you! And who's this?" She glanced at Everest.

"Um, this is my boyfriend." Urban scratched her arm.

"Boyfriend?" Aunt Song asked, her eyes lighting up.

Her son pushed toward them. "Let's link!" He extended his tatt at Everest.

Everest didn't move. "Sorry. Can't."

Song's eyes narrowed.

"I'm participating in the Lunar New Year tatt fast," he explained, not missing a beat. He gestured at the yellow blinking in his eye.

"Good for you." Aunt Song nodded approvingly. "I keep telling my son he needs to do an hour or two with his tatt deactivated, but he never does. Kids these days." She clucked her tongue.

"I told you, I'll do it once you do." The young boy rounded on his mom. "But you haven't ever deactivated your tatt."

"Yes, well, it was nice seeing you dears! We're off to get this one to bed." Aunt Song turned and practically dragged her child away.

Everest folded his arms across his chest. Urban noticed how toned they were, even through his smart wear. Had he been working out more?

Why am I noticing his arms?

"You okay?" Everest cut into her thoughts, watching her with concern.

As okay as I can be with my ex back in my life as my fake boyfriend. Urban nodded and began walking again to clear her head. They entered a narrow hallway with dark glass walls. Glowing jellyfish floated by on all sides.

"I'm really sorry," Everest said. "I knew AiE was preparing me for the Metropolis, but I had no idea their plan involved us."

Urban let out a long breath as they reached the end of the walkway. "Well, looks like we'd better figure this out fast."

They entered a circular room with spotlights shining down on deadly weapons and strange inventions. One plaque even had a tiny beetle pinned to it.

Everest read the description. "Cybug?"

"The Lees are Inventors and Aquas," Urban explained. "These are some of their creations. That's a cyborg bug. Implanted with a receiver chip that takes in the chemical makeup of the air as a larva. When it grows up, its flesh combines with the device. That one over there"–she gestured at another bug–"picks up sound, and the one over there can record."

"Does the Asian Federation know about these?" Everest asked.

"My family has tons of stuff like this they've invented. Usually, it's for personal use or fun."

Everest studied the cybug. "Invented by Kim Star . . . who's that?"

"I think it's someone who married into the family, but he's dead now."

Everest bowed his head respectfully before approaching a platform hovering at the center of the room with a helmet next to it. A holo projection of a thundercloud spun slowly. "And what's that?"

"That's my family's most prized possession." Urban stood next to Everest. "Have you heard of the Race to the Clouds?"

"Who hasn't? But one of your family members actually qualified to race?"

"My father. Not just qualified–he won."

Everest stared.

"That's the helmet my father wore when he won the championship. He used to be a pretty daring Inventor and competed with one of his own inventions."

"Incredible." Everest fingered the helmet next to the trophy. It was made of gold, with reinforced blue gears and shiny attach points that smoothed into aerodynamic lines to look like small fins streaking behind it.

"Don't touch that," Urban ordered. "My father doesn't let anyone go near it."

"Sorry." Everest pulled his hand away, but remained staring.

"Come on, let me see your tatt." She reached for his wrist, fingers tingling when they brushed up against his.

Something passed between them, a spark zipping up

Urban's arm. She jerked back and spoke quickly to hide her embarrassment. "I manually transferred a list of relatives with their names. Now, here's what you need to know about my family." She ran through each member along with their name, gene pool, and sosh.

"Since you won't be able to link with any of them, this guide should help you," Urban explained. "Most of them won't think twice about you supposedly being an Artisan like me. The only ones to watch out for are Uncle Chang, who's an Inceptor, and my cousins Jade and Jem. They hate Naturals. Be very careful around them."

The sounds of raucous laughter and the beat of music grew louder as they headed toward the dining hall.

"Got it," Everest said. "Anything else I should know?"

My brother's a jerk, half my extended family is psycho, my relationship with my parents is rocky, I never fit in, and now you're going to see all of it.

Urban forced a smile. "Nope."

A THICK SILENCE DESCENDED AS URBAN AND Everest drew nearer to the banquet hall.

When Urban had first met Everest's family, she'd thought she would pass out, she'd been so nervous. But they had all been welcoming, and Everest had done his best to put her at ease.

His family's apartment was so small–nearly the size of one of Auntie's restrooms–but it had been homey, peaceful, even. She wondered what Everest must be feeling now, in this mansion with the pressure of meeting her extended Enhanced family.

Urban sneaked a glance at him. He walked with confidence and back straight, in an almost leisurely stroll. A barely perceptible hardness lined his features, but she doubted anyone other than herself would recognize it.

She wanted to say something to put him at ease, but what? *Don't worry about being a Natural, my family won't care?*

Lies.

Her extended family didn't even know Urban was a Natural.

My family's not drowning in wealth. It's not a big deal you come from the Outskirts?

More lies.

"Be on your guard and keep your head down," she whispered instead.

Everest gave a barely perceptible nod as they rounded a corner and paused at the entrance.

The room was a shrine of red festivity. Rich, rose-red carpets blanketed the floor, decorative red fans lined the walls, and red cherry blossom trees stood spaced between the tables, filling the room with a floral, earthy scent. The ceiling far above, drowning in paper lanterns, glowed brightly and cast a warm red hue. Natural attendants dispensed hand towels with the character *fu* embroidered on them.

Auntie has really outdone herself this year.

Birds chirped happily in cages, though they were nearly drowned by laughter, and shouts ricocheting off the walls. Urban recognized a few familiar faces among the hundred or so relatives wearing red silks and elegant ball gowns. She broke into a cold sweat at the prospect of having to introduce them to her boyfriend.

She'd once wished for this moment, to introduce Everest to her world, but that was before, when they were still dating. Now everything was different. Despite the awkwardness between them, there was something else she couldn't put her finger on. But it sparked a warning in her chest, even as his arm edged closer to hers.

She wiped sweaty palms on her silk XR slacks.

Everest's calloused hand slipped into hers, and Urban's breath caught. She looked over at him in surprise and he offered an encouraging smile.

Urban turned back to the hall, trying desperately not to think about the warm, steadying hand she held.

They caught up to the rest of the family.

"You're doing great," Lillian whispered. Leave it to her to always seem to know what to say. Urban gave her sister a grateful smile.

"Come, come, I'll show you to your place." Auntie led the Lees past huge circular tables. Each one had a blooming lotus flower arrangement, the family's emblem. Surrounding the display, every delicacy imaginable ladened the tables: roasted duck, home-made *jiaozi*, pumpkin soup, swan intestine, *chaomian*, pork rinds, spring rolls, and more. There was also a wide variety of vegan seafood dishes, since the Aquas in the family all found eating real seafood distasteful. Auntie stopped at a table with Uncle Chang, Jade, Jem, a younger cousin, and two other relatives Urban didn't recognize.

Of course we get seated here.

Several of the relatives at the table were pink-faced and shouting. Either they'd already had a plethora of drinks, or they'd chosen to reduce the alcoholic metabolism in their livers, so as to feel a little more than lightly buzzed tonight.

"About time!" Uncle Chang said, noticing them.

Chairs scraped the floor as Urban and her family took their seats.

One of the relatives Urban didn't recognize motioned at Everest. "Urban, who's this? Introduce us!"

Urban had no idea who the relative was, and checked her retina display. Unfortunately, there was a yellow blinking light in the corner of his eye, and Urban had no way to pull up his avatar.

Urban felt Everest's gaze on her and silently pleaded for help.

The corner of Everest's lips twitched upward, and her cheeks warmed.

"I'm Everest." He smiled genially.

"Very nice to meet you, Everest. I'm Shard. I see you're doing the augmented-free challenge."

Everest brightened. "You too? How's it going?"

Urban released a breath.

Shard and Everest talked about the pains of not having their retina displays, laughing over shared experiences.

"I'm trying to get her to go augment free." Everest nudged Urban playfully.

Urban nearly fell over with surprise. How was Everest so calm and composed right now? And how was he pulling off the whole dating act and being Enhanced with such ease? She could hardly focus on the conversation with him sitting this close.

"Have you seen the latest news on the Western Federation's Revolutionaries?" Shard asked.

That caught her full attention.

"The killings?" Everest asked. "I read about it right before I took off my overlays."

Urban did a quick search in QuanNao to see what they were talking about. She held in a gasp. Her stomach churned at the gruesome images. A caption read: *Radical Western Revolutionaries Attack Shoppers. Twenty Fatalities, More Injured.*

"The Western Federation is out of control." Father joined the conversation. "Thank goodness there's an ocean between us. They have way too many lethal enhancements and weapons, easily accessible to the general population. I don't understand why their government doesn't crack down on them."

"Don't think they haven't tried," Shard told him. "There's too many of them to completely snuff out. Hope is a dangerous commodity. The Revolutionaries have had a taste of it, and I don't believe they'll stop until they get what they want."

"What's wrong with their hope?" Everest interjected. "The hope that all people, regardless of genetics, will be treated equally?"

Urban stiffened.

Shard studied Everest as if only seeing him for the first time. "That's a fine thing in theory. But reality doesn't work that way. We will always have the rich and the poor. The strong and the weak. The Enhanced and Naturals. It's how things are. Nothing's going to change that."

"Maybe nothing small. But maybe that's why the Revolutionaries are so radical," Everest pointed out.

Shard's eyes narrowed. "You agree with them?"

"I think what they're fighting for, equality between Naturals and Enhanced, is a worthy cause."

"But do the ends justify the means?"

Everest gave a quick half smile. "You tell me."

Urban's chest tightened. Surely Everest would never agree with the crazy Radicals that killing and blowing things up was the answer? Was he really that open to their ideas? And what was he doing, debating it here, of all places? She could strangle him.

Fortunately, the conversation shifted to discussing the pros and cons of legalizing a variety of obscure enhancements.

"Let's have some fun tonight!" an Aqua yelled, voice filling the room. The woman flashed a brilliant smile from a stage at the other end of the banquet hall. Bright crimson lights swung around the stage and over her. "Who here is the best singer?"

Several people stood or raised their hands.

"*Lai lai*!" The MC motioned both of them to join her on the stage. "Come up here and give us your best shot!"

As two young men and a woman climbed onto the stage, the crowd shouted and hooted. "Let's see who can sing along best to this tune."

The lights dimmed so that only a spotlight focused on each of the individuals. There were several chuckles as the famous tune began to play. The contestants belted out the song, growing louder as each tried to drown out the other.

The crowd roared with delight. They held up holo signs with numbers ranging from 0, meaning auto-tune would have been better, to 10, Artisan-level skills.

"I hear many of you are Inventors here," the MC called out. "Is that correct?"

The crowd cheered.

"In that case, let's see some tech!"

One of the contestants pulled out what looked like a barbell, but Urban realized was actually a giant voice enhancer. The device floated inches away from the man, converting his voice into that of a famous pop star.

A smattering of signs displaying 10s projected around the room.

Another contestant, a woman, started dancing. While her moves were incredible, there was something slightly off about them. Urban studied her closely and realized she was wearing the auto dance suit. Supposedly it wasn't even on the market yet. This time, the signs displayed 8s, 9s and 10s.

The third contestant, an Aqua, roared the last note to the song so loudly, the woman nearly fell off the stage and everyone held their ears. When the music ended, he grinned widely, even while the crowd booed and several of the virtual signs flashed 0s.

Still grinning, the Aqua and other contestants made their way off the stage.

The family's Lunar New Year's gatherings always reminded her more of a wild party than a family dinner. But that was the way of her Auntie. She was never one to miss an opportunity to host an extravagant gathering.

Urban's attention returned to the table as another song started up. Uncle Chang picked up a jug of rice wine and filled Lillian's and then Lucas's shot glasses. He paused at Urban's. "Are you still abstaining?"

"What?" Jade's ginormous eyebrows lifted. "Not drinking? Why?"

The table turned its attention to Urban. She shifted in her seat.

With her Natural genetics, Urban would end up drunk way too fast to be a believable Enhanced. Then again, most of them had lowered their alcohol threshold for the night. But Urban despised the idea of drinking. Her father drank enough for the entire family.

"She's morally opposed to it." Lucas jumped at the opportunity to embarrass her. "Thinks alcohol is made from the slave labor of bots and the chemicals and toxins used to harvest it will erode away her digestive system."

Several relatives stared at Lucas, not sure if he was serious.

Urban shrank further into her chair wishing she could disappear.

"It is a pity, not being able to drink." Everest spoke evenly.

"I guess that's the price to pay when you sign a Key Opinion Leader partnership." He turned to Lucas. "Urban and I envy you, really. You have so much freedom when you're not a KOL."

Lucas blinked, unsure of how to respond. Heat crept up his neck. He glared at Urban, then turned to their cousin and began talking rapidly.

"Thanks," Urban whispered to Everest once the conversation around the table had picked back up.

After everyone had eaten way too many sweet rice balls, *jiaozi*, and *fagao* cakes, the MC began shouting from the stage again. "Another round of competitors!"

"You should go up there, Everest," Lucas prodded.

Everest laughed. "Oh, I wouldn't want to put everyone here to shame."

Lucas's gaze was unwavering. "No, really. You're an Artisan, right? Let's hear it."

"Lucas–" Urban began.

"It's fine." Everest rose to his feet. "I wouldn't want to disappoint."

Uncle Chang slapped him on the back with a good-natured cheer, but Urban's stomach twisted as Everest walked onto the stage.

"Who's this?" the MC asked, giving Everest a once-over. "Our next victim? I mean, volunteer?"

The crowd laughed.

"Hmm . . . augmented free?" The MC appraised Everest. "So private."

"Sorry." Everest inclined his head. "I wanted to start the year out right."

Several people booed at this, Aunt Song among them. A few 0s flashed across the holo signs to express disapproval, but some, including Shard, held up 10s.

"I suppose we'll have to wait in suspense." The MC turned to the crowd. "Give our next volunteer a round of applause!"

The room broke out in a smattering of applause, hoots, and drunken shouts.

As the music began to play, Urban recognized it and groaned. It was a slow song with impossibly low notes. By the vindictive look on the MC's face, she knew it. Even Lucas smirked as he sipped his rice wine.

The song intro finished and Everest began to sing. It was a low, haunting tune, not at all fitting to the lively festivities around them, but his deep baritone voice was strong, clear, and pure.

A stillness descended, as if a trance had been placed upon the room. Chills crept up Urban's arms at the beauty of the song and Everest's voice. She'd forgotten what he sounded like.

He swayed slightly to the melody, eyes closed, completely immersed in the music. His stylish combat boots and loose pants rippled around him as he moved.

Urban had heard him sing before, nestled against his shoulder as the guitar echoed softly in her ear. But she'd never seen him *perform*. It made sense that if he was going to be a musician, he would be good at it. But she'd never imagined he was this talented.

He was good. Enhanced good.

Maybe pretending to be an Enhanced Artisan really would get him to the Metropolis. Maybe they *could* be together someday.

The last note of the song stretched on, and Everest held it an impossibly long time. There was a moment of silence as he finished. When he was nearly back to his seat, Urban broke out of her reverie and clapped. Those around her followed suit, until a defeaning roar overtook the room. Tens glowed everywhere.

Next to her, she overheard Jade speaking to Jem. "What a *shuaige*. Where do I find a man like *him*?"

They both erupted in giggles as Everest sat down.

"Great job, babe," Urban said. And she found she wasn't

pretending. Somehow, Everest, who'd never spent more than a few hours in the Metropolis, was holding his own. With her family. With the *Enhanced.*

His eyes met hers, and a low, hot flame shot through her stomach. The one that was so familiar and yet foreign. Their eyes remained locked and the room faded around them.

"To Everest!" Uncle Chang said, jarring them out of the moment. "*Gan bei*!"

Glasses were raised in the air and the words were echoed before everyone downed their drinks.

Surrounding relatives heaped more food on Everest's plate, and another round of volunteers sang a festive tune.

As the night wore on, and more people allowed themselves to get drunk, the karaoke grew wilder and less comprehensible. Even Lucas, red-faced, stumbled his way onto the stage.

As soon as he started belting out off-key, Father roared his drunken approval and clapped his hands, knocking over the jug of alcohol and spilling it all over the table. Several other relatives cheered as they clinked glasses and continued drinking. Mother was at another table, flattering a relative with a high sosh. Lillian made small talk with Jade and Jem. Urban knew she should be doing the same, but she was too exhausted. Instead, she sat in silence.

Closing her eyes, she tried to put distance between herself and her family. Why couldn't they be normal, like Everest's?

"They're all you've got."

Urban's eyes flashed open in surprise. Uncle Chang leaned forward, head bent close, the acrid scent of rice wine strong on his breath.

"Sorry?"

"We can't always choose our family." Uncle Chang nodded at Lucas, who had collapsed in a fit of hysterical laughter on stage. "But we can choose to make the most of the family we have."

Uncle Chang straightened and looked pointedly at Urban.

She tried to remember what his enhancements were, then shuddered.

Inceptor, of course. She would have to be more careful around him.

"Thanks, Uncle. I'll keep that in mind." Urban turned to her tea, hoping he would leave her alone.

He doesn't know anything about me or my family. If it weren't for a mistake in my paperwork, I wouldn't even be in this family.

Urban found her mind kept drifting back to the lead on her birth origins. *Who changed my paperwork and placed me with the Lees? What if I do have another family out there somewhere? Would I belong with them?*

So many obstacles stood between her and finding her birth origins.

Tuneless singing pierced the air, and garbled laughter grated against her nerves. A wasted relative spilled greasy food on her lap.

Urban wiped it up with a napkin, wishing she was anywhere else.

Her mind began to drift when a blinding light flashed, followed by an ear-splitting explosion.

Suddenly, the room plunged into darkness.

SOMEONE SCREAMED.

"What's going on?" a voice demanded.

A low buzzing sound emanated from the front stage, then the lights flickered and popped back on.

Auntie leaped to her feet, blushing furiously. "My apologies! I'll have maintenance look into that."

Two Supers marched toward Auntie. They lowered their voices, but Urban was close enough to overhear: "You don't have any reason to suspect an attack, do you?"

"No–no, I don't think so." Auntie's face paled. "Why? Do you think that's what it was?"

One of the Supers put out a reassuring hand and guided her past Urban's table. "We're not sure of anything yet. We'll have the security team look into it, but it's highly unlikely that was a maintenance issue."

"But–surely it's nothing. Why would someone attack us?"

Auntie and the guards were now out of earshot, but Urban had heard enough. Dread crept down her spine. Auntie didn't have a reason to be attacked, but someone else in this room did.

Me.

As if reaching the same conclusion, Lillian caught her eye.

She wore a grave expression. In fact, Urban's entire family kept casting quick glances at Urban. Or, in Lucas's case, glares.

Everest stood. "I feel the need for a walk after all the . . . excitement." He flashed a charming smile, then left.

Urban picked at her food as the off-key singing resumed.

It wasn't until Everest returned a few minutes later that she realized how tense she was. It eased only somewhat when he slid back next to her, offering a barely perceptible shrug.

Nothing.

Could it be a coincidence? Or had Urban's attacker found her, even here? She was grateful for all the Inventor tech protecting them in Auntie's mansion. But was it enough? Her attacker had also been an Inventor and an Aqua.

Everest leaned toward her, shaking her from her thoughts. "Is now a good time to talk?"

"Sure." She gestured at the nearby table. "Everyone will be drinking and singing until the fireworks start."

"I can't host an XR meeting." Everest gestured at the yellow blinking in the corner of his eye. He bumped tatts with her. "Can you start one with Coral, Ash, Trig, and Lillian? I sent you the setting. I'll meet you in your room."

Urban nodded then loudly excused herself from the table and went to ask a Natural attendant for directions.

"Of course, madam. This way," the Natural said, leading her.

The Natural stopped in front of a steel door, and Urban couldn't help but notice that he wasn't much older than she was, yet he kept his eyes submissively downcast.

"Lee Urban, these are your quarters for the night. Please let me know if they are satisfactory." The Natural's voice was soft, almost a whisper.

Urban smiled. She tried to make eye contact with the Natural, but he continued to keep his eyes on the ground. "Thank you. I'm sure it's fine."

The Natural dipped his head and left, but a weight descended on her chest. *This is why AiE has to find the hybrid. Things will change then. We will finally see equality between Naturals and Enhanced.*

The sharp tang of oranges greeted her inside the room. A stand with two bowls and three oranges in each sat in a corner. Lucky numbers, according to Auntie.

But Urban didn't believe in luck.

"Winners make their own luck," Father had always told them. Then, he had pushed them harder, Urban being challenged the most.

A mash-up of Western and ancient Asian influences decorated the room. The pastel-colored love seats, coffee table, chest of drawers, and makeup stand were all reminiscent of the plush Western style. But the walls adorned with paintings spoke of the Asian Federation's influence.

Urban changed into her full-immersion XR suit and face mask. Cool, soft smart fabric brushed up against her skin as the external plates conformed across her body, extending from her face to her toes. She sent out the group invite and entered the meeting setting Everest had shared with her.

Her retina overlays transported her to a dilapidated warehouse. Her smart suit temperature dropped to mimic the shack's cold atmosphere, and she instantly regretted wearing it.

Most of the others hadn't joined yet. Only one person was there, waiting.

Coral stamped her high-top sneakers for warmth. Her avatar's blue hair was tied up in a messy bun and her yellow, owl-like eyes studied their surroundings. She rubbed at her sleeves, and Urban caught a glimpse of her embedded flamethrowers.

Urban still couldn't believe Qing Angel, the influencer who'd hacked into her system on the last day of her job, was her ex-roommate, Coral. Last semester, she'd been following Urban and had warned her about several upcoming attacks.

Her parents had been convinced Coral was the attacker,

but Urban wasn't so sure. Since then, Coral had proven her innocence by providing valuable intel via encrypted channels to AiE, as well as warning Urban of another attack. This was the first time since then that Urban was seeing her ex-roommate, even if it was in XR.

Urban glanced around, though the warehouse looked deserted. "Is it a good idea for you to be here in XR?"

"I got rid of the bugs they planted on me. I'm not being watched anymore."

Urban breathed a sigh of relief. "Who do you think was spying on you?"

"The usual suspects. SAS."

Urban startled, surprised by Coral's casual tone when it came to the group who brutally murdered Naturals.

But so many questions came to mind. "Coral, why did you hack me last semester? Was it just to warn me?"

Coral studied Urban a moment, her expression maddeningly neutral. "How much do you know about WEO?"

"The World Enhancement Org? They're the global governing body overseeing all enhancements at the Federation level."

"They're more than that. They also have a security division ensuring each Federation adheres to those laws." She stomped her feet again.

"Gosh, it's cold in here." A black hoodie suddenly materialized on Coral's avatar. "Anyway, I'm a part of WEO's security division. I was sent to PKU to check up on some suspicious behavior. AKA *you*."

Urban's eyes widened. "Wait. You're not even a real student?"

Coral gave a short laugh. "I was. But uni was never my priority. Finding you was."

Urban's brain reeled from the information. "But how did you find me?"

"You tripped a few of our traps with your Natural genetics," Coral explained. "I was sent to investigate. When you opened my file from work, you gave me root access to your system. I was able to access your location and messages after that. That's how I figured out which dorm you'd be in and conveniently rearranged our rooms so that I was your roommate."

"I knew I shouldn't have opened that file." Urban groaned. "Are there other traps set in place I might have tripped? Does SAS have similar tests in the Metropolis?"

"Actually, yes." Coral pulled the hood up over her head. "It's been a huge pain for me to keep them off your tail. Even had to sign up for that awful motorcycle race."

The memory of the race came flooding back. Adrenaline from the heavy bass pulsed through her. Wind rushed past her as she made the jump. Terror clouded her mind as her motorcycle shut off and plummeted down.

Urban pushed the images away. "But why does SAS want me dead? I get that they think I'm the hybrid, but why kill me?"

"Because," Coral spoke slowly, as if explaining to a child. "They're Supers Against Soups. They're prejudiced against all Naturals. They like their superior genetics and want to keep it that way. If the hybrid were discovered, and everyone were given the choice of enhancements, they'd lose their edge."

"Would I be safer in the Western Federation?"

Coral eyed Urban a moment, then said, "No. SAS's global headquarters are based there, actually."

Urban's chest constricted.

There was a knock on the door, and Urban switched to dual vision mode so she could see her immediate physical surroundings.

Everest stood outside. "Sorry, I got caught up in a conversation with your parents."

"Are they joining?"

Everest shook his head. "AiE doesn't want them involved. They have obligations with your relatives for the holidays, and their absence would be missed."

Urban didn't know if she was disappointed or not. "Is anyone from AiE joining us?"

He shook his head. "No. They try and stay anonymous. Betrayal from the inside is what destroyed them over a decade ago. They take extra precautions now to keep each unit and all members separate and safe. They weren't too happy when I suggested we pull in Coral and Ash for this operation." Everest gave Coral a wry smile. "Sorry."

Coral shrugged.

"They wanted their own agents to work this mission," Everest continued. "But for reasons you'll understand in a minute, that wasn't possible."

Mission. The word sent a thrill of excitement up Urban's spine. *Maybe we'll finally start getting some answers.*

As they waited for Lillian, Urban couldn't help but notice how different Everest seemed. His eyes were a focused fire, his stance, confident and alert. Even the way he spoke was commanding in a way she'd never seen before.

Urban realized she watched the side of Everest he'd kept secret the whole time they'd dated. She had recently learned he was one of five Outskirts Captains reporting directly to the AiE Premier of Operations. Now, seeing him take charge, she believed it.

Urban squashed the sensations flooding her.

He broke my heart once. I don't know if I can trust him with it again.

Urban changed back to full virtual reality mode as an avatar resembling a cyborg with robotic limbs but a human face appeared.

"Welcome, Lillian," Everest said.

Ash's avatar appeared next in the warehouse. He resembled a speckled Tyrannosaurus rex, the coloring matching the shade of his wings in reality.

"A dinosaur?" Coral eyed Ash. "Seriously?"

Ash grinned, revealing jagged rows of teeth. He nodded at Urban, then winked flirtatiously at Lillian. Her sister tried not to laugh.

Trig appeared next, wings fading into the background while his body remained clearly visible. He looked almost the same as he did in reality. But in XR, his skin glowed silver and his hair was red-hot lava.

"Want to tell me why we're gathered at this hour of the night?" A virtual beanie appeared on Ash's head, but started to slip off. He caught it and tried to put it back on, but his tiny little T-Rex hands couldn't quite reach. He finally gave up and the beanie disappeared.

"We have a lead on the scientist who created the hybrid, but we need to move fast," Everest told the group. "His name is Dr. Liang. He's the researcher who invented the microneedle patch. He's connected to the scientist who created the hybrid and might be able to lead us to him. We've found their encrypted messages. If we can access them, we think we can figure out where the scientist is."

"That's not super helpful," Coral pointed out. "Brute-force hacking their messages could take a minimum of ten years to get one line of info."

"Or?" Everest prompted.

"Or finding the decoder key would be awesome. But if the only person to have it is Dr. Liang, we'd have to access his physical tatt . . ." Her words slowed. "That's your plan, isn't it?"

Everest nodded.

"How is that possible? Liang is dead." Urban live projected an obituary of the researcher dated over a decade ago.

"So where do you think that tatt might be now?" Everest asked.

Urban hesitated. "In a tatt temple?"

"So you're suggesting we become tomb raiders or something?" Ash looked hopeful.

"Why don't we hack the temple and get the decoder key that way?" Coral asked.

"Liang's tatt is in a special division of the temple with an air-gapped system."

"Oh." Coral nodded. "No remote access. We'll have to go in person."

"We're not exactly trained hackers and heist men," Urban said. "Well, not all of us." She glanced covertly at Coral.

"That's why *you* won't be stealing anything," Everest said. "You'll be our distraction."

"Distraction?" Urban's brow arched.

"What better way to divert attention off of us than a KOL showing up?" Coral said, catching on. "I would volunteer, but I don't have any relatives in temples in the Asian Federation. It wouldn't make sense for me to be there, unless it's as one of your guests."

"Whereas you"–Everest turned knowing eyes on Urban–"happen to have a deceased relative in the exact one we need access to: *Sunsi* Temple."

"*Popo*?" Urban blanched. "Our grandma?" She looked to Lillian, whose mouth was slightly opened. Urban had been too young when *Popo* died to understand what was happening.

She had a few memories of *Popo* picking them up from school when their parents were busy at work, but otherwise, didn't remember much of her. Lillian and Lucas, on the other hand, had spent the majority of their early years with her. She was their built-in childcare.

Not that the Lees had real need of her, with all the nannies and servants. But *Popo* had insisted her grandchildren not be raised by strangers.

After *Popo's* death, Urban had been forced to attend the funeral rituals. The eerie melody from the gong, drums, and Sheng mouth organ still haunted some of her dreams.

She remembered mourners dressed in white, wailing and crying in a tent. She remembered the overpowering scent of yellow and white mum wreaths in a cramped space. She remembered little white envelopes with candy and virtual tokens passed out. And . . . that was all she remembered.

Since then, both of her older siblings and Mother had faithfully visited the temple every year to pay their respects. But Urban couldn't remember the last time she'd been there. She was pretty sure she'd gone at least once since the funeral.

"Urban will be the distraction," Everest was saying. "Coral and I will be Lillian's guests. Trig and Ash will accompany Urban as guests. Once inside, we'll break off to hack Dr. Liang's tatt."

"Why do they get to do all the cool stuff?" Ash grumbled, his tiny arms not quite folding over his reptilian chest.

Coral rolled her eyes. "'Cause they don't want your dinosaur brain slowing them down."

Lillian ignored their banter, a crease forming on her forehead. "I don't see how we are going to pull this off. There are all sorts of security measures to prevent that from happening. All entrances require special access and could be easily sealed off in case of a breach. There are no windows, no other possible escape routes. Not to mention, they have facial recognition readers everywhere, human guards, and bots. If they engage lockdown protocol, there's no getting out."

"That's why timing is everything," Everest replied. "The temple is closely monitored and rarely receives visitors. We will be instant suspects on most days. There's just one time of the year when the temple is overrun."

"Lunar New Year," Urban said thoughtfully. "The temple will be full of people hoping to boost their sosh by paying their respects."

"Exactly. If we can pull this off during that window of time, we'll be safely hidden within the masses."

"But that's tomorrow!" Lillian exclaimed.

"That's why AiE sent me here," Everest said pointedly. "We'll meet in the real world version of this abandoned warehouse tomorrow morning." He faced the others. "Coral, Trig, Ash, can you take an overnight pod to get here?"

"There's a strong possibility I can make that work," Trig spoke up in his thick accent.

Urban often forgot he wasn't from the Asian Federation. His pronunciation was smoother and he had a lighter inflection on some of his tones, distinguishing him as from the African Federation. Even in XR, he was impeccably dressed, wearing a suit making him appear much older.

Coral grinned. "That's easy for me."

"Not so easy." Ash glanced over his shoulder as if looking out for someone in real life. "My family will be furious if I go missing. But," he added, "they usually sleep in late on New Year's Day. They probably won't notice if I'm gone a few extra hours."

"There's one more thing." Everest hesitated. "I have some good news . . . but also some bad news. The bad news is, if we get caught, we're in serious trouble with the Asian Federation. Temples are under their jurisdiction, and breaking into their data is a federal offense."

The room grew silent and Urban's stomach tied itself in knots.

"And the good news?" Ash prompted.

"The good news is, because of that, apparently no one's ever attempted it. Their security system has grown lax over the years." He took a breath. "I'm confident my plan will work."

"I know what the consequences are for committing a federal offense in the Western Federation," Coral said, concern coloring her voice. "But what exactly are we talking about for the Asian Federation?"

"If the Federation catches us"–Everest's jaw tightened–"our sosh will zero out."

It was as if the air was sucked out of the room.

Urban grew suddenly dizzy. She thought about her own sosh of 90 dropping to zero. If that happened, she'd lose her motorcycle license. She wouldn't be able to purchase things in

QuanNao, or even ride public transportation. All her avatar's accessories would be taken and auctioned off.

She'd once stumbled upon a Flyer in the Outskirts whose sosh had zeroed out. He was destitute, begging on the side of a road for food. If her sosh went to zero, she'd end up like him.

The knots in her stomach tightened. "Then we'd better not fail."

IT SOUNDED LIKE A WAR ZONE OUTSIDE FROM the pop, crackle, and boom of fireworks. They grew increasingly loud as each minute to Lunar New Year ticked by.

Urban was still thinking about her conversation with Everest and the fact that they were about to steal a tatt. *What if tomorrow doesn't work? We need a backup plan. But what?*

She turned on a holo of the Dragons' last game against the Scorpions. She hadn't watched a game in ages. She'd grown up like most other kids, dreaming of joining the team. But once Mother squashed that hope, Urban rarely watched anymore. It was another painful reminder of something she wasn't and could never be because of her genetics.

An odd feeling stirred in her chest. If she accepted Dr. Gong's offer, that could be her facing the arena in the coming weeks.

Of course, she would have to find a way not to compete so she never actually ended up in the arena. She couldn't have Samson crashing and sending the school into chaos again.

As Urban continued to observe the Games, she noticed Willow, the team's captain, never played any B-string players—only the A team. If Urban joined, she might not have to worry about competing at all.

But what about the attacks? They won't stop because I'm on campus.

We're already in danger, no matter where I go. The attacks won't stop until we find the hybrid, then they'll leave us alone.

I think.

The door flew opened and Lillian barged in. She looked like she was about to say something but stopped. "You're watching the Games?"

Urban debated telling Lillian about Dr. Gong's offer, but her older sister was so protective, she might try and talk Urban out of it.

"You have something better to watch?" Urban asked instead.

Lillian eyed Urban a moment before flopping onto the bed. "I can't believe AiE is sending a bunch of college kids to do their dirty work."

Urban paused the holo, surprised at the vehemence in Lillian's voice. She rarely saw her sister this upset. "But you and I are the only ones with a believable excuse to visit the temple. They can't send a bunch of AiE operatives. It would be suspicious."

"First the lights getting cut, now this. I don't like it."

Dread pooled in the pit of Urban's stomach. "Do you think it's the attacker from last semester?"

"I don't know." Lillian sat up. "I'm glad Trig and Ash will be with you tomorrow. I've trained with Trig and trust him with my life. And from what you've told me of Ash, he seems highly qualified. And if you trust him, so do I."

"Ash is on the military-commander track, so I should hope he's trained," Urban remarked. "Not to mention, he's saved my life more times than I care to admit. He's a good guy."

"Don't try your sales pitch on him again." Lillian huffed, though the corner of her lips lifted.

Urban gave an innocent shrug.

"Anyhow, I came in here for a reason." Lillian bounded off the bed. "Time for some fun!"

"Why do I have a feeling our ideas of fun are not aligned?"

Lillian grinned. "Let's practice jiujitsu. It's been too long. And"–for a moment, her face grew somber–"you need to stay in shape."

Urban groaned. "It's the holidays. Can't I be lazy for one day?"

"Come on." Lillian pulled Urban off the bed, and then immediately proceeded to trap Urban in an armbar.

"Fine!" Urban grimaced. "I'll practice with you, just make it stop!"

Lillian freed her triumphantly.

"You're the worst sister." Urban tightened her ponytail.

"Would you rather I be a normal sister and steal your clothes and fight over the bathroom and boys?" Lillian quipped. "Now, what to work on? How about chokes?"

"Ah, yes! Chokes. Sooooo fun."

Lillian ignored the comment and gained side control on Urban. She released, then stood and turned to Urban, waiting expectantly.

Somehow, Lillian always made moves look easy. Urban knelt to the ground and concentrated, trying to remember the steps.

"First, it's getting around my guard," Lillian instructed.

Urban followed her guidance, until she completed the move. She practiced several more times until she could execute it without hesitation.

"Good job." Lillian nodded her approval. "Keep practicing until you have the muscle memory. In a real attack, you tend to forget most of your training. You want to make sure your body knows what to do without having to think about it."

"More practice, wahoo!" Urban grumbled, though she made a mental note of it. While jiujitsu had started off as something her mother had forced her into, after multiple attacks on her life, she was beginning to appreciate and value self-defense.

"Say," Lillian said slowly, "you and Everest. How's that going?"

Urban looked at her sister. Her face was expressionless. *So this is the real reason she's here.* "It's . . . awkward."

"Do you want to be with him?"

It was a simple question, and yet it resurfaced layers of buried emotions. Being with Everest was like constantly unearthing new things about herself and the world around her. It reminded Urban of the reopening of the Terracotta Soldiers she'd been lucky enough to attend.

The museum's bot tour guide had given a live demonstration on a fake statue, showing the effort that went into carefully removing layers of dirt to restore each work of art. New features on the soldier became gradually visible as the dirt slowly vanished.

Sometimes, Urban felt like that soldier.

Everest always pushed past the layers and walls she put up. He saw the real version of her–the version she kept tightly locked and hidden away.

Urban hesitated. "I . . . I don't know."

Lillian tilted her head, watching her younger sister with speculative eyes.

Urban sighed. "I'd be lying to say I don't care about him. But he hurt me so badly, I want to be sure I can trust him before taking another risk like that again. Sometimes, it seems like all he really cares about is AiE. I get that it's important, obviously. But he broke up with me because of them, and now he's willing to be back together with me because of them. I feel like all he does is follow orders, and I'm secondary."

Lillian was silent a moment, considering her. "Have you asked him about it? Why he cares so much about AiE?"

"Well, no," Urban confessed.

"I'm not going to give you any dating advice, since clearly I'm not an expert in that department," Lillian said. "But, I will say, don't push him away. From what I've seen, Everest knows you. I mean, really *knows* you." She looked Urban in the eye. "He's one of the few people who sees and accepts the real version of you. That's a rare gift."

Urban's throat constricted.

For everyone else, Urban was always trying to be what they wanted. Though she'd finally learned to accept herself, she still wasn't sure how to fit in to a society of Enhanced and Naturals, since she wasn't sure she belonged to either.

She sighed. "I just need more time to think before jumping back into a relationship. I have enough decisions to make as is." Urban immediately bit her lip, realizing her slip.

Lillian frowned. "What decisions?"

Urban chose her words carefully. "For one thing, whether or not to pursue the lead on our bio parents."

"That's an easy one. Don't."

"Don't you want to know who our parents really are?" Urban asked.

"Not at all," Lillian said adamantly. "They left us. They didn't want us. Finding them, if they're even alive, would be a mistake."

"But why didn't our parents enhance both of us?" Urban pressed. "Why put us up for adoption? Hack my paperwork? Don't you ever wonder about these mysteries?"

"There's no mystery. This happens all the time. Someone has their sosh tank and can't afford to enhance their kids or keep them anymore. That's how half the kids end up in the orphanage. You can put on your detective hat and spend years trying to track our parents down, but if you find them, in the end, it will only cause you a lot of grief."

"You don't know that."

"No, I don't." Lillian sighed. "But what I do know is, we are lucky to be adopted. Our family cares about us. Why mess all that up for some fairy-tale family that probably doesn't exist?"

"Easy for you to say," Urban shot back. "You have enhancements. You fit in. I'm a Natural pretending to fit in with an enhanced family."

"That's not true," Lillian insisted. "We both belong–"

"No. *You* belong. Not me–never me." Urban's eyes stung. *Don't cry.*

Lillian put a hand on Urban's arm. "Look, I know Lucas is being a pain right now, and Father . . . well, he's being Father. But Mother really does care about you. And so do I. Isn't that enough?"

"Maybe," Urban said in a quiet voice. "But sometimes I wish I knew where we came from, you know?"

Lillian's tone softened. "I know."

They stood together for a moment.

"Speaking of family," Lillian suddenly said brightly. "It's almost time for the fireworks. I'm going to go get my invention ready. See you soon?"

Urban nodded. But when Lillian left, she collapsed onto the bed and tried to clear her mind. She must have dozed off, because a knock jolted her out of sleep. Reluctantly, she opened the door.

Her parents stood outside. "May we come in?" Mother asked.

A very inebriated Father teetered into the doorframe. Mother's mouth thinned as she helped him stand.

Urban opened the door wider, and Father stumbled in, then flopped onto the plush love seat.

Mother faced Urban, all business. "We received AiE's message about Everest being here and tomorrow's mission."

She fingered one of her giant diamond rings. "It's unsafe, and I'm displeased they didn't notify us first, but your father and I will do our best to make sure your absence goes undetected tomorrow. We'll also cover for Lillian." Mother frowned at this.

A couple days ago, Lillian had come clean about being an AiE member to their parents. Apparently, the news hadn't been received well.

Mother wouldn't be too thrilled if Urban did decide to go back to uni and join the Dragons, either. *One more thing to consider before choosing whether or not to accept Dr. Gong's offer.*

Mother stood, hesitating. "Also, I . . . wanted to give you something." She extended an empty hand.

Urban switched on augmented reality, and in her mother's hands rested a scroll tied by a silky red ribbon.

"This was my grandmother's. She was an Artisan back before it was a gene pool. She was a true master of the craft. All her paintings in real life have been ruined by mold. Your father was able to save two of them by converting them into NFTs before they were destroyed." Mother shifted. "I know we don't see eye to eye regarding your decision to become an Artisan, but you had our word. Last semester, you managed a high enough sosh that we must allow it. Your father and I still think it is a foolish decision, but if that's what you've decided, then I wanted to give you this." Her face had a slight flush. "I thought it might be inspirational."

"Thank you." Taken aback, Urban accepted the virtual scroll. With her XR gloves still on, she felt the smooth texture and lightweight paper of the NFT. Gingerly, she unraveled it, her breath catching.

In the painting, a pond of goldfish swam together in harmony. The bright oranges and reds of the fish contrasted sharply against the deep blue of the water. It spoke of peace and–for some reason–Urban was sure it was meant to represent family.

Her throat tightened.

"It reminds me of your style of paintings," Mother said softly. "I hope you like it."

Urban nodded, unable to force words out.

Mother straightened, suddenly transforming back to the polished woman Urban was used to. "It's almost time for the fireworks display." With that, Mother guided Father out the door.

Urban carefully packed the scroll away in her avatar's accessories compartment. The hallway outside her room grew louder as relatives flocked to the roof.

As she made her way to join them, a warm bustle filled the mansion and a cheeriness permeated the air. The same holiday tunes, with their familiar drumbeats and clanging symbols, played throughout. The smell of ginger, orange, and more holiday treats wafted through the house. Normally, it was Urban's favorite time of the year. But this night, she couldn't get into the spirit of it.

The lingering threat of a potential attacker stole the holiday's usual delights, and a chill settled over her.

I can't live like this, forever endangering my family. What happens if the tatt temple is a dead end? How will we find the hybrid? There has to be another way–a lead somewhere.

She climbed onto the rooftop, her mind running round in circles like the pinwheel fireworks above. A frigid wind snapped her in the face as the night sky filled with flashes of light and the delayed booms of their sources. Most of the relatives stayed huddled close together, cupping steaming teas and talking loudly to be heard above the thunderous blasts.

Scanning the crowd for Everest, Urban spotted him with Lucas and the more adventurous relatives farther out on the deck, surrounded by large boxes. She breathed a sigh of relief. He really was holding his own.

"Real fireworks? Again?" a nearby uncle complained.

Urban glanced at him.

"Why don't we ever use those hologram ones?" he griped. "Much safer and cheaper. Not to mention *legal.*"

"It's not the same," a cousin argued.

Urban couldn't help but agree. While the holographic fireworks were as loud and beautiful, they weren't the same as the real thing. The scent of burning paper and the reverberating booms in her chest couldn't quite be matched by XR. Not yet, anyway.

Children lit some of the smaller boxes with their long-distance matches, then giggled with delight as the fireworks popped, or spun in circles and lifted off the ground in sparks of cerulean and white.

Then came the larger boxes. Lucas, Everest, and two other cousins retreated before shooting the crates with their lighters.

Urban adjusted the settings on her hearing to dial down all the volume.

Her retina display marked the first box as designed by Father. It sparked to life, then shot up far into the air. At first, Urban thought it had malfunctioned. Then, with a blinding explosion, fiery green sparks filled the sky. It took Urban a second to recognize the pattern forming: a star.

She frowned. It was an easy one to make–too simple for him. He didn't even seem to want to try. She gave his firework design a generous 7 rating.

Everyone politely clapped. His ratings fluctuated as the votes came in, starting high at an 8, probably a pity vote from Mother, then dropping to 5. It stabilized at a collective 6.1.

Lillian's box released next.

Four flames streaked skyward then burst into a dancing dragon, just like the ones sure to be on all the XR feeds from the New Year's parade. The dragon pranced across the sky, then exploded in twinkling *hongbaos.*

The votes came in hovering around 9 and 10.

The younger cousins screamed with delight and pushed and shoved each other in their eagerness to catch the red envelopes. It was with much disappointment that they watched the *hongbaos* vanish before reaching them. But then, with shouts of glee, the children motioned at their tatts, realizing crypto points had been transferred to each of them. Lillian grinned, watching.

More family fireworks boomed above–a horse, red paper lanterns, and every kind of flower imaginable, their scores ranging from 6s to 9s.

Only the Lees would turn everything into a competition.

Singing, fireworks, tomorrow it will probably be who can eat the most jiaozi.

Lucas's fireworks came next. Once lit, a hissing sound emanated from the box, but nothing happened.

Everyone waited with bated breath.

"It's a dud." One of the cousins headed toward the box but Everest yanked him back.

With a shriek, flames shot skyward like missiles.

A moment later, the roof trembled in a giant explosion. An enormous seahorse bloomed above in cobalt and navy blue. It swam across the night sky, then burst into a million glimmering blue dots.

The circular lights converged into a giant wave that fell from the sky. Urban took a step back as the wave rolled toward them. The younger kids screamed and scurried away as Lucas laughed.

At the last second, the wave crashed above them, vanishing into foam and mist and leaving a salty spray in the air. Adding scent to their fireworks was new.

Despite the incredible displays, anxiety gnawed at Urban, aggravated by the shrill booms and giddy laughter. Tomorrow they had to find answers.

Her mind wandered to the times she'd searched for the hybrid in QuanNao. It all but didn't exist. The only place she'd received any real information was in one of her classes last semester.

She jolted from the realization.

My probot last semester! It taught me about the hybrid. Whoever programmed the bot must have known something. Her breath caught. *If I join the Dragons and go back to uni, I'd have a shot at figuring out who that was.*

An explosion went off so close, one of the cousins dove for cover. All around them, the night air lit up with flowers, spinning wheels, and streaking stars. As midnight drew nearer, the fireworks reached a frenzied crescendo. Usually, the sight made Urban thrum with happiness. But now, she felt burdened with weight.

I have to protect my family and find the hybrid.

The smoke grew so thick, Urban couldn't see more than a few meters in front of her. Her thoughts, too, felt foggy and shrouded in ominous smoke.

Tomorrow we're breaking into a temple and stealing a tatt.

If that fails, I'm accepting Dr. Gong's offer.

A SECURITY-BOT CHASED AFTER URBAN THROUGH a dark, chilly corridor. No matter how fast she ran, she couldn't escape it. She felt like she was running in slow motion, getting colder and colder. Her vision kept going dark and she couldn't see. Her sosh zeroed out as she was captured.

Urban awoke from her nightmare to a loud beeping noise and a bright gold light filling the room. Her tatt continued flashing until she shut off her alarm.

Shuddering, she realized her blankets had fallen off. A knot of dread remained firmly lodged within her as she got ready and then holstered her stun shield before making her way downstairs.

Hardly any of the relatives were up at this hour. Urban knew from years past they would probably sleep until noon before rousing from their drunken slumber.

A maidbot handed Urban a cup of hot green tea and a *mantou.* Urban nibbled on the steamed bread.

Popping noises made her jump. It started to grow light outside in the courtyard where two younger cousins set off fireworks and a thin sheen of smoke hovered over the ground from last night's festivities.

Urban thought about when she used to set off fireworks. How simple those days were. Mother hadn't been so strict. Things with Lillian were always good. Father was more easygoing and happy. Even Lucas had been Urban's partner in crime when it came to pranks and adventures. The two of them used to follow unsuspecting relatives and throw firecrackers, watching them jump with surprise.

The memories faded as sunlight spilled into the room. Urban headed to the back driveway to wait for the others.

Outside, frigid air crept down her back and she rubbed her arms as she waited for her XR suit to warm. She ordered a vehicle and it pulled into the driveway right as Lillian and Everest arrived.

"*Zao.*" Everest nodded.

"Morning," Urban replied and they all climbed into the vehicle.

With an almost silent electric hum, they took off. The Metropolis was quiet as they sped away. Warm red light reflected off of towering skyscrapers, and little bits of glittering snow remaining on the sidewalks.

Soon, the New Harbin Metropolis gave way to frozen tundra. Stick-figure trees and ghost-white fields lined either side of the road. They drove in silence past the white and brown landscape.

Urban's retina display pinged her a warning as they crossed over from the clean Metropolis and into the polluted Outskirts air.

<Entering yellow zone. Exercise CAUTION.>

Urban had only ever been in New Beijing's Outskirts, and she was curious to see if it was similar here.

Many of the buildings had rusted window panes and peeling paint. Some of them had dead vines climbing up their sides. Holo signs of varying neon colors flicked off as the sun rose. The streets had dirty puddles of melted snow, and steam rose from many open windows where aunties and grandmas were up early to get a head start on cooking.

Bits of trash were frozen to the ground, and a cluster of beggars sat huddled in a caved-in alcove for warmth. Delivery drones buzzed through the air, delivering last-minute cooking supplies and presents.

Urban decided it was very similar to New Beijing's Outskirts, only it didn't smell as bad, and was less crowded and noisy. Then again, that might have been due to the holidays.

They reached the end of the Outskirts and pulled into an abandoned parking lot next to a dilapidated warehouse. There were two sets of dirty tire tracks in the otherwise pristine snow.

"Looks like the others are here." Everest pulled a mask on over his face, and Urban and Lillian followed his example.

<Entering orange zone. Exercise CAUTION.>

Once, those warnings had caused fear to ripple through her. Now, after two weeks of living with Everest's family, she felt more comfortable with them. She almost felt safe–like she could belong.

Almost.

Despite how easy it was to blend in with Naturals compared to the Enhanced, there was always a sliver of doubt as to whether she belonged. Even though she was a Natural, she'd spent more of her life in the Metropolis, which was a world of its own.

When she interacted with Naturals, she had learned how to blend in well enough from her days at the AI training factory. But given enough time, the cracks in her façade began to show.

The physical things were easy enough to change: carry old tech (or pretend not to have tech at all); wear clothes less of a fashion statement and more utilitarian in nature; and keep a constant hunch to the shoulders.

But some of the differences were harder for Urban to replicate and left her feeling lost. There were certain phrases that were different from the Metropolis. Urban would nod along when Naturals said them, then would search in QuanNao for what they actually meant.

It was in those moments she felt lost in the space between two worlds.

Urban snapped out of her thoughts as Everest exited the vehicle and she followed. An icy wind hit her and her eyes watered and blinked as she entered the warehouse. Despite the mask covering her mouth and nose, the scent of urine permeated the air. Ash, Trig, and Coral were already waiting in the main room.

Behind them, a broken-down metal staircase led to what looked like a control center. Sagging shelves, crates, metal boxes, and bins that looked alarmingly like eroded toxic waste containers surrounded them. With a click, her mask's filtration system came on.

"Good to see you again in the flesh." Coral's face was mostly covered by her red mask, but the corners of her eyes lifted up in a smile.

"Same." Urban smiled back. She surveyed the others. Trig gave her a head nod. Ash winked, though it was directed at Lillian. Everyone was garbed in festive red smart wear to blend in at the temple.

Everest went over the plan again and then distributed circular balls, one each to Urban, Trig, and Ash. "This is your ticket out. Don't waste it."

He turned to Urban. "While we're at the temple, make sure to actually pull up memories of your grandma. If security looks into the records, we want a plausible excuse for why we were there."

She nodded and they broke into two teams and made their way out.

Ash and Trig rode in Urban's car. They were all quiet on the drive over, no doubt contemplating the ramifications of zeroing out their sosh. Urban focused on the landscape, trying not to think about that.

All too soon, they were pulling into a small but festive town.

Holo lanterns dangled across the streets, with decorative couplets projected above every alcove. As they approached the temple, the traffic picked up. Despite the early hour, vehicles littered the side of the road, and streams of people surged around them.

They got as close as they could to the temple before disembarking and joining the crowds. Urban led the way through the maze of people until the outer building came into view.

A thin, cold mist hovered around the ancient walls, partially shrouding its curved tiled roof and blood-red doors from view. Temple goers shuffled silently forward, the air thick with memories of the dead.

The group made their way up a set of wide concrete stairs, and the temple's entrance came into view–a giant *paifang* arching over sharp steps. Brilliant seafoam blues, cherry reds, and rich greens decorated the structure with painted characters and designs.

On the other side, the temple loomed above a stone garden with leafless trees and stone statues. The entry was sealed off and guarded by several *Jingcha* bots. Each had armored legs that allowed them to jump super high and run incredibly fast. At least, that's what the *Jingcha Showdown* episodes Urban had watched showed.

The bots' bulging metallic arms were clunky, but Urban knew they stored a comprehensive list of supplies and weapons, from stun pikes to first aid kits to tatt freezers. Hopefully, none of which would be necessary.

One of the *Jingcha* stepped forward, square head twisting to screen their faces. "What is the purpose of your visit, Lee Urban, Ding Ash, and Trig Dlamini?"

Urban extended her tatt. "We're here to pay respects to my *popo*."

The *Jingcha* scanned her, then waved them in. A panel in the stone wall slid open, revealing a narrow walkway. Inside, it was musty, dark, and cold, even colder than it was outside, if that were possible. A gong sounded from somewhere deep within. Urban couldn't shake the feeling it was warning them.

The door shut behind them with a dull thud, and they followed the line of temple goers.

Large columns supported the high arched ceilings, with golden dragons wrapped around each one. The dragons had black, unseeing pits for eyes and razored teeth drenched in painted blood.

"That's not creepy at all," Ash said as they passed.

They reached a large set of stairs, then descended into a lower room with four doors, leading north, south, east, and west. Giant bells covered the ceiling. The sides of the walls had a continuous chained fence with hundreds of bronze locks on it.

The room was loud and packed with all sorts of Enhanced. Using Gene-IQ in her retina display, Urban identified a woman with enhancements of extreme speed and agility modeled after a flying squirrel. A man in colorful garb and tiny bells attached to his boots sashayed by. Artisan, of course. Another man, with limbs covered in a black exoskeleton like that of a beetle, flexed and unflexed his boulder-like arms.

Urban and her companions squeezed their way into the throngs of Enhanced. At the center of the room, a giant bronze basin stood with incense sticks protruding from it. Tendrils of smoke wafted into the air, filling it with a sickly sweet aroma.

Something about the place made Urban's skin crawl. She weaved quickly through the swarms of people and past the main arrival hall, noting the vid monitoring devices before ducking through another doorway.

The narrow hall had fewer people in it. Both sides had what, at first glance, looked like tiny wooden filing cabinets. Studying them closer, Urban realized they were actually holo projections over dull gray cement. The cabinets rose from the floor to the ceiling, and each one had a name embossed in gold. Every few paces, the shelves would stop, and a small viewing room would open up.

Urban faced the wall, eyes scanning it for "Liu," her grandmother's surname. Since wives kept their surnames while children took their father's surname, Urban's mother was a Zhou while the rest of the family were all Lees, and her maternal grandmother was a Liu while the rest of her family were Zhous.

Her hand reached up toward a wooden cabinet emblazoned with familiar characters: "Liu Mingchen."

She scanned her tatt and the faux wooden door opened, the cement cool on her fingertips.

Urban reached inside, pulling out a metal scroll, and wiped off a thin sheen of dust. The smooth parchment weighed hardly anything. She stared at the scroll in her hand–all that was left of Liu *Popo*.

It was hard to imagine an entire life could be reduced to something so small.

Is life really so fleeting? You get a sosh, a family, some accomplishments that only matter to a few people, and then you're gone, sitting in a tatt temple collecting dust. Is that really all there is to it?

For this reason, Urban didn't come to the temple. It was too depressing.

She shook herself and searched for an unoccupied viewing room.

A window on each door indicated whether the room was in use. Frosted glass windows meant the room was occupied, clear meant the room was available. Most of the rooms were frosted over today, but toward the end, she found one that was clear.

The door slid shut behind them with a soft click. They were in a tiny wooden room the size of a closet in the Metropolis. A sagging bench sat ready for use, and across from it, a circular hole protruded from the wall. Urban slid the scroll inside the hole and a holo projection flickered to life.

She returned to the bench and Ash and Trig squeezed in on either side of her, their wings taking up most of the space.

"Welcome, Lee Urban, to the Temple of North Mountains," a melodious voice seeming to come from all directions addressed her. "You have come to pay your respects to Liu Mingchen, correct?"

"Correct," Urban said.

"One moment please."

The display changed from white to an image of a woman in her mid-forties with a kind smile and mischievous eyes. Her grandma was the last generation to live openly without enhancements. For a Natural, *Popo* had aged well.

Urban had never seen her grandma this young before. It was weird being reminded that her grandmother had once been so vibrant and full of life.

A carousel of moving images appeared, each a separate vid recording from the view point of *Popo*. Urban's eyes caught on a vid recording of herself and Lillian making *jiaozi* with their grandma.

Urban's two pigtails stuck straight out. Lillian was missing one of her front teeth and grinning up at *Popo* as she held up a *jiaozi* falling apart at the seams.

"There's your gal, Ash," Trig said.

"Lillian isn't *my* girl. Yet," Ash corrected, then grinned.

"Right. Asking her on an XR date last week worked very well in your favor."

"Hey. She was busy. It happens. So, I'll ask again when she's not busy. A girl can only resist this–he gestured at his face– "for so long."

Ignoring their banter, Urban flicked through the menu options. The recordings of her grandma made her wonder what growing up must have been like for her mother. "Bring up memories with Liu MingChen and Zhou Flora," Urban ordered.

The vid recordings vanished, replaced by new ones. "Show me Flora's childhood."

Several vids appeared, representing different time periods. Urban zeroed in on one where her mother looked eight. Several more recordings populated, all around that age. A vid recording of a birthday flashed by, next was a Dragon Boat Festival, then school, and next, one of Mother crying.

Urban paused, then selected the latter, curious what could make her stone-faced mother upset. The full-body immersion experience began as the memory played.

Urban was in a cluttered apartment that smelled of burnt rice. Her XR suit became warm and humid, mimicking the climate of the memory. Bright sunlight shone through a crack in the closed window.

Mother sat hunched and small in her seat at a rickety table.

"These scores are completely unacceptable," Urban said in a shrill voice. Only, it wasn't her saying it. It was disorienting reliving a memory from her *Popo's* point of view.

"How do you expect to get into a decent university with such abysmal grades?"

Guess I know where Mother gets it.

Urban studied the memory of her mother, so lifelike. The younger version of Flora sank further into her chair, as if trying to hide from sight. Urban actually felt sorry for her.

"I'll work harder," Mother whispered.

Popo studied her daughter a moment before speaking. "You have to. You know what will happen if you are to be–"

Her words died on her tongue.

Blackness.

With a dizzying jolt, the vid recording stopped. Urban found herself back in the tiny wooden room, squeezed between Trig and Ash.

"Hey! I want my money back," Ash complained.

Trig frowned. "That was odd."

Urban selected the memory and re-entered it. At the exact same point, it stopped again.

After a short delay, it picked back up in the same setting. Mother now had wet cheeks and Grandma was standing above her.

"You will leave tomorrow for the EuroAsian Federation. The schools there will prepare you." She stooped down and patted Mother's head. "Don't cry, you'll make new friends. It will be fine. You'll see."

The recording ended as Mother slowly stood and left the room.

Urban knew her mother had studied abroad growing up but she'd never known why. Why would the EuroAsian Federation have a better education system? Why send her away? Her mother avoided any talk about her time abroad.

Urban returned to the main menu and selected another memory, when her mother was older. This time, a crowded street came into view with the faintest hint of fried potatoes in the air. It was hard to tell if it was in the Outskirts or the Metropolis. Back then, the two weren't so segregated. Both Naturals and Enhanced flooded the streets.

A hooded Super stopped suddenly a couple meters away in front of a Natural woman. The woman tried to sidestep the hooded figure but he blocked her.

The Natural said nothing, just brushed past him, in the process knocking his hood off. Upon seeing his face, she stumbled, tripping on a curb.

The Super's hand shot out, gripping her around the wrist and jerking her upright. The woman screamed as if in pain and shook herself free.

At this point, the crowd had given them a wide berth.

The woman grabbed at her wrist, where he'd touched her, moaning in agony. Someone shouted for a medbot. The Super, only a teen, stood watching, a grin slithering across his toad-like features.

Suddenly, Urban lurched forward in the memory as *Popo*

ran toward the injured woman. "Are you okay?" she asked. "What happened?"

"My hand." The woman struggled to speak. Her veins bulged and pulsed in her temples.

Popo examined the woman's hand. It had swelled to the size of a balloon. Then she turned to look at the Super. "What have you done?"

The Super remained expressionless, tiny eyes gleaming. "What should have been done to every Natural. *Justice.*"

Then he walked away as a medbot arrived. "Everyone back away," it ordered.

A young version of Mother trembled and *Popo* put a steadying hand on her.

The woman on the ground began to convulse.

Popo turned her daughter away. "It's time to go."

The memory ended and blanketed the room in a dark silence. Urban was left trying to piece together what she'd witnessed.

During the Genetic Revolution, many of the first Enhanced had been persecuted. Naturals were jealous of the Enhanced superior genetics and had bullied them. In some instances, even killed them.

But once the Enhanced claimed power, everything changed. The bullying stopped. And then the tables reversed and it was the Enhanced attacking the Naturals, getting revenge for family members and friends that had been hurt and killed.

Most of such crimes had died off as the distance of time had smoothed over the wounds of the Genetic Revolution. But remnants remained, cracked, bleeding, and festering in secret.

Still, seeing the blatant violence was jarring. *I can't believe Mother lived through that.*

"Was that who I think it was?" Ash asked.

Urban turned to him. "What do you mean?"

"Was that one of the original Deadly Five?"

Urban's eyes widened. She had seen the feeds on the Deadly

Five, but these days, they operated in the shadows. Open killings were practically nonexistent.

"I'm sorry." Trig looked at them. "What is the Deadly Five?"

"Something you all from the African Fed are lucky not to have." Ash shuddered, his wings ruffling in the process. "They're named after the five deadly poisons said to come out in the month of May."

"They're also the founders of SAS," Urban added.

Trig frowned. "I've read multiple volumes on Asian Federation history. Are the deadly poisons from the origin stories for the Dragon Boat Festival? If I recall, it was poisonous snakes, scorpions, toads, centipedes, and spiders–all creatures that come out in the warmer months of May?"

"Looks like your studying paid off," Ash remarked. "Just like the five deadly poisons, the Deadly Five are five Enhanced with genetics lethal to all Naturals. One of them, the Deadly Fifth, has enhancements like that of a poisonous tree frog. Any Natural who touches him dies."

"Which is highly illegal," Urban said. "He must have gotten his enhancements from one of the underground labs." She was still picturing the Natural woman convulsing on the ground when her alarm went off. "Time to go."

The three of them left the viewing room and returned to the main hall. The eerie dragons seemed to watch Urban, waiting for a misstep. She took a deep breath, then changed her social settings from private to public, ensuring Gene-IQ's DNA reader was still set to private. Her social score of 90, suddenly was on display for the world to see.

Her sosh had increased since the tryouts, and staring at the glowing number now still felt unreal to Urban. She'd tried so long and hard to achieve a high sosh, and now it meant so little to her. She rarely even thought about it. Then again, that was a luxury only a KOL could afford.

People flowed in and out of the rooms around them. Urban's

retina display picked up their soshes, ranging from the upper 50s to low 80s.

At first, nothing happened.

But then, some of the people around her began to slow as they passed, noticing her sosh. One of them took a tentative step forward. "Excuse me, Lee Urban? Would you mind if we snapped?"

Urban smiled, for once not minding at all. "Sure."

Soon, the viewing rooms were all but forgotten as a crowd formed around her. What started as a few people wanting to snap, quickly turned into a mob. This was exactly the scenario most KOLs wanted to avoid, and she was willingly walking into it.

As the crowd pressed in tighter, Trig slipped away unnoticed.

Ash did his best to shield Urban, but the heat from the surrounding bodies stifled her. The scent of too many perfumes and sticks of incense, suffocating. The bodies, soft flesh and hard bones, swept her in a tide of claustrophobic movement. Just then, an explosion rocked the room.

Dust and wooden splinters fell from the ceiling. Fractured beams left a gaping hole overhead, exposing the dull gray sky. It looked so life-like. Even though Urban knew it was a projection, she was still tempted to cover her head.

Pandemonium broke out.

A wailing alarm cracked through the air. "Engaging lockdown protocol," a mechanical voice announced.

"Come on." Ash grabbed Urban by the arm. "That's our cue to leave."

THE *JINGCHA* WAVED SIZZLING STUN PIKES, blocking the exit.

"No one leaves until we identify the source of the disturbance," one of them said in a monotone.

Urban backed away from the door, palms sweating. Without a word, she dropped a metal ball out from her sleeve, careful to use Ash as a shield against any monitoring devices.

The ball rolled away of its own accord.

A second later, another deafening explosion rocked the room. People screamed. The mob stampeded toward the exit. The two *Jingcha* held out their stun pikes and shocked a few people at the front of the stampede, but then were overrun.

The mob banged on the locked door.

Urban held her breath. This was the one weak point in their plan.

If the human security team monitoring the room decided it was in their best interest to detain all the visitors in order to find the breach, the door would remain locked and they would be trapped. If, however, for the sake of tourism and reducing mass hysteria, they opened the door, they would be letting the perpetrator get away.

As Urban watched the local news on her retina display, a string of angry pings and live streams popped up. The Temple's sosh started to drop.

They need a little more encouragement. Urban nodded to Ash and he dropped another ball. This one rolled away and hid behind a pillar.

Another ear-splitting detonation.

"It's going to collapse!" a woman screamed, peering up as more dust fell from the roof. "We're trapped in here to die!"

"Let us out of here!" a Flyer demanded as he pounded the exit with his wings.

The Temple's sosh dropped faster than the fake particles falling from the ceiling. At this rate, the temple would be out of business if it didn't unlock its door in the next few minutes.

The temple's owners must have realized this, because a short moment later, the door's locking mechanism released and the *Jingcha* stood asidc.

Throngs of people pushed their way through, sweeping Urban up with them.

Back outside, the crowd began to disperse and she slipped away. Her breathing finally slowed as it grew calm and quiet around her.

A green triangle appeared in her retina display. Trig was already back to being invisible again, but his familiar presence loosened some of the tension in her gut. *Where are the others?*

"Hey," a familiar voice said.

Urban whirled and spotted Everest, relief flooding her. As he approached, she couldn't get over how different he looked without his outdated eye covering and worn XR suit.

In their place, he wore a black fitted jumpsuit, accentuating his toned muscles, and with square patches giving him a military look. His retina displays were still colored that brilliant blue. Even his normally tousled shock of black hair was slicked to the side in the latest fashion. He really did look Enhanced, and it was jarring.

As he caught up, Urban tried to calm the maelstrom of emotions within her.

Then she noticed his expression. Something was wrong.

"Come with me," Everest whispered as he called a vehicle over.

Once inside, Urban pressed her hand on the leather seats as they zipped through the streets. "Where are we going?"

"Somewhere we can't be overheard." Everest left it at that.

Urban noticed that Trig, faithful as ever, managed to keep up. Lillian really had found the best bodyguard when she'd selected him for her sister. Being both a Flyer and a Camo made him nearly impossible to shake. Urban would know.

Soon, they pulled to a stop back at the warehouse.

"Change into these." Everest handed her Outskirts tech and clothes.

He popped off his blue retina displays and his eyes immediately shifted to their deep, starry-night black. He switched his slick, shiny shoes for his familiar, worn boots, XR jacket, and headset.

Urban bit her lip trying not to laugh as Everest attempted to rid himself of the hair gel. Sighing, he gave up and left his hair a tousled mess. All of a sudden, she was looking at the old Everest–the Natural she knew so well. The one who knew *her* so well.

Everest looked up and they locked eyes.

Urban's heart beat faster. *We're going to have to talk soon about us.* Both excitement and anxiety filled her at the thought. *I need to know more about his reason for working for AiE. But now isn't the time.*

She broke away to find a private place where she could change.

Once they were both fully in Outskirts tech, Everest led the way to two shiny motorcycles outside. "I had these delivered. It will be faster this way."

Urban took a seat and linked her retina display to the control. Then they were off.

For a moment, it was like old times, riding side by side on their bikes. Urban could almost trick herself into believing they were still together and her biggest worry was fitting in at uni.

But as they drew nearer to the Outskirts, Everest pulled ahead, leaving her and her wistful dreams behind.

A Natural stepped into the street in front of Urban and she had to slam on the brakes. The back of her bike fishtailed on the slushy road and she fought to get control. Once her bike straightened out, she glanced in her mirror to see the beggar stumbling carelessly across the street. A quick sosh scan showed his low score of 4.

Urban shuddered.

Maybe he'd meant to do that–to be hit.

Urban's jaw tightened.

Pulling back on the throttle, she shot forward, trying to keep up with Everest.

Her retina display sent her a ping as she entered the Outskirts, but she ignored it.

<Entering yellow zone. Exercise CAUTION.>

Everest slowed, then stopped in front of a tall, decrepit skyscraper with peeling paint and sides battered by graffiti. Inside, the lobby smelled of cigarettes and was almost the same temperature as outside. Urban wondered if they cut the heat to help lower rent rates. A lone holo projection displayed reruns of the Lunar New Year parade, and several sets of sagging and stained couches clustered around it.

Two Naturals sat talking, cigarettes dangling. One of them turned at their approach, and his face hardened. He lowered his cigarette. Something dark swam in those eyes as he watched their approach. "I suggest you leave, *Farmed*."

Everest tensed, and Urban grew very still. *How did he recognize me as from the Metropolis? But I'm not Enhanced. He shouldn't be able to tell.* She double-checked that her retina display color was set to black and not a showy Metropolis color.

Yep, still black.

Her hand crept slowly toward her stun shield. In her augmented maps, she saw Trig waiting outside the building. Not good.

"Did you hear me?" the man growled.

"You don't own this trash heap," a voice snapped.

A man appeared from behind Urban and Everest, arms crossed over a shiny metallic suit. His eyes glowed silver, and an extra mechanical limb waved over his head in crude gestures.

The Natural stood and looked at the man behind her. "Don't think because you're an Inventor, you can take on a dozen Naturals. My fellow Natural brothers will be here faster than you can say '*si ding.*'"

The Enhanced stood his ground and the three men stared at each other. The tension in the room was so thick Urban could have sliced it with her stun shield.

Finally, the Inventor backed down. "I was leaving anyway."

He turned and exited the building, the tension in the room instantly releasing. The two Naturals acknowledged Urban and Everest with brief nods before sitting back down.

If they found out I'm from the Metropolis, what would they do to me? Does it matter that I'm not Enhanced?

Urban couldn't dispel the tightness in her chest.

I'm one wrong word, one slipup of tech away from being attacked.

A warm touch startled her. Everest's hand rested on her shoulder, almost as if he knew Urban's thoughts. He squeezed once and then led the way toward an old elevator.

How does he always seem to know what I'm feeling?

Everest swiped his tatt and the elevator shuddered, then lurched upward.

What if AiE sends new orders to break up? What would he choose?

Urban shook her head at herself. First, she needed to know

if they'd found out anything about the hybrid.

The elevator stopped, and she followed Everest to a metal door where he entered a PIN and it slid open.

"Where are we?" Urban asked, studying the small space.

They were in a cold room, with large glass windows enabling them to see the Outskirts beyond. Holographic signs, AC units, and XR tech cluttered the spaces between buildings, blocking out most of the natural light. Instead, azure fluorescent signs bathed the space in wintry lighting.

Inside, several black couches with the leather peeling off in small patches sat back against the wall. A tea set and fake flora provided some decor. By the dust collecting on them, Urban got the impression no one had been there in some time.

Everest reached behind one of the couches and clicked on an air filter before taking off his mask. He set a pot of water to boil, then sank into one of the seats, which immediately sagged under his weight. Urban sat on the couch across from him.

"This is one of AiE's safe houses." Everest ran a hand through his hair. "I thought it would be a good space to talk."

Urban's thoughts returned to the scene she'd witnessed in the lobby.

"Are things between Naturals and Enhanced getting that bad?"

Everest stared at the windows so long, Urban thought he wasn't going to answer. "You're not supposed to know . . . but you deserve to." His sharp jawline grew taut. "Things are becoming more divided between Enhanced and Naturals. There's a bill being drafted right now that could change everything. It would be a big leap forward and would give Naturals a say in politics again and allow them to hold a position within the party. But many people–Enhanced–don't want to see it passed."

The boiler clicked off and Everest rose to pour the steaming water into a pot along with some tea leaves. "As you know, all enhancements are purchased by parents and inserted in vitro. The more money you have, the better enhancements you give to your children. Thus, the cycle of wealth and poverty continues. But this bill proposes a way to level the playing field for those in the Outskirts."

Urban knew what was coming.

"It all rests on the hybrid. Once found, if indeed it is possible to leverage hybrid genetics, no one would have to be born with enhancements. Instead, everyone would be injected with hybrid DNA in vitro. Then, when they enter puberty, they would select a gene pool and become enhanced via the microneedle patch. But it would be based on merit–a performance and aptitude test, if you will."

"That would change everything."

Everest nodded soberly. "That's why it's AiE's key initiative."

Urban was silent a moment, processing the information.

Everest poured tea into two cups and handed one to Urban, who took it gratefully. "But first we have to find the hybrid. After that, we have to get the bill some PR. All the media outlets are controlled by the Enhanced. None of them will cover the bill for fear of losing their funding from shareholders. To make matters worse, every time we find a backdoor into hacking a network, officials launch another augment-free challenge, thus lessening the number of people who see our messages."

Urban thought back to the Augmented Free campaign she saw at the parade. "Is that what they're doing right now?"

Everest nodded. "They already gained back control of the network, and I don't think our broadcast made it to more than a few thousand people. We're running out of time. The bill will go to the Capitol Prefects sometime later this year. If we haven't found the hybrid by then, and if we lose the vote, that's it. There might not be another opportunity in decades."

Urban's stomach plummeted. *We have to find the hybrid.* "Did you get what you needed today?"

"We had no problems getting into the air-gapped system, and managed to plant the backdoor in their physical hardware.

But"–Everest paused–"there was one already there."

Urban gasped. "What? Someone is one step ahead of us? Who?"

"I have no idea," Everest said. "I thought it was just AiE, SAS, and then the WEO looking for the hybrid. But with Coral's insider info on Supers Against Soups, we know they haven't figured it out. The World Enhancement Org is aware of the hybrid, but doesn't have any leads. And AiE wouldn't have sent us on this mission in the first place if they were the ones who hacked it. Which leads me to believe there might be a fourth party involved."

Urban was silent a moment, considering. "So does that mean we can't hack the tatt?"

Everest shook his head. "The good news is, with our own backdoor planted, Coral can still hack into the system to find any vulnerabilities, and then break in and get access to Dr. Liang's tatt. But whoever went before us has most likely already exploited the easiest way in. Not to mention, if the Temple's security detected the breech, they might have updated their software, making breaking in even harder."

It could be another dead end. Who knows how long it will take Coral to hack in now? There's only one sure way to find the hybrid, and it's up to me.

Her gut clenched at the implication.

Urban realized he was waiting for her to say something. "So, what now?"

"We wait and see if Coral can hack into the tatt temple."

"No, I mean"—Urban hesitated–"what's next for you?" *For us?*

"Oh." Everest gazed at her with his raven eyes. "I'm heading back to New Beijing. I'll arrange a fake date for us later."

Urban tried not to show her disappointment. *I get to explain to everyone why my fake boyfriend ditched me.*

Everest was sympathetic. "Sorry, AiE needs me back there."

"Yeah, for sure. I get it." She mustered a smile.

Everest made to leave, but Urban impulsively stopped him. "I wanted to tell you–great job with my family, and . . . your music, it was incredible."

"Thanks." Everest's cheeks tinged. "I've been working on it."

"It's paying off."

They both stood there a moment in silence.

"Well, see you around, I guess?" Urban asked. She hated how squeaky and hopeful her voice sounded.

"Yeah." Everest shifted his feet. "I think I'll be staying at a flat in the Metropolis. So I should be seeing a lot more of you."

Urban swallowed. "Cool."

Another moment of silence.

"Well, we should probably go."

"Right." Urban leaped up and helped clear the tea away before they locked up and made their way down to the lobby.

Urban called a vehicle and Everest waited until it arrived before he left.

"Bye, Urban," Everest said softly.

"Next time around! I mean, until soon." Urban bit her lip. "Bye."

She climbed quickly into the vehicle to hide her blushing cheeks, kicking herself internally. *What's wrong with me? I know Everest really well. It's not like I've never had a conversation with him before.*

And yet, it felt like they had just met. Like the relationship they'd once had was gone, replaced by something unfamiliar and fragile. One wrong word, and it might all come crashing down around them.

As the vehicle sped through the dirty, cluttered streets, Urban replayed their conversation. Their one lead might turn up to be a dead end.

"Everything hinges upon finding the hybrid," Everest had said.

She ran a finger over the tatt on her forearm, considering Dr. Gong's offer.

Her family was sure to disapprove of, or worse, forbid, her decision. It would be dangerous, but so was not doing anything–staying hidden in the Outskirts. Urban's resolve hardened.

She sent a quick response to Dr. Gong.

[Urban: Thank you for the offer to join the Dragons. I accept.]

FROZEN TRASH CRUNCHED UNDER URBAN'S feet as she stepped into the deteriorating warehouse.

Inside, dim lighting illuminated a lone figure wrapping her arms around herself for warmth. Lillian's face lit up once she noticed Urban. "Oh my gosh, I'm so glad you're safe!"

"You too," Urban replied. "I thought for sure we were all going to get caught."

They ordered a vehicle, and Urban quickly changed back into her Metropolis clothes, before they sped toward Auntie's house. Urban considered how to bring up her decision to join the Dragons. *I should also tell Lillian about my memories of the microneedle patch.*

Last semester, Urban realized she had seen the patch before being adopted. Urban hadn't told her sister about the memories, for fear of her telling their parents and keeping Urban from returning to uni.

Lillian is going to hate my decision to join the Dragons. If I start talking about weird memories that don't make sense, she'll think I've totally lost it.

But why would I have seen one of the microneedle patches before? Is it still possible the hybrid is me?

Urban mentally shook her head. Lillian already confirmed she was not. *It was probably all a strange dream or my imagination.*

"So, I heard about the network backdoor," Urban said.

"Can you believe it?" Lillian exclaimed. "Someone beat us to it. Who else knew about Dr. Liang's connection to the hybrid?"

Urban gave a helpless shrug. "I don't know. Do we have a backup plan if Coral can't hack it?"

Lillian sighed. "Don't worry, I'm sure AiE will come up with something."

"Actually, about that," Urban began carefully. "I have an idea."

Lillian looked up sharply.

"There was a probot from my genetic engineering class last semester that knew about the microneedle patch. Which means it might also know about the hybrid. I think if we could figure out who programmed it, we might get some answers."

"And how do you suggest we do that?" Lillian asked.

Urban hesitated. "I'll go back to uni and enroll in the advanced genetics class."

"Why does it have to be you?" Lillian sounded suddenly defensive. "It could be me, Coral, or Ash."

"You and Coral are on the wrong tracks for that to be possible," Urban pointed out. "And Ash is already enrolled in all his classes, which leaves me."

"Have you forgotten you were almost *killed* last semester? Twice."

Urban tried not to shrink under her sister's growing anger. They rarely fought, and when they did, it was usually petty arguments. Urban wasn't used to this. She swallowed and forced a confidence she didn't feel. "Dr. Gong has offered me a room in the KOL dorms where I'll be safe."

Lillian's eyes flew wide. "Why would he do that?"

Urban took a breath. "In exchange for joining the Dragons."

An awkward silence descended.

Lillian crossed her arms. "You wouldn't." Her voice deadly,

like a red zone's mist, stretched out to kill.

"I'd be on the B-string, which means I'll never even play. But joining would guarantee a safe spot on campus from which to find answers."

"And to foolishly endanger the whole family?" Lillian's eyes burned.

"Our family is already endangered," Urban protested. "Even last night, you said it yourself, that blackout was not an accident. This is the only way to stop the attacks."

"Which is why returning to the spotlight is dangerous," Lillian stated firmly. "You need to stay in the Outskirts."

"I can't live the rest of my life in the Outskirts. I want to help. This might be the only other chance we have to find the hybrid."

"It's not safe."

"I'm sorry, Lil." Urban tried to keep her voice steady. "But I already accepted Dr. Gong's offer."

Lillian remained silent a moment, then turned to the window, signaling the end of the conversation.

As they sped back toward Auntie's house in silence, a ping from Dr. Gong appeared in Urban's retina display.

[Dr. Gong: Congratulations and welcome! The PKU Dragons are lucky to have you.]

Urban reread the message. She knew she should feel excited, proud even, to have made the elite team and to have another lead on finding the hybrid.

Instead, she felt a sense of dread.

I hope I made the right decision.

Back at Auntie's mansion, Lillian darted away the second the vehicle's doors opened.

With a sigh, Urban went up to her own room. It was nearly

time for the annual family Ice Festival trip. The last thing she wanted to do was make small talk with her relatives, but they would be suspicious if she didn't attend. So instead, she forced herself to get ready.

She examined her appearance in the bathroom mirror. Large, dark eyes, black hair straightened and cut at the shoulders. She was still too skinny, her skin not porcelain smooth, and her jaw too sharp, to be Enhanced. But after last semester, and everything she'd been through, she no longer cared. And with her impossibly high sosh of 90, no one suspected anymore.

She could hide in plain sight.

She threw on an XR jumpsuit in her favorite color, rose gold, then applied a stick to her lips, extracting the natural pH levels and turning them a glossy red. Any sort of family outing was sure to involve meeting KOLs, check-ins, and posts. Urban was convinced half the family only came to boost their sosh.

By the time she was ready, her extended family stood gathered in the main parlor. Most of them wore bright red XR suits. Lucas stood at the center of a circle, animatedly telling a story, most likely an embarrassing one from Urban's past. Lillian turned her back to Urban when she entered the room.

Urban's heart plummeted.

"There you are, dear," Auntie said, taking her by the shoulder. "We're nearly ready to go." She looked around. "Where's your boyfriend?"

"He had to leave. Urgent business."

"What a shame." Disappointment filled Auntie's face. "He was nice to look at."

Urban flushed.

"You two were adorable together last night. If only your uncle looked at me that way." She sighed, then turned to the milling relatives trying to take selfies with Urban in the background and clapped her hands. "Time to go!"

A fresh layer of snow coated the yard outside. Urban noticed with relief the tracks from when they'd left for the temple were already covered.

The annual party bus awaited, blasting its festive tunes out into the frigid air. Only, this year, the vehicle had been upgraded to . . . well, Urban wasn't sure what it was. It looked like a giant spider–the body of the car in the air and thick metal legs supporting it.

"*Tiana.*" Urban overheard Lillian gasp. "It's the SpideX."

"What's that?" Urban asked.

"How have you never heard of it?" Jade was the one who answered. "It's a car that can climb over traffic using its legs and convert into a submarine."

"Submarine?" Urban's face fell. "Why would we need to go underwater? Aren't we going to the Ice Festival?"

Jade merely shrugged, her eyes never leaving the SpideX. She wasn't the only one. Several of the Inventors in the family snapped images of the vehicle with their retina displays or ran their hands over its smooth exterior.

"This year we have a special surprise for everyone," Auntie announced cheerily. "But first, get in!" The body of the vehicle lowered to the earth and retracted its legs, the metal folding against its side like columns. A door opened and Auntie shepherded everyone inside.

It was cramped with fifty or so relatives, despite the massiveness of the pod, and Urban couldn't stretch out her legs. Thankfully, none of them were Supers.

Urban surveyed her seat options. Lillian talked with Jem, and Lucas sat on her other side. Lucas made a show of pushing a bag on the open seat next to him.

Urban swallowed and chose a spot next to Mother, instead.

"Incredible," Father declared, taking a seat next to them.

"See that?" He pinged Urban and Mother a lens filter which overlaid all the inner workings of the SpideX. "That's what generates a vortex for when it's underwater." He pointed. "It reduces the drag, enabling it to propel through the water at 110 kmph."

Jade sat next to Urban. "Are you talking about the SpideX's underwater features?" Her eyes sparked in excitement. "Have you heard they actually modeled it after the sailfish?"

Father's face lit up. "Why, yes!"

They launched into a discussion about the evolution of its design and rattled off stats about the SpideX. It was as if they switched to a foreign language. Urban tried to follow along but found her interest waning.

She scanned the pod for a drink dispenser and requested a snowy, cheese-flavored latte. Available only during the winter holidays, they were one of her favorites. Foam covered her lips as she sipped the sweet, buttery drink.

Urban had just regained her seat when the vehicle left the complex and zoomed along, its wheels on the street, taking up both lanes. At the speedway, cars littered the road, all headed toward the Ice Festival. Snow-covered roads had turned to black slush under the vehicles stalled to a stop.

The SpideX lifted spindly legs and picked its way over the long line of vehicles.

Several relatives applauded and cheered.

The movement felt like they were riding some sort of animal. It was unsteady, not riding along solid ground like cars, nor humming steadily in the air like a hovercraft. Instead, they swayed to and fro as they sidestepped traffic, and then left the road altogether.

As they reached the top of a small hill, a new sight awaited them. They were at the base of the *Songhua* River, where other SpideXes skittered across the frozen lake.

"Who's ready for some fun?" Auntie called out, then instructed, "But first, please discard all your drinks and loose items and strap in."

With a shudder, the SpideX took its first step onto the ice, shoving what looked like a giant spiked foot into the ground and securing it. Each step was firm, but required more effort and swaying.

Urban noticed Lillian clutching her stomach.

"No, no, no." Auntie fiddled with the controls. "Where's the 'fun' mode?"

The spiked feet retracted, replaced by smooth-tipped ends. Instantly, the vehicle lurched to the side and slid down a slight incline. There were several shrieks of delight.

The SpideX attempted to take a sharp left, but clawed at the ground in vain as it continued straight on its original trajectory. When it skidded to a stop, it finally managed to pivot directions.

"It's being steered manually," Father observed. "That's why we're sliding."

The course finally straightened.

"Now, onto the real fun!" Auntie declared happily. "Because it's the Year of the Water Horse, there are special water activities this year. We're going to get a closer look."

The SpideX made its way smoothly past the other out-of-control vehicles still slipping across the ice. They headed straight for a giant hole in the frozen lake.

Urban gripped her seatbelt, hoping she was wrong about where they were headed.

The SpideX slowed its approach. It came to a stop directly above the hole, legs holding it up. Then, slowly, the body lowered into the water until they were floating on it.

For a second, Urban dared think they might stay there. But then the legs retracted, dipped under the water, and latched onto the bottom of the thick layer of ice. With a thrust, the pod sank under. The SpideX's legs swirled and formed underwater propellers, forcing them downward.

Urban's chest constricted. She was getting better at controlling her fear of being underwater, but it still wasn't eradicated. Closing her eyes, she forced her breathing to slow.

When she opened them again, the relatives were gaping out the windows in awe. Urban turned to look and caught her breath.

Outside, the cobalt-blue water darkened from the thick layer of ice above. But natural illumination wasn't needed. Undulating flashes of light in pink, red, and white filled the water. The light streamed forth from giant ice structures spiraling up from the bottom of the murky lake.

Auntie beamed. "Welcome to the Underwater Ice Festival!"

PSYCHEDELIC COLORS DANCED IN THE WATER beneath the surface of the lake as awe-inspiring ice sculptures bobbed around the SpideX.

Some of the works of art started at the murky bottom and worked their way up, while others started from the top and expanded downward. Still more floated mid-lake. There were castles, a giant clock with all the animals from the zodiac calendar, temples, dragon boats, emperors of old, and of course, all kinds of horses–stallions, ponies, and warhorses–all celebrating the Year of the Water Horse.

Some carvings were as large as the Aquas swimming among them. Others were built bigger than life and made the hovering SpideXes seem like grains of rice.

"All the award-winning sculptures are underwater this year," Auntie said proudly. "Exclusive to those with SpideXes or other underwater transporters."

"Can I go out there?" Lucas pointed at a giant sculpture of a pyramid with several Aquas floating near it. "Looks like the architect is doing a meet and greet."

"We have the latest thermal smart suits for any Aquas who want to go," Uncle Lee said as he held out several suits.

"Thanks, Uncle, but I brought my own." Lucas was already in the changing room and emerged looking like a red salmon in his festive thermal suit.

Lillian raised a brow. "What are you, a clown fish?"

Lucas tugged at several stylish frills on his wetsuit. "You're just jealous of my Aqua abilities. My sosh is going to get an incredible jump after I meet all these ice designers." With that, he went into a separate pod that sealed him off from the main compartment.

A moment later, outside Urban's window, he made a face before swimming off.

All the Aquas decided to take Auntie up on her offer.

With half the pod empty, Mother scooted closer to Lillian and Urban. She cupped a mug of tea that clicked on as it reheated in her hands.

But Lillian rose to her feet. "Excuse me, I'm going to the washroom." She smiled quickly to ward off any inquisitions, then left.

Mother's gaze narrowed ever so slightly as it followed Lillian, but then drifted out the window. She pursed her lips and pointed. A flash of something caught Urban's attention.

A growing cloud of black dust swept away from a giant pig. The black liquid looked like squid ink leaking from the sculpture's snout.

Father frowned. "Is that coming from the pig?"

Urban searched the water for the source. It wasn't hard to spot. A frilly red suit was swimming swiftly away from the scene ahead of the growing ink.

Several underwater security-bots, designed to look like robotic sharks, zoomed over to investigate. A dark cloud already enveloped half the ice sculpture. But Lucas had activated a pair of propellers on his feet and now shot toward their pod. A moment later, he climbed through the door.

Urban's retina display picked up a change in Lucas's social

score. It had jumped to 76. No wonder the relatives were all out there swimming in the freezing water.

"Did you get dusted by that ink bomb?" a relative asked, examining Lucas from head to toe.

Lucas just grinned. "Wasn't it awesome?" He wiped at the stains on his wetsuit, but they only smeared more. "Works like squid ink."

"*You* set it off?" Mother was horrified.

"One of the ice designers gave me an ink bomb," Lucas told her quickly. "He told me to try it out."

Urban doubted that. Fortunately for Lucas, their parents weren't Inceptors, and he had always been a good liar. Though she did wonder where he'd come by such a device.

"Pull another prank like that, and your semester to the Dominican Islands Federation will be canceled." Father's voice was stern and his face rigid.

"Of course." Lucas shuffled his feet. But the second Father's gaze was off of him, he sauntered back to his seat and grinned at Lillian.

"*Tiana,*" Lillian hissed, "don't ruin my chances of getting a trip abroad."

Lucas waved a hand. "Don't worry." He rolled his eyes. Then he lowered his voice. "Next time, I won't get caught."

Urban glanced to her father to see if he'd heard, but he was deep in conversation with Auntie.

Sitting alone, her thoughts drifted back to their trip to the temple that morning. Remembering the glitched memory, she glanced around before facing Mother to ensure no one was near enough to overhear.

"Mother," Urban said slowly, not sure how to start. "When we went to the tatt temple today, we found something interesting. One of your memories was . . . well, something unusual happened to it."

Mother stiffened.

"There was a memory of when *Popo* sent you to study abroad. Parts of it were missing."

Mother took a long sip of her tea. "Technology wasn't as reliable back then. It was most likely a malfunction in *Popo's* retina display."

Urban watched Mother, not believing her for a second. "So why did you study abroad?"

"I've told you before." Mother's voice grew taut. "They had better art schools in the EuroAsian Federation."

"But–"

"Laoshen!" Mother quickly stood and made her way over to a seated relative. "Which of the ice sculptures is your favorite?"

Urban gazed after her.

What is she hiding?

As the water began to grow dark and the Aquas of the family had snapped and linked with nearly all the KOLs, the SpideX finally made its way back to the Lees' mansion.

The time before their late dinner was spent exchanging gifts of sweet fruits, fine teas, and, for the children, receiving little *hongbaos*. Urban watched as the youngsters received the red envelopes and ripped them open eagerly to examine the amount of crypto points they'd been gifted. With a scan of their tatt, they'd upload the funds to their accounts, then offer their relatives obligatory thanks.

Eighteen was too old to receive the *hongbaos*, and it was Urban's first year not being a recipient. *At least I have my own money now.*

She had yet to do any ads for Croix, but they'd already given her a significant deposit into her previously dried-up account.

After gifts, the relatives dispersed. The Aquas went swimming in the heated pond outside or lounged in the hot springs. They looked ridiculous in their swimsuits, pasty, bare arms and legs flashing in the dead of winter. Through the light snowfall they ran, laughing, across frozen pathways between steaming pools.

Lucas chucked a snowball at someone sitting in a jacuzzi and nailed him in the back of the head. An uncle sputtered and swore, but Lucas was long gone. Turning, he spotted Urban watching. He looked as if he were about to call her to join him, but then he scowled and turned away.

Urban let out a sigh.

The remaining relatives were gathered in the parlor, playing cards, *mahjong*, or an XR game designed for Inventors.

Urban didn't feel like joining them. Almost every one of the Lees was either an Aqua or Inventor. The rare exceptions were spouses who'd married into the family. But even then, many of them were also from those gene pools. Families in the Asian Federation typically tried to give their offspring enhancements from their own family gene pools. Urban supposed it was the same appeal as seeing a child with your own eyes or nose and recognizing yourself in them.

With genetics so precisely selected, why not make your descendants have your same strengths? Not to mention that it was much easier to build a house around one or two than try to accommodate every gene pool. Mother was one of the rare exceptions among the Lees with her Artisan genetics.

Back when they were kids, Urban used to join Lucas swimming, but that was before her near-drowning episode. After that, she'd switched to hanging out with Lillian and the Inventors.

Now, she sat in a wicker chair watching them.

Alone.

She sipped her tea, its warmth spreading through her, but doing nothing to dispel the coldness in her chest.

Urban thought about her own birth origins. The familiar ache to find her parents resurfaced.

Lillian thinks it will only cause pain to find out about them. But what if she's wrong? What if the greater pain is spending my whole life wondering 'what if'?

Urban suddenly sat up. The Dragons' first game was usually abroad. She pulled up their schedule.

Her breath stilled.

Sure enough, their first match was against the Scorpions in the Western Federation. *Is this my chance?*

"*Lai lai*!" Auntie called out. "Come! It's time for dinner!"

All games were stopped midway, even the gambling left off with virtual money still on the table while relatives headed toward round two of feasting. The swimmers outside snatched up red towels and made a beeline for the house.

In the dining hall, family units sat together again amidst platters of steaming noodles, fish, and a variety of stir-fry dishes.

Dinner seemed to stretch on and on. More fattening dishes were brought out, then there were more *gan beis* and laughter, followed by *fagao* cakes for dessert.

Finally, after most of the relatives had drunk themselves into oblivion, Urban escaped to her room.

Tomorrow I'll be back on campus looking for the hybrid.

But with that also came a conversation with her parents. Not wanting to think about that, she adjusted her sleeping headset over her eyes and nose. As she breathed in the gas, her awareness gradually slipped away.

The next morning, the family quickly packed up and said their goodbyes. Mother and Father had bags under their eyes, and Urban wondered if they'd slept at all.

Everyone lapsed into silence on the ride home. Urban used the time to wade through her backlog of pings.

"Ah!" Lucas burst out, making them all jump. "The lead player for my school's team just got injured. We're going to get crushed at the Games." He glanced at Lillian. "How are the Dragons looking this semester?'

"I don't know. Why don't you ask *her*?" Lillian's voice was like ice as she pointed to Urban.

Everyone's eyes went to Urban.

"What is this your sister is talking about?" Apprehension laced Mother's voice.

This was not how Urban envisioned telling her parents. "Uh . . ."

"Oh, I'm sorry." Lillian's voice was saccharine sweet. "She hasn't told you yet? I didn't mean to ruin the surprise."

"What surprise?" Lucas demanded.

"I–uh–" Urban swallowed. "I got an interesting offer from Dr. Gong."

"Dr. Gong." Father nodded. "He's an important guy."

Mother eyed Urban. "What did he say?"

She took a breath. "I've been accepted onto the Dragons' team."

"You turned down the offer?" Mother wasn't so much asking as warning.

Urban cleared her throat. "I–I was thinking it could be a good opportunity."

Mother stiffened.

"I mean, I can't stay in the Outskirts forever," Urban rushed to explain. "He offered me a room in the KOL dorm, which has crazy good security measures. And it would give me a chance to discover more about the hybrid. My genetics probot last semester knew about it, which means someone had to have programmed it with the information. If we knew who programmed it, we'd have a lead." Her words tumbled out. "You know, in case the whole hacking into the temple doesn't work out. Did AiE tell you someone beat us to it? It could take a lot of time to get the encrypted key and find our lead on the hybrid." She looked pleadingly at her mother. “This is our best option.”

Urban bit her lip. Mother stared at her in a way that was discomfiting.

“I would be on the B string of the Dragons, which means I’d never compete,” she assured Mother quickly. “And I could always feign an injury or something. There are only two tournaments this year, and they’re around the same time. It would be easy to miss them.”

When Urban finished, there was a heavy silence. Even Lucas remained quiet.

“Where are the tournaments?”

Urban hesitated at Mother’s question. “One’s on campus and the other . . . is in the Western Federation.”

Mother studied her face. “Is this at all related to finding your birth parents?”

“It’s about finding the hybrid,” Urban replied. *And while I’m there, I can search for my birth origins as well.*

Mother continued watching her daughter. “Will you look for your biological parents?”

Urban saw Lillian’s eyes widen in realization. “N–no.” Urban’s own eyes darted away from Mother’s accusatory gaze.

Mother closed her eyes, but when she opened them again, her voice was soft. “Even if you manage to locate your biological parents, we don’t know why they gave you and Lillian up for adoption. Finding them might cause . . . pain.” Mother sighed. “Our job as parents is to protect you from harm. The Western Federation isn’t safe.” She leaned forward. “If you want to search for answers, while I strongly advise against it, I will support you so long as it’s here, in New Beijing. But I cannot allow you to travel abroad to one of the most dangerous Federations. Especially not with the Dragons and the potential threat of ending up back in the Games.”

Urban gathered her courage and braced herself. “I’m sorry, but I have to find the hybrid. I’ve already accepted.”

A palpable shift hit the air.

It was as if the weight of the largest ice sculpture were suddenly crushing Urban's chest. She had rarely dared to go against her parents' expressed wishes. Then again, she'd never had the ability to do so, with her parents tightly controlling her crypto points. Now, as a KOL, Urban had what she needed to give her the freedom of choice.

"Well then," Mother said, an edge to her voice. "I guess it's settled." She turned away.

Lillian glared.

Guilt twisted inside of Urban. *They don't understand. They all belong in the Metropolis with the Enhanced.*

New Beijing's Metropolis bloomed into view. This time of year, most of its residents were out visiting family, and deserted streets stretched below them. She turned on her favorite holiday playlist and closed her eyes, trying to focus on the melodic and upbeat tunes. But instead, each song grated on her nerves, until finally, she shut the music off and opted for staring out the window in silence.

Their pod zipped quickly through the streets and landed gently on their gardened rooftop.

Urban was the first to hop out, but her mother caught her arm before she could head to her room. "I need to tell you something. Follow me." She led Urban downstairs into her studio and scanned her tatt. The door slid open with a click.

Urban stepped gingerly in. Mother's studio was always off limits growing up, and she'd rarely even managed to get a glimpse of it.

The circular room had no corners or hard edges, which was odd, given the rooms around it were all square-shaped. Everything in the studio seemed to be circular in some form, from the light fixtures, to the two art tables covered in supplies. The windowless walls were filled with paintings hanging to dry.

Urban had read most of her mother's poetry and knew

she dabbled in painting and other art forms, but Urban had never seen any of it. Mother's tutor, Mako Moss, was one of the renowned artists to rise from the Outskirts and enter the Metropolis purely based on skill. Despite his upbringing, he was revered by the art community and had a sosh of 90. He was every Natural's hero. And every Artisan's dream mentor.

In one of the paintings, a Natural sat regally in a chair. A mother and child, both Naturals, held hands in the next painting. In fact, most of the images were of Naturals.

Urban glanced at her mother, startled. Mother turned ashen.

A moment later, all the paintings disappeared, replaced with ones of Enhanced.

"Someone's been in my studio." Mother's voice shook. "You shouldn't have seen that. Someone changed my settings." Her eyes shifted as she scanned the room, then landed on Urban. "Check our encrypted channel later," she whispered. "I need you to trust me."

Mother rummaged around in a drawer, her normally steady hands trembling. Slender fingers slipped something into a fold of her jacket.

Straightening, she embraced Urban. "Enjoy the semester, dear," she said loudly but then added, almost inaudibly, "stay safe."

Urban caught sight of what looked like a syringe. Before she could react, Mother stabbed her in the arm.

AT THE SHARP PAIN, URBAN JERKED AWAY, BUT Mother's vice-like grip tightened and held her still. A cool sensation crept through Urban's veins before the syringe was pulled out and hidden back in Mother's sleeve.

Urban resisted the urge to look at her arm, knowing the importance of discretion, since they still weren't entirely sure what parts of the house might be bugged. She would inspect it once she'd left for campus. She stumbled out of Mother's studio.

I need you to trust me.

Mind reeling, she collected her bags. She stood for a moment, gathering her thoughts. One more goodbye was needed before she was ready to go.

Urban headed down the hall, slowing as she drew near the door. Normally, she barged into this room, but then again, the door wasn't usually closed.

Raising a hesitant fist, she knocked.

"Come in," an out-of-breath voice said from within.

Urban tentatively opened the door.

Lillian dodged a projected attacker. She bobbed, weaved, then shifted her center of gravity, coming up beside the attacker and nailing it in the head with her elbow.

The holo projection flashed red and then disappeared. Lillian turned to face Urban.

Urban's pulse quickened and her mouth felt as if it were stuffed with rice cakes. "I wanted to say goodbye."

"Well, goodbye," Lillian said flatly.

Urban tried again. "And I wanted to say . . . sorry."

Lillian shrugged. "It's your life. You can do what you want. Don't let any of us get in the way." A new attacker materialized, and she took it down with vicious precision.

Urban lingered at the doorway, hoping her sister would turn to her again.

She didn't.

Slowly, Urban went back into the hallway, a hollowness creeping through her chest.

She made her way down to the building's garage, and immediately, a green triangle appeared in her retina display. She turned her head in Trig's direction, but he had Camo mode enabled and she saw nothing but the garage wall.

Feeling slightly comforted by his unseen but familiar presence, she climbed onto her motorcycle. With a silent pull of the throttle, she shot out of the garage and onto the wide Metropolis streets. The sky was overcast, and cold air stung her cheeks. Most of the shops were still closed for the holidays, the absence of their usual music and tantalizing scents leaving the air empty and quiet. A few smart cars still occupied the Zeolite-coated road, but otherwise, Urban sped through quickly.

Soon, the familiar structure of the university came into view.

<Peking University Academic Building. Sosh: 75. Average number of visitors per year: 1,557,000.>

Urban gazed past the information on her retina display as she parked.

The last time she had headed toward the registration building, everything had felt new, exciting, and terrifying.

How things had changed.

Now, the trees lining the streets were no longer lush and green, but brown and resembling inverted human nervous systems. The colorful traditional buildings seemed duller than she remembered.

Her worries back then seemed so small. Now, Urban was at uni to get access to the Western Federation and answers about her birth origins. She was voluntarily going into the AI arena to train with the Dragons. And in her spare time, she'd be attempting to hack a probot.

No problem.

Urban climbed the set of glass stairs overlooking bald, dry grass. The familiar holo images of Dragon members lined each step.

Some smirked, others waved, still others stared stonily into the distance. Urban recognized a few of them–Olive's white hair and chalky skin, Orion's honey eyes, Brooke's impressive height and confident stance. There was a new holo too.

Urban stopped abruptly.

This one was shorter and skinnier than the rest. She had short, straight black hair blowing behind her in an imaginary gust of wind. Her defiant jaw was titled upward in challenge. Large, ink black eyes flashed back at her.

Urban stared at her reflection. *They must have already updated the team roster.* Seeing her real image and not her avatar was disconcerting.

She began to wonder if she could avoid going into the Games if on the team.

I have to.

She instantly made a mental list of all the possible excuses she could use. Most of them involved feigning illness the night before the Games.

She made her way past shiny windows reflecting ominous gray clouds overhead as she went toward registration. Inside, a gust of warm air blasted her until her suit's thermals clicked off. She crossed the marbled floor, huge pillars towering over her like giants.

Relieved by the absence of other students or a line, she stepped into the see-through tube with reinforced metal cylinders. Her pulse quickened as the door whirred shut behind her, a cold gas brushing against the part of her skin not covered in her suit–her neck and face.

Urban fingered the fake nail her father had given her at the start of last semester. The DNA in it belonged to Lucas and would cause the scanner to pick up his enhancements, not her own suspicious lack thereof. She still found it ridiculous that students had to go through this process each semester. It wasn't like someone was getting enhancements over the holidays.

A moment later, it beeped and flashed green.

Urban let out a breath.

Of course her "enhancements" were deemed green or safe. Still, it always unnerved her going through the genetics detector.

A registration bot waved its hand in greeting. "Welcome, Lee Urban, to the spring semester. Your course catalog is now being transferred to you." Its lemon-yellow eyes focused on Urban. A moment later, a ping popped up in her retina display.

<Access to Peking University's classes granted. Please follow the recommended course guideline for your respective track.>

As Urban left the warmth of the building, a course catalog appeared in one corner of her display. In the other section, she enabled dual vision mode, with directions to her new dorm. A pulsing green arrow showed her which way to go.

She knew the *Xiama* Dorms were for KOLs, but the campus was huge, and she'd never been to this side before. Urban passed arched bridges, frozen streams, dried-up willow trees, and a slew of buildings on the three-kilometer walk to her new dormitory. A few other students passed her with their breath swirling in the air. Urban hardly noticed them as she perused the class options.

Last semester, she'd been forced to follow the generic track. Since she didn't have any enhancements, selecting a gene pool track was more complicated for her. Mother and Father had wanted her to select the Giver track, thinking it would be the easiest to disguise her lack of enhancements.

After making headline news for over a week and her sosh hitting 80, her parents had reluctantly agreed to allow her to join the gene pool she wanted.

So now, Urban selected the Artisan GP track. Technically, students weren't able to declare a gene pool until their second year, but she could at least get a jump start on some of the classes she'd need.

First, Urban made sure to enroll in Advanced Genetics, double-checking it was the same probot from her class last semester. Her heart skipped a beat at the thought of hacking into it. But that was a problem for after registration.

Next, she selected one upperclassman course, Advanced AI, in the hopes of learning hacks for how to better out-maneuver the Games' AI. The remaining three classes were specific to the Artisan track.

She eagerly selected Art History, Elements of Design, and Mixed Media & Art. Of course, in addition to those, she was continuing her jiujitsu elective. Though, this time, she looked forward to that class. Thoughts of Lillian drifted into her mind, and she quickly pushed them away.

As she submitted her finalized course schedule, her retina maps marked her arrival at the dorms. Urban blinked out of her dual vision mode and focused on her surroundings. Her head bent back as she stared at the building. Her mouth gaped.

It wasn't the height of the building that stunned her, but rather, the waterfall cascading from the top of it. It had to be larger than some of nature's biggest waterfalls, yet here it stood in the middle of campus, a sight to behold. She'd seen it in XR before, but it couldn't compare to reality.

The waterfall disappeared into a large hole below ground. An icy spray of mist kissed her cheeks as Urban leaned over the railing to get a better look. Shivering, she turned away and headed for the entrance, Trig's familiar green triangle following her.

Inside, it smelled of oranges and dried dates. A student lazed behind the front desk.

"Welcome to *Xiama* Dorms." The student yawned. His eyes zoned out, no doubt using Gene-IQ's software to try and discern Urban's genetics and sosh. Too bad for him, Urban's parents had paid big money for privacy mode in Gene-IQ. He wouldn't be able to find any info on her genetics. Though, by the way he straightened, she guessed he recognized her from the vids.

"You're Lee Urban? You're the one who destroyed the Games last year!" His face lit up. "That was the coolest thing ever. I was totally about to fail a class but then you saved us all by forcing the campus to close down for a couple days."

He extended a platter of rice balls. "Leftovers from the holidays. Want one?"

Urban politely declined.

"I'm Bak Clay. I'm on the team too. I'm a B-string player, so you've probably never heard of me." He laughed in a self-deprecating way, but Urban wasn't sure if she should laugh too or not.

His statement sparked her curiosity. She studied him more carefully.

Clay's enhancements and sosh were all public, indicating he was a Giver. He had a relaxed, easy smile that made him feel approachable, but there was something about his brown eyes. They seemed simultaneously welcoming and yet sad.

Givers always had positive mantras, affirmations, and life hacks. Urban didn't even think it was possible for them to be sad. It seemed silly, now that she thought about it. Of course

Givers experienced sadness like the rest of them. Yet, hadn't their brains been wired to feel fewer emotions? Or was it the other way around?

Her retina display showed Clay had a sosh of 87 and an impressive list of check-ins at the top parties and events of the year. So what was he doing here, working a manual-labor job, one a bot could do no less, while everyone else was on New Year's break?

"Seems Dr. Gong himself assigned you one of our best rooms," Clay noted. He smiled a full, wide smile that warmed her. "I'll give you a quick tour and then show you to your room."

They made their way across silver and gold floors, over to a Belgian black marble staircase. "The *Xiama* Dorms are only for the elite. You need a minimum sosh of 85 for your application to even be considered," Clay explained. "It's home to several flicks stars, as well as a few singers, prodigies, children of important people, blah, blah, blah.

"That's the boring part of the tour speech." Clay gave Urban a lopsided grin. "I can tell you're not interested in the name dropping. What's actually cool about the dorms, and I think you'll like, are the amenities."

Urban tried not to balk at how easily he'd read her body language. While not as gifted as Inceptors, Givers were still a dangerous breed for people like her. But Urban didn't feel threatened. She felt safe with Clay.

"Check it out." Clay pushed open a doorway revealing a room filled with warm steam. "I give you the 24-hour spa!"

Pebbled pathways filled the space leading from pools of different shades of blue water. Small fountains and shrubbery filled the spaces between, giving them a natural feel. In one corner, a holoprojector displayed the New Year's festivals taking place. Clay pointed at it. "Usually, it's set to the Games so you can watch them as you soak. Sometimes, the team will watch replays of our performance while we're in here."

Hopefully not my *performance*, Urban thought.

Clay had moved on. "There are several cafes, study lounges, and a restaurant over that way." He pointed. "But what's really cool is our immersion room." He led her inside another doorway and flipped a switch. The room began moving, causing Urban to sway on her feet.

A moment later, the room transformed to resemble a peaceful, snowy landscape. She took a step forward and snow crunched under her feet.

"It's real," Clay affirmed. "It's like a mini version of the arena used by the team to train. Some of the other KOLs also use it for various purposes. Of course, there aren't any of the animals or bigger game items like the arena houses, but it's still impressive."

"How often does the team train?" Urban asked.

"Depends on the captain. This year, with Willow, the requirement is daily on your own workouts and team training every other day."

"How do you have time to study?"

Clay snorted. "We don't. That's why I nearly failed one of my classes." He leaned closer. "You find other . . . creative ways of passing."

He then turned and quickly started off again.

Urban followed him with a creased brow. She had a few guesses at what "creative" might mean, none of them good. *Aren't Givers supposed to have life figured out? Why would a Giver of all people be using "creative" means to pass classes?* Urban herself used natural energy boosters to enhance her performance when it came to physical training, but she doubted that's what Clay was referring to.

Clay led her to the living section of the building, pointing at a scanner next to a door. "This should be yours."

Urban held up her tatt to it, and the door slid open.

Clay led the way in and gestured at the giant floor-to-ceiling glass window. Outside, water poured down.

"The rooms behind the waterfall are the most secure. Getting in from the outside through the water would be extremely difficult. The walls are all reinforced and the only way in is through the door."

Urban surveyed her room. "Do you stay in a room like this?"

Clay's laughter turned into a coughing fit. "Only A-team players are high profile enough to need the security," he explained, recovering himself. "You're an exception."

He gestured at the room. "Anyhow, your room has top-notch tech, gadgets and stuff. But you're not dumb. I don't need to explain it to you." He turned to the door. "Let me know if you have any other questions. We have pretty much everything in this building. Besides class, you wouldn't ever need to leave."

Then Clay was gone and Urban was left alone in her room. A queen bed sat in the corner next to a tiny square table with chairs, a miniature kitchen, even a bathroom. Not only was it bigger than the one from last semester, she didn't have to share it with Blossom, Hazel, and Coral.

And since she didn't have roommates, she could completely customize her room the way she wanted. Dropping her backpack on the bed, Urban logged into QuanNao and located her bedroom's controls.

She programmed her walls to take on a velvety texture and rose gold hue. Then she switched the smell, and a second later she heard a tiny squirt. The room filled with the aroma of jasmine. She told herself it was because she loved tea. It had nothing to do with Everest, of course.

She pulled up one of her favorite instrumental playlists and music reverberated from all sides. She opened a pair of new slippers, burying her toes in the fur.

Now it felt like home.

Urban explored the kitchen until she found a smart mug and a tea bag, setting it to brew. Then, steaming drink in hand, she climbed onto her bed and accessed her pings.

As usual, there was a backlog that seemed longer than the Great Wall of the old Federation. She pulled up the ones her system had prioritized for her. There was a message from Croix about her first upcoming photo shoot, an invitation to the Back-to-School Bash, and several messages from Hazel wanting to know if Urban was returning to campus soon. She noticed an encrypted message from Mother and quickly opened it.

[Zhou Flora: Urban, I'm sorry I wasn't able to explain. I thought my studio would be a safe place to talk, but it seems even that is now being watched. I implanted you with a more sophisticated tracker than both the bracelet Lillian gave you and the Safe Child App. Which, you'll be happy to know, we have deactivated. For now. Your new tracker can't be hacked, removed, or go offline unless you're far enough out of range. That can only happen if you travel into space or underwater. Your father and I feel safer about keeping an eye on you this way.]

Urban wasn't sure if she should feel grateful or annoyed. She peered over her shoulder at the tender spot where her mother had injected her. She couldn't see anything, but knowing there was a tracker there that she was incapable of removing made her want to run. And run and run.

Her gaze drifted out her window to the water pouring down. Clay said it was impossible for anyone to break in. Didn't that also make it impossible for her to escape? Was she protected or trapped?

With a growl of frustration, she went back to her messages. There was a new one from an unknown sender at the top of her prioritized inbox.

[Wu Willow: Hello Urban. Congratulations on joining the team and welcome! I'm the Dragons' captain and wanted to let you know about our first upcoming mandatory orientation dinner on January tenth at 21:00. Please make sure to be there.

I've also granted you access to our exclusive XR room where you'll find the training schedule, helpful exercises, game replays, roster, playbook, and our code of conduct. Please familiarize yourself with our team and strategy before the tenth. We look forward to seeing your talent contributing to our team.]

The tenth was tomorrow.

Clay wasn't kidding about Willow. *Most of the other students are still at home in a food coma, and I already have homework.*

But a thrill of excitement washed over her. She was actually going to be training with all the KOLs on the team. It was followed quickly by a wave of dismay. She had nothing she could contribute.

Urban thought back to last semester when she'd destroyed the arena with her Natural genetics. The AI should have evolved by now and would most likely be able to withstand another encounter with a Natural. Still, the thought made her break into a cold sweat. If Samson broke down again, everyone would be suspicious. They might even want to test her DNA or boot her off the team.

She would have to make sure training mode was always selected. Which should be easy, since entertainment mode was never used except in games. *So long as I'm not playing in an actual game, I'll be fine.*

Yet, she couldn't fight off the tsunami of dread barreling toward her.

"WELCOME TO THE DRAGON'S LAIR!" A DISEMBODIED voice announced.

The Dragon's Lair sat wedged in the side of a huge mountain. As Urban's avatar went into the cave, it grew dark and chilly. It smelled musty, like she'd remembered it from the first and the last time she'd visited. Back before Mother found out about her obsession with the team and used the Safe Child App to block her from exploring.

Now, here she was again, years later, on that very team. Urban shook her head.

A woman approached. Golden locks of hair flowed over her shoulders and a mischievous smile danced across her face.

"Hello, I'm Hong, Peking University's one and only Game Announcer. Are you here to explore the Dragons?"

Hong gestured at a square of solid jade on the ground. There were sixteen in all. Urban watched as the one Hong gestured at came to life. A person with spiky, neon-green hair and moss-green eyes appeared, blinking at her.

"I'm Kang Hickory, Camo team lead. Would you like to see my stats?"

Urban pushed past the automated Hong and Hickory, feet

crunching over a floor disconcertingly covered in human bones. She stopped in front of a towering oak door.

"That entry is for the team members only," Hong said. "It seems you have the access code. Would you like to enter?"

Urban didn't bother responding as she pushed the door open. The scene shifted to display a room with high, arched ceilings and three walls made of floor-to-ceiling windows. She inhaled a sharp breath at the view.

Jagged black rocks rose majestically into the sky, putting New Beijing's tallest skyscrapers to shame. Urban had seen mountains before in the Outskirts, but these were different. The snow-capped peaks pointed upward in rebellious defiance. Rocky sides, having survived thousands of years of wind, ice, and harsh conditions, yet standing strong. Outside, the wind blew so loudly, Urban nearly forgot she was in virtual reality.

She stepped into the room, inhaling scents of frankincense, cedar, and rum, which baffled her until she noticed a bar.

Silver pendant lights dangled from the ceiling and covered half the space, like wind chimes. At the center of the room, on a small black velvet stage, sat a collection of hologram trophies from the last few championship games.

"2122 Eastern Conference Champions."

"*Sun WuKong* Most Athletic Player Awarded to Wen Brooke."

"Global MVP Awarded to Wu Willow."

Urban stared at that one. She hadn't remembered Willow winning the most prestigious award for individual players. Then again, she hadn't been paying attention to the Games much the last few years.

Impressive.

Urban plopped onto a white sofa facing the mountains. "Show me the Dragons' exercise regimen."

A wispy figure appeared in the room. Urban was fascinated by her clothing. She wore what looked like a jiujitsu robe mixed with exotic silks. Her black velvet top had a golden dragon embroidered on it and a white belt tied in a knot. The pants were flowy and white with strips of see-through mesh.

"Hello, I'm Willow, team lead for the Artisans." Her face was pale, but her lips were painted dove gray. She had thick eyeliner to match. It was a stunning contrast and tastefully done. Urban's artistic eye could appreciate the look.

Willow pirouetted in mid-air before landing gracefully. "I'm also the team captain of the Dragons. Our team motto is: work smarter *and* harder."

Great. Because I have so much free time.

Willow smirked and Urban wondered if the avatar was responsive.

"We value grace, creativity, and teamwork," Willow continued. "That's why we have a lot of exercises expected of the whole team. First, all members need to be in top physical condition."

The room faded and turned into the gym where Urban and Lillian had worked out last semester.

"Our partnership with Infini-Fit will allow you to gain access to several exclusive Dragons' training rooms. Should you choose to publicly check in during your training sessions, the gym will give you free food, drink, massage, and use of their recovery room."

Willow's avatar took a selfie, then posted it before picking up a smoothie from the bar and sauntering out.

"In addition, you are expected to excel in your area of genetic enhancement." The gym changed to display an Aqua swimming in the middle of a vast ocean, then to a Super charging into battle on a field, bombs detonating all around. The scene shifted to a Giver studying the faces of people around her and offering a helping hand. Next, they were in a forest and a Camo shimmered into view, then the image transformed and they were in a crowd of people with an Inceptor giving a speech. It switched again, and this time an Inventor wearing goggles grinned at a bubbling concoction. Finally, it ended with Willow herself dancing serenely in a studio.

"Whatever your gifting," Willow continued, "you will be the best. However, I expect you to be well-rounded, which is why you will practice in training mode."

At least that's doable. If Willow wanted to use entertainment mode, I'd probably get injured and everyone would find out I'm a Natural. Urban let out a sigh of relief.

A shuffling sound behind her made Urban freeze.

She wasn't alone.

Urban turned and found a girl with sharp features, straight black hair, and intelligent dark eyes watching her.

"Blossom?" Urban hadn't seen her former roommate since last semester. She was convinced Blossom was a secret SAS member, after finding a member badge in their dorm room. Urban put on her friendliest smile to ward off any suspicion. "What are you doing here?"

Blossom strode further into the room. "Don't look so surprised."

"You're on the team too? But . . . how?" Urban thought back to the previous semester. She'd forgotten Blossom had tried out as well. She had been too distracted with nearly dying in the Games to notice.

Blossom ran a skeletal finger over the base of one of the trophies. "While you were busy showing off, I tried out. I made it onto the reserve team. Then, when Chang Slash, the Inventor house lead, was seriously injured, I got bumped to the actual team."

"So, if Slash is no longer the Inventor team lead, and we're both . . ." A chill crawled down Urban's spine.

Blossom's eyes darkened as they studied Urban. "One of us will be the new A-team lead."

"LET ME GET THIS STRAIGHT, NOT ONLY DO YOU have to play well enough to not attract attention, you have to *not* play well enough so as to avoid getting bumped to first string where you would actually compete?" Ash scratched his head.

Urban paused from slurping noodles. "Basically."

They had both returned early to campus and were at the underground food courts. Most of the restaurants were still closed for the holidays, but they'd managed to find one open. Peppy holiday music played in the background.

Ash let out a low whistle. "I swear, you know how to get yourself in more trouble than anyone I know."

"At least getting first string shouldn't be a concern." She expelled a breath. "Though, it doesn't help things with Blossom. She's convinced we're now rivals."

Ash chewed in silence, digesting her words.

"Anyhow." Urban swirled her food with her chopsticks. "I just enrolled in Dr. Huang's Advanced Genetics class."

"Yeah?" Ash tipped his bowl and drained the rest of the noodle juice. "Any ideas on how to hack it?"

"I was hoping the guy who managed to trick a probot would know."

Last semester, Ash and Urban had been enrolled in a class where the probot would give the students the day off if anyone could cause its AI to trip up. No one had been successful except for Ash.

"Brilliant, if I do say so myself." Ash grinned. "So . . . how could we hack *this* probot?"

Urban studied her surroundings, thinking.

Everything was slick and mirrored except the plush chairs they sat in. Ash was across from her in a half-dome seat, an XR pod split in half, allowing for partial immersion while still enabling the user to sit at a table and eat. The dim, cool room had muted colors and décor to allow for minimum distractions while in XR.

Urban was pretty sure they were the only ones there not immersed in extended reality. A student at the table next to them sat hooked up to a specialized pair of XR pants. Urban grimaced, recognizing the Recycling Relief Pants, or the ones that allowed people to use them without having to get up to use the restroom. They were standard fare for serious XR gamers, but they still grossed her out.

"Actually, I might have an idea," Urban said, her mind focusing again. "I remember my brother telling me about a prank he pulled on his probots once. Apparently, they all return to a secure warehouse each night to recharge. He and his friends kidnapped one on its way to its station. If we kidnapped ours, so to speak, I'm sure it wouldn't be too hard to physically hack it from there."

Ash grinned. "Well if that doesn't sound like fun, I don't know what does."

"My brother said it wasn't hard to do," Urban continued. "You have to make sure to wear a full-face mask so they can't recognize your identity, of course. And you have to use a location scatterer device. Otherwise, campus security will track you down right away with the trackers installed inside the probots. Granted, my brother goes to New Shanghai Ocean University," Urban added. "So it might be different here, but I think it could work."

"I've been watching the probot's schedule," a voice said.

Urban spun in her seat. She couldn't see anyone at first. A moment later, the air began to shimmer and Trig materialized next to them.

Ash clutched at his heart. "You Camos are the worst."

"Sorry, I couldn't help listening in." Trig looked genuinely apologetic. He straightened his glasses. "The probots on this campus, at the end of each day's final class, head straight to the warehouse. I can ping you their route."

"Perfect!" Urban smiled. "Anyone have a location scatterer?"

Ash shrugged and looked to Trig.

Trig shook his head delicately. "Sorry, I do not."

"Hmm . . ." Urban pursed her lips. "I think I know who might be able to help."

When Urban returned to the dorms, she studied up on the Dragons. She was nearly finished with their code of conduct manual and starting to doze off when a knock sounded on her door.

Urban's retina display showed the security feed.

<Alert! KOL Qing Angel at the door. Would you like to allow her in?>

"Yes," Urban commanded, and her door unlocked and slid open.

Coral entered wearing a backward hat and her trademark high-top shoes. "Well, aren't you living the high life?" She took in her surroundings. "You're going to be too fancy for us plebeians soon."

"I bet you could get a room here too. You're a KOL–"

"Nah. I was teasing." Coral waved her off. "You know me. I like to keep things simple." Coral lowered herself onto the floor and sat cross-legged. "So, what's up?"

Urban bit her lip. "I was wondering if you have access to a location scatterer? They're outlawed here, but I know they're legal in the Western Federation."

"A scatterer, huh?" Coral studied Urban carefully. "Why do you need one of those?"

Urban quickly explained her plan to hack the probot.

Coral rubbed her forearm over her tattoo. The characters *weiji*, or crisis, stood out sharply in black ink across her pale skin.

"That could work," she said slowly when Urban was finished. "I actually have two on hand back in my dorm. The only thing is, there's still a small flaw in your plan."

Urban frowned. "What?"

"Trig said all the probots leave at the same time to head to the warehouse, right?"

Urban nodded.

"Well, that's going to be tricky," Coral said. "The model of probot used on campus is equipped with a deadly self-defense mechanism. If it's three against one, we can totally best it. However, I wouldn't want to take my chances against more than one. If we kidnap your probot as it's heading back, the other probots will be alerted and will come to its aid. Then we'll really be in trouble."

"What do you recommend?"

Coral cocked her head. "What time is your class?"

"It's the last one of the day."

"Perfect." Coral grinned. "So here's what I'll need you to do. At the end of class, go up to your probot and ask a dumb question about the syllabus or something. Stall for time. If you can give us even a few minutes, all the other probots should be far enough out to no longer be a threat. That gives us a wider window, time-wise, to nab the probot."

"I can do that."

"The only thing is, you'll need some sort of alibi," Coral

pointed out. "Otherwise, you'll become the prime suspect."

"I know!" Urban's face lit up. "After I talk to the probot, I'll stay in the classroom and go straight into QuanNao. There's a virtual Back-to-School Bash I can attend. Not only will the other students vouch for my presence, if campus authorities look at the virtual time stamp, they'll see I was there during the time of the botnapping."

Coral nodded her approval. "I'll get you your location scatterer and go over the plan with Trig and Ash before tomorrow."

"Great!" Urban beamed.

Coral made to leave, but then stopped. "I think I found something else." She paused. "Something about your origins."

Urban looked up sharply.

"You know I've been hacking into the orphanage database to try and figure out who was behind your adoption and paperwork."

At Urban's nod, Coral continued, "Well, I found something."

Urban reached out and clutched Coral's arm. "What?"

Coral live projected an image of a man. "This is Rai Reed." She gave Urban a sideways glance. "He's the one who erased your records when you were adopted."

Urban stared at the man's gaunt face and thin beard and swallowed. "Do you think he's my bio dad?"

"No clue," Coral confessed. "That's the really weird part. I can't find anything in QuanNao about him."

Urban's eyes widened slightly. "How's that even possible? Doesn't he have a sosh?"

"Apparently not. Otherwise, the facial recognition software should be able to pick him out. It's like he's a ghost."

Urban's forehead creased. "I didn't know people could live without a sosh."

"Me either. As you know, we've tracked your origins back to the Western Fed. It all lines up. He's living in Texicana."

Urban leaned forward. "You think that's where he is now?"

"That's where he was ten years ago. Of course, he could be anywhere by now." Coral shrugged apologetically. "Sorry, I know it's not much, but it's a start. I'll keep digging around and see what else I can find."

Urban smiled at her friend. "Thanks, I really appreciate it. You've already done so much."

Coral stood. "See you tomorrow after we've nabbed a probot." She wiggled her eyebrows mischievously, then left.

Texicana . . . why does that state sound so familiar? Urban conducted a quick search in QuanNao.

[Texicana is the capitol of the Western Federation and also houses the Global AI Games. Their local team, the Scorpions, competes at the local arena and is a major tourist attraction for people around the globe.]

Urban smiled to herself.

Despite everything, it looks like joining the Dragons will get me exactly where I need to be for answers.

URBAN AND EVEREST WORE MATCHING RUGGED leathers and leaned up against their motorcycles. In the photo, Everest had an arm around Urban and they were laughing at something, but Urban couldn't remember what.

Urban sat on her dorm bed staring at the photo. She sighed, missing the familiar warmth and security he brought. She missed *him*. His strength, gentleness, kindness, and the freedom she always felt to be herself. The way she could talk with him about anything–art, music, life as a Natural, motorcycle racing.

Before she could stop herself, she ordered QuanNao's AI to use facial recognition and sort through her other top replayed memories. A ping arrived, interrupting her search. Her heart leapt.

[Everest: Want to grab some tea? We could get those rumors started.]

She should probably study more for the Dragons, but Everest needed help getting his sosh up.

[Urban: The news has certainly been pretty boring as of late. Let's give them a real story to talk about!]

She got a ping back almost immediately.

[Everest: You free now?]

[Urban: Now works.]

[Everest: Race you to our usual bubble tea spot. Loser pays.]

[Urban: I love free drinks!]

She threw on a jacket and ran out of the room.

[Everest: Keep dreaming.]

A familiar warmth filled Urban's belly at his reply. It felt almost like old times.

Once to the garage, Urban climbed onto her motorcycle. Her bike shot up the spiral ramp and past the waterfall as she exited the underground parking.

Wind beat against her as she accelerated through the cold twilight of the Metropolis. Urban had never gone this fast downtown, but usually it wasn't this empty. She was surprised the tea shop was open during the holidays.

After parking, Urban sprinted toward an old elevator and into the cafe. The familiar scent of sugary milk teas and fresh boiled bobas brought back waves of memories. This had always been one of her favorite spots. Coming back to it, and being in a state of quasi dating, made her heart thump with a confusing array of emotions.

Everest stood to meet her with a smug look on his face. "About that drink."

"How did you beat me?" Urban demanded.

"You assume I started elsewhere." Everest grinned.

"Cheater!" Urban growled, trying to smother her own smile. She still paid for both of their drinks with a swipe of her tatt. A few other patrons sat at various seats scattered throughout the shop. Most seemed deep in conversation, but one was watching them discreetly. With Urban's identity now changed to public, it was only a matter of time before someone realized she was a KOL.

Everest led them to a table near the wall. They sipped their drinks.

"So . . . how were the rest of your holidays?" Everest leaned back in his seat, a casual expression on his face. A barely visible crease in his forehead was the only indicator of his discomfort.

Somehow, seeing his unease helped Urban relax. "This year, the Ice Festival was underwater. So that was fun."

Everest raised a brow. "For someone with a fear of water, you've had more unfortunate encounters than anyone I know."

"You'd think I'd be over it by now." Urban shuddered.

"Did I ever tell you about my fear of the giant toad from the XR kiddie experience *Frogs*?"

"You mean Toddy?"

"Yeah, him." Everest sipped his drink. "Used to give me nightmares. I was convinced he was hiding in my closet. My parents had to come into my room and turn on the lights to show me he wasn't there."

Urban's lips quirked at the mental image of Everest hiding under his covers from an XR toad.

"One day, I forced myself to stand in the closet with the lights out. When Toddy didn't devour me, I realized it was just my imagination. It still took me a while not to be afraid of him."

"You're saying I should face my fear of water?"

Everest locked his gaze on her, tiny flecks of amber shining in his black eyes. Why had she never noticed that before?

"I'm saying sometimes deep-rooted fears are hard to overcome."

Urban swirled the boba in her drink. "So, what does the great Chong Everest fear? Anything?"

Hesitating, Everest scanned their surroundings before focusing back on her. "I guess I fear living my life in vain."

"But you're already making a difference!" Urban blurted.

"Am I?" Everest ran a hand through his thick black hair. The exhausted lines creasing his sharply angled face seemed more prominent than ever.

The thought crossed Urban's mind that they both were avoiding the elephant in the room.

"Anyhow, I didn't invite you here to talk about my fears."

Everest lowered his voice. "We have a rumor to start." He suddenly leaned forward, dark eyes sparkling.

"Think it will work?"

"Already is." Everest pinged her a live forum.

[New Beijing KOL Sightings: This just in! Beijing's trending KOL spotted on a date! Who's the lucky guy? Is it official? Share your spotting with us along with any voice recordings and vids!]

Urban tasted ash in her mouth. What if a voice recorder had already been used? Thankfully, they'd been careful. Still, all it would take was one slip. One conversation leaked, and it would be obvious they were both Naturals and everything they'd worked so hard for would be destroyed in an instant.

Everest leaned in closer and a ping appeared in her retina display.

[Everest: We should probably confirm the rumors.]

Urban looked at him, and an electric jolt shot through her. He was gazing at her with such intensity. Was he going to . . . kiss her?

Heat flooded her, but then a tingling sensation crept through her.

Everest remained leaned forward, centimeters away, still staring into her eyes.

She yearned to be the way they used to be. *But I'm not ready to be hurt again.* She jerked back.

Hurt flashed across Everest's face and his jaw tightened.

I'm sorry. I don't know if I can trust you, Urban wanted to tell him. Instead she said, "I have to go. Practice starts soon."

"Yeah, I should head out too." Everest's voice was clipped. "Great seeing you, *meinu.*"

Urban's stomach dropped at the familiar nickname. Everest hadn't called her that since they'd really been dating. What did he mean by using it now? Was he pretending everything was okay?

Everest stiffened. "Sorry. I didn't mean–" He stopped abruptly, then stood, his eyes watching as a person walked past. "I'll see you later."

Urban watched him go, then slowly walked back down to the garage and climbed onto her motorcycle.

Urban's retina display informed her of several tags in trending articles and vids. She wasn't able to restrain herself from projecting the KOL gossip channel on the wall.

In the recording, Everest leaned forward. Urban paused it and admired his chiseled jawline, then–berating herself–unpaused it.

As the vid played, she watched herself jerk back and saw the surprise on Everest's face. The vid ended and she scrolled the comments. There were already over two hundred.

[Zhou Jade: Wow, what an awkward first date.]

[Tin Vine: Who is her hot date? Why does he have privacy mode enabled?]

[Tang Tong: What a *suige*! Where's the scoop on HIM??!]

Urban closed her eyes. Her life involving Everest was getting more complicated. And now, the whole world had a front-row seat to watch.

A MULTI-LEVELED PAGODA STOOD SILHOUETTED against the backdrop of New Beijing's bright Metropolis lights. The structure had been restored several times since its original build and now stood taller than ever.

The top floor of the pagoda spun slowly, lights streaming out like a twirling disco ball. Jazzy colors danced on the white snow of the frozen lake surrounding it.

Cold wind nipped at Urban as she speed-walked into the warm lobby. Everything was made of wood and had an earthy scent to it. She spent a few seconds searching for the elevator before realizing there wasn't one.

She checked the time. Five minutes 'til.

Locating the staircase, she took them two at a time, round and round, seven flights up. Midway, she stopped to catch her breath, then continued on again at a slower pace.

Finally, the stairs stopped their spiraling. She tugged at her rose gold pantsuit and smoothed her hair. Then, with head high and shoulders back, she opened the door.

Heat, light, and sound blasted her.

She stood in a small banquet room with enough space for two tables. Most of the players had already arrived and were seated. Their social scores ranged from the high 80s to mid 90s–all KOLs. Urban continued to be grateful for her sosh of 90 to ward off suspicions.

The smell of roasted duck, stir-fried vegetables, and rice permeated the air, despite the tables being empty of food. A remixed song by a local Artisan boomed over the speakers, the beat trembling the wooden floor beneath her. The Dragons shouted out each lyric ending in “er,” laughing and cheering. The Artisan was one of Urban’s favorites for his self-deprecating lyrics and play on words.

The current song, “On My New Beijing Turf,” was sung using local slang. The slurring of words to end in “er” was a deviation from the usual pronunciation and only used in New Beijing. It annoyed citizens of other provinces in the Asian Federation to no end, making it all the more fun to sing.

Urban suppressed a smile. *Maybe pretending to belong here won’t be so hard after all.*

Digital nameplates projected at each table. Urban searched for hers, then slid next to a pasty girl with white hair and pale blue eyes who was dressed in white silk and pearls.

“Urban, so good to have you on the team.” Olive batted her long, white eyelashes, but looked anything but pleased.

Urban smiled back politely, being sure to mask her emotions. *Stupid Inceptors, why do I always run into them? I’m still indebted to her, thanks to that useless motorcycle race she got me into.* She hated owing anyone a favor, least of all Olive.

“I’m honored to be here.” Urban turned to introduce herself to the others at the table, hoping Olive would stop watching her.

There were six other seats at her table, four of which were already occupied. She spotted Clay, and he gave her a head nod.

“Welcome to the team, Urban,” an accented voice said.

Urban brightened at seeing the muscular guy with sharp eyes and blond stubble. She hadn’t seen her jiujitsu instructor since last semester.

"Hey!" she greeted him. "Good to see you!"

"As you." Orion's smile was dazzling as ever. It was no surprise Lillian was practically in love with him. Urban instantly put her sister out of her mind.

"I hope you've been keeping up with your jiujitsu training over the holidays." Orion's amber eyes were intense as ever.

"I–uh–" Urban stammered.

Orion winked. "I'm kidding. But I'll see you back at the gym soon, yes?"

"Yes of course," Urban replied quickly, grateful he'd helped her save face.

Next to Orion sat a Super polishing a razored stud in her leather jacket. Wen Brooke, the Super GP lead who killed all the saber-tooth tigers in the Inauguration Games.

"Brooke, it's nice to see you again."

Brooke's head snapped up to Urban. She stared a moment, then, no doubt with the help of QuanNao, smiled. "Urban! You still haven't taken me up on my offer to roll or spar sometime."

"Yes, well. Someday." Urban mustered a smile before turning to the last person at the table. A girl with blood-red eyes, and hair to match, sat with steepled fingers, observing. There was something familiar about her eyes, but Urban couldn't quite place it. Fortunately, the girl didn't have privacy mode enabled and Urban was able to pull up her stats.

[Jeong Dawn. Sosh: 90. Dragons' team lead for the Giver's Gene Pool. Dragons Vice Captain. Total Games competed to date: 5.]

Urban straightened. "Hi, I'm Lee Urban."

Dawn appraised her with her beady red eyes. "Are you on the A team or B team?"

"That's still to be determined," Blossom interposed as she took a seat at their table.

Urban gave her former roommate a tentative smile, trying to reassure her she had no intentions of competing. Blossom sniffed and turned away.

The last empty seat shimmered, and a man with spiked black hair and dancing hazel eyes appeared.

Urban started.

The figure grinned widely. "Kang Hickory. Camo."

Dawn flashed a look of annoyance at Hickory. "You Camos think you're so funny." She glanced at Urban. "Now that you've officially joined the team, you should link with the others so that you're aware of future training sessions, events, and parties."

"Thanks."

Urban extended her tatt to Hickory, Clay, and Dawn. Her sosh jumped .19% just from linking with the other KOLs.

Dawn nodded her head in approval.

Steaming dishes arrived on the table and everyone dove in.

"How are the Scorpions looking this year?" Orion inquired.

Urban knew firsthand from her jiujitsu training sessions how much of a strategist he was. Dawn might be the vice captain, but Urban wouldn't be surprised if half the plays actually came from Orion.

"They're good." Dawn projected a holo above the food, displaying some of the Western Federation's highlights. "They completely dominated their inter-federation games."

"As did we," Orion pointed out.

"I heard the Scorpions' team captain got suspended over the holidays." Olive delicately picked some food off the slowly hovering lazy Susan. "He failed out of classes." Her eyes glimmered to life as if juicy bits of gossip fed her soul. Yet another reason for Urban to keep her distance from the Inceptor.

"Kal Roberts?" Dawn raised an eyebrow. "The idol of all the women?"

"It will be all over the news in a few days," Olive declared. "I hear they're scrambling to find a new captain."

"Finally, an easy win." Clay cheered. "Put me in, coach!"

Dawn shook her head. "I wouldn't be so sure. Their Camo-Flyer-Super trio is the best out there." She glanced quickly at Brooke and Hickory. "No offense." She changed the projection to show some of the clips from the three Western Federation team members working in perfect harmony to complete near impossible feats.

"Yes, but we have all the brain power," Blossom piped up. "Willow is the best Artisan alive, and the two of you"–she motioned at Dawn and Orion–"are brilliant Givers and Inceptors. If it's an intellectual challenge, we'll win."

Orion nodded politely, but Dawn eyed Blossom skeptically, completely unaffected by the attempted flattery.

Next to Urban, Clay made a quiet gagging noise, and she turned her head in surprise.

"Is she always like that?" Clay asked.

"Blossom?" Urban's mouth twitched. "Only when she really wants something, apparently."

"For your sake, I hope you make the A team." Clay's eyes darted past Urban to Blossom. "But for mine . . ." He made a comical face. "Please don't let her join us on the B team."

She had to smile. *At least there's one person on the B team I might be friends with.*

The Dragons continued to debate their strengths and weaknesses as opposed to their upcoming competitors'. Urban listened silently, not feeling comfortable enough to contribute.

"What do you think, Urban?" Blossom dabbed a napkin to her mouth. Her eyes on Urban held something in them. A challenge?

Urban hesitated. "I think we're going to stomp out the Scorpions." She mustered what she hoped was a confident grin.

Clay slapped her on the back. "That's right!"

Several others laughed, and the conversation shifted away. Urban relaxed again. Only Olive's eyes remained on her, wary as ever.

Why can't Inceptors leave me alone? Urban focused on the food. There were many of her holiday favorites, and she was starving.

Clay lowered his voice. "I wouldn't eat too much if I were you."

It was too late for that.

At that moment, Willow scooted her chair back and stood. "Welcome, Dragons!"

Cheers and applause filled the room and Urban joined in, her stomach a little queasy.

"We have some tough competition this year from the Scorpions, and later, the Jaguars, but I'm confident the championship trophy will end up at PKU again."

Whistles and more whoops.

"But as you all know, to be the best, we have to work smarter and harder than everyone else. That's how we'll win."

Clay groaned.

"And it begins now!" Willow clapped her hands. "To the arena!"

Urban noticed for the first time how the other players had barely touched the food on the table. Clay's warning now made sense. Anxiety, mixed with way too much rice and braised beef, knotted her stomach.

Thankfully, Urban always kept her power-boosting energy pills and an extra steroid shot for her asthma with her at all times. She was very thankful her asthma hadn't flared up over the past few weeks. Discretely popping one of the energy pills in her mouth, she desperately hoped it would kick in soon.

As the team went outside, their suits clicked on, and a collective hum filled the air.

"For our warm-up," Willow had to shout above the howl of the wind, "we'll start with a light jog to the Coliseum."

She took off, slender legs moving gracefully, and the rest of the team matched her pace.

They jogged over deserted bridges, through bamboo forests, and toward the other side of campus. Urban was near the back of the group, food sloshing in her stomach. Blossom, the only other new recruit, and equally ignorant, also fell behind. Clay shot them a sympathetic glance, but everyone else seemed oblivious to their struggle.

It would have been a comfortable pace had Urban not been so stuffed. She tried concentrating on anything other than her growing sense of nausea–the wind biting into her face and burning her lungs, the puff of heavy breathing, the jolt of her legs as they struck against the pavement.

She gritted her teeth. *This will all pay off once I find the hybrid.*

By the time they reached their destination, she was red-faced and sweating. PKU's bone-white structure loomed above as they slowed their pace and filed into the Coliseum. Her retina display flashed in the corner of her eye.

<Now arriving at Peking Coliseum. Sosh: 91.>

Inside, the arena seemed very different without its throngs of amped-up students, flashing lights, and music. In the still darkness, it was almost peaceful.

The team made their way onto the stage, and Urban's breath staggered. Memories assaulted her from when she'd been forced into the arena to compete. When her Natural DNA had broken Samson and resulted in it releasing all its obstacles at once. Several of the front row seats still had gashes on them from the wildlife.

Thankfully, this time she wouldn't be caught unaware.

Make sure training mode is always selected. If for some weird reason it's not, feign injury or illness.

Willow whistled for silence. "Alright, most of you have been lying around for the past few days and stuffing your faces with *fagao* cakes. That's why this practice will be all about getting back into shape. Everyone suit up," she ordered.

Urban dragged herself to the women's locker room. Most of the players were already inside changing. Brooke, two heads taller than Urban, bounced up and down with way too much energy, as if the jog had been nothing.

Please don't let me get partnered with Brooke.

"It's too tight on me," someone complained, cutting into Urban's thoughts.

Dawn stood in nothing but her fitted underlayer. Her glittering red eyes roamed over the other girls, stopping on Urban.

"You. Give me your suit," she demanded.

Urban took a surprised step back.

The room grew quiet as the other girls discreetly watched the interaction. Dawn tried to snatch the suit, but Urban pulled back just in time.

"What's wrong with yours?"

"Does it matter?" Dawn snapped. "I'm on the A team. You're not. Now give me your suit."

"And you're a Giver," Urban countered. "Aren't you supposed to be the giving type or something?"

Willow entered the room and Dawn's expression instantly changed.

"Oh, Willow, there you are. Would you mind helping me?" Dawn's voice was honeyed, and Urban felt some of her own anger dissipating at the soothing tone. "My suit doesn't fit. I will just have to trade with someone."

Willow sized up the team members. "Urban, you're a little smaller, why don't you trade with Dawn."

The second Willow's back turned, Dawn flashed a triumphant smile and yanked Urban's suit out of her hands. She tossed her own at Urban before sauntering away.

Urban schooled her expression, despite the rage simmering underneath.

She slipped on Dawn's suit. At least it fit. Urban emerged from the locker room and back onto the stage.

Everyone spread out across the platform. Individually, they were confronted with a variety of challenges tailored to their weaknesses. Blue bubbles, each the size of a small apartment, formed around the players.

Blossom stood her ground against a masked ninja and snatched up a dagger to defend herself. Brooke faced some sort of stratagem game, and Clay a blank canvas. Urban noticed in the bubble closest to her, Dawn circled a muscled lion. Urban almost felt sorry for her.

She held her breath as a blue ball formed around her. For several seconds, nothing happened. Her heart pounded. It was like the tryouts all over again.

But training mode was selected, and since the AI was constantly evolving and had encountered her Natural genetics before, it shouldn't break again.

All the same, Urban was both relieved and anxious when the two tiles closest to her flipped over and two robotic soldiers emerged. They heaved stun spears and guns, but remained frozen in place until another tile flipped over, revealing a shield and a stun sword.

Urban raced toward the weapons. As soon as her hands closed around the pulsing sword and shield, they activated, turning blue. Her retina display showed her information on the weapons.

<All weapons with blue setting will temporarily disable any opponents. Red setting indicates kill mode. Red mode disabled in all trainings.>

Urban remembered how the Flyer who'd attacked her and Ash last semester with a laser hand ax had a pulse that was red. Not that she hadn't known he was attempting to kill her, but something about the confirmation made her shudder.

The two bots jerked to life, lifting their own weapons, and circled her. One stabbed a spear at Urban's midsection.

Diving to the ground, she rolled into a crouch and kicked out at one of the bots. It stepped out of the way.

A powering-up sound had Urban instinctively pull up her shield. Several stun blasts exploded into it and warmed her arm from the force.

Behind her, the other bot stabbed her leg. Urban felt a moment of pressure but then her suit absorbed the blow. Her damage counter dropped from 100% to 85% and she spun around to face the bot, furious.

A blood-curdling scream pierced the air.

Is that normal for training? Urban tried to peer out her bubble. Distracted, she didn't block as one of the bots fired again, striking her in the chest. The force of it threw her backward, and she watched as her damage counter dropped twenty more points.

"Samson, shut down all training!" Willow was shouting.

Urban's tough exoskeleton suit deflated against her skin, no longer protective. Just like in the tryouts. Shutting down the obstacles deactivated their suits. The bubble encapsulating her disappeared, along with the attacking bots. Only this time, the obstacles all retreated underground of their own accord. Urban watched as the two bots disappeared.

All the other obstacles around them retreated underground–except one.

Dawn's.

It was hard to tell what was happening. With a start, Urban saw that blood smeared the ground.

She followed the trail of crimson to where Dawn lay curled in the fetal position. Her bubble and damage counter were gone.

Something moved.

A lion, teeth bared, claws sharp, shook its bloodstained mane before biting into Dawn's arm. The girl screamed again.

Urban gasped. *Why is there still an obstacle when everything has been shut down?*

More blood appeared, and Urban's stomach revolted at the sight.

"Supers, Camos, get over here!" Willow yelled. "Someone call the medbots."

Urban was the closest one to Dawn. She knew firsthand how deadly it could be to get caught in the arena without a working suit. *The rest of the team may not make it to her in time.* She had to do something.

She glanced down at her hands, which still held her shield and stun sword. Reactivating them, she dashed toward Dawn.

Urban brought her shield down with a crack to the lion's head. An electric pop filled the air. The lion's filthy mane stood on end with the current. For a moment, she thought she'd stopped it.

Then the lion roared.

Jaws snapping, it lunged. Urban rolled away just in time.

Dawn whimpered and tried to scoot away, her one good arm pulling her slowly across the floor. The lion turned back to her, and a claw darted out and sank deep into her flesh.

She didn't scream this time.

Urban rolled to her feet, and, in desperation, she brought the sword down on the lion's head with all her strength, this time slashing into its sinewy neck.

The lion swerved to Urban, momentarily forgetting Dawn. It slinked toward her.

"Force it into the cage!" someone yelled.

Behind the lion, several bots lowered a giant metal cage. A mechanical clicking filled the air as the arena, in its attempt to recalibrate, flipped over several of the tiles.

Urban tripped on one of the uneven tiles and fell backward. She caught herself before hitting the ground, but dropped her sword.

Now, nothing but her shield could keep the giant creature at bay.

Sensing her vulnerability, the lion crouched, ready to pounce.

Suddenly, something buckled the lion's leg. The beast swiveled and faced empty air, as another invisible force slammed into it from the other side. This time, it caught ahold of something. Hickory shimmered into view and let out a grunt of pain.

Then Clay and Brooke were there. The giant woman poked at the lion with a sword and stopped its movement. It looked from left to right, either seeking out an escape or easier prey, but the Flyers flapped their giant wings and drove it back.

Slowly, the lion retreated. Its paw halted on the cage.

Brooke arced her sword and brought it down. The lion growled, but retreated into the cage, out of reach of the slicing blade. The door instantly slid down, trapping it.

Willow and several other team members were already crowded around Dawn as Urban hurried over. Urban's stomach lurched.

Dawn's face was an unnatural white and glistened with sweat. Blood seeped through her suit, and one of her legs bent at an unnatural angle.

Several medbots landed next to her and gently moved her limp body onto a stretcher.

"Take her to the triage unit below and alert the staff," Willow ordered. "I want a live surgeon here ASAP."

The stretcher carrying Dawn descended, tiles lowering like an elevator, allowing them to retreat faster to the emergency med center below.

Several heavily armed bots and Supers arrived. Each had a golden hammer and sickle emblazoned on their uniform, identifying them as the *Jingcha*.

"Practice is canceled for the rest of the night," Willow said shortly, and went to talk to the law enforcement.

There was a moment of silence as the team watched them go. Several bots whirred to life, cleaning up the blood on the platform while other bots lowered the giant steel cage and lion away.

Orion's voice was quiet. "What happened?"

"I think her suit malfunctioned." Blossom pointed at the streaks of blood on the arena floor. "I was watching her when the lion came. From the start, she had no protection. Her suit never even came online."

"But the suits have triple fail-safe mechanisms built in," Clay protested. “A suit malfunction should be impossible.”

“Not if someone tampered with it,” Orion pointed out.

“But why would someone want to hurt Dawn?” Blossom asked.

“I don’t think anyone did.” Olive’s eyes went to Urban. “That was Urban’s suit.”

BACK IN HER ROOM, URBAN PACED THE FLOOR, mind spinning.

She thought of all her close calls the previous semester. Being trapped in a purple zone, her motorcycle shutting off right as she made a jump, the attacker who'd crashed her car into the bottom of the Reservoir.

Coral had said all the incidents were from SAS and, going forward, she'd warn Urban if they tried to attack. Was someone else other than Supers Against Soups targeting her? Could it be the same Enhanced attacker who'd nearly drowned her? With his Camo enhancements, he could still be following her.

K-pop played in the background, agitating an oncoming headache. She turned the music off.

She couldn't shake the image of Dawn–in *her* suit–out of her mind.

Is it the attacker from last semester, and here on campus? You have to have special security clearance to get into the arena.

With a sinking heart, she realized it was probably someone on the team.

But who? Blossom? She thought of the SAS badge found in the dorms the previous semester. *But if she wanted to hurt me, she could have done it at any point when we roomed together.*

It made perfect sense, and yet, it didn't.

Olive's calculating eyes came to mind.

Rubbing her temples, Urban knew she had to keep busy or her mind would implode. She took a deep breath and stilled herself for a moment.

Her suitcases had been delivered to the room, but she hadn't had a chance to unpack them yet. Squatting next to one, Urban sorted through its contents until she found what she was looking for. She pulled out a paintbrush, ink stick, ink stone, and scroll. After changing into her silk nightgown and preparing her ink, she gazed at her walls.

A *chengyu* her elementary school teacher taught her resurfaced: *ju mu wu qin*, or, 'to be a stranger in a foreign land'. *How fitting.* She dipped her fine rabbit-hair brush in the watery ink and brought it to the canvas.

Her fingers, of their own accord, copied the characters while her mind drifted again.

Maybe it's not Blossom or Olive at all.

Urban flipped through a mental team roster. She didn't know most of the students that well. There was Orion, but it would have been tricky for him to get into the women's locker room.

There was Brooke, the huge Super who, at a party last semester, had worn something with the SAS logo on it. She had been in the women's locker room. With each player's suit clearly labeled, Brooke would have had the opportunity to tamper with Urban's suit.

Urban dipped her brush back in the ink before resuming her work.

Should I leave the team? She considered the possibility.

Leaving the Dragons before their first game would probably tank her sosh. Even though she could spare more than a few hits, if she lost her KOL status, her sponsorship with Croix, the athleisure brand, would most likely be cancelled. And if that happened, she wouldn't be able to finance her trip to the West.

Not to mention, she needed access to data, people, and information in order to help track down the hybrid. To do that, she had to stay a KOL.

Urban's tension grew as she completed the last stroke. Setting her brush down, she examined her work. With a sigh, she put her supplies away but left the scroll to dry.

She climbed into bed and cranked her headset to the highest sleep setting. Even as the cold gas infused her breath, the last thing filling her vision was Dawn's blood smearing the arena platform.

The next day, Urban quickly got ready and headed to Mixed Media & Art. Trig's familiar green dot showed up in her maps, though he remained invisible as she made her way toward the Choo Building of Design and Art. She'd passed the impressive structure several times before, admiring its curved angles and aesthetic textures and colors. An entire side of the building appeared to be a giant wave captured in a ten-story-high box. An illusion of course, but impressive nevertheless.

The Artisans inside wore bright colors and fashions she'd never seen before–each one looking like something off a KOL landing page. Their unique makeup consisted of bright colors, and many of them had pulsing tattoos snaking around their necks. One carried a boom box on his shoulders. Some wore shiny retro headphones or watches from generations ago, while still others went further back in time and wore *kimono* and *qipao*-style dresses mixed with netting and smart fabric.

Urban's retina maps guided her to the top floor of the building where there were fewer students. The space overlooked the main lobby, and students talking on the ground floor echoed sharply up.

The Mixed Media & Art classroom was hard to miss. Bright blue waves resembling *The Great Wave off Kanagawa* covered the door. One of the walls to the left lit up in a holo projection of the tops of trees, swaying and glistening in sunlight.

On the other side of the door, music played, old Federation opera mixed with a modern beat. There were four statues against that wall, each displaying the same elegant woman with flowing smooth hair and wearing a traditional *qipao*. But the materials from which each statue was made differed. The first was carved from stone, the second beaten out of metal, the third made from a 3D printer, and the final one was a flickering holo projection.

Inside the classroom, there were no tables, just a variety of chairs ranging from bean bags, to pillows, to stiff-backed wooden armchairs, to shiny metal stools. A lone beam of light dimly illuminated the room, the odd assortment of seats clustered around it.

A man wearing a black hooded robe stood at the center of the light. Urban couldn't see his face, but she got the impression he watched her and the other students filing in. She took a seat on an embroidered pillow and waited for class to begin.

The rest of the twelve students seated themselves and quieted down, turning their attention to the still figure at the center of the room. Urban counted a full two minutes before the professor moved.

With the slightest shifting and a click, a projection displayed out from under his hood. It looked like it might be coming from his eye socket. Only fully replaced metal eyes had the ability to display 3D holos. Urban wondered if he had lost an eye.

Another cloaked figure projected out, a duplicate of the professor. Only, this one removed his hood, revealing a bald, scarred scalp, eye patch, and a grave expression in his one remaining blue eye.

The projection opened his mouth and a gravelly voice

came from all corners of the room's sound system. "Hello. I'm Dr. Yukio. I was rendered deaf, mute, and partially blind in an accident. Now, I speak, listen, and see with the help of technology.

"This partnership of technology infused in my body has taught me much about seeing art from new angles. It's enabled me to push the limits of my own creative boundaries in ways I wouldn't have anticipated. My hope is that each of you will walk away from my class with a new appreciation for the different mediums in which art can be displayed. The number one trait I value and encourage in this class is boldness."

He snapped his fingers and a bot emerged from a side room holding a burlap bag.

Dr. Yukio's projected figure studied the students. "Who's first?"

"First for . . . what?" a student asked nervously.

"I repeat, who's first?"

The class fell silent. Urban raised a hand, determined to prove she belonged on the Artisan track.

"Very good." Dr. Yukio motioned the bot toward her. It hovered to a stop in front of Urban and extended the burlap bag.

Urban glanced up at the professor, unsure of what to do.

"Stick your hand in and pull out one object."

Urban did as she was told, trying not to think of what might be in the bag. To her relief, her fingers didn't touch anything slimy or moving. She shuffled through, trying to guess what things were. Her fingers brushed up against cold smooth objects, rough splintered ones, soft ones, even a warm one. She couldn't figure out any of them so decided to grab the most baffling object of all, something circular and squishy.

Pulling her hand out, she saw that a tiny water drop encapsulated in a flexible plastic rested in the palm of her hand. She examined it as the bot proceeded to extend the bag out to the next student until everyone held an object. The student on Urban's right withdrew a block of wood, the one to her left had a square made of felt, and the one behind her pulled out a tangled mess of wires.

"What you hold in your hand," Dr. Yukio continued, "is the medium you will be using to create for the duration of this semester."

A student holding a clear ball with fire inside groaned, while several others murmured excitedly. *Of course I get water.*

Dr. Yukio held up his hand for silence. "Some of you may be wondering how this is possible with your selected medium. Like I mentioned, boldness is the highest valued trait in this class. It can be done. Leading up to your midterm project, we will workshop your ideas to ensure you're on the right track."

Dr. Yukio's projection glided closer to them. "Now, I don't believe in wasting time, so we will start on your first assignment, an invitation. In your digital folder you will find all the details you need to incorporate. I suggest you start brainstorming."

The projection pointed at the bot which had now moved toward a door. "Follow my assistant to the supply room for ideas. You may use anything in there for this assignment. That is all."

With that, Dr. Yukio's projected image vanished, leaving the real Dr. Yukio with his hood pulled up, silent and watchful.

Urban and the rest of the class followed the bot through a deceptively small doorway into a massive storage room. A lone skylight illuminated the dark room.

Urban stared in wonder.

Rows upon rows of shelves stood filled with the oddest assortment of items. One row had every kind of paper imaginable, from crinkly brown bags to sheik gold, and even old-school lined paper. Another had a variety of live plants along with different kinds and shapes of wooden boards and particles. Another row had live and dead animals alike. Urban picked up a dried, shiny beetle and studied it before setting it back down.

But the row that caught Urban's eye was the aquatic row. Different-sized fish tanks sat with plants and marine life swimming inside. Fish food, Aqua suits, fountains, mermaid statues, lamps with glowing bubbles, and all sorts of experimental test tubes filled with colorful liquids lined the shelves.

From somewhere above, the sound of crashing waves and clapping thunder melded together in deafening tones. The row smelled like fish, salt, and earth after a rain–a confusing combination that had Urban's brain short-circuiting trying to categorize it.

There was also a section of books about marine life, rain, and water. Urban picked up one titled: *The Natural Waterflow of New Beijing: A Complete Journey.* She pulled up her class resources to see if she could check out the book virtually, but the book wasn't available except in hardback. She couldn't remember the last time she'd read a printed book, but she tucked it under her arm.

She fingered through another book called *H2O: The Elemental Makeup of Water and How to Alter It* and checked that one out, as well. Several textured papers with designs of waves, rain, and fish caught her eye. She selected a few and placed them carefully into one of the books.

Urban wasn't sure how long she had been there, but when she looked up, the rest of the class was gone. Quickly returning, she found Dr. Yukio to be the only one remaining in the main room. His projection was back and the head swiveled ever so slowly following her movement.

"Ms. Lee," he called out. "Come here a moment, please."

Am I in trouble? Does he know I'm not a genetically enhanced Artisan? Slowly, Urban made her way toward the middle of the classroom where he sat.

Dr. Yukio remained staring at her from under his hood, until she shifted uncomfortably. "Are you aware of PKU's Artisan Leadership Program?"

"I think I've heard of it," Urban said.

"It's typically only open to upperclassmen students, but in your case, the Board of Directors has made an exception. Congratulations on being accepted."

Urban blinked. "Oh. Um . . . I'm sorry, but I'm not exactly sure what that means." *Please don't let it involve more homework.*

Dr. Yukio's projection offered a small smile. "It won't require much time, if that's what you're concerned about."

Urban smiled sheepishly in return, wondering how he had read her so easily.

"At least not right now. As a third year, you'll have some additional classes, and in your fourth year you'll intern with one of the big five art conservatories. But for now, all it means is you'll receive private mentoring from one of the Artisan professors."

"Oh, wow. Great."

"I volunteered to be your mentor."

"Oh." She was saying that a lot. Something about Dr. Yukio made her uncomfortable. Maybe it was that she couldn't see his face, or how intuitive he was. The last thing she needed was someone highly observant noticing she wasn't like most other enhanced Artisans.

Dr. Yukio remained silent.

"Thank you!" Urban hastily added.

Dr. Yukio stood from his chair. "I'll set up some time for us after next class period for our first mentoring session. Congratulations again."

Urban took her cue to leave.

She spent the walk back to the dorms looking up the Artisan Leadership Program in QuanNao, and she almost couldn't believe her eyes. Apparently, it was highly prestigious and competitive. It was also nomination-based, and Urban wondered who had nominated her and why the Board of Directors had made an exception.

Her emotions flitted from excitement to terror. On the one hand, Urban was thrilled and excited to be accepted into the program. It would open so many doors to her art career. But on the other hand, it would invite a whole new level of scrutiny.

What if Dr. Yukio finds out I'm not really an Artisan when he spends time mentoring me?

Urban was a good painter, but she didn't have enhancements that steadied her hands and allowed for greater precision. It was the whole reason her parents hadn't wanted her to pursue the Artisan track–the risk for exposure was high.

Urban's plan had always been to practice her artwork in the safety of her own room, not in front of a mentor or at one of the big five conservatories. Now, she would have to be much more careful.

As if I didn't have enough to worry about.

By the time she returned to her room, a headache pounded against her skull. She made a pot of tea and lay down to rest before her last class of the day. But resting was out of the question. They were actually going to kidnap a probot.

A knock sounded on the door and her system alerted her to Coral's presence.

"Come in!" Urban said as she sat up.

Coral entered and took a seat on the tile floor.

"Tea?" Urban offered.

Coral nodded, but there was something troubling in her gaze.

Urban measured out several spoonfuls of shriveled leaves into a pot. The aroma of sencha filled the room, but did nothing to calm Urban's nerves. "Any more news on the hybrid? Are we on for this afternoon's mission?"

"That's actually why I'm here." Coral crossed her legs. "Yes and no. So, I've managed to get access to Dr. Liang's public tatts, but his private ones are behind an added layer of security. I'm still working on those."

Coral paused. "Urban, when I was going through his public memories, I found something."

Urban poured hot water into the teapot and looked at Coral as it steeped. "A lead on the hybrid?"

"I found something else . . . weird. My system flagged it since the data had been altered. In one of Dr. Liang's memories, I found Rai Reed."

Urban frowned. "What does the person who hacked my adoption paperwork have to do with the founder of the microneedle patch?" She poured both cups of tea and, steaming drinks in hand, sat on a chair next to Coral.

"Watch." Coral projected on the wall in front of them.

The memory took place in an old apartment with broken tiled floors and a wobbly table with two bowls of noodles and chopsticks set on it.

It was from Dr. Liang's view. He watched a tiny figure crouched in the corner playing with two pieces of scrap metal. Black hair covered part of her dirty face as she made the jagged metal pieces walk across the floor like humans.

"*Lai, chi fan.*" A man gestured at the two bowls on the table. He wore a stained turtleneck and had a gaunt face with a straggly beard. His eyes blinked rapidly. Urban recognized him as Rai Reed from the image Coral had shown her the day before.

The toddler waddled over to the table. She pulled herself up onto the too-big chair, the table's edge coming to her eyes.

The girl's arms reached above the table to pull her bowl closer. She was about to spill it, when Reed caught the bowl just in time. He adjusted her seat so she was tall enough to see over the table.

Another chair was pulled up and Dr. Liang sat. The girl had managed to splash noodle juice all over her face as the other man sank into the chair with a deep sigh.

Reed inclined his head to Dr. Liang. "I'm very sorry, we weren't expecting you. We don't have any more food."

Dr. Liang waved his hand dismissively. "Food is the least of my worries."

Reed reached into his faded jacket and pulled something out and set it carefully on the table. "I did manage to recover your work."

Dr. Liang was very still as he surveyed the device.

Urban experienced a sense of déjà vu as she gazed at it, as well. Two bowls of noodles. A microneedle patch.

With a jolt, she remembered.

The smell of cilantro and juicy noodles. The cut from the metal she'd been playing with on the palm of her hand. A nasally voice.

This was the same patch she'd learned about last semester in her genetic engineering class. It was also the same one from her own memories.

Urban dropped her cup–shattering it on the floor.

The little girl she was staring at was her.

CORAL WAS ON HER FEET. "ARE YOU ALRIGHT?"

"I don't–I don't know." Urban shook her head, trying to clear it. "That girl." She gestured with a shaky hand. "That's . . . me."

"How do you know?" Coral studied the frozen image.

Urban felt like her voice was coming from far away. "Because I remember this."

Coral's eyebrows shot up. "But you had to be what? Three? Four?"

Urban stared at the recording. "I don't remember everything, just the bowl of noodles and the microneedle patch."

Urban's mind bounced around. How was Reed connected to the founder of the microneedle patch?

The recording unpaused.

"Thank you," Dr. Liang breathed. "You saved my life's work. I am indebted to you, Dr. Rai."

"Things are getting more dangerous." Reed's chopsticks trembled slightly as he struggled to wrangle slippery noodles. "I've nearly been caught twice in the last week. Our allies are dwindling. It's hard to know who we can trust. And this"–he waved a chopstick at the microneedle patch–"has a hundred thousand crypto reward on it."

Dr. Liang delicately fingered the device. "I am aware. I will be leaving the country soon. You should do the same. I suggest you get your daughter"–he gestured at the younger version of Urban–"off your hands."

Urban gasped.

Reed was silent a moment considering, sending Urban's heart strings twisting within her.

"You are free to do what you want," Dr. Liang continued, "but I'm going to the Western Federation with my experiments."

Reed looked at little Urban, who was happily using her chopsticks to stab at a floating cabbage. She hummed a little tune, oblivious to the conversation around her.

"You're right. We cannot risk the fate of the next generation." A pained expression shadowed Reed's face. "I'll find her a new home and come with you."

The memory faded to black.

Coral turned slowly to Urban. "You okay?"

Urban could hear her, but the words sounded muffled, distant, like something from a dream. *Get her off your hands. Your daughter. Find her a new home. The fate of the next generation.* The words cycled on repeat until they no longer made sense.

Urban began to hyperventilate.

"Urban?"

Urban closed her eyes briefly and breathed deep. "Send me the recording."

Coral looked like she was about to protest, but then decided against it.

A moment later, Urban pulled up the vid and played it again, this time freezing on the split second where Reed placed a hand on the little girl's back to help adjust her in the seat. She stared at the image. Reed's eyes were big and black, matching her own. And if she looked hard, the slant in their nose looked similar too.

That's my real dad.

Suddenly, she was crying into a pillow.

A hand touched her back. Urban had totally forgotten Coral was in the room, but she still couldn't stop herself from crying.

It wasn't until her pillow grew soggy with tears that she managed to sit up. "Sorry," she choked.

Coral extended a box of tissues.

"Thank you." Urban's voice was thin.

"Don't thank me." Coral was trying to sound lighthearted. "They're your tissues."

Urban tried to hide her embarrassment as she blew her nose. She thought about how her parents had traced her adoption agency to the Western Federation. Now, it made sense. She looked at Coral with what she knew had to be puffy red eyes. "Reed has to be involved with the work being done around the hybrid. Why else would he need to flee?" *And put me up for adoption?* She swallowed hard.

"You could be right," Coral acknowledged.

Urban's brow furrowed. "I don't understand why he doesn't have a sosh."

Coral shook her head. "I wrote a script to search the rest of the memories using facial recognition. Nothing came up."

How is that possible?

"Sorry, I have to go, but I'll keep looking," Coral promised, standing to leave.

Urban's thoughts spun wildly long after her friend had left. She finally made herself some more tea. Her throat kept itching and she was nervous it was her asthma coming back. As she sipped the soothing liquid, her thoughts returned to the puzzle of her origins.

She rewatched the vid recording over and over. Something was not quite right. She couldn't quite put her finger on it, but something about the recording was odd.

Lillian.

Her sister had been missing from the entire vid. Was it possible that . . .

No. Lillian's my birth sister. She wasn't in the vid because she was probably back in another room out of sight. Playing. Alone.

Urban bit her lip.

A ping startled her.

It was time for her final class of the day. Nervous adrenaline spiked through her as she realized which one it was, Advanced Genetic Engineering. All other thoughts fled.

Time to get answers. And hack a probot.

“WELCOME TO ADVANCED GENETICS!” A PROBOT said. Its canary-yellow eyes darted across the classroom like a cat chasing a laser beam, tracking students’ attendance. Its metal but mostly humanoid form paced in front of the podium. “I’m Dr. Huang, your professor for this general education course. I will be guiding you through the marvels of human DNA.”

Urban’s palms left moist sweat marks on her smart suit. *We’re actually going to kidnap him. This is madness.*

“I recognize a few of you from last semester. Welcome back. Glad I didn’t scare you away.” The probot’s face shield lit up in a fluorescent smile. Why engineers programmed some of the bots with their own lame sense of humor, Urban would never know.

The probot continued on about the course schedule and expectations, but Urban tuned him out. Busy rehearsing the plan, she gradually had a prickling sensation, like someone was watching her. Urban double-checked her ID was still set to private. Had a student recognized her without the help of QuanNao?

Casually, she turned to glance behind her. Her gaze scanned the other students, then locked with familiar golden eyes. Blossom, her blood-red lips unsmiling.

What is she doing here?

Then again, Blossom's keyword was 'genetic engineering' and she was on the Inventor path. It made sense.

Urban kept her eyes straight ahead, but Blossom's gaze seemed to bore into her back, making it hard to concentrate.

The probot started lecturing. "Now, for the rest of today's period, we will cover a brief history of enhancements. To be Enhanced, an embryo must be injected with AOG–Anti-OncoGene 2719, which prevents the body from seeing the enhancement tissues as foreign matter and attacking them. This attack by the immune system was suppressed for many years by medications such as mycophenlate and tacrolimus, which allowed a person to carry a kidney from a donor."

Urban leaned forward in her seat. She'd heard all of this before of course, but in primary school they'd breezed over the topic. This in-depth breakdown into the process was fascinating.

"Unfortunately, the immunosuppressive medications to allow this were often worse than the disease itself," the probot continued. "That is, until 2039, when the genetic cloaking procedure won the Nobel Prize and genetic swapping of organs and tissues became commonplace. This free-swapping era was the precursor to enhancements which allowed the human body to accept and use outside resources. Enhancing began shortly thereafter when laboratories merged gene cloaking with gene splicing. But there was a problem."

A holo projection at the front of the classroom flicked on, displaying a human lung.

"A small portion of the Enhanced, less than 1%, through molecular mimicry, experienced hypertrophy and proliferation of lung fibroblasts in random areas of the lung tissues."

Urban squinted, trying to look up words in QuanNao almost as fast as the probot could speak. She was having difficulty keeping up.

"Not only was this random, it was also roving, occurring in

some areas of the lung at one time, but in other areas of the lungs at a different time. Thus the R designation. It took the research group at the New São Paulo Genetics Lab a mere sixteen months to isolate the cloaking defect and the genetic profile of susceptibility of affected individuals. But no cure was found. Thus, individuals with RSP492 are left with a chronic intermittent cough that slowly causes more and more scarring of the lungs."

Urban shuddered. While she wasn't following everything the bot was saying, she understood one thing.

The probot was talking about RSP492–or RSP for short.

It was the single most deadly disease among the Enhanced. As a Natural, Urban had nothing to fear, but she still worried for her family and Enhanced friends.

"The World Enhancement Organization is the governing body overseeing all genetic engineering globally. They are still working on a cure but have yet to find one. Please continue reading on your own about the research being done by the WEO around RSP492. That concludes today's class."

Urban blinked. She had been so intent on the lecture, she had actually forgotten what was about to happen.

It was time.

Taking a deep breath, she headed toward the probot as students filed out of the classroom.

"How may I help you, Lee Urban?"

"I was wondering when our first test is and how to get a jump start studying for it." Urban wondered if the probots were programmed to read people's facial movements, breathing, and pulse. Would the probot know she was lying?

"I can help you with that," a voice said.

Blossom was right behind her. "If you read the syllabus at all you'd know that's in three weeks. The study guide is already there too." She gave Urban a quizzical look. "You coming to the virtual bash tonight?"

"Uh . . . of course." Urban was frantically trying to come up with another question as the probot began to whir silently away.

"Great. Want to walk to an XR pod together?" Blossom asked.

What is happening? Why is Blossom suddenly being so nice? "That would be great, but I have some other things I need to ask Dr. Huang about." She caught up to the probot. "Dr. Huang! One more question." She turned and gave Blossom a wave. "See you there, alright?"

For a moment, Urban thought Blossom was going to join them again. But then she nodded and left.

Urban exhaled a sigh of relief.

"Yes, Lee Urban?" the probot asked. "How may I assist you?"

Urban scrambled for a question. "Actually, I have a question about something from last semester. You mentioned a microneedle patch that can . . . someday maybe change the world of genetics."

The probot stared, its bright lights for eyes unblinking.

"I'm wondering if there's any update on that," Urban went on. "Do we know who invented them? Where they are today? Anything?"

The probot was silent a moment before responding. Its yellow eyes darkened to a burnt orange. "I'm sorry, but that information is restricted."

Urban's heart jumped. "So, there is an update?"

The knobs and gears on the side of the probot's head purred as if the question required greater computing power. "I'm sorry, but I am unable to divulge any additional information on the subject."

Urban did a quick time check. She still needed to delay the probot another three minutes. She changed tactics and began babbling about grades and asking how to get high marks in the class. The bot, unlike a real human, never seemed to grow impatient.

As it reached ten past, Urban couldn't think of any more

questions to stall for time. "Thank you for all your help." She tried to smile. "I hope to do well in your class."

As the probot exited the room and headed toward the center of campus, Urban went in the opposite direction toward several XR pods.

Sliding into one, she logged into QuanNao and accepted the invitation to the back-to-school bash.

A moment later she was transported to a swanky ballroom. The hall was already full of students talking and laughing. A DJ set up in the corner on a stage.

Urban quickly found Blossom, and the two of them mingled with several of the other students. Now that both Urban and her former roommate were KOLs and on the Dragons team, it seemed everyone wanted to link with them. There was practically a line around them.

How different this kickoff party is from the one last semester, Urban thought.

After she'd lost count of how many people she'd snapped and linked with, she checked the time. *They should be finished by now.*

Excusing herself, Urban logged back out of QuanNao and stepped onto campus.

Veering from the pods, Urban walked down a quiet street toward a small shopping center. The doorway to the first store was constructed to look like something out of the old Federation.

Stepping inside, she was greeted by warmth and the scent of matcha, barley, and oolong tea. She took a bamboo seat at a table next to the window. She watched as the few people who were outside walked or hovered past.

She ordered a buckwheat tea, trying in vain not to check the time repeatedly. *Three minutes past.*

Four.

A fist squeezed Urban's heart.

Five.

A bot came and placed a delicate teacup in front of her. It lifted a pot with a spout as long as her arm and poured the tea, first close to her, then hovered slowly away, all while still pouring. The final bit was poured from several meters away, and yet, not a drop spilled.

Urban focused on the process, trying to distract herself from her worried thoughts. Her mother had told her humans used to do this and it was considered an art form. With the bots' mathematical precision, they never spilled, something very difficult for most humans. It was one of the many dying arts replaced by the bots.

"Hey."

Urban quickly turned her head to see Coral, Ash, and Trig take the other seats at the table. She let out a breath of relief.

They ordered, then waited for the bot to leave.

"So?" Urban leaned forward, voice hushed. "How did it go?"

"We're a little worse for wear." Ash grinned, despite a huge bruise forming on his temple. "But it worked. And we don't think anyone suspects anything."

"We got a name," Coral interjected.

Urban sat upright. "Anyone we know?"

"Unfortunately, it's another dead end."

"As in some old guy who's dead." Ash made a face.

Urban's heart sank. But Reed had worked with Dr. Liang. If they could find Reed, they still had a shot at finding the hybrid. "It looks like our best bet is still in the West," she said slowly.

"I agree." Ash stretched out his wings, careful to avoid hitting another table, and looked at the group. "So apart from Urban, who's already Western Federation bound, how are the rest of us going to tag along?"

Urban looked at him in surprise. "You want to come?"

"Of course. What are friends for?"

Urban's heart filled with a sudden warmth. She wasn't sure

when this small band of AiE members had become her friends, but she trusted each of them with her life.

"We just need an excuse to go," Ash said.

"All my family is there," Coral mused. "I could claim a family emergency."

"I go wherever you go," Trig said. He straightened his stylish suit jacket.

"I have an idea," Ash offered. "I could volunteer as the Dragons' official bag boy."

Urban scrunched her forehead. "The what?"

"Bag boy." Ash waved a hand. "Not to worry. I have it all figured out!"

Coral rolled her eyes.

Ash grinned. "Western Federation, here we come!"

URBAN'S MOTORCYCLE SKIDDED TO AN ABRUPT stop. A glossy high-rise loomed in front of her. The fading rays of the sun reflected off of the surrounding buildings. Holographic signage advertised new openings for rent and boasted of access to a luxury spa, pool, XR facilities, and other features to try to entice new residents.

She had decided to pay Everest a visit to update him on the news and, according to her retina display, this was his new place.

Urban buzzed the apartment's intercom, and a moment later, it clicked open. Passing through an empty lobby and up a set of stairs, Urban crossed over a glass walkway with bright lights flickering all around.

She rode up an elevator, tucked a strand of hair behind her ears, then knocked.

The door flew open and Everest stood wearing sweats and a hoodie, black hair wild and messy. An electric current zinged Urban as their eyes met then darted away.

Everest offered her a pair of slippers. "These should be your size."

"Is this your new place?" Urban bent down to the slippers to hide her burning cheeks.

"AiE got it for me. Pretty swanky, huh?"

Everest shut the door and Urban followed him into the living room. It was dimly lit with fluorescent purple blacklights in the wall paneling, under the black marble coffee table, and around the various plant life and statues decorating the room. The entire place had a modern, trendy, and yet empty feel to it.

Urban wondered how Everest felt about living here. It had to be a shock from the grungy two-bedroom apartment he shared with his parents in the Outskirts.

"Nice view," she commented. She walked over to the floor-to-ceiling windows taking up an entire side of the living room.

The bustling, bright city life beyond spilled a riot of colors into the room. Outside, delivery bots and hovercrafts traversed orderly in the air. Below, autonomous vehicles waited in never-ending traffic and pedestrians walked or zoomed along the crowded sidewalks.

Urban took a seat in the chair next to Everest. Her eyes snagged on a wall. It was empty except for a single painting. She'd seen it before. It was of two goldfish chasing each other's tails in a circle–her painting.

The one she'd given him back when they were dating.

"So," Everest said. "What's this I hear about hacking a probot?

"That's the plan I came up with last week."

Everest's eyebrows shot up. "It was *your* plan?"

"Don't look so surprised."

Everest sat back. "You've changed."

Urban made a face.

"In a good way," he amended. There was something in his gaze–admiration, pride, respect?

Then it was gone and Urban wasn't sure if she'd seen it at all. She quickly explained the probot hacking.

"That was a pretty good idea," Everest commented.

"Coral also found something else." Urban hesitated. "A lead on my dad."

Surprise flashed across Everest's face.

Urban told him about the vid recording of Rai Reed.

"Wow." Everest's gentle voice held a note of uncertainty, as if he wasn't sure how to react.

"I feel so close to so many answers. I wish we could find him," Urban added wistfully. She sighed. "To top it off, I almost got killed on my first day of practice."

"What!" Everest's eyes went wide, and he bolted upright.

"It's okay. I'm fine," Urban told him. "I wasn't hurt, since the Giver team lead took my suit for herself that day. *She* was the one nearly killed instead."

Everest shook his head. "I'll see if AiE can spare the resources to look into it. We need to make sure you're safe." He leaned back again in his seat. "I wish I could help more. I feel so useless, trying to pretend like I'm on a tatt fast everywhere I go. I have AiE work piling up, and all leads to the hybrid are stalled until Coral can hack the tatt." He ran a hand through his hair. "I should be spending my time boosting my sosh, but I'd rather focus on the hybrid. Once the Lunar New Year tatt fast ends, I have to have it high enough."

He was talking to her in his old way, which touched something deep within her.

Focusing on their immediate conversation, Urban's eyes grew round with worry. "That's not a lot of time."

"No, it's not. Which means, if there's any chance I'm going to make this work, I need to go with you to the Western Fed to mingle with KOLs. It will help the sosh algorithms. Not to mention, there's an AiE summit taking place that I need to be involved with." He regarded her as if gauging her reaction.

She hadn't thought about the possibility of Everest coming. "Oh."

"I can try and give you space and stay out of your way–"

"No," Urban interrupted. "It's fine. I just wasn't expecting it."

Everest's face flickered. "Sorry, incoming location request

from AiE. I have to take this. Do you mind?"

Urban stood. "Do you need me to leave?"

"No, it's fine." Everest motioned her to sit back down.

A moment later, a holo projection appeared above the coffee table. A bearded man with a buzz cut and combat boots surveyed them.

"Who's this?" The man eyed Urban.

"She's with us," Everest explained. "Urban, this is the Premier of AiE's Operations, Sung Ray."

"Ah, Urban," Ray said, his holo projection smiling. "You're the one helping until we can get Everest's sosh up?"

"That's me."

"On behalf of the Advancements in Enhancements, I thank you for your service." He inclined his head, then turned immediately to Everest. "We have some things to discuss."

"Actually, before we get started, I have a request." Everest glanced at Urban. "I was wondering if we could have someone look into PKU's campus security?"

The man stroked his beard. "I think we can spare a resource."

The two of them eventually began talking about the best strategies to boost Everest's sosh–all things Urban was well versed in–and her mind wandered.

Soon, the conversation with AiE wrapped up and the holo vanished.

There was a moment of quiet, then Everest shifted in his seat. Was he avoiding something? His eyes met hers.

"Urban, I don't know how to say this. This whole fake dating act is killing me. Being this close to you and yet . . ." he trailed off, his dark eyes filling with an intensity she couldn't turn away from. "I can't do it. I want us to be together again. For real–not for some fake pretense."

Urban's heart began to pound as he leaned closer.

"I know things between us have been difficult. And I can't stop berating myself for the way I hurt you. It wasn't fair of me to break up with you so suddenly or to have you pretend to be back with me because of AiE." His eyes searched hers. "Can you forgive me?"

Urban's eyes grew moist. "Thank you. That means a lot." She bit her lip. "And . . . I do forgive you." She still felt shaky about the trust component.

Everest's face lit up and he began to speak, but Urban stopped him. "Everest."

He waited.

"Why did you join AiE?"

Everest stilled. He seemed to be debating with himself before he spoke, voice quiet. "When I was just a kid, my mom died. She was killed by Supers Against Soups."

"Everest, I'm so sorry." Urban blinked in confusion. "Then who is it I met?"

"My step-mom." Everest's eyes were distant. "I was there when it happened. Several SAS members came in and I–I froze. I did nothing to stop them from killing her." His voice hardened. "After that, I learned to fight so that would never happen again to anyone close to me.

"I threw myself at every street rat in town until I never let fear freeze me again. Eventually, my dad moved on and remarried. Things were rocky at first with my step-mom, but we've worked through things as a family. We've all had to fight to stick together. Things aren't perfect, but they're good now." His tone grew somber. "But I've never forgotten that day."

How had she never known this about him? When they were dating, Urban felt like she had known everything. His eyes were tinged with pain.

"So," he continued, "I know if we can't find the hybrid and bring change, my family will always be at risk from hate crimes. It's why I work so hard with AiE. We *have* to find the hybrid."

We have that in common. Finding the hybrid is the only way to keep both our families safe.

"Sometimes sacrifices will have to be made to change the world," Everest said.

"I know." Urban's eyes pleaded with him. "But Everest, I don't want to be your sacrifice."

Everest's face fell. "What I did wasn't fair to you. To be honest, I don't always know what's right these days." He ran a hand through his hair. "I'm trying to balance protecting my family, bringing equality to Naturals, coordinating AiE members, and boosting my sosh. But I do know that I want to be with you."

Urban regarded him. "I want to believe you. But I feel like you're so dedicated to the cause that I'll always be a second thought."

"But don't you see how important this is?" Everest argued. "If we don't fight to find the hybrid, we'll never be able to be together–to be free. I get that I'm not perfect, but I'm trying my best."

"I'm not asking you to be perfect," Urban told him. "I just want to be more than a distant second."

Everest was silent a long time before speaking again. "We're on the cusp of something great, Urban. I don't know if I can promise that right now."

Urban's voice trembled. "Then maybe it's best if we keep our distance."

"Urban." Everest tried to take her hand but she pulled away. He regarded her a moment, eyes darkening. "Very well, then."

Urban's throat constricted. Why did it suddenly feel like they were breaking up again?

Everest leaped to his feet. "Almost time to go."

"Go?" Urban looked at him, taken aback. How could he change so fast?

"Lillian suggested I train with you guys to boost my sosh. I believe jiujitsu class starts soon."

Urban had completely forgotten about her classes with

Orion and Lillian. And Everest was joining them? She swallowed.

"She also suggested I race."

"Race?"

"Coral has some connections to the Western Federation's underground racing league," Everest said. "She's getting me a spot in the upcoming competition. Afterward, we'll reveal my sosh. The AiE council thinks it's too dangerous for me to risk revealing my sosh in the Asian Fed. But the Western Fed is open to Naturals and Enhanced mixing. If I make my sosh public there, no one will bat an eye while I start low and link my way up."

He grabbed his bike helmet and headed out the door.

The sun had set by the time they rode out onto the main street. Rush-hour traffic had subsided and the streets were flooded with blue and purple light from the surrounding shops. Techno music and floral perfume wafted from the bright stores.

After weaving their way through the city, they came to the edge and stopped in a dark alleyway.

Everest leaned his bike against the wall, then locked it. "What better place to go on a date than a gym?"

Urban rolled her eyes. "Working out isn't really a date."

"And we're not really dating."

His comment stung, but Urban was worried. "It's risky for you to come here. I've almost been discovered as a Natural multiple times."

Everest was unfazed. "It'll be fine."

"It won't be fine if you jeopardize everything we've been working for," she countered.

"Trust me, Urban."

Urban was about to respond when a voice interrupted their conversation.

"Hey." Orion stood at the alleyway entrance.

"I don't believe we've met." Everest draped an arm over Urban's shoulder. "I'm Everest. Urban's boyfriend."

Orion's eyes flicked briefly over Everest. His face split into a smile that didn't quite reach his eyes. "I'm Orion. It's nice to meet you."

"Are you going to this joker's class, too?" Everest motioned toward the building. "Let's see what he really knows about jiujitsu, huh?"

Urban tensed.

Orion cleared his throat. "Yes . . . well, I'll see you inside." With a parting nod, he left.

As soon as he was out of earshot, Urban rounded on Everest. "He's the instructor!" she hissed.

"Oh." Everest had the grace to look abashed. "Isn't that what someone Enhanced would act like?"

Urban gritted her teeth. "Try not to attract attention, alright?"

After changing into her gi and removing her shoes, she lined up on the mat with the rest of the students. Orion started one of his monologues about discipline, but Urban's gaze drifted to the other end of the mat where her sister stood. Lillian had a scowl on her face. *I didn't think she'd be mad at me this long.*

She noted Orion's eyes on her. She straightened and masked her emotions.

"Alright, everyone partner up and practice side control," Orion ordered.

Inwardly, Urban groaned. *Lillian, Everest, or someone with enhancements?* Everest was the best option, but the last thing she wanted right now was to train in close proximity with him.

But with a flick of her ponytail, Lillian turned and partnered with a Flyer. Disconcerted, Urban scanned the room for another option.

"Want to be my partner?" Everest asked.

Urban's eyes went sideways to Orion. He watched their interaction.

She pasted on a wide smile with her nod, doing her best to look enthused, knowing Orion was probably reading them and knew something was up.

They moved to a corner of the mat and waited for instructions.

Orion gave a demo, then everyone began practicing.

Everest turned to Urban. "Do you want to go first . . . ?"

"You can start." Urban sensed her own uneasiness reflected in him.

She lay down on the mat and Everest lowered himself to her side. His black hair hung around his eyes. Urban found herself staring at his lips, remembering what they felt like against her own.

Stop it. Remember, distance, safety. This is just an act.

"The first thing to do is make sure you block the hip from escaping," Orion called out to the classroom.

Everest placed his hand in front of Urban's hip so she couldn't turn into him. Then he pulled her shoulder up and lowered his arm under her neck, trapping her.

Urban felt her heart racing at the sudden proximity between them as Everest leaned in closer. Mercifully, Everest released her and they switched places.

Urban tried to focus, but the old Everest kept coming to mind. The only person who hadn't discouraged her from going to uni, who'd taught her motorcycle racing, and who'd believed in her–the real her–from the start. Gentle, kind, strong, Everest, who could understand her creative struggles with art and yet was tough enough to survive the worst of the Outskirts.

Her concentration slipped, and she moved. They ended up in an awkward tangle of limbs and nervous laughter.

A voice cut the air sharply. "Let me show you two how it's done."

Urban jerked away, surprised to find Orion standing over them. His eyes were focused on Everest.

Picking himself up from the mat, Everest faced Orion squarely. "We're fine," he said coolly.

Orion held his gaze evenly. "I don't think so." He pointed at the mat. "Let me show you."

But Everest remained standing. There was a fleeting moment where Urban thought he'd refuse, but then he nodded. "Alright, *master*, teach me your ways."

Orion smiled, a glint of something dangerous in his eyes.

Urban's chest tightened.

The two circled each other, predators sizing up prey, then suddenly, Orion lurched forward, so fast Urban almost missed it. He landed smoothly with his back to the ground but his legs protectively up, one on Everest's hip, the other tucked underneath his back side.

Both shuffled across the mat, trying to get the better position, moving hand-holds and adjusting their grip. Everest slowly lowered himself to the mat, knee digging into Orion's stomach and grabbing a hold on the top of his gi.

Orion used the opportunity to grip Everest's leg.

Each vied for a better position in a mad scramble. They looked like fighting crabs, all arms and legs tangling and locking. Urban wasn't sure who was winning.

When they stopped again to regroup, Orion was squatting on Everest and his hands gripped his gi around the neck, pulling Everest's head toward him.

Both were panting heavily, and even Orion had beads of sweat glistening on his head. Everest's gi was half open, revealing the muscled planes of his bare chest. Orion's black belt was half untied and slipping off.

Still, neither seemed to have the upper hand.

The tangle of limbs moved slowly across the mat, their movements becoming sluggish as their faces reddened with exertion.

Orion had one of Everest's arms trapped in what looked like an incredibly painful angle, but Everest seemed to be choking Orion out. Both had faces contorted in agony, neither yielding.

The fools are going to kill each other. "Stop!" Urban cried.

Both Everest's and Orion's heads turned slightly to her.

Then they returned to each other, eyes flashing.

Finally, Orion spoke. “Call it?”

Everest nodded.

Cautiously, as if worried the other might trick them, they released each other.

Everest climbed to his feet and helped Orion up.

Orion surveyed Everest a moment, then smiled. This time it was genuine and filled with respect. “Not bad.”

Everest tightened the white belt around his gi and shook his head. “Nah, I’m not that good.”

“No, really.” Orion studied him with interest. “You’re definitely more than just a white belt. What school did you go to?”

Everest uttered a laugh. “I like to spar a lot.”

“Whatever you’re doing, it’s working.” Orion slapped him on the back. “Alright, class, that’s it for tonight.”

As the students dispersed, one of them approached Everest and tried to link. “Oh. You’re doing the augmented-free week,” she said with disappointment. “That’s over in a couple of days, right? I wanna link with you then!”

A chill raced down Urban’s spine. *Only a few more days.*

“Sure.” Everest smiled.

Urban spotted Lillian and started toward her, but her sister left before she had the chance to speak. In the back alley, she found Everest unlocking his bike.

“Hey–”

“See you later,” he said and zoomed away.

Alone, Urban wound her way through the streets.

This is for the best. So why does it hurt so much?

THUNDER CLAPPED LOUDLY OVERHEAD. COOL mist sprayed Urban and the scent of fresh rainwater filled her lungs. The supply closet to her Mixed Media Arts class almost seemed as if it had grown since the last period.

Eyes scanning the rows of supplies, she stopped at one full of fish tanks. There were tiny, bottled-sized glasses, huge aquariums, ones in the shape of a heart, and more. She selected a simple glass bowl with a goldfish swimming gracefully inside, its swishy tail fanning the water.

Back in the classroom, Dr. Yukio's projected figure roamed around, occasionally stopping to observe a student and provide feedback.

Urban pulled out her supplies and set them on the floor around her. Cutting out several circles, she began to make a collage of mixed green papers. She glued the pieces together in circles so that they resembled a lily pad.

While she waited for them to dry, she pulled out her paintbrush and prepared her ink. Urban scrolled through her class files and opened the one with the invitation details in her retina display. With careful precision, she painted the invite onto the green lily collage. She applied a sealant and let it dry before placing it in the fish bowl.

"Your medium is water, yes?" Dr. Yukio and his projection stood over Urban, observing.

"Yes." The sealant had held and the characters stayed dry. However, the lily pad-shaped papers had sunk to the bottom.

"That's not exactly what I had planned," Urban confessed.

"It's creative. Once the invitation floats, you will be on the right track." Dr. Yukio turned to inspect the next student's work.

Urban returned to the supplies room. She was able to solve the sinking invite by using magnetic levitation to keep it afloat, and she added a smart screen to the lilies. After programming the screen, each time one of the goldfish swam close to it, a trickle of water flowed over the lilies and back into the water. She surveyed her work with pride as class came to an end.

"Remember, your invitations are due next class," Dr. Yukio said. "Be ready to present them and tell us more about working with your selected medium, as well as defend your aesthetic decisions.

"Ms. Lee, why don't you remain for a minute?"

Urban packed up her supplies before following Dr. Yukio to the adjacent office.

The walls in the room resembled a slow-motion waterfall, but in reverse. Instead of trickling down, a glowing purple river floated up toward the ceiling. An odd, suctioning gurgle accompanied it.

As Urban entered the room, a drop of water splashed onto her shoulder, startling her.

"It's real," Dr. Yukio said without turning. "Took a while to figure out how to make it flow up instead of down, but it was worth it."

Urban stared at the waterfall with renewed interest before turning her attention back to the rest of the room. The office was sparse, but tastefully decorated. Several pieces of artwork projected or hung from the ceiling. The center of the room had a simple white desk with a water boiler, several glass containers of tea, and old-school pens and paper, and several hovering stools clustered close by.

Dr. Yukio poured boiling water into a beautiful teapot. It looked as if it had been shattered and then glued back together with gold.

After pouring them both a cup of jasmine silver needles, Dr. Yukio motioned for Urban to sit. He gestured at one of the paintings. “Have you seen this one before?”

“No,” Urban admitted.

“It’s one of my favorites. It was painted by a relatively obscure artist, Bai Yungtai. He died in the Genetic Revolution, right as he was reaching his peak potential.”

Dr. Yukio showed Urban several more pieces of artwork he had collected and inquired about artists who had inspired her.

Urban realized this was more of a get-to-know-you conversation than any sort of real lesson or mentoring. She relaxed as they chatted about favorite artists, collections, and museums.

“Well, it was delightful spending time with you, Ms. Lee,” Dr. Yukio concluded their time together. “I look forward to future sessions with you.”

“It was a pleasure for me also,” Urban said politely. But she realized it was the truth. Maybe this mentoring program wouldn’t be too bad after all.

By the time Urban arrived at the arena, the Dragons were already gathered and stood clustered together, speaking in hushed tones.

“What’s going on?” Urban whispered, sliding beside Clay.

“Not sure.” Clay shrugged. “Willow is waiting for everyone

to get here before she tells us."

The team captain clapped her hands. "I have an announcement." She paused, ensuring she had everyone's full attention.

"Security looked into the damaged suit to try and understand what happened." Her sharp gaze took in the whole team. "The results were . . . troubling, to say the least. Someone hacked the suit."

Dawn gasped.

Urban was surprised to see the Giver already back at practice. Several sickly bruises and smart bandages covered her arm and head, but otherwise she looked fine.

"We think we know who it is," Willow declared. Her eyes grew hard as they pinpointed a player.

"Ito Olive."

Murmurs erupted. Several players cast sideways glances at the Inceptor.

"What evidence do you have?" Somehow, Olive was as calm and composed as ever.

Willow projected a vid recording. "This."

The time stamp for the recording was a few hours before the first practice took place. It looked like security footage of a bright room filled with benches and lockers. In it, Olive slinked toward Urban's locker, and after attaching a device to it, she forced the door open. Looking both ways, she withdrew Urban's suit. Her back was turned to the camera and so it was impossible to see what she was doing before she placed the suit back in the locker and left.

Willow cut the recording and rounded sharply on Olive. "Would you like to tell us what you were doing tampering with Urban's suit?"

Olive stood unmoving. "I wasn't tampering with it. I was inspecting it."

Willow's brow shot up. "*Inspecting* it?"

"Yes."

"And why would her suit need *inspecting*?"

"Your evidence is inconclusive," Olive maintained. "I'm not the culprit."

Willow's face was rigid. "For an Inceptor, I'd think you could do a better job lying."

"She's telling the truth!" Blossom stepped forward, then shrank under Willow's glare. Her voice faltered. "She didn't do it."

"Then who did?" Willow demanded.

Blossom and Olive exchanged glances. "We don't know," Blossom said quietly.

Willow studied the two girls a moment. "I'm sorry, but your story is completely unacceptable. I won't tolerate lies and attacks made out of jealousy or vain ambition." She pointed to the Inceptor. "Ito Olive, you are suspended from the team."

Olive's face went crimson, and Blossom's mouth dropped open. "You can't do that!"

Willow's eyes bored into Blossom. "Would you like to leave the team as well?"

She fell silent, but her eyes lingered on Olive as the other girl departed, head down.

As if nothing had happened, Willow gave a whistle. "Now, shall we train? Jogging, go!"

The team made several laps around the arena before Willow stopped them to start practice. She seemed distracted, however, and training wasn't nearly as brutal as the last time. Although unsettled by what had taken place, Urban was grateful for an easy day.

When they finished, Willow gathered them once more. "We're leaving for the Western Federation on a private hypersonic aircraft tomorrow. I just sent everyone instructions on how to request international tatts, as well as a few other logistical items. Before we go, I have one final matter to discuss."

She spoke succinctly. “It’s the matter of A and B team players for the Inventor position.”

Blossom straightened and Urban tried not to let her panic show.

“After careful observation,” Willow announced, “I have decided that Blossom is the superior player.”

A smile played at the corner of Blossom’s lips.

Urban breathed a quiet sigh of relief.

“However.” Willow looked directly at Blossom. “After your display of defiance today, my decision to move you to the A team is not final. You will play on probation. Should I catch the slightest hint of trouble, Urban will take your place. Am I clear?”

Blossom stood still for a moment, then nodded begrudgingly. Urban felt a rising panic.

Willow now addressed the rest of the team. “Practice is finished for today. See everyone at the landing tomorrow morning at 0600 sharp. Anyone late will not be going.”

Urban headed back to the dorm to pack. Nervous adrenaline coursed through her at the thought of flying the next day. She had never left the Asian Federation before. She’d had her AI assistant apply for an international tatt via the KOL expedited channel and received approval hours ago.

But she kept feeling as if she were forgetting something important.

At least the person who hacked the suit isn’t coming.

Olive had been suspicious of her since they first met. She was also at the motorcycle race when Urban got hacked.

But something still nagged at the back of Urban’s mind about that too.

Urban cast her doubts aside and focused on packing things into a suitcase lying on the floor. She turned on a projection of the local news and let it drone on in the background. On another wall, she pulled up her pings and, using voice commands, responded to a few of the urgent ones.

“In breaking news, the Deadly Five have made a reappearance in New Beijing.”

Urban glanced up sharply.

"The Deadly Five were the bedrock and founders of the prejudice group toward Naturals, Supers Against Soups, or SAS," the newscaster continued. "After the Deadly Fourth was convicted of murder in a trial many years ago which went all the way up to the Capitol Prefects, the Deadly Five have all gone into hiding. But earlier today, the Deadly First was found deceased in an orange zone in the Outskirts."

"Rumor has it, the Deadly First was an Inceptor who used her abilities to mesmerize victims. If they were able to resist her powers, she used her weapon to temporarily paralyze them until she could get close enough to attack. Her fangs held a poison found in the deadly *Scolopendra subspinipes* centipede–an enhancement now banned."

The image cut to show an insect with a long black body and hundreds of unnaturally bright red legs crawling surprisingly fast across the ground. Urban shuddered.

"Authorities are still investigating the cause of her death, but it appears she was killed after using her poison on several Naturals. This jarring news seems to indicate that the Deadly Five do, in fact, still exist, and aren't as dormant as originally supposed. The question is, how many of the Deadly Five are left, and are those remaining still operating in hiding?"

Urban's gut clenched.

The newscaster went on to report an upcoming vote on a bill to change the social score rating system.

The divide between Naturals and Enhanced is going to keep growing if we don't get answers about the hybrid.

Her mind wandered back to Coral's finding about Rai Reed's connection to Dr. Liang. *If we could find Reed, he could lead us to the hybrid. But how will we ever find him without a sosh?*

Absently, Urban added stylish clothes and workout gear into her suitcase.

Her mind reeled. *As a KOL, I have access to everything I want.*

There has to be a way to leverage my status to find Reed.

She wasn't sure how much time had passed when a live vid interrupted her thoughts. Everest stood in the Metropolis in a pristine white XR suit.

[Everest: Hey. Just checking in to see how you're feeling.]

He gave a short wave.

Urban stared at his eyes, a Metropolis gold rather than his usual black. The blinking light in the corner of his retina display was the only indicator he didn't belong.

[Everest: I'm leaving tonight for the Western Fed, but I'll see you there.]

He offered a smile, then the connection cut.

Urban watched as the yellow light in his eyes slowly vanished along with his holo.

She straightened suddenly.

In QuanNao, she quickly pulled up one of the popular KOL gossip discussion boards. She took a few minutes to craft her post, rewriting it several times.

[*Challenge alert*]

[Hello! Some of you may know me as the girl who crashed PKU's AI. Since then, I'm thrilled to have been accepted onto the Dragons' team and will be traveling with them to the Western Federation to compete. While there, I'm hoping to meet up with an old friend of mine. Unfortunately, he's doing the augmented-free week and I can't get ahold of him.]

[He's based in the Western Fed, but doesn't have his profile or info publicly available. Here's an image of what he looks like. Anyone who can find him or provide any helpful info on his whereabouts will be awarded a prize. I will personally fly you to have coffee with me for an hour and link with you.]

[This challenge will run starting now through the end of the augmented-free week. Challenge is open internationally. Not sponsored by Croix. Winners may choose to meet in person or via XR. Best of luck, Lee Urban.]

With a smile of satisfaction, she leaned back. *If Reed is still alive, surely someone will find him.*

Urban hefted her suitcase and swung it over her bed, accidentally knocking over her jewelry box. Beads, bracelets, and pendants clattered to the ground. In their midst, something silver sparkled.

She stooped to pick it up and her breath caught. A necklace with the character "*mei*" glimmered brightly in her hand.

The sight of it brought back a wave of memories. Everest placing it gently around her neck and whispering in her ear. "*A reminder you have a boyfriend who thinks you're beautiful.*"

Urban gazed at it, then slipped the necklace into her suitcase. She was still standing there when a ping flashed in her retina display.

[Lillian: Are you really going tomorrow?]

Urban's heart leapt.

[Urban: Good to hear from you! How are you?]

[Lillian: I'm going to take that as a yes.]

Urban tried to location request her sister, but it was denied. There was no additional ping.

She rubbed at her eyes before crafting a simple message in reply.

[Urban: Don't worry, I'll be safe.]

Yet, she couldn't shake the feeling that safety was only an illusion, and it was danger that was on the other side of the ocean waiting for her.

URBAN SAT DOWN ON A WHITE PLUSH ARMCHAIR of the slim Hypersonic X8, stifling a yawn. It smelled new and too strongly of cleaning chemicals. A chill from the wide-open door swept through as groggy students filed in behind her.

"Not gonna lie, this is amazing." Ash took the seat in front of her. "Totally worth it."

Urban still couldn't believe Ash had managed to convince Willow to allow him to travel with the team. He'd volunteered as bag boy, errand runner, and even a mob scout. Urban hoped Willow had been kidding when she'd mentioned the need for that last part.

Ash adjusted the settings of his seat to accommodate a Flyer, then nestled his giant wings in a gap that formed in the chair.

With a rumble, the aircraft's engines warmed up for hypersonic speed.

"Please fasten your belts and remain seated for take-off," a disembodied voice advised.

Nervous adrenaline spiked through Urban as the hypersonic propulsion system grew to a dull roar outside the window. Then it boosted upward, and the skyrise launch pad dropped out from under them. Buildings passed below in a blur.

Urban absentmindedly twisted the bracelet Lillian had given her last semester. A knot in her stomach formed as she realized what she was doing. Her fingers fell away from the jewelry, and she tried not to think about everything she was leaving unresolved in the Asian Federation. Instead, she pulled up her post on the KOL discussion board.

Her jaw dropped.

Urban's KOL status certainly had garnered the attention she was hoping for. There were already over a thousand entries in her inbox and over ten thousand comments. The post had gone viral. Several news outlets had even picked up the story and were attempting to aid with the finding of her friend.

Urban opened the first few entries. They looked nothing like Rai Reed. One was a picture of a red panda and some tween girl gushing about how she'd named her furry friend Rai Reed. Another was wanting to ask Urban out.

With a sigh, she ordered her AI to prioritize the messages that had attached images or vids of men with similar facial matching to Reed. That reduced the number to 321 valid entries. Slowly, she waded through them.

After one hour, Urban was no closer to finding the elusive Reed. Frustration built and her eyes burned. Exhausted and discouraged, she drifted off to sleep.

A popping in her ears awakened her.

Bright morning sunlight blinded her as she tried to orient herself. The cabin filled with excited chatter and the sharp scent of coffee. Out the window, a glittering blue ocean faded into the distance and land stretched in all directions.

A patchwork of blotchy browns, terra-cotta orange, and green dotted the earth. Cities, smaller than New Beijing, sprawled out, disconnected. Urban noticed these cities didn't have any barriers over them. Perhaps the air was cleaner, or the residents simply didn't care to pay the extra taxes for air filtration domes.

The aircraft descended, causing her ears to pop again.

The cities and farmland came into sharper focus. In the place of familiar bushes and trees were wiry shrubs and thin palm trees. The streets looked practically empty compared to the Metropolis back in the Asian Federation. No one walked or rode hoverboards. All that occupied the sparkling clean roads were autonomous hovercrafts and a few flying transport units.

Soon, they were landing atop an airway strip at the city's center. The team disembarked quickly, but Ash lagged behind collecting the luggage, his giant wings wrapped around a towering stack of suitcases in his arms.

The airway reception was a large building made mostly of glass, sitting on the tallest high-rise in the city. Despite the bright light shining through, it was surprisingly cold inside. Urban pulled out a cardigan from her bag and tugged it on. She'd heard the southern part of the Western Federation was supposed to be warm this time of year. Had she mis-packed?

Urban glanced back at Ash. He was in the middle of dumping the last of the suitcases on the landing, earning him a look from Willow.

Noticing Urban, he grinned. "Don't worry, I've got this." He wrapped a rope through all the hovering suitcases and dragged them in a long row, like ducklings following their mother.

Around them, other passengers waiting for their flights sat sipping drinks and laughing. Their sosh ranged wildly from the high 30s to mid 80s. One of them caught Urban watching, smiled, and waved.

Urban waved back in confusion. She'd heard of the Western Federation's so-called friendliness, but had always assumed it was an exaggeration.

Music poured out from the overhead sound system. The scent of buttery pretzels and sweet cinnamon drifted toward them from one of the automated snack stalls. Urban's mouth watered, but instead she flashed her tatt at the international customs scanner.

A moment later, it beeped green. "Welcome to the Western Federation, Urban Lee," a robotic voice said. "Enjoy your stay."

A virtual stamp appeared on her international tatt, and Urban couldn't help but smile. She had really done it. She had left the Asian Federation. The accompanying sense of freedom was exhilarating.

"Keep up, people," Willow ordered. She turned and led the way again.

Urban followed close behind until they reached the exit.

"There's a slight disturbance outside the terminal," Willow informed them. "Our hired guards will be out these doors waiting. I want everyone to stick together and be quick about getting into your vehicles."

Urban pulled up the local news feed through her retina display. A platinum-blond reporter was speaking.

[. . . this is one of four demonstrations taking place today throughout the city by the Revolutionaries. They are known for their violence and extreme measures. Residents are advised to keep clear until military personnel have neutralized the threat.]

Urban closed the feed as they exited the building into the warm, muggy air.

A mass of bodies moved across the street like an amoeba, chanting loudly. Digital signs flashed with slogans: "Equal genetic regulations for all" and "Be done with genetic classes" or "No more *Soups* or *Farmed*! We're all equal."

Urban cringed at the genetic slurs. It jarred her to see both Primordial Soups, or *Soups* for short, and *Farmed,* referring to the Enhanced, on the same sign.

They were an odd mix of Naturals, but also a few Supers, Flyers, and some other Enhanced. Urban had never seen Naturals and Enhanced working together like this.

The Western Federation's flag had been torn down and, in its place, a new white flag with the words "Equality for all" waved in a slight hot breeze. Several Supers in blue military suits were attempting to pull the flag down, but the mob drove them back.

"This is your last warning to disband, or force will be necessary," said a military Super.

"We'll show you force!" One of the protesters launched a glass bottle. The Super dodged, and it sailed harmlessly overhead.

The Super withdrew what looked like a giant metal belt and booted it up so that it hovered in the air, pointing toward the crowd. Other military Supers did the same, and then they began distancing themselves from the mob.

"Remote area denial systems in place," a Super said.

Upon noticing the devices, the protestors at the front of group turned back, shouting and pushing the other protesters away.

The air cracked with electricity. A moment later, each device turned blue and undulated like a wave.

Pop! Sparks flew.

The protestors closest to the devices seized up, then fell stiffly to the ground.

Urban gasped.

Chaos ensued. Some of the Revolutionaries tried to run away, but most seemed all the more infuriated and ran at the devices.

Another two rounds of sparking darts went off, felling the first two lines of protestors. As the third wave approached, the devices hummed and rebooted. But before they could strike, they were smashed to the ground by the stampeding crowd. The military personnel retreated.

A deep humming drew Urban's attention skyward to a small swarm of drones. The bots sprayed the protestors with a putrid yellow gas which descended slowly.

Then the screams began.

Panicked, Urban reached for her stun shield.

People dropped to the ground trying to avoid the gas. Some clawed at their faces, while others tried to shield their mouths and noses with their shirts.

Urban watched in horror, unable to turn away. Hadn't the Revolutionaries seen this coming? "Get in! Now!" Willow bellowed.

The Supers accompanying the Dragons swiftly shepherded the team into waiting armored vehicles. Several of them stood guard with Magtouch M600s drawn and at the ready. Coral had told her the weapons were legal here, but to see them out in the open was still odd.

Heart pounding, Urban scrambled into the vehicle with Ash, Willow, and Brooke. The door shut behind her with a click, trapping the cool air and pleasant car smells in with them.

"What are they protesting?" Ash asked.

Willow sat down and turned on the local news. Images of violent protesters displayed in the background, but missing was the military spraying the crowd with gas.

"Western Federation officials must decide on the upcoming election what to do about the freedoms around genetic enhancements," a blond reporter said. "This past year alone, many troubled Revolutionaries have killed hundreds of innocent children and bystanders in the name of so-called freedom. Will officials crack down on them or will they–"

The recording flashed, then died. Urban and Ash exchanged worried glances before the image came back to life.

Only this time, it wasn't the blond reporter, but a woman with a flickering face. One second it resembled a beautiful woman's, the next, it changed to display an old man, then a young girl, then a middle-aged man.

"Don't let the news fool you." The voice was modulated and the image shifted to show the military releasing the shock wave. "The politicians control the news. The narrative. The enhancements. They control *us*. Not anymore. It's time for us to take a stand and take control of our own destiny."

Images flashed, showing a new scene of a subdued mob

moaning. One protester, a girl with amphibious skin, poured a water bottle over her face trying to blink away the pain, her eyes bloodshot. A close-up showed a boy, not old enough for university, balled into the fetal position and rocking back and forth. Sparks zipped across his skin. A family sat weeping and hugging each other tightly.

"We are everywhere. And because we are many, the truth will prevail."

The image flashed back to the flickering face. Both arms crossed over an armored chest in the form of an X.

"What a stupid signature for a bunch of Revolutionaries," Willow scoffed.

"Our government tells us that by programming genetic enhancements to become artificially hereditary, they have brought about equality," the voice continued. "Nothing could be further from the truth.

"So-called hereditary enhancements work for 5% of the population who have two enhancements and pass two of those enhancements down to their children. But what about for the rest of us? Over half the population who are Naturals don't get any enhancements. Their only option for equality is marriage. *Marriage.*" The newscaster spat the word.

Urban cast a furtive glance at Brooke and Willow. Both sat stiffly, but while Willow's upper lip curled, Brooke had a thoughtful, almost curious expression.

"You wonder why our Federation has the lowest reported satisfaction among family units?" the Revolutionary continued. "Maybe it's because half of the families were forced together out of need rather than love. Out of a desire to enhance their children–the only way to do that is through marriage alliances. It's also why we have one of the highest rates of child abandonment globally."

The recording switched to show footage of a Flyer in labor giving birth to a Natural. She eyed her crying Natural baby with disdain before bots delivered the still-crying infant to an overrun orphanage.

Urban's stomach turned.

"If the past century has taught us anything, it's that genetics are programmable. Why use an archaic system of deciding who gets to select the best genes for their children?"

Willow turned the recording off.

"Wait." Brooke leaned forward. "I want to watch."

"It's all Revolutionary propaganda," Willow stated, but she turned it back on anyway.

". . . end now. Our government wants you to believe this system is normal, fair. It's not. This system perpetuates a widening gap between genetic classes.

"The Board for Genetic Enhancements only allows for a certain percentage of each enhancement to exist within each Federation. Otherwise, one Federation could enhance everyone with lethal enhancements, becoming the dominating Federation."

The image switched to a half-human, half-wolf creature sparring and slicing into his opponent with razored claws.

"Our Federation hoards the best enhancements for a select few. If it were evenly distributed, equality could be realized. We could–"

The recording jerked, then returned to the now frazzled blond reporter. "We apologize for the interruption. As I was saying, local military personnel are attempting to gain control of the situation. Clearly, these terrorists are dangerous–"

Willow shut the recording off again, and this time no one protested.

The rest of the trip to the hotel was in silence.

The Western Federation was not at all like Urban had imagined. She thought over the Revolutionaries' message. Were they looking for the hybrid too?

She wondered if Everest had arrived yet. He had mentioned

AiE had a larger presence here. Would they work with him? Or would they see Everest as a threat if he found and brought the hybrid back to the Asian Federation?

If the news feeds were any indicator, the Western Federation's politics looked messy, at best. Not something Urban wanted to get near. Everest had mentioned agreeing with some of the activists' methods. Now she understood why–the Revolutionaries were cunning and knew how to game the system. But hadn't the news reporter mentioned the activists also killed innocent children? Or was that a lie? Urban felt like she was looking at the tip of an iceberg. It was hard to discern what was really going on below the surface of politics and news.

Outside, sunny streets lined with tall palm trees flashed by. Giant decked out smart trucks filled the streets and country music blared from their force field windows. The moving sidewalks were interspersed with a diverse group of genetics. Even though Urban's retina display pegged many of them as having high soshes, they didn't wear the trendy silks and cutting-edge fashion of the Asian Federation. Instead, they wore simple smart blouses and rugged jeans. Despite the formidable greeting at the airport, the people seemed relaxed and welcoming.

The sidewalks had a disproportionate number of Supers on them. Urban noticed most of the shops were bigger to accommodate them. A sign with a Super holding a pumpkin-sized beer read: "Everything's bigger in Texicana."

"Finally, a Metropolis my size," Brooke said, perking up. "I hear they have more Supers per capita living here than anywhere else in the world."

Urban wouldn't be surprised. She felt small and out of place surrounded by the oversized city. Her sentiments increased as they pulled up to their hotel.

"Is that where we're staying?" Ash asked. It wasn't an idle question. Everyone's retina displays labeled the formidable structure as the Atlas Hotel. Only, it looked nothing like a hotel. A bunker would have been more accurate.

A giant gray structure stretched across the earth. Surrounded by force fields, vid monitoring devices, and bot guards, security did not appear to be taken lightly. They passed two check points before making it down a ramp and to an underground entrance.

"I wanted to take a few extra precautions." Willow's tone was overly nonchalant.

After a valet bot took their autonomous vehicle, the group headed into the main lobby. The opulent room that greeted them was in complete contrast to the drab exterior. It smelled of cinnamon, and the sounds of a tinkling fountain and a violin echoed in the large room. A chandelier hung overhead, brightly illuminating speckled fur rugs and leather armchairs surrounding oak tables. Longhorn trophies hung from the walls, along with gold-trimmed deer heads, giving a posh log cabin vibe.

Once checked in, the team descended in the elevator to the rooms.

Urban dropped her backpack and suitcase on the carpeted floor of her suite. She ignored the wooden furniture as she made straight for the king-sized bed. With a sigh, she sank into a cloud-like comforter.

She decided to check her messages one more time before going to bed. There were several more categorized as ones from her competition, but Urban knew better than to get her hopes up.

She opened the first one, and sure enough, the man didn't look remotely like Reed. But her pulse quickened on the next one, until her system flagged it as an AI-generated face. The third one was actually decent, but the man had a sosh, so he couldn't be Reed.

There were twenty-one messages to go, and jet lag was

kicking in. Urban decided to open one more.

The message had an image of a gaunt-faced man with a beard. Urban's breath caught.

It's him. That's Rai Reed.

SHE WAS WIDE AWAKE NOW.

The image looked exactly like the man Coral had shown her in the hacked memory. Urban pulled up the details on him. The man didn't have a sosh. The person who'd reported him said he'd seen him come out of a walled compound at Burb Town of the Texicana capitol.

Rai Reed is here.

Her heart ballooned with hope.

Could I actually have a chance to meet my father?

Urban checked her jam-packed calendar for a good time to track him down. Every spare moment over the next few days was filled with obligatory practices, banquets, and her first KOL duties. *The only spare time I have is tonight before practice.*

She mapped out the fastest route and found he was under an hour away. She quickly had a motorcycle air dropped. She was tempted to leave immediately, but paused. Even though she wasn't a known KOL here, if her attackers had followed her, it would be foolish to go somewhere by herself. She could practically hear Lillian's voice warning her.

She sent Trig a quick ping letting him know about her plan. He was supposed to be staying at the same hotel, but she wasn't sure if he had landed yet.

She sent another ping to Ash, then, hesitating, one to Everest. If she didn't hear back from any of them, she was heading out on her own. Otherwise, she'd miss her one chance.

[Trig: I am sorry, but I have not yet landed. Might I advise you to wait until my arrival?]

One minute.

[Ash: Are you serious? I'm coming with. Give me a minute.]

Another ping arrived two minutes later.

[Everest: Wrapping up a meeting with AiE. Meet at the entrance to the hotel?]

Within moments, Urban was out her door.

When she arrived at the hotel entrance, Everest was already there. There was a stiffness to his posture that made her throat tighten. He was probably wondering why she'd called on him.

"Thanks for coming." Urban eyed the red motorcycle propped next to him. "Nice bike."

Everest shrugged. "I need something for the race. Coral promised me this is the fastest model in the West."

The race.

Urban had almost forgotten about it. Her stomach twisted.

Everest's coal-black eyes searched hers. A yellow light blinked in the corner of his retina display–a constant reminder of his limited days augmented-free. After tomorrow, he wouldn't have that excuse and would be forced to launch his sosh.

"You didn't tell me *he* was coming." Ash joined them with an exaggerated once-over directed at Everest. "I hate third-wheeling."

Urban rolled her eyes. "It's not third-wheeling if we're not really dating."

"Good point." Ash flashed his boyish grin. "In that case, I suppose I'll come along for the adventure."

Everest held up a hand to interrupt them. "Are you sure this is a good idea?"

"I couldn't get ahold of Trig, but I think you two should be enough protection–"

"No," Everest clarified, "I mean meeting your birth father."

I'm not sure at all, but I have to know. "Yes." Urban mustered a smile.

Everest regarded her a moment. Almost reluctantly, he climbed onto his red racer. "Then let's go."

Urban turned to Ash. "I pinged you the address. Meet us there?"

"Sounds good."

Once astride her own motorcycle, Urban adjusted several of the settings, set her maps to the coordinates, then pulled back the throttle hard.

Her bike leaped forward into the dark street. Urban raced through the muggy night with Everest close behind. They flew over a bridge, down a tunnel, and out of the city.

They pulled up to a stop in front of a gated compound. A heavy thud made her jump as Ash landed next to them.

Urban focused on the slab of ominous concrete that was the back gate. Despite the warm air, her fingers were icy. Nerves tingling, Urban forced herself to climb off the bike.

She ran trembling hands through her hair in an attempt to pull it into a ponytail. It felt like she was moving in slow motion–her fingers wouldn't cooperate.

"Hey." Everest stepped closer.

Urban attempted to speak but choked on words. Why was her throat suddenly so tight?

Everest leaned forward, hesitated, then ran his fingers through her hair, pulling it back, his hand tender and steady. Urban relaxed against his familiar touch. She extended a hairband and he tugged the last strands into a ponytail.

Urban turned her head and found Everest's eyes, kind and supportive, looking back.

"Just be yourself." There was a gentleness to his tone.

Urban nodded and strode toward the entrance, where several vid recorders pointed down. Urban looked for a tatt scanner or some sort of doorbell but didn't find one.

Instead, she waved up at the vid recorder. "Hi there. I'm here to see Rai Reed." Her cheeks burned.

Nothing happened.

Urban inhaled a breath and tried again. Still no response.

What now?

She'd come so far. *I can't give up.*

Her mind jumped for a solution and went back to their time at the tatt temple and how everyone had flooded her to link when she'd turned her sosh on public. Time to leverage her KOL status again.

She turned her sosh to public. If this vid recorder was like most, it would pick up her sosh and alert them to her presence. "I'm Lee Urban and I'd like to speak to Rai Reed."

Nothing.

Urban's throat constricted. *I was so close.*

Then, with an eerie groan, the gate slid open.

A moment later, Dr. Rai emerged, flanked by five Supers. He looked identical to the man in the vid recording of the microneedle patch, only older. He had the same big black eyes.

Like mine.

Urban found she was trembling.

Dr. Rai and his entourage approached her, and Urban noticed his shirt. It was simple smart wear, but the color . . . rose gold.

Do we have the same favorite color?

The slab of a gate remained open and she caught a glimpse of a garden within. Green and full of growth. Despite the dark night sky, light from inside the house hovered over the grounds in a warm halo.

Cautiously, she took a step forward and cleared her throat. "Dr. Rai?"

The Supers trained their Magtouch M600s' muzzles on her.

Urban lifted her hands in a gesture of peace. She forced her words to be even and steady, a difficult task when facing a loaded barrel. "I'm here to speak with Dr. Rai."

"What are you doing here?" Dr. Rai asked.

"I wanted to meet you."

The Supers made no indication they'd heard, and Dr. Rai just looked at her.

She began again. "I thought perhaps you might–might be related to me."

Dr. Rai arched an eyebrow. "And how so?"

Urban moistened her lips. "It's possible you might be . . ." The words seemed stuck in her throat. "You might be my father."

"I have no children."

"Maybe you would"–Urban was taken aback at her own boldness–"if I hadn't been given up for adoption."

The moment following her statement seemed to stretch on for eternity. Urban's breath bottled up in her chest, threatening to explode.

Dr. Rai stared at her. Then his hand moved ever so slightly and the guards lowered their guns.

Dr. Rai motioned behind Urban at the building where Everest and Ash were hiding. "They stay where they are."

Urban didn't have time to wonder how he had known they were there, before he turned and beckoned her to follow.

THE GATE SHUT WITH AN OMINOUS THUD, trapping Urban inside the compound.

It gave her pause for a moment before she followed Dr. Rai over a red, sandstone path that cut across the grounds in a jagged line. Cacti sprouted through rocks, their fiery flowers filling the air with a sickly sweet aroma.

Urban climbed up bone-white steps toward the house. Lion statues by the door, traditional good luck charms, bared sharp teeth. Their stony eyes seemed to follow her.

Two dually enhanced Super Flyers flanked the doorway, standing at full height with stun clubs by their sides, eyes unblinking. The door they were guarding slid open automatically and Dr. Rai didn't look back as he led the way.

Inside, it smelled of lacquered wood and dust. The sharp clip of Dr. Rai's shoes echoed loudly in a strange quiet. Urban couldn't remember the last time she'd been surrounded by such deep silence. Even in places of relaxation in QuanNao, there was always the gentle hum of the XR pod's noise cancellation.

They passed through several empty hallways and stopped in front of a large, black door. Urban felt uneasy, as if unknown eyes were on her, and glanced over her shoulder.

Nothing.

She looked up and froze.

A figure clothed in black, perched on the ceiling like a bat, watched them. Urban remained unmoving, heart racing, until she noticed the deactivated stun pike.

It's just a guard.

The black door slid open and Dr. Rai stepped into the room. Urban followed, trying to shake her nerves.

The space had a table and two chairs, like that of a tea house. It was surprisingly cool, and hanging lanterns bathed the room in blood red. Urban realized the reason for the temperature drop. On the other side, an entire wall was missing. The cracked wooden floor stopped abruptly over a dimly lit pond, and a chilled wind blew across it.

"Please." Dr. Rai gestured at a wooden chair across from him. He really did look almost exactly like the man from the vid recording Coral had shown Urban. The same long, unkempt beard hid his thin face, reaching all the way to his collarbone. Though he'd aged, only his eyes seemed truly different. Something about them had changed, but Urban wasn't sure what.

She took the seat next to the table. Her gaze shifted outside, where orange and white koi fish broke the pond's surface and then swiftly darted back into the murky water. A bird somewhere in the garden trilled a sharp tune and then stopped abruptly.

A bot poured two sets of jasmine tea. She cupped her warm tea, trying to ward off the growing chill creeping up her spine.

The bot laid out a cheese platter with tiny crackers, fresh fruits, blue cheeses, dried figs, and two types of jam. Dr. Rai took a sip of tea and then set the cup down delicately. "Are you really . . . her?"

Urban straightened. "I am."

Dr. Rai watched her with an unreadable expression. She became uncomfortably aware of the fact that they were alone and a long way off from Everest and Ash. Maybe coming here by herself hadn't been the best idea.

"I'm sorry for being overly cautious, but may I take a blood sample?"

Urban choked on a sip of tea.

"To confirm we are related," Dr. Rai explained, his voice honeyed. "You never know these days. But DNA never lies."

A bot entered the room bearing a tray with a syringe.

Urban eyed the bot warily. "No."

"No?"

"No DNA samples."

Dr. Rai gave a small smile. "Don't you want to know if we're related?"

Urban forced a confidence she didn't feel. "Answers, first."

Dr. Rai looked like he might protest. Urban wondered if she really had the power to make demands. But then he spoke again. "Very well. What would you like to know?"

"Do you . . . like it here?"

He stared at her a moment as if confused by the question. "Yes."

"And how long have you been here?"

"Fifteen years."

Urban took a sip of her tea, trying desperately to still her trembling hands. "Have you been back to the Asian Federation at all?"

"No." A look of annoyance crossed Dr. Rai's features. "I'm sorry, but what does this have to do–"

"Why did you leave me?" Urban's voice was no more than a whisper. Her eyes remained on the tea cup in her hand, its warmth gone.

"There was nothing I could do," Dr. Rai finally said. "I was hunted by people who wanted to kill me for my technology. My former colleague, Dr. Liang, put you up for adoption. He hacked your paperwork, sent you to an Enhanced family, and covered your trail."

He admitted it. It was true!

"Why?" Urban's voice hitched.

"To protect you."

"No. Why didn't *you* do it?" Urban amended.

Dr. Rai's face was taut. "I was on the run. I nearly lost my life. There was no time. Dr. Liang did me a favor."

Favor.

Urban's eyes smarted and she bit her tongue to keep from crying.

"What about my sister?"

Dr. Rai shook his head. "You don't have one. All your paperwork was forged."

Urban felt like her whole body was shaking. *This can't be happening.*

"And my mother?" Her voice was nothing more than a choked whisper.

Dr. Rai's eyes flickered to the syringe before he spoke again. "Your mother was . . ." His eyes grew distant–and hard. "They took her. Now I have no family."

There was more silence.

"But I'm family," Urban said in a small voice.

Dr. Rai's attention came back to focus on her. The brief smile appeared again. "Yes. Now, dear family, would you mind?" He indicated the bot with the tray still hovering by the door.

The way he said the words made Urban nauseous. Despite what she had discovered, it all felt wrong.

She needed to get out of there–she needed air. Urban contemplated bolting for the door, but remembered the Supers outside. She'd never make it past all of them. If Rai wanted to take a blood sample, he could use force. Better to comply than give him a reason for that.

Nodding in defeat, she eyed the bot as it picked up a sharp syringe.

A shaft of fear stabbed her.

"This will only take a second," Dr. Rai was babbling. ". . . nothing more than a prick . . ."

Urban's vision swam.

Her invincible exoskeleton cracked. She was sinking, drowned by Lucas all over again, dragged to the bottom of the water tank. The last of her air bubbled around her as the syringe pierced soft flesh.

Urban's lungs caved inward, desperate for air that wouldn't come.

"We'll have our experts analyze your data and get back to us within the hour." Dr. Rai's smile was directed at her, but his eyes followed the bot.

Urban sprang to her feet.

Dr. Rai stood up abruptly as well.

Urban rubbed her palms against her smart suit. "I'm going."

"Don't you want to find out the results?" Dr. Rai asked.

Urban had the distinct impression he didn't want her to leave. She shrugged, feigning nonchalance. "I know the results."

"You know, you were meant to be the hybrid."

Urban stopped in her tracks and turned slowly to Dr. Rai again.

He had her in the palm of his hand, and by his smug expression, he knew it.

Calmly sipping his tea, he waited for her to take the bait.

Urban hesitated. She needed answers. "What do you mean?"

Dr. Rai smiled, but it didn't reach his eyes. "Dr. Liang invented the microneedle patch and I developed the hybrid technology. We worked closely together."

"*You* invented the hybrid?" Urban thought back to the vid recordings Coral had shown her. *This whole time I thought Dr. Liang was the one working on the hybrid.*

Dr. Rai sipped his tea again.

Meant to be the hybrid . . . "I–I'm not the hybrid, am I?"

"You were the closest to succeeding. I hoped maybe my calculations were wrong, that you were. But"–he shook his head–"my calculations are never wrong. There is none. Not yet."

The last of Urban's mask cracked.

Too many emotions warred within her. Without caring about the guard, she turned and fled the room.

"Wait. Wait!"

Urban ignored Dr. Rai, hoping desperately he wouldn't try and detain her. She felt his eyes follow her as she left.

Back in the hallway more eyes bored into her. Looking up, she saw the same figure cloaked in black watching her again. Urban quickened her pace, almost running until she burst through the main door. She nearly tripped as she took the stairs two at a time, sprinting across the garden, and back out the gated door.

No Supers stopped her.

It wasn't until she'd left the compound behind that she let her guard down.

Everest and Ash were instantly by her side.

"What happened?"

"Are you alright?"

She couldn't see through her tears or make sense of the words. Suddenly, the world turned dark and she was falling.

URBAN PITCHED BACKWARD INTO AN ABYSS.

But something stopped her. Warm hands. Though she couldn't think whose.

"Easy there," a gentle voice cautioned.

"Let's get her back," another voice said. "She's in no condition to drive. I'll call a ride."

Urban found herself staring at a dark, haunting alleyway, thoughts exploding in the deepest recesses of her mind. Parts she'd kept locked away were suddenly laid bare, secrets exposed, buried memories resurrected.

If she were an Aqua, she would roar until every glass window shattered. If she were an Inventor, she'd explode a bridge. If she were a Flyer, she'd fly far, far away.

Instead, she was the failed hybrid.

There is no hybrid.

The thought lanced her with pain. She barely registered climbing into a vehicle with Everest and Ash. Urban tried to focus on the cold leather seats, to stay present, but as soon as the vehicle lurched forward, her mind pressed full speed ahead.

I finally got what I wished for. I found my real dad, but I'm nothing more than an experiment to him. I was warned.

Urban didn't realize she was shivering until something warm draped over her shoulders. Startled, she looked up and found Everest, eyes filled with concern, his leather jacket wrapped around her.

Urban opened her mouth but nothing came out. She swallowed, and suddenly, she was crying.

She sensed him hesitate, then he gently pulled her into him. With a sob, Urban nestled into the crook of his arm and let the tears flow.

Everything she'd been working toward shattered around her. She wanted to curl up and disappear.

Urban wasn't sure how much time had passed. She was half asleep, rocking gently with the slight movements of the vehicle. Everest's clothes were damp from her tears and her neck hurt from the odd angle she'd been leaned against him. She shifted her head and rested it against his warm chest, then fell asleep. The last thing she remembered was Everest caressing her hair.

When she awoke, they were stopped in front of the hotel. Ash got out first, and with a sympathetic smile at Urban, left.

Everest walked her to her room, stopping at the door. "Do you want to talk?"

Urban nodded.

Everest followed her in and took a seat near the back wall, a respectful distance from Urban as she collapsed on the bed. He didn't say anything, just waited.

Urban picked at the comforter. "My bio dad . . ." She swallowed. "He doesn't . . . care about me. I don't think he ever did. And I think he–he wanted my DNA."

"Why would he want that?"

"He said he wanted a DNA sample to confirm I'm related to him. But I'm more of an experiment to him than a daughter." She choked on the last word.

"Urban." Everest's tone was gentle.

"He's the very scientist we've been looking to find." Urban

blinked away fresh tears. "All this time, he was right under our nose. He was the one working on the hybrid."

Everest straightened. "The hybrid?"

"I was supposed to be it, apparently." Urban stared down at her fingers tracing a pattern on the bed. "But I'm not. It didn't work. I'm not the hybrid, and there isn't one."

Everest ran a hand through his black hair, making it stand on end. "Maybe that's not true. Maybe he lied and that's why he wanted a DNA sample, to see if you *are* the hybrid."

"Everest, it's over. There's no hybrid." Urban looked at him, eyes dull. "If I were the hybrid, he wouldn't have given me up for adoption. He would have kept me. He would have loved me." Her voice broke.

"Urban." Everest was by her side in an instant. "That's not true."

"Isn't it, though?" Fresh tears threatened.

"Some people are brilliant in their careers but idiots when it comes to being parents," Everest said, his voice firm. "It has nothing to do with you. You could have the most amazing DNA in the world and you'd never be enough for a man like that."

Urban's throat tightened.

"Real family fight for each other."

Urban's eyes went to Everest's scarred knuckles. He'd done his best to fight for his own family, even if it had been hard at times.

The thought of Urban's own family made her heart wrench.

"Everest, Lillian isn't actually related to me. I never doubted she was my sister. Now I need her more than ever, and she isn't speaking to me. My whole family is a disaster."

He lightly touched her face. "What's stopping you from being the first one to reach out?"

"It's a waste of time."

"I don't believe that." Everest looked about to say more, when he sat up straight. "So sorry, but it's the Premier of Operations from AiE again. I have to take this."

Urban nodded.

Everest accepted the request, and a man in a buzz cut appeared.

"Hello, Ray."

"Ah, Everest. I see you're with Urban. Seems you two are taking this dating act quite seriously, which we appreciate." Urban's face reddened. "That's actually why I called." Ray tapped his virtual combat boots. "It's dangerous having two Naturals dating in plain sight, and we need to limit it as much as we can. After you race, Everest, we need you two to end the dating charade."

Urban hadn't thought her heart could sink lower.

Everest became very businesslike. "Why not date a little longer? One race alone won't get my sosh where I need it. The longer I'm with Urban, the more chances I'll have to–"

Ray cut him off. "It's too dangerous. The board has already decided. You two break up after the race."

Everest looked like he wanted to argue, but Ray moved on. "Any news on the hybrid?"

"Actually, yes." With a quick glance at Urban, Everest gave an update.

Ray's expression grew grave. "I'll let the board know. It's still possible there's another lead or a hybrid out there. If not . . ." Ray blew out a long breath. "We're in for trouble. Keep attending the AiE meetings and boost your sosh in the meantime. That's all. Good luck."

The holo vanished.

Urban looked at Everest, waiting for him to say something, hoping against hope that he'd change his mind, stand up to AiE, and fight for their relationship.

Everest's expression was troubled. "There has to be a hybrid."

Urban knew her disappointment was uncalled for–they wanted the same thing, really.

"Everest, I'm so tired. I think you should go."

Everest looked at her a moment, then gave a silent nod and quietly left the room.

Tears pricked at Urban's eyes.

Her retina display sent her a reminder for an upcoming meeting with her professor.

She'd forgotten. Urban swiped at her eyes, sniffed, and let out a shaky breath. She wearily changed into her full XR suit and face mask, grateful in virtual reality no one would see her tears. Then she accepted the invite from her professor. Her surroundings changed to a room moving with color and an odd sensation under her feet.

"Good morning, or should I say, evening for you?" Dr. Yukio greeted her. In XR, Urban was surprised to see Dr. Yukio's true form as his avatar. His hood was pulled back, revealing what must have once been a handsome face. The damaged skin and robotic eye were jarring.

Urban tried not to stare while orienting herself. "Where are we?"

"This is my virtual study room."

Tiny bulbs of light floated throughout a darkened space. They shifted from rice-ball white to matcha green and then bean-paste red. The colors changed in a flowing motion, giving the illusion of waves passing through the room. The effect was both soothing and dizzying. The ground was made from a crushed pagoda roof. With each step, Urban's XR suit vibrated.

"The AI doesn't know how to interpret the ancient crushed tiles. That's why you feel the odd vibration in your foot," Dr. Yukio explained. "Like you, I enjoy pushing the boundaries of AI."

Urban wasn't sure how to respond. Little did her professor know, she hadn't done anything to challenge Samson. It was a fluke it crashed.

Dr. Yukio pressed his way through the lights and they floated away. "How are you feeling about tomorrow's presentation?"

"Alright."

"Your project looked good last I checked. And how is your next one coming?"

The truth was, she hadn't even started. "It could use some work."

"Are you feeling a creative block?"

Urban hesitated. "You could say that."

Dr. Yukio nodded knowingly. "There are three stages to every great work of art. First, it seems insurmountable, then it becomes challenging, and finally, it is complete. I have found the same to be true of life. Whatever it is you're facing that seems impossible, it's only a matter of perspective."

Urban thought over the last few days. She sincerely doubted the wreckage of her family and the lack of a hybrid was a 'matter of perspective,' but she nodded along. No need to offend her mentor.

"You don't believe me." It wasn't a question, but a statement.

Urban's face grew pink.

Dr. Yukio was an Artisan, right? She double-checked his enhancements using Gene-IQ. No Inceptor abilities. But then how could he always read her so easily?

"It's strange what happens when one acquires a disability." Dr. Yukio gestured at his missing eye. "I may have lost the ability to hear, speak, and see on my own, but in the process, everything has changed. I once was blind, but now I see."

I'm a painter, not a poet or mystic. Urban tried to will herself to be patient. *I'm sure there's a lot he can teach me.*

"My accident has enabled me to be more perceptive." He offered a smile. "Don't worry, I'm not an Inceptor. I can't read your mind. But I'm told I read hearts."

Urban sighed inwardly. The last thing she needed was her professor seeing her messy heart. She offered a polite smile. "I'm just here to become a better artist."

Dr. Yukio smiled, his first true smile, in return. It made his features less intimidating, brighter. "That's what you think."

Before Urban could respond, he stood. "Come, let me show you something."

The setting around them shifted to a virtual playground. Avatars of children, all faceless due to privacy laws, ran laughing and shrieking through glowing slides and on hovering swings. AI nannies, in the forms of talking animals, chased after them.

Urban stared at Dr. Yukio in surprise.

"Sometimes, I find the best place to look for inspiration is in the simple joys of life."

He took a seat on a bench and Urban joined him.

They sat, watching the children play. At first, the silence was uncomfortable–awkward. But then Urban grew used to it, and even relaxed. By the end of their time, she was almost sad to go.

Somehow, sitting in silence at a children's playground was exactly what she needed. How had her professor known?

"Hopefully you've found some inspiration for your next project," Dr. Yukio said. "Or, if nothing else, a rest from the daily demands of life."

"Thank you," Urban said, truly grateful.

The connection cut and the bright light from the playground faded as Urban's dimly lit hotel room came back into focus.

She stripped out of her full XR suit and mask. Alone in her room again, exhaustion and jet lag hit. Setting an alarm before her next practice with the Dragons, Urban fell asleep.

A knock at the door startled Urban awake. She checked her retina display and saw Ash standing outside the door.

Urban rubbed sleep from her eyes as she let him in.

"Hey, are you ready to go?"

Urban squinted. "Go where?"

"Practice? It's ten 'til."

"*Tiana*! I overslept." Urban raced around the room, throwing her hair into a ponytail and getting ready.

Locking the room behind her, she sprinted down the hotel corridor. "Are you coming too?"

Ash grinned wide. “Of course. Bag boy goes everywhere.”

“I could use you there.” Her throat constricted.

“Urban using me. What else is new?” Ash let out a dramatic sigh and winked.

The rest of the Dragons were already waiting when she arrived in the lobby.

“There you are,” Willow said sharply. “You’re both late.”

“So sorry,” Ash apologized with a dazzling grin. “Bad hair day.” He patted his perfectly styled wavy hair.

Willow pursed her lips, but then turned and led the way to a waiting line of vehicles.

“Thanks,” Urban mouthed to Ash.

The drive through the city and past Burb Town went slowly. Every second of numb silence was a battle within Urban as she tried desperately not to think–to feel. Otherwise, she knew she’d never make it through practice.

Finally, the agonizing ride reached an end. The engine’s hum changed pitch as the vehicle slowed near an ancient Aztec pyramid mixed with modern tech. Urban had seen the giant structure a few times on the feeds when the Dragons competed at the Scorpions’ stadium, but it was much more impressive up close.

“Today we’ll be training on their turf,” Willow said as she flashed her tatt at several security-bots.

Urban tried not to gape as they walked through the entryway. It felt like walking into an enormous, cool, dark cave. The structure looked as if it were made with giants in mind, with a ceiling so far above them, it disappeared. Everything was industrial gray, with square columns of cement rising on all sides. A few stiff, communal seats lined the long walkway, but otherwise, it was completely empty.

“I want everyone to get a feel for their AI,” Willow instructed, unfazed by their surroundings.

“Jack is nothing compared to Samson.” Hickory appeared out of thin air to stand beside Willow.

"True, we have the best AI. But that also means we have a bigger home-court advantage. Here, we'll have to figure out how to cater to Jack's games." Willow stopped as they reached the end of the walkway. Her eyes were unfocused for a moment while she checked her maps, then led the team through several more doors and hallways. She flashed her tatt again, and they stepped into a new room.

Not a room, Urban realized as the lights flickered on, but the stadium. Thousands of empty seats lit with electric blue surrounded them on all sides. Urban tried to imagine what it would be like full of people, and a spike of nerves ran up her spine. The platform itself stood removed from the stands on a raised metal dais.

Smart, Urban thought. *No chance of getting splashed or attacked by rogue animals.*

Blossom was also looking around in a daze.

"Come on," Willow said with annoyance.

"New recruits," Dawn scoffed as she followed Willow to a large glass elevator.

The team piled in with plenty of room to spare, and shot up toward the stadium's platform.

Above, in each ridge of the pyramid, square rings of blue light flashed. Combined with their upward momentum, Urban felt dizzy and had to look away. The elevator slowed to a stop far above the ground and level with the platform.

Urban's feet hit bouncy synthetic turf as Willow led the team jogging across it. After one giant lap around the turf, she stopped and led them in a light stretch before going on.

"Everyone form two lines, A and B teams." Willow motioned them to one end of the stage and took her place. "Sprints. Go!"

The A team took off, then turned and ran back.

Brooke, with her lengthy legs, came in first, way before the others. After her were Willow and Orion. Urban's hair fluttered in her face from the rush of wind as the rest of the A team charged past her.

"B squad, go!"

Urban took off across the stage, running so fast everything but her destination blurred. But even as she reached the other side, she fell behind. The B-team Super easily took the lead. By the time Urban turned back, she was in last place. Shame would have colored her face if it weren't already red from exertion.

The A team immediately took off again, while, panting, Urban caught her breath.

The next time they sprinted, Urban felt sick from the effort. She was pushing herself too hard and she knew it. But the pain was a welcome distraction.

"Again," Willow ordered, and the next group took off.

Clay leaned in close to Urban, chest heaving. "I swear, that girl has more energy than three Supers combined."

Urban was too tired to reply. She slumped to the floor and watched the A team sprint back across the platform.

They went twice more. Most of the players were a little winded, but seemed fine. Only Clay seemed to be struggling as much as Urban. She was weighing which option was worse, throwing up in front of the team or walking the next round, when thankfully, Willow ordered a break.

Urban grabbed her bottle. Never had water tasted so sweet. She was careful not to drink too much, for fear of it coming back up.

After the break, the team did a series of group challenges, with Jack spitting out a variety of obstacles. Urban found with relief she was able to hold her own. She was halfway through an obstacle course when Willow clapped her hands.

"Everyone gather around. I have two announcements. First, I'd like to congratulate Blossom on her exemplary performance in practice." Willow turned to face her. "You will officially remain on the A team, representing the Inventor GP for the duration of the season."

Urban let out a breath. At least she didn't have to worry about playing time at the upcoming games. She'd been studying the Dragons' games, and Willow never played a B-string member.

"There's one other thing." Willow's expression sobered. "It has come to my attention that Ito Olive, who we believed to be the culprit who hacked Urban's suit, is innocent."

Someone gasped.

"According to the Asian Federation privacy laws, we cannot force anyone to show their retina display memories unless they choose. Until recently, the locker room footage seemed to incriminate Olive. However, today, she chose to send me her retina display recording. It seems she was telling the truth. Olive was, indeed, merely examining Urban's suit."

"So, is she coming back?" Blossom asked hopefully.

"She's flying here as we speak."

A murmur rippled through the team, but Willow continued, "I also had security double-check all the locker room footage, and there's a section the day before our practice that seemed off. It looks like someone altered that data."

"So, the real culprit covered their tracks and is still out there?" Dawn's eyes were wide.

"Yes," Willow acknowledged. "But we will catch him, or her, and when we do, they will deeply regret their poor decision." She glared at all of them.

Urban's mouth went dry. *Whoever tried to kill me could be standing right next to me.* She glanced around.

Clay looked shaken. Blossom relieved. Dawn puzzled.

Orion glared.

But Brooke was staring straight at Urban, her giant arms crossed over her chest, a grin on her lips.

WHO HACKED MY SUIT?

The thought shuffled on replay through Urban's exhausted brain all the way back to the hotel. Back in her room, she didn't even bother changing out of her practice uniform before sinking into bed.

When Urban wiggled out from under her comforter the next morning, her sweaty uniform, now damp and cold, clung to her. The past few days all came flashing back.

Dr. Rai, her bio dad. The DNA sample. Practice. The attacker. Lillian.

Pull it together! She glanced at her schedule, taking deep breaths to force the swirling emotions to settle.

Everest's race to boost his sosh was in an hour. She'd totally forgotten about it. Hurriedly, she checked her pings, and sure enough, one from Everest awaited her.

[Everest: Hey. Just a reminder today's the day AiE wants us to stage . . . you know what.]

As if Urban needed reminding.

[Everest: After the race.]

Urban squeezed her eyes shut for a moment, then looked at her schedule for the rest of the day.

After the race, she had to present her assignment in her Mixed Media class, then she had her first KOL obligation, and after that, the Games kick-off party. Tomorrow, the actual games began.

And I have to pretend everything is fine throughout all of it.

Peeling out of her sticky clothes, she hopped into the shower and let the warm water beat against her skin and her emotions. Later, wiping away the steam on the mirror, she stared at her reflection.

The girl who stared back was one she wouldn't have recognized a year ago.

Thanks to her jiujitsu training and workout regime, she was more toned and muscled than ever before. She looked like someone who actually belonged on a professional AI team. It was the closest to Enhanced she had ever been.

Yet, the hollowness in her eyes, the dark shadows that lined her face, were a portal into her heart and hinted at her "otherness."

Her secret.

Swallowing back dark thoughts, she rummaged in her suitcase until she found what she was looking for. Carefully, she pulled out the silver necklace Everest had given her. She held it a moment before fastening it around her neck.

Her stomach twisted.

As she made her way toward the lobby, Urban noticed a familiar green triangle in her retina display.

[Urban: Trig! You made it to the Western Fed!]

Relief flooded her at the sight of his icon on her maps. He was supposedly ten meters away, but in reality, there was no one visible except a speckled rug and a coffee table. Invisible, per usual.

"Ready for some fun?"

Urban turned and found Ash grinning at her. She mustered a smile before climbing into a waiting vehicle with him.

As their vehicle zipped along the early morning streets, Urban's stomach was churning with nerves. She had been so anxious when she'd competed in the underground races last semester. But somehow, this was worse. Watching Everest compete and having no way of empowering him made her feel helpless. She wondered if this was how Lillian felt when she had tried to talk Urban out of racing and was forced to watch instead. Thoughts of Lillian filled her with a dull ache.

"Think he's ready?" Ash asked.

Urban exhaled a breath. "He has to be."

"I'm sure he'll do great."

Urban shifted in the seat. "Thanks for coming. I know you don't have to be here."

Ash grinned boyishly. "So I could stop snoozing through all my virtual classes? You know I wouldn't miss this!" He winked.

Urban couldn't help but smile.

"Though, I will say, my parents aren't too happy about my decision." Ash's expression sobered. "They think it's a disgrace to be a bag boy."

"How can they think you're a disgrace when you've rescued a KOL multiple times now?" Urban teased.

He snorted in reply. "Yeah, well, unless I'm a top military commander, I'm a disappointment by my parent's standards. That's what my DNA was designed for, anyway."

Urban looked at him. "What do you want to be?"

Ash was silent so long Urban thought he hadn't heard her.

When he spoke again, Urban had to lean forward to catch his words. "Honestly, I wish I were an Inventor or Giver, helping people and making the world a better place. All the clichés. But since those genetics will never be an option for me . . . I wish I could be a professor. I know everyone thinks Flyers don't study, but I'm secretly a nerd and love geeking out on stuff. It would be a blast to be the most irreverent, hilarious professor around. One who actually makes learning fun."

"Maybe you can," Urban encouraged.

Ash shook his head as their vehicle pulled to a stop. Taking a breath, she climbed out and gazed up at a row of high-rises with reflective panels. They entered one with circular sides, following their maps to a hoverstop overlooking the city. Several people were already there, one of whom she recognized.

"Hey!" Coral motioned them over. "This is going to be so much fun!"

"Are you sure this is a good idea?" Urban surveyed their surroundings. The balcony was several stories off the ground, in the middle of a skyscraper. The entire floor was open air and full of lush trees. Thick, supporting beams held the rest of the building up above them.

Below, giant autonomous trucks hovered over the Zeolite-coated streets. The streets were much wider than in New Beijing. They seemed emptier too. A hoverbus stopped at their platform, a few people got off, then it continued on.

Urban turned back to Coral and Ash. "Won't racing in the city get the police called?"

"Oh, definitely." Coral waved a careless hand. "As we like to say, 'There's two kinds of people in underground racing. The quick and the imprisoned.'"

"Is this safe?"

Coral leaned in. "Look, do you want Everest to get a high sosh or not?"

Urban swallowed and nodded.

Coral's gold and black eyes sparkled with excitement. "He'll be on a bike, so he's fine. All *you* need to do is get away fast." She beckoned to a girl with a speckled black-and-white mohawk and cargo pants. "Meet my friend. I'll be leaving you all in her capable hands while I get ready." Coral saluted them and left.

"So, you're Coral's Asian Fed friends?" The girl with the mohawk gave them an appraising glance, her black eyes warm and friendly. She smiled. "Chrissy. But I usually go by my last name, Salt."

She extended a hand, and Urban remembered just in time to

shake it. "Lee Urban. And this is my friend, Ding Ash."

Salt linked with them before walking to the wall. "The route we're following via hover bus is planned as far away from the stationed police bots as possible," she explained. "But at the end of the race, where the final stop is, you'll only have forty-five seconds to get off the bus and hide before they arrive. Get into the building next to the stop. One of our guys will cut the power so the lights will go out for twenty seconds. Get as far as you can in those twenty seconds."

She handed them each a hoodie, hat, and mask. "When that all happens, remove the hoodie and mask right away, and put on the hat. When the power comes back on, keep walking."

"That's the plan?" Urban pulled the hoodie on over her head and instantly regretted how hot it was. "What if the police catch us?"

"They won't. We do this all the time across the country. Only two people have ever been caught, and it was because they got trampled. Don't trip and you'll be fine."

Urban tried not to gulp.

"Stick with me," Salt said with another smile.

As they waited for the racers to come into view, the humid heat made sweat cling to Urban's body. Bright sunlight reflected off shiny glass buildings and warmed the parts of the road not in the shade from the surrounding skyscrapers.

The store titles below were in Federation English. Her retina display translator seemed off, with names like: "Heart Attack Grill," "Howdy Hamburgers," and "Friendly Guy Bail Crypto."

The city also smelled different, like hot cement and cilantro. Which could have been pleasant, if Urban liked cilantro. Unfortunately, it reminded her of a stink bug.

As it grew closer to the time, more people filed in around them. Tatts bumped against each other as crypto points were collected and bets placed.

It was three minutes until noon when she caught sight of

the first motorcycle rounding the corner. Several more followed, and she spotted Coral and Everest among them.

Even though his helmet was on, Urban recognized Everest's slim but muscular frame. And while most of the other racers wore white suits to ward off the heat, Everest wore his black leathers.

She fingered her necklace.

The crowd around her grew restless. Some argued over who would win. Others craned their necks in search of any law enforcement. Still others nervously pulled hats low over their eyes.

A transparent hover bus drew near. It stopped, and the few patrons inside, noticing the masked crowd at the stop, moaned. Most exited the vehicle, one of them grumbling something about being late for work.

Salt rushed Urban and Ash onto the hover bus. It smelled of lingering body odor and cheap cologne.

A short woman with a blond ponytail plugged a device into the vehicle and then began speaking. "Ha! It works!" her voice broke over the intercom. "Now that I've hacked the public transport system's sound, I will be your commentary for the race."

The people on the bus cheered.

"And here we go! Ten! Nine! Eight!" Everyone joined in the countdown.

Urban's skin tingled with anticipation. The base of the hover bus was made of transparent wood and she could see Everest leaning close to his bike below.

"Seven! Six! Five!"

Engines revved.

"Four! Three!"

The hover bus doors shut.

"Two! One!"

The vehicle lurched forward.

"Goooooo!"

Coral and Everest jumped to the front along with a Flyer, and they sped down the empty road.

The hover bus floated up in the sky until Urban could no longer see the racers. When they lowered back toward the streets, the racers came into view again.

Everest had slipped nearly to the back of the pack, and a tiny little racer on an orange bike was now in the lead. Some of the watchers on the bus cheered all the more while others groaned. The racers sped around cars, swerving into oncoming traffic to pass vehicles. Urban bit her lip as Everest zoomed straight toward a Honeybee G6.

While the other Enhanced riders could take a hit, Everest's Natural body couldn't. It was the most dangerous part of the plan. Not only did he have to win the race, he had to stay alive.

A horn blared. At the last second, Everest swerved out of the way.

Urban let out a breath. As the racers passed below, she noticed Coral was missing. Hopefully, she was stirring up the trouble she'd promised.

A rider with white-and-black stripes began gaining on Everest. There was something odd about his bike. It was closer to the ground and it lurched oddly. Instead of wheels, it had four moving parts–muscled legs. The entire thing looked like a cyborg tiger.

The machine increased in speed, straight toward Everest. As the rider pulled on the handle bars, the front popped into the air, exposing razored claws.

"Everest!" Urban screamed.

Sensing the danger, he swerved, right as the claws came down.

"A close call for our newest rider," the announcer commented.

The tiger rider drew nearer, and Everest slid into oncoming traffic trying to lose him.

The cyborg cycle rose up again, giant razored claws aimed at Everest's head. At the last second, Everest ducked back into the opposite lane.

An oncoming vehicle crashed into the tiger motorcycle. The

biker flew into the air, hit the pavement, rolled, and came to a stop next to the curb.

"Another down!"

People near Urban cheered. The bus stopped at another station and lost sight of the riders. Several people got off to help the injured rider. Urban sat, wishing desperately there was something she could do to help Everest.

When they caught back up to the racers, Everest was in fourth place. One of the riders pulled out what looked like an electric mace and began swinging it at a Super on a fully-armored rev machine in front.

"Looks like someone's in trouble," the announcer said. "You've got to watch out for those Inventors."

The Super's bike beeped a warning and he slapped his back, activating a set of heavy-duty armored plates. They formed a protective shield, but also slowed his speed.

With a flash of electricity, the mace flew forward and struck the shield. The Inventor tried to jerk the mace back, but it was stuck.

Glancing back, the Super grabbed hold of the mace's chain. Too late, the Inventor realized what was happening as the Super used the chain to whip him into the side of a vehicle. The bike smashed the rider's leg and he screamed.

Cheers and whoops broke out across the hover bus. Urban felt sick.

Everest was now in third place and gaining ground on the Super. Suddenly, the Super clipped seemingly thin air and lost his balance. He wobbled, trying to regain control of his motorcycle before slamming into a car.

"He's down!" the announcer shouted. "The second-place rider is down!"

The crowd on the bus roared.

At the next stop, several people leaped off the platform and ran back to help the downed riders.

"And this, ladies and gentlemen," the announcer continued, "this is the last leg of our journey. When we disembark at our next stop, the race will be over and we'll have our winner!"

Urban held her breath.

As the hover bus took off again, the racers came back into view. Everest was now in second place and close behind. Coral was still nowhere to be seen, though occasionally riders would be scorched by flames if they got too close to Everest.

Traffic came to a stop on both sides of the road, slowing the racers down. Everest weaved around the vehicles, but it was slow going.

"We have Everest coming up from behind!" declared the announcer. "Will he be able to steal Zita's lead?"

Everest tried to cut around the stalled cars, but the oncoming traffic was too thick. Zita's small bike zipped through, putting more space between them.

"Zita keeps her lead!" The announcer's blond hair had escaped her ponytail and clung to her face wildly. "Can Everest catch up?"

"Let's go, Everest!" Urban yelled.

As the traffic grew thicker, even Zita was forced to slow down, and Everest caught up to her.

He was nearly to Zita, but wasn't catching up fast enough.

He's not going to make it.

Everest leaned closer to his bike and tapped several settings. The sides of his bike began to glow yellow. A second later, they exploded into bright light.

"An illegal light blaster," the announcer yelled. "A daring move by our newest racer!"

Urban couldn't see anything. Horns blared. When her vision returned, the lead rider slammed on her brakes to avoid hitting a delivery truck. Too late.

Crunch!

Her bike clipped the side of the truck and spun out of control, smashing into a wall.

"We're almost to the end!" The announcer's excitement pitched her voice.

Urban cheered at the top of her lungs amidst the shouts of the other spectators.

Everest passed the rider and delivery truck. He shot to the front right as the hover bus lurched to a stop.

"And that's the end!"

Screams and cheers erupted.

"Everest steals first place at the very last second!" The announcer had shouted herself hoarse. "What a race!"

Everest pumped a fist in the sky. The other racers stopped next to him, exchanged a word, then walked their bikes off the main road.

A wailing siren pierced the air.

"Time to make yourself scarce!" The announcer jerked a device out of the control panel and stuffed it into her pocket.

The doors to the hover bus opened and everyone spilled out.

"This way!" Salt dragged Urban and Ash into a large, mostly empty shopping center. Despite an open courtyard filled with clothing, the air was stale. Above, a smart glass ceiling allowed sunlight to filter through. At the other end, a holo projection displayed ads: "This week, watch the big match! Scorpions vs. Dragons! Tickets on sale now!"

Then the display cut out and the mall plunged into darkness. Someone screamed.

The overhead nano glass dimmed to block out the sunlight.

Salt nudged her from behind. "That's our cue."

Urban ripped off her mask and hoodie, stuffing them into Ash's backpack. She pulled the baseball cap on, and the three of them began walking in a different direction.

The lights flickered back on as the siren continued to wail.

Urban kept an even pace, despite her heart galloping in her chest.

The three of them exited, using a glass crosswalk over a road, and entered another building. When they were back together out in the open, Salt grinned. "And that's what we call a successful race! Come on, the after-party is out of the city."

Urban thought she would melt with relief.

Several hover stops later, they arrived at what looked like a renovated barn. The exterior was made of faded wood, but the inside was smooth cement walls, floors, and ceilings. The space was already crowded with racers and fans alike, and music blared from a live band performing on stage, with Coral as the lead singer. It was odd seeing her in her natural element. Urban's gaze quickly shifted off Coral and found Everest, grinning and surrounded by a circle of people at the center of the room.

"Everest!" Urban shoved her way through.

A slow smile spread across his face.

As she approached, Urban's breath caught. The blinking yellow light in the corner of his eye was gone, and her retina display picked up his new public identity.

[Chong Everest. Age: 19. Social score: 55. Key words: motorcycle racing.]

It was too low to be an elite Enhanced, but so far, no one was complaining, and there were no hateful or suspicious comments. As the other racers linked with him, his sosh climbed steadily upward.

Urban flung herself into Everest's arms. Though, she wasn't entirely sure if it was to help boost his sosh or because she actually wanted to. The crowd gave them space.

"Great job," she whispered in his ear. "Be sure to link with and take as many snaps with people as you can. Tonight's your night. Aim for a sosh of 60. Stay as long as you have to." She let go and snapped with him in the hopes that it would encourage others to do the same.

"Who's this?" the announcer asked. "Your girlfriend?"

Urban ducked her head shyly, before remembering she was a KOL.

"The one and only." Everest draped an arm over Urban's shoulder.

The announcer made a clucking noise of disapproval at Urban. "I know you Asians can be modest, but honey, where's the steamy kiss for the champion?"

Heat crept up Urban's face.

"Yeah, we want a kiss!" someone shouted. It was Coral.

I'm going to kill her.

"Kiss! Kiss! Kiss!" The crowd began to chant.

Urban furtively glanced at Everest and saw him looking down at her, something unreadable in his eyes.

Fireworks erupted in her stomach as he brought his hand up to her face.

He was going to kiss her.

URBAN'S HEART THUMPED WILDLY. SHE COULD pull back.

Instead, she found herself lifting her head to his. She could smell the familiar scent of jasmine and smoke.

Everest's charcoal eyes shifted down to her necklace. Then he closed the gap between them and his lips pressed against hers.

Urban melted as his arms tightened around her. The crowd was cheering, but it was white noise.

How had she forgotten this? The safety, warmth, and comfort Everest brought? Lost for a moment, she came to and heard the cheers.

Crimson-faced, she pulled quickly away.

What have we done? This certainly didn't look like the planned break-up.

Emotions spinning, she darted into the crowd. Soon, she was past them and running down the street.

Urban wasn't sure where she was going. She had to get away from it all. Everything was too confusing. From social scores, parties, Games, her bio dad, the staged dating and breakup–all of it.

She ran until she found a deserted street. After calling a vehicle, she climbed in and pulled up the already trending vid recording of Everest's win. And there she was, bounding into his arms like an overjoyed puppy.

The comments were flowing in.

[Crossthorn: They make a stunning couple!]

[Rappel Flower: They're so cute! I wish it were me with such a *shuaige*.]

Urban forced herself to stop scrolling through the comments.

She suddenly realized she was afraid. Afraid of her feelings, afraid of possibly losing Everest again to AiE, afraid the hybrid truly did not exist.

When the vehicle stopped at the hotel, tears streaked her face.

Gathering herself together, she made her way to the empty diner. She had to be productive.

"Table for one, please," she said.

A bot with a cowboy hat led her over a plush, carpeted floor and past dimly lit seating to a leathered booth. The scent of bacon filled the air.

"Today's special is served all day: the Farmer's Breakfast, which comes with toast, bacon, and scrambled eggs."

Urban didn't even bother opening the digital menu hovering at the corner of her retina display. "I'll take that and a latte."

The bot returned carrying a steaming plate piled high.

Urban focused her attention on her upcoming Mixed Media class. She nervously nibbled on the toast, while quickly outlining her speaking points for the presentation.

All too soon, it was time.

Once she accepted Dr. Yukio's XR invite, Urban found herself seated at her usual spot in the classroom on the other side of the planet. Several students kept glancing her way, no doubt wondering why her holo projection was in the room rather than her physical body.

At the center of the class, the projects sat on a display stand.

Dr. Yukio's projection gestured at the table. "I will be grading each project based on four criteria. One, presentation quality. Two, creativity. Three, how well you've incorporated your medium. And four, legibility of the invitation itself."

Dr. Yukio turned toward the projects and selected one made of glass. Inside, flames raged. The invite was written in fire-resistant characters.

A student with fawn-like eyes but deadly spikes on his back strode to the front of the class. Urban's retina display showed his sosh was 73 and his enhanced barbs were poisonous.

With a confident, relaxed stance, the student gave an overview of his project. When he was finished, the student flashed the class a radiant smile, then returned to his seat.

Dr. Yukio stared at him until an uncomfortable silence descended. "Presentation quality was excellent. So was creativity, the ability to incorporate your medium, and legibility. That's a 95%."

The student grinned smugly.

"Except," Dr. Yukio continued, "I've seen this exact project before. Ten years ago, by a student named Wu Cleon."

The student flinched.

"I never forget a project." Dr. Yukio's voice took on a cold tone. "Which means, for finding your answer in QuanNao's *heiwang,* you receive a zero."

The boy's face reddened. "I–I didn't use the d–d–dark web."

Dr. Yukio looked at the student unblinkingly until his stammering came to a stop. "Cheating is the highest insult you could pay a professor, and a deep wound you inflict upon yourself. Anything from the *heiwang* in my class hereafter will result in an instant zero."

"Who's next?" he asked brightly. He was met with complete

silence. "How about Lee Urban?"

Somewhat jarred by the previous exchange, Urban hurriedly ordered her avatar to the front of the room and picked up her project. Without her full-immersion XR suit, she couldn't feel anything. Only the coolness of the cafe's air, as sweat beaded on her forehead.

Dr. Yukio's hooded figure turned toward her. It was discomforting not being able to see his face.

She took a deep, calming breath. "My medium is water."

She explained her design decisions and process. With the class's attention on her, she found herself talking faster and faster.

Dr. Yukio held up a hand. "Slow down. You won't get extra marks for speed talking."

Urban flushed and made a conscious effort to speak at a normal pace. *Why is it so hard? I'm a KOL now. Shouldn't I be good at this? Where's the confidence I thought it would give me?*

When she was done, she returned to her seat.

"Presentation quality was acceptable," Dr. Yukio said. "Creativity was excellent. Ability to incorporate your medium was very good. Legibility is very good. That's a 91."

Urban felt like she could sink to the floor in relief.

When the rest of the class presentations were done, Dr. Yukio motioned for silence. "Now, for your midterm project, which will be the majority of your grade. For that, I want you to create something showing a new perspective."

A student raised her hand. "What exactly do you mean by 'new perspective'?"

"That is open to interpretation," said Dr. Yukio. "That's part of being creative."

"What medium will we be using?" the same student asked.

"The medium you selected at the start of the semester is your given medium for the duration of this course."

Several students groaned. Urban was one of them, but inwardly. *Always water. Wherever I go.*

Logging out of XR, Urban drank the last of her latte and then followed her maps to the location for her KOL shoot, which was in a conference room inside the hotel.

The space Croix had rented out was already abuzz with activity when she arrived.

"There she is!" A Super strode over. "I'm Eliza, head stylist."

Urban tried not to stare at the woman. She'd never seen a Super stylist, and Eliza seemed to break every Super stereotype. She wore clothes like that of an Artisan, unique and trendy, and her makeup was bold and colorful, usually traits Supers avoided. Her hair was in a long braid that draped all the way down her back and to her knees. Tattoos of cannon balls, dancing skulls, and the Western Federation flag covered her bare arms.

Eliza guided Urban to a hovering chair and offered her some ice water.

Urban's throat started itching. *Not now!* She glanced at the cold water. She'd prefer something hot, but it would have to do. She took small sips, but the itch grew stronger, and with it, her concern.

Eliza clapped her hands twice, and the assistants scattered. Urban's reflection in the smart mirror changed as the Super played with her appearance in XR.

Urban's black hair turned a slight shade of blue and hung in sharp, jutting strands around her face. Her eyes became larger, darker, sparkling cobalt. Her eyebrows were deeper and longer, her lips a matted red, and her facial features sharper.

Eliza turned back to her assistants. "Alright everyone, this is the look we're going for. Let's make this vision a reality."

Instantly, a half dozen stylists twirled around Urban, working quickly. But all Urban could think about was her throat. The glass of water was now empty, and she suppressed a cough. *No, no, no. Please don't let me have an asthma attack right now.*

She'd left her steroid shot in her room, knowing they'd want her to change into their own clothes when she arrived. She tried to steady her breathing, even as it came in shorter, sharper gasps.

As she watched, Urban's face and hair transformed into the image she'd been shown. Eliza added the finishing touch before extending clothes for her to wear.

Back in the changing room, Urban coughed several times, and her throat felt slightly relieved. When she reemerged, Eliza guided her through heavy black curtains.

The room on the other side was warm and looked like it was typically used for meetings. A conference table had been pushed to the side, along with several leather chairs. In its place, an LED wall took up half of the room, programmed to look like a black brick wall.

Camera and lighting bots hovered around the set while Artisans leaned over a display at a table cluttered with coffee mugs and croissants.

A man wearing thick-rimmed red glasses jumped up. "There she is. I'm Dan, first producer."

"Nice to meet you." Urban shook his hand.

"Come stand over here." Dan motioned Urban to enter the set. "We want to get a visual before we start shooting."

Urban did as she was told, and stood awkwardly in the middle of the set as the Artisans crowded around. It was even warmer under the heat of the lights.

"Hmm . . . the angle isn't quite right." Dan pointed at something on the display. "Wait. There. Yes, that's perfect." He looked up at Urban. "We're going to take a few stills first."

Urban nodded. Several lights flashed, blinding her. The urge to cough resurfaced, but she stuffed it back down.

"Can I have you look straight into this front camera?" Dan asked. "Good. Now I need you to act like I've slapped your mother."

Urban looked at him in confusion.

"Is that what you would do? Stare dumbly?" Dan asked. "No, you'd be enraged, my girl! Now show it."

Urban crossed her arms and glared into the camera.

"That's it!" Dan coached. "Hold it right there."

More flashing lights. A cough escaped.

"Let's get a few more, then move on to vids," Dan said to one of his assistants.

When the blazing light finally subsided, Urban had spots in her vision. In the corner, she could make out the Artisans gathered around the display. There was someone new with them. Something about his broad shoulders and large wings gave her pause. He seemed familiar.

"This time, Urban, we're going with a vid, so I want you to add a little movement," Dan instructed. "Toss your hair, lean back, do whatever you want, but end with a glare."

Urban did as she was told, feeling foolish flipping her hair over her shoulder.

"A casual flip, darling," Dan instructed. "You're not trying to hit someone."

Urban blushed, then gave a less dramatic hair toss.

"Better," Dan said. "Now this time, don't forget to add the glare."

Cough. Cough. Cough. Urban couldn't help it, she had to relieve her throat.

"Are you alright?" Dan snapped his fingers. "Someone get her a drink."

Urban gratefully took a few sips of water and felt temporary relief. *This had better be over soon, or I'm in trouble.* She mustered a smile and a thumbs-up. "I'm good."

The Flyer next to Dan yawned and ruffled his wings. That's when Urban saw it–the blood-red scales.

She had definitely seen those wings before.

They were the exact same as the Flyer who'd attacked her last semester.

Urban froze.

Dan was giving more instructions, but she wasn't listening.

He's here.

"HELLO!" DAN WAS WAVING HIS HANDS. "I SAID glare at the camera. Not look at it in utter terror. It won't hurt you, I promise."

"Sorry." Urban cleared her throat to alleviate the building pressure.

She glanced back at the Flyer, but his wings were folded out of sight. *I'm probably imagining it. Plenty of Flyers have wings like that.*

"Amateurs," one of the Artisans muttered.

"Let's go again," Dan said.

Urban flipped her hair and looked into the camera, but it was difficult to concentrate. She tried to remember exactly what the Flyer who'd attacked her had looked like. He'd been wearing a mask and full body armor. The only part of his face she'd seen was where a piece of the mask had been broken off–his jaw. It was sharp and stubbled.

Her eyes darted to the Flyer's jawline. Firm. Clean shaven. It was impossible to tell if it was a match.

"We still need a wide angle," someone said when they'd finally gotten what Dan deemed a decent shot.

"Vance, can you show her what we need?" Dan asked.

The Flyer nodded. Urban drew in a sharp breath, which now had a slight wheeze to it. Her pulse quickened with each step he took toward her.

Did he recognize her? He only appeared curious and relaxed. Before she could look him up in QuanNao, he extended a hand. “Vance.”

“Lee Urban.” She coughed, blushed, then shook his hand, waiting for him to offer to link. He didn’t. Urban could view his public sosh, a whopping 94, but nothing more.

“I’m one of the other KOLs for Croix.” Vance had a smile on his face. “Don’t worry. You’ll get the hang of this soon.”

Either Vance was hiding his emotions miraculously well or they really hadn’t met before. *Then again, given my attacker’s long list of enhancements, I wouldn’t be surprised if he’s an Inceptor too.*

Vance brushed aside a wave of black hair and Urban noticed his facial features.

He looks like he’s from the Asian Federation. But if he was born there, it’s not possible for him to have that many enhancements. Unless his parents moved to the West and had him here, it can’t possibly be him. But she couldn’t be sure . . .

“Let’s try again, shall we?” Dan asked.

Vance demonstrated, and she carefully mimicked his stance, trying desperately to reel in her thoughts and her coughs. She managed to swallow another wheeze that was tightening her chest.

“That’s more like it.”

The lights flashed several times before they switched positions and tried again.

Finally, Dan clapped his hands. “Alright, enough torture–I mean, trying–for now. That’s a wrap.”

Holding back another cough, Urban rushed off the set, eager to get away from Vance and the hot lights.

Back in her room, she was overcome by a bout of coughing

and was wheezing more intensely before she found her steroid shot. She quickly stabbed it in her thigh, then sank to her bed. While waiting for the meds to kick in, she searched Croix's KOL list for Vance, but with no luck.

Why isn't he showing up? She tried conducting a general search, but without linking, and with only his first name, there was still nothing.

Her retina display chimed an alarm notification.

<Reminder: The Games Kick-Off Party commences in six minutes.>

Urban stopped her search and grabbed an energy bar off the counter on her way to the elevators. The invite said the party was located on the lowest floor of the building.

As Urban stepped off onto the -34th floor, she followed the distant thumping bass. Soon, she was in what looked like a magical cave. The walls were made of harsh rock, the ceiling high above was filled with stalactites. Each jagged piece of stone had glowing fairy lights in it, giving the cave an otherworldly appearance. Colored strobe lights flashed across a nano-glass dance floor, and beneath it yawned a darker part of the cavern.

Some partygoers were showing off their best moves, but most were clustered around the buffet tables or lounged on metal couches hovering around the room. Urban scanned the faces for anyone she knew.

Suddenly, she felt oddly alone without Everest. She'd grown used to his constant presence. The way he easily diffused tension and played the part of an Enhanced so well. He was confident, interesting, and a natural leader in every setting. People always wanted to talk with him and treated him with respect.

His presence made her relax, and going to a party alone reminded her of how much she hated such things.

Urban took a moment, then, seeing Brooke, Blossom, and several people she didn't recognize, she made her way toward them. Brooke was in the middle of a conversation, but stopped when she noticed Urban. "Hey guys, this is Urban. She's an Artisan, but through a weird stroke of luck, the Inventor GP."

"As the *B-team* Inventor," Blossom amended.

Urban's jaw twitched, but Brooke didn't pick up on the tension. "That's right. She's also the one to single-handedly break our AI and cancel school for an entire day."

"I remember hearing about that," said a guy who towered over everyone but Brooke. "I'm Trall, the Western Fed's Super lead."

Urban tried to hide her surprise. She'd gotten the impression the team rivals were always at odds with one another. She'd expected the teams to keep to themselves and not converse freely like this.

"Ah, there you are!" said a familiar voice.

Urban turned in relief. "Coral!"

"I heard there was a fabulous bash happening and didn't want to miss."

"Angel?" Brooke asked in awe.

It took Urban a moment to realize Brooke was talking about Coral. Technically, Angel was her real name. But after introducing herself as Coral and an entire semester of calling her that, she was always Coral in Urban's mind.

"Your song, 'The Dance of Death,' is one of my favorites," Brooke breathed.

"Why, thank you. It's not that impressive, really." Coral deflected the compliment.

Urban's eyes widened a little. She had never seen this side of her former roommate before. Coral had never played the sosh game or attended parties when they'd roomed together. In fact, she seemed not to care at all about her sosh, and Urban had been convinced her strategy was to do the opposite of what was expected. Now Coral tilted her head, eyeing Urban. "You look different."

"Oh, I had a shoot with one of my sponsors and haven't had time to change," Urban explained.

"It's fabulous."

"Gives off low-key rebel vibes," Brooke agreed. "I'm a fan."

A bot holding a platter of miniature waffles with fried chicken approached the group.

Coral took one of the skewers and popped its contents into her mouth. "This is the best of what the Western Fed has to offer," she declared. "Well, this and their beds. I finally got a decent night of sleep, now that I no longer have a rock for a mattress."

Conversation turned to favorite foods, international travel, and adventures abroad, and eventually, the group dispersed. Urban wandered over to Clay, who was surrounded by a Super, Dawn, and a Flyer with red wings.

Vance.

Urban tensed and slowly backed away. Too late.

Clay spotted her. "Urban!"

She reluctantly joined them.

"Have you met Emin? She's a star from the local vids." Clay waved a hand at Dawn. "Of course you know Dawn."

Dawn's face was expressionless, and Urban tried to keep hers likewise.

"And this is the Scorpions' new captain, Vance Vaughn," Clay finished.

Vance gave Urban a nod. "We've met."

Urban's brain raced. Vance was the Scorpions' captain. *That must have been why he was snatched up by Croix as a KOL, and also why there aren't any ads with him in them yet.*

"You've met?" Clay looked inquisitively at Urban. "And you didn't think it worth telling us?" He leaned forward and pretended to whisper. "We could have been gaining valuable intel on our rivals."

Vance laughed good-naturedly, though his eyes went to Dawn, and something seemed to pass between them. "Just a few hours ago."

"You didn't mention you're the new Scorpions' captain," Urban remarked.

He cocked his head. “And you didn’t mention you’re the girl who destroyed the Dragons’ arena.”

“Fair enough,” Urban conceded. She sized him up. The Scorpions’ captain was constantly being watched by thousands of fans. There was no way he would have had time to escape to the Asian Federation just to chase her down.

She relaxed.

Besides, it was illegal for players to have more than two main gene-pool enhancements. His genetic material would have been flagged instantly. He wouldn’t have made it past tryouts.

Then again, neither should I.

“How do you guys know each other?” Clay asked.

“We had a KOL shoot for Croix,” Vance said. “We’re their newest reps.”

“Wow, Croix? What I wouldn’t give for a sponsor like them.” Clay sighed dramatically. “Alas, I’m stuck with brands such as Titanium Tights and Floosel Dog Treats. I told Floosel if they ask me to do one more post holding that ridiculous little yap-yap dog of theirs, I’ll cancel the contract. Little creature panics in terror every time I get near it. And let’s just say the results are not pleasant.”

The conversation shifted to bemoaning terrible contracts and one-upping each other’s KOL horror stories. Urban laughed along with them, but couldn’t help feeling like a fraud. Everyone else in this stalactite-filled room of luxury was a KOL because of their talents and enhancements.

Only Urban was here by a fluke. A mistake.

Just like her bio father said. She was nothing more than a failed experiment. Tears pricked at her eyes.

“Caviar?” a bot asked.

Urban blinked and reached for the food.

Everyone in the group did likewise. Except Vance.

“Is it vegan?” he asked.

“No sir, this is made from the freshest–”

Vance waved the bot away. "No, thank you."

Sometimes Urban forgot how realistic fake seafood could appear. She actually had been wondering the same thing about the caviar.

Urban's brow furrowed. Something about this detail bothered her, but she couldn't put her finger on it. She was still pondering this when another person sauntered up to their group.

The newcomer wore a trendy jumpsuit and had perfectly styled, ink-black hair.

Urban blanched.

"Hello, Urban." Lucas smiled, but it didn't quite meet his eyes.

"Lee Lucas?" Clay confirmed, scanning the newcomer's profile. He turned back to Urban. "You two are related?"

"Unfortunately." Lucas gave an exaggerated sigh.

Everyone laughed, but Urban regarded him warily. "What are you doing here?"

Lucas swiped a drink off a passing bot's tray. "I was in the area and decided to check on my little sis."

"Aren't you supposed to be in the Dominican Federation?"

Lucas downed the drink before answering. "That's the thing about ships. They tend to move around."

"You're on a boat?"

Lucas grinned.

Urban wanted to ask if their parents knew about this, but was pretty sure she already knew the answer.

"Anyhow, it's nice to meet a few *real* KOLs," Lucas said to the circle.

Urban felt her cheeks burn with fury. Who did Lucas think he was, showing up like this and risking her cover? She was contemplating how to exit gracefully when another bot approached.

"Shrimp?" The bot extended a silver platter full of fried shrimp.

Urban and the others all took one–except Lucas and Vance.

Noticing, Clay grabbed one and extended it to Vance. "Oh,

come on. You have to try these. They're the best."

Vance stiffened. "No thanks."

Urban watched him. There was something in his gaze. Something about it was familiar, and yet . . . she couldn't put her finger on it.

The conversation had drifted on to local tourist traps, when her stomach knotted.

Lucas never ate any sort of seafood. It was a common trait for Aquas. They loved marine life and found eating fish distasteful.

And Vance hadn't touched the seafood. *My attacker was an Aqua. It could be a coincidence . . .*

Their eyes locked, and she knew her answer.

In that split second, the familiar spike of fear shot up her spine. It was the same as when he'd stood over her with a pulsing blade, ready to kill her.

HE'S HERE. SHE'D BEEN RIGHT THE FIRST TIME.

Urban excused herself from the conversation and raced back to her bedroom.

She sat on the bed with her head in her hands, stomach churning. After a moment, she pinged her friends. Everest was in the middle of an AiE summit and she received an auto reply from him. The others were on their way.

Restlessly, Urban stood and began pacing the carpeted floor, waiting.

Why would the Scorpions' captain be trying to kill me?

Trig, Ash, and Coral soon arrived, and Urban bypassed all greetings. "I think my attacker is here."

"What? Where?" Ash flared. "I'll teach him a lesson."

While Urban appreciated the sentiment, she didn't want Ash going anywhere near him. If Vance was the attacker, he'd nearly killed Ash once already.

Trig scowled. "I despise that weapon of a human."

"How do you know?" Coral's eyes were unusually serious.

Urban explained what had happened. "I'm not positive it's him, but what are the odds it's not?"

"Hmm . . . 4%, to be precise," Trig said. "According to my analysis."

The others looked at him.

"If you take the number of individuals to have that exact combination of enhancements and run a query of those in the Western Federation, that leaves you at 18%. Then, if you narrow it down further by selecting wing color and type, the odds are high that the attacker and this individual are one and the same."

Urban glanced at Coral. "What do you know about him?"

"I already told you everything last semester." Coral furrowed her brow. "Not much. I intercepted one of his messages in SAS and heard his plan to kidnap you. But his identity was scrambled. I could tell it originated from the Western Federation, but that was all."

"Can't you search for him?" Urban asked. "You're an SAS member. Between being a triple agent, I'd think you have plenty of ways to find him."

"You'd think." Coral made a face. "But SAS, the World Enhancement Org, and even AiE, all keep me separate from their main members for safety purposes. I can't look for him without arousing suspicion."

"You've got to stay away from him," Ash advised.

"I can't." Urban swallowed. "He's the Scorpions' new captain."

"That's impossible," Coral said. "No one with more than two GP enhancements is allowed to compete. They screen for anyone with multiple genetic enhancements."

"I've managed to fool the genetic readers for the past year," Urban pointed out.

Coral pursed her lips, considering. "You think he's cheating the system too?"

"So, we expose him and he's kicked off the team," Ash proposed. "Problem solved."

Urban looked at him. "And while they're doing an in-depth screen of everyone's genetics, I also get discovered as a Natural."

Everyone fell silent at that.

Urban collapsed onto a stiff armchair. "I don't think there's any way for me to expose him without incriminating myself."

"We'll stick closer to you," Trig stated. "And notify AiE. They can investigate further."

"Don't go anywhere alone, in case," Coral warned.

Urban nodded wearily.

"See you tomorrow. Stay safe." Ash's words floated behind as they left Urban.

The second the door closed, exhaustion hit Urban. She forced herself up from the chair and prepared for bed. Donning her sleep headset, she immediately drifted into one nightmare after another–all of them involving a faceless Flyer with blood-red wings.

The next day, Urban focused on finishing up homework assignments before checking out the gift shop in the main lobby. She was tempted to get a collection of shot glasses with actual bullets welded into them for her father and Lucas, but in the end decided not. *Why bother?*

She did, however, buy a pair of cowboy boots. Everest had a performance that evening to help boost his sosh, and Urban, Ash, and Coral were planning on attending to support him. Urban had thought about bailing now, but Coral had promised it would be safer for her to be with them than sitting alone in the hotel.

The venue had a dress code that was Western casual, and based on images Urban found in QuanNao, that appeared to be jeans and boots.

As it drew near time to leave, Urban returned to her room to change. Her new boots were clunky and heavy, but she felt oddly safe in them, like she could kick down a door or knock someone unconscious. *Is something wrong with me that I now think of footwear in terms of how practical they are in a fight?*

A moment later, a ping from Coral let Urban know they were waiting with a vehicle.

It was hot outside and Urban instantly regretted her choice of jeans. *How is it so warm this time of year?*

Ash and Coral were already in the vehicle, along with several of Coral's security guards. Trig materialized beside them a moment later. Urban slid into a seat next to Coral and they were off.

"Thanks for the invite." Ash bounced in his seat. "I love dancing." He wore sweatpants, a baggy t-shirt, and a pair of sneakers.

"The attire is country, not streetwear." Coral rolled her eyes. "You look like you just rolled out of bed."

Ash just grinned. "I heard Western, and this is what they always wear in the flicks."

Trig hadn't deviated from his usual formal attire, and so had on a crisp, collared shirt, with his curly black hair styled perfectly.

Coral had traded her classic high-tops for a pair of black cowboy boots, and wore denim shorts with frayed edges. Her normally backward baseball cap was pointed forward and pulled down low over her eyes.

Coral caught Urban's eye on her. "Let's hope no one recognizes me, or we'll spend the evening snapping with strangers rather than dancing."

Urban kept forgetting her ex-roommate was a famous Western Federation KOL. While fewer people were recognizing Urban now that she was out of the Asian Federation, Coral had the opposite problem.

Their vehicle eventually slowed and stopped in front of a historical trading post converted into a dance hall. A Super with wings stood guard at the entrance.

As they approached, the Super examined their tatts. "Sorry, you're underage."

He took Urban's wrist and scanned it, changing her tatt to a glowing pink. "That will disappear within twelve hours. Try and buy a drink with it, and a sosh infringement will be triggered."

Urban nearly laughed. That's what this was about? Trying to prevent drinking? They had nothing to worry about with her. She wondered what the legal drinking age was in the Western Federation and if the Enhanced didn't have increased drinking thresholds like they did back home.

The temperature dropped inside the dance hall, a mister in the corner working overtime to keep it that way. Deafening music assaulted them. Coral said something, but the words were indecipherable.

"What?" Urban yelled back.

Coral leaned closer. "I said, welcome to my old stomping grounds!"

"This is awesome," Ash shouted.

Coral pulled her hat lower. "Come on!" She led them past a bar glowing in neon lights, where patrons laughed and lounged on hovering stools, then the four of them squeezed their way toward the dance floor.

A slow ballad came on with heavy guitar and vocals. Country music, Urban realized, from back when Coral used to play it in their dorm.

"Here we go!" Coral shouted.

People started pairing up and going onto the dance floor. They shuffled and swayed in an odd pattern.

"It's called the Federation two-step," Coral yelled. "It's super easy. Two steps backward and one step forward. Here, I'll teach you guys."

Coral helped position Ash and Urban and then paired up with Trig. She modeled the steps with Trig, then guided Urban and Ash.

"Like that." Coral nodded. "Easy, right?"

Urban wasn't convinced, but Ash grinned and scanned the room. "So how do I meet girls here?"

"You go up to them and ask them to dance," Coral said.

Ash's face fell. "Maybe if Lillian were here."

Urban smacked his shoulder. "Get out there!"

Ash's dazzling smile returned. He leaped into the air, wings thrusting him upward, and joined a group of Flyers sitting at some of the hovering barstools. Urban watched with amusement as Ash extended a hand to one of the girls and the two of them flew above the dance floor where a group of Flyers danced.

As the next song came on, a Camo appeared out of thin air beside them. He inclined his head to Coral. "Care to dance?"

They both disappeared, except for their feet. Urban grinned at the sight of two pairs of cowboy boots moving along the dance floor. Soon, she lost sight of them among the other dancers. Though, every once in a while, a couple would seemingly trip on thin air.

Urban watched as Supers stomped together across the floor and Artisans glided smoothly, swaying effortlessly. Inventors spun, tech shimmering around them. There were even Naturals.

Urban wondered what it must be like to live in a society where Naturals and Enhanced coexisted. Despite the riots at the airport and the fact that tension was high, she was still envious of the Naturals able to live openly among the Enhanced.

Next to her, Trig watched the dance floor in peaceful silence. Urban wondered what he thought about. It had to be a boring job, following her around. Maybe he was actually watching vids with dual vision enabled.

Above them, Ash and his partner spun and danced, wings beating in time with the music. Their grace was breathtaking. The way they moved as one caused an ache in Urban's stomach.

"Want to dance?" A warm whisper caressed her neck.

She spun around and saw Everest close to her.

"Hey!" For a brief moment, a thrill of excitement washed over her.

Everest's hair was hidden beneath a baseball cap with the logo to a minor league AI team. The look suited him.

Urban's retina display showed his sosh had jumped to 62. *He should be safe now. No one will suspect he's a Natural.*

Everest said something more, but the music drowned out his words.

"What?" Urban yelled.

He motioned Urban to follow and led her to a booth near the back where it was quieter.

"We need to talk." Something about Everest's expression made butterflies erupt in Urban's stomach.

"I'm going against AiE's orders. I know you've been concerned, and it's created too much conflict between us. You mean too much to me to let that happen."

"Wh–what?" Urban stammered.

"I talked to them. They weren't . . . happy, but you're worth it." He leaned forward. "Urban, I can't do this without you. Plus, I care about you too much to let you go again."

Urban's breath caught.

She thought back to all her interactions with Everest, from the first day they met in the Outskirts, to riding their bikes together, even interacting with her family with him around. Kind, fierce, brave Everest, who knew her better than anyone else.

Her smile felt like it would burst. She couldn't speak, only give a happy nod.

Everest broke into a radiant smile himself, and they gazed at each other for a long moment.

Everest cleared his throat. "Do you want to dance?"

"I'd like that."

Everest took her hand and gently led her through the throngs of sweating bodies, stopping once they were on the slick wooden dance floor. The twang of guitar strings and a slow beat grew louder as the next song started up.

Everest spun Urban in a slow circle, then pulled her close. He placed a hand on her lower back. Tentatively, Urban rested her own hand on his shoulder.

They started slow, both of them getting their footing.

Everest guided them first backward two steps then forward one, just like Coral had showed Urban. Though he hesitated slightly, there was otherwise no indicator this was new to him.

Urban stumbled over his feet, the giant points of her boots unfamiliar and clumsy, but Everest smiled encouragingly and they reset.

As the song wore on, their movements grew steadier, slow and rhythmic. Here a spin. There a step. They shuffled and swayed from one end of the dance floor to the other.

Everest twirled her, and when Urban returned to his arms, his ink-black eyes locked with her own. The crowds around them, cool air, loud music–all faded.

Everest pulled her closer and her heart did jiujitsu rolls within her chest. They continued dancing, oblivious to anything else. Gone were the worries about the attacker, upcoming Games, strained relationships with family, the hybrid, AiE, SAS, her bio dad. They were in a bubble of happiness only punctured as the song came to an end.

Everest attempted to dip her, and they fell in a tangle of limbs. They burst into laughter, silly grins on their faces as they stood back up. It was like when they were in the Outskirts racing motorcycles. Back when life was simpler.

I missed this.

"It looks like I'm up soon." Everest glanced toward the stage. "I should probably warm up for my performance."

A flash of light suddenly blinded them. There was a huge blast of sound.

Urban fell to the wooden floor.

Screams and smoke filled the air.

Urban's ears rang, and she blinked, trying to clear her vision.

Blasts rang through the space.

More screaming. Blurred figures ran through the smoke.

"Get down!" Everest was shielding Urban with his body. Trig

crouched protectively in front of them, withdrawing a weapon before disappearing.

The smoke lifted, and street light poured in through one of the walls. Or at least, where a wall had been. Now, there was nothing but a gaping hole. Several masked individuals brandished weapons and shouted as they plunged through.

More blasts resounded. A siren wailed, and the room filled with flashes of red and blue light as law enforcement arrived.

Running. Scrambling. More blasts.

"On your knees!" someone yelled.

Scuffling. Another blast. Moaning.

Silence.

The air grew thick and still.

When the smoke began to clear, masked figures lay on the dance floor, with a Super and law-enforcement bots standing over them. Pulsing red weapons aimed at each of the moaning figures.

An emergency squad of medbots flooded the room, administering aid.

Everest's body still protected Urban, his eyes constantly scanning the room. Urban finally noticed several people tied up at the center of the room, surrounded by law enforcement.

Everest looked down at her as he eased away and stood. "You okay?" He reached out a hand to help her to her feet.

Urban nodded, dust falling from her as she stood.

Trig appeared at Urban's side and touched her arm. "We need to get you out of here."

"Wait." She looked around for Ash.

Relieved, she spotted him perched atop one of the bar tables in the air. He flew to the ground and joined them.

Coral suddenly appeared beside them, her embedded flamethrowers sparking and at the ready.

"Let's get you out of here," Trig repeated, and this time Urban relented. The others followed, forming a protective ring around Urban.

"They weren't after her," Coral informed them, though she kept her pulse weapon at the ready.

Urban had so many questions, but Supers and Flyers clad in military armor flooded the room, barking orders.

The group picked their way over debris and shattered glass to the exit. Outside, the words: "We won't stop until the *Farmed* stop" were graffitied on a wall in crude letters.

"Who are they? What do they want?" Urban asked.

Coral's jaw tightened. "Revolutionaries." She hailed a vehicle and ushered them inside. "Now get going."

"Aren't you coming?" Urban asked.

Coral shook her head. "I'm going to see what I can do to help. You guys get out of here. Who knows if more of them will come." She quickly shut the car door and disappeared.

Urban stared after her. *Revolutionaries? Here?*

"Do you know much about the Revolutionaries?" Urban asked Everest.

"In today's AiE summit, there was a lot of talk about them," he replied. "They are a big problem here. They keep derailing the efforts of the local AiE members."

"How?"

"They split from AiE over disagreements on how to bring about change. AiE is for peaceful change. The Revolutionaries want immediate results and are willing to use violence to get it. AiE is a total mess in the Western Federation, because the Revolutionaries keep poaching their members. Seems many people are so sick of things, they're willing to take extreme measures. The citizens here have such differing ideologies and so little respect for each other."

Urban thought back to the riots outside of the airport.

"The Western Federation has turbulent times ahead."

"What do you mean?" Urban asked.

Everest looked out the window. "If they don't find a way to respect each other's differences without tearing everything down . . . they could be looking at civil war."

BLUE AND SILVER FLASHED AS MUSIC BLARED. Crowds rose and fell like a wave around the entrance to the stadium as Urban's vehicle hovered toward the pyramid-like structure. Security-bots attempted to hold back fans and make way for the Dragons.

Urban sat in a seat next to Brooke, Clay, Ash, Blossom, and Olive on their way to their first game. It was a little odd seeing Olive again, after she had been suspended. Her normally shrewd eyes had a dulled gleam and black circles under them. She avoided Urban's gaze.

Their vehicle pulled into a heavily guarded side entrance, where an escort and several armored Supers led the team through a back tunnel under the arena. They stopped in a large room smelling of lemons. Someone activated the lights, illuminating a set of semicircle couches, XR pods, and water dispensers.

"You have one hour," Willow announced. "At 1400, I expect everyone in uniform and ready to go."

Urban found a training room and climbed onto a running device. After a short warm-up, her nerves were a little calmer. She stretched, then explored the other rooms. There were several spacious showers, a recovery room equipped with cryo, pressurized air massages, and nano tech compression devices.

One room was dimly lit and quiet. A diffuser spritzed the air with the aroma of eucalyptus. Several team members lay face down on massage chairs, getting suctioned cupped by bots. Others sat in swimwear in hot tubs or ice ponds. One even dangled from the ceiling wrapped in silk.

Intrigued by the latter, Urban called a bot over. "How do I use that hammock thing?"

"It would be my pleasure to assist you." The bot led Urban to a plump mat, where she lay down on a soft, stretchy rope. The edges were wrapped around her, then she was hoisted into the air.

It was a strange feeling, suspended weightless, slowly spinning in the dark. Urban relaxed into her cocoon, turned on some of her favorite soothing music, and let her mind go blank.

At least, she tried to.

Her thoughts spun round and round with her body. She had to survive the ordeal of the Games. Which would be starting in less than an hour. Her pulse quickened at the thought. She was confident she would watch from the sidelines, but whoever had hacked her suit was out there. A ping appeared.

[Everest: Stay safe tonight. I'll see you at the after-party back in New Beijing.]

Urban opened the ping. There was a vid recording of Everest winking. She smiled.

She checked Everest's sosh. It had climbed several more points since the race and was now 64–a little low for the Enhanced in her circles. *Hopefully, he can pull it up more before we go back to the Asian Federation.*

She switched her music to a guided breathing exercise and enabled do not disturb mode so she wouldn't get any more messages. Then she hung, spinning, and finally relaxed.

Urban wasn't sure how much time had passed when the

others left the room. Lowering herself, she wandered into another dimly lit room, trying to find her locker. A figure wearing a white hoodie was huddled in a corner, shaking.

Urban recognized the broad, hunched shoulders. “Clay?”

The hood turned in her direction, but Urban couldn’t see a face. Hesitating, she approached. “Are you okay?”

He hastily shoved a bottle into a pocket, but his hands shook so violently, he dropped it and pills spilled everywhere.

Urban bent to help him pick them up, but he swiftly scooped most of them before she could. Urban handed him the few she’d collected.

“It’s not what you think.” As he tucked the pills away, Clay’s hood slipped, revealing bloodshot eyes.

Urban just stood there. She wasn’t sure what to think. If Clay was using performance enhancers before a game, he wouldn’t get far. The pre-game genetic screening process was sure to catch that. Surely, he wasn’t that senseless. Urban blinked. Clay looked like he’d been crying. That wasn’t a side effect of any drugs she was aware of.

As if reading her thoughts, Clay’s red eyes pleaded with her. “Don’t tell anyone. I’m . . . I’m sick.”

Urban’s brow creased.

“Like really sick.”

“Why not let Willow know?”

Clay vigorously shook his head. “Not that kind of sick.”

Confused, Urban wasn’t sure if he meant mentally or physically ill. It would be very strange for a Giver to have a mental illness; then again, Clay did seem uncharacteristically sad. She remained silent to see if he’d elaborate.

“I–I have . . . RSP.” It was almost a whisper.

Urban choked back a gasp. She didn’t know what to say.

It suddenly made sense why he had a cough and why he had been the only other player winded in the team practices.

“No one on the team knows. I don’t want Willow cutting me

because she realizes I'm dying." He let out a strangled laugh. "These pills are the only meds I can take without flagging the drug screening."

Urban regarded him with concern. "So, you're not getting the actual treatment you need?"

"The disease has gone too far, and I don't–" He took a breath. "I don't have much time. Growing up, my dream was always to play for the Dragons. And now here I am, on the team, but I've never had the chance to play. I'm a benchwarmer. All I want is to face the arena before I die."

He gave a wan smile. "I'm supposed to be a life coach, giving people advice that will make their lives better, all while my own life is falling to pieces. I have all the tools to put on a smile and a good show, but what's the point? My parents are ashamed of me. They want me to quit the team and live at the hospital, but since I won't, they won't pay for any treatment. That's why I have to work a manual-labor job and secure as many KOL sponsorships as I can."

Clay shook his head. "Givers are supposed to be perfectly balanced and in control of their emotions and lives. I mean, look at Dawn. She has Willow wrapped around her finger. Technically, Brooke should be the vice captain, or maybe even Orion, but instead, it's Dawn."

"Ten-minute warning," a voice boomed over an intercom.

Clay straightened somewhat. "*Anyway*, thanks for listening to my sob story. Hopefully you never get RSP." His voice was back to his self-deprecating and humorous tone. A lump rose in Urban's throat, now understanding why there was always an undercurrent of sadness.

She almost told him. After he had bared his soul to her, she felt she owed him the truth about her genetics. It seemed like telling him she was a Natural would somehow make him feel better. Only a distant stirring at the back of her brain restrained her.

"Thanks. Me too," she responded instead.

At the lockers, Brooke's music pumped loudly, chanting words of victory in a southern dialect. The floor vibrated with each beat.

Urban took out her suit and examined it closely. The image of Dawn being gored by the lion made her shudder. The suit had obviously been fixed since the accident.

Not that I'll need it. The sidelines are perfectly safe anyway.

Still, the thought made her uneasy as she tugged on the form-fitting smart fabric. A minute later, she rejoined the team in the main room.

Willow surveyed them. "As you all know, the Scorpions are tough competition. They're smart, innovative, and fast. Last year, we almost lost to them. This game will be challenging." She paused. "But we've trained for this. We've worked harder than their team. We play smarter. We are Dragons. We never lose."

She raised her voice. "Now let's get out there and carry on that tradition!"

The team cheered, then stacked their hands.

"*San, er, yi,*" they counted down. "Dragons!"

An attendant poked his head through the door. "Five minutes."

Willow gave a thumbs-up.

The energy in the room was palpable. Hickory jumped up and down on his toes, while Brooke and Orion lightly sparred in a corner. Urban took a seat on the couch and leaned forward, knees bouncing.

The attendant returned. "One minute. Get into position."

The team made their way through the door and into a dimly lit room with rubbery floors. Sixteen helix-shaped slabs spread out across the space. Urban stepped into one and a glass casing rose up around her. She tensed.

The last time she'd been in one of these was when she'd been thrown into PKU's tryouts. It had been going up onto the stage while Coral and Lillian hacked the AI to avoid exposing her DNA. How different things were now.

A cold mist sprayed through the glass. Urban fingered the fake thumbnail given to her by Father. She tried not to think about what would happen should the AI detect her Natural genetics.

Her gaze crossed the tubes to Clay. He, too, looked nervous. He wasn't shaking anymore, but his face gleamed, wax-like.

The room flashed green, and all sixteen platforms pushed upward toward gaps in the ceiling.

With an explosion of light and sound, the arena came to life. Blinding red lights flashed wildly over them, making it hard to see. The glass encasing Urban lifted and the sound sharpened. Some in the crowd cheered, but most booed as they stepped onto soft synthetic turf.

The Scorpions were already waiting. They stood on the opposite end of the arena in shinning blue and silver suits, with an enormous projection of their school flag waving in an imaginary tempest. A projected storm hovered over that side of the stadium, with flashes of lightning bolting through the sky and striking at the feet of the Dragons. A few team members jumped back and the Scorpions laughed.

But Willow charged straight toward the center of the stadium, the rest of the team keeping at her heels. Urban kept her eyes on Blossom's swinging ponytail in front of her, gut clenching, tuning out the thousands of people watching.

The team stopped at the center of the platform, but Willow went a bit further as Vance strode forward. The team captains met in the middle.

"Ladies and gentlemen, the most anticipated match of the year has arrived," a voice boomed.

Vance and Willow fist bumped, their tatts igniting in a riot of color. A circle of light encompassed their arms, pulsing brightly.

"May your minds be illuminated, and your steps light," the AI boomed. "May the ones truly worthy be victorious in might."

Urban shaded her eyes as the light became blinding.

"And let's all ya'll have a great time tonight!" The AI finished in a southern drawl and the crowd roared.

The light faded to darkness. Willow and Vance returned to their teams and led them to opposite ends of the turf.

“Captains, assemble your players,” the announcer ordered.

Willow stepped forward, along with Brooke, Orion, and the rest of the A team. Urban and the B team moved back into an alcove off to the side.

“Jack,” the announcer said. “Initialize genetic screening.”

The stadium grew quiet.

“Genetic screening complete,” Jack’s mechanical voice echoed.

“Excellent,” the announcer said. “Let the Games begin!”

THE STAGE'S TILES FLIPPED OVER, CREATING an arid desert terrain. The temperature in the stadium ratcheted up until Urban's suit struggled to keep her cool. The air was filled with particles of dust and the smell of burning rubber. The stadium's noise cancellation activated, and everything fell silent except an artificial wind blowing.

Urban wondered what sorts of unseen peril lurked behind dunes or in rocky nooks. Everything appeared silent, foreboding. At the center of the stadium, a floating package, which would determine the winner, appeared.

"We're going to use Storming the Castle," Willow said. "Does everyone remember that play?"

"It's where we blitz them, right?" Brooke asked.

"Yes. We break into three groups, but go straight for the winning package. Two teams stay back to delay attacks, while the Flyer/Camo group carries it back to our territory. It's brute force, but we haven't used it in ages and the Scorpions won't be expecting it."

"Game play commencing in five, four . . ." Jack counted down.

The Dragons lined up at the point where the platform disappeared into sand and a holo line appeared.

"Three, two, one. Begin!"

The team charged forward with Brooke, Willow, and Orion running in one group and the Aqua, Giver, and Blossom in another. The Camo disappeared, and the Flyer flew above them all. From the opposite end of the stadium, a lone girl tore across the dunes to meet them. The rest of the Scorpions were nowhere to be seen.

Suddenly, out of the sky, a wooden obstacle course dropped into the air. The Flyer pulled up sharply to avoid slamming into a spiked wall. His flight slowed as he maneuvered around walls, under giant logs, and through other odd shapes and barriers.

On the ground, Brooke and Willow were nearing the first dune when one of the bushes moved surprisingly fast. One second it appeared rooted, the next, it was rolling like a giant tumbleweed straight toward them, growing every second.

"Run!" Willow ordered as she faced off with it.

The plant tried to tangle Willow with its roots, but she sidestepped easily. It became a flowing dance, swinging roots lashing at Willow as she spun, leaped, and dodged out of the way.

Her steps quickly grew tired, and she was now only a millisecond ahead of the tangle of roots. Soon, she'd be too slow and trapped by the barbs and root netting.

Meanwhile, Orion raced toward a power-up package. "Use this!" He flung the package back.

Brooke caught it and smiled. Attaching it to her boots, she leaped into the air, going much higher than a normal Super was capable of, then crashed to the ground. The force of her landing shook the ground and sent sand spiking into the air around her like a wave.

The roots and thorns attacking Willow flew into the sky. When the bush came down, Brooke punched it and it shattered into splinters, cascading like dry rain.

The three of them sprinted up the dune toward the winning

package. Brooke tossed it to the Flyer, who'd competed the obstacle course, and flew back toward their end of the stadium with it.

The Scorpions were still nowhere to be seen.

Then, from the opposite end of the stadium, one of the Scorpions poked his head out. He looked nervously up, then scurried away.

Willow glanced back to see what he was looking at and gasped.

Black tar fell from the sky like an enormous sticky waterfall. It formed a solid line, covering one end of the stadium to the other. Thick and bubbling, the waterfall moved forward, forcing the Dragons back toward the Scorpions' end of the stadium.

"Take cover!" Willow yelled.

They scrambled toward several power-up packages and activated them. One was a giant hammer. The other was a small metal box with the ability to blind an opponent.

"Over here!" Brooke held a wooden shield above her head.

The others sprinted toward her as the tar followed them.

The Flyer landed hard on the ground, rolling under the shield just in time. Brooke braced herself as blackness fell.

When it cleared again, Brooke was trembling and had sunk to her knees from the exertion of keeping the shield raised. Their Aqua, Giver, and Inceptor hadn't been so lucky. All of them zeroed out except Blossom, who'd managed to use a force field to save herself. Their Camo was still alive, but invisible somewhere.

"Can you fly?" Willow asked the Flyer.

He nodded, then leaped back into the sky with the winning package.

A bazooka powered up from the Scorpions' Inventor. He targeted the Flyer in the chest, causing him to spiral down and zero out. The package bounced across the sand, leaving skid marks as it came to a stop.

Willow swore. "New plan. Let's go with play Mount Tai."

The remaining Dragons nodded and split into two groups of two, with the Super and Willow in one, and Orion and Blossom in the other. Only Hickory remained by himself.

A giant scorpion the size of a hover bus appeared from behind a dune, but luckily, charged one of the Scorpions players and left the Dragons alone.

The team converged around a group of three Scorpions and attacked from both sides. They'd managed to take out the Scorpions' Super when Vance and the full force of the team swooped down on them. The team captain spun a reaping scythe so fast its glowing tip blurred in a silver arc.

The Dragons scattered, but not before Orion had his damage counter drop 50% after several ballista attacks from the enemy Inventor.

Suddenly, everything froze.

Each player's suit locked them in place. A snapshot of the arena flashed on the jumbotron above for the crowd to see.

"Timeout," Jack boomed.

The suits released the players and they were free to return to their respective sides.

"Who called a time out?" Brooke demanded the second they were off the turf.

"Me." Willow shut her up with a look. "They've been studying us too carefully. They're familiar with all our plays."

Dawn whispered something to Willow.

Willow frowned but then grew thoughtful. "Yes, I see what you mean." The team captain turned to face the others. "New plan. We're going to change it up a little."

Willow assessed her players. "B team, you're in. Except I'm still playing too."

Urban paled.

Clay cheered and raced onto the stage to fill the marked spot where Brooke had been. The others on the team joined him–except Urban.

She became conscious of a single bead of sweat making a slow trek down her neck and back. Her breathing suddenly seemed too loud.

"What's this?" the announcer declared. "Looks like the Dragons are changing up the roster by throwing in most of their B squad. This has never been done before!"

People in the stadium booed.

Urban remained frozen as she watched her teammates go out onto the arena. *Training mode won't be selected.* Dark spots filled the corners of her vision. *This can't be happening.*

Dawn waited until Willow's back was turned before giving Urban a push forward, a smirk on her face. "That means you too, Urban."

SAND CRUNCHED UNDER URBAN'S BOOTS AND a sharp pain clawed at her chest. *No. No. No!*

Blinding light from the stadium made it impossible to see anything except the dunes directly in front of her, shimmering in heat. She tried to think of a way out, but her brain was short-circuiting in panic.

"For some of these players, this will be the first time competing," the announcer said. "For example, Lee Urban, the legendary player reported to have temporarily broken PKU's AI during her tryouts. We haven't seen Urban since then, so let's see what she's been up to."

Urban hardly cared that her landing page was being broadcast to thousands, both in the stadium and virtually.

Jack is about to analyze my DNA and I have no idea what will happen.

"Looks like she's keeping a pretty low profile," the announcer continued. "Except . . . wait. What's this? She's one of the new Croix Rebel reps. An impressive feat for a first year."

Urban wiggled her feet into the sand, wishing desperately she could disappear with them. *How did I let this happen?*

The announcer moved on to cover Clay, as Urban made

her way to the pulsing marker at the base of a dune where Blossom had been. If she remembered correctly, there was a giant scorpion on the other side of this dune, but it had been heading toward a Scorpion player. At least, she hoped it was.

"The game will resume in ten, nine, eight."

Her pulse was pounding. *Please don't break. Please, please!*

"Seven, six, five . . ."

Urban quickly took a look around her. What if her suit deflated again because they had to shut off the arena? What could she use to protect herself?

Checking her inventory, she was dismayed to find Blossom had no special packages, plays, or weapons. She was entirely at the mercy of her surroundings. Nearby, there was a shrub, an ominous-looking hole, and lots and lots of sand.

"Four, three, two."

Wait. There was something else.

"One."

It looked like a mesh delivery net.

"Resume game!"

A horn blasted and then everything fell silent again as the noise cancellation was activated. In the distance, there were muted shouts and striking metal.

Urban waited a moment.

Nothing.

Hesitantly, she edged up the sand in the opposite direction of the scorpion toward the netting and tore it open.

"A fan?" She stared in disappointment at folding silk and bamboo.

Urban scanned her surroundings. Jack didn't seem to be losing it like Samson had back when she'd destroyed the PKU arena. *Maybe with a whole team to analyze, I can't break it.*

Urban allowed herself to relax a little and examined the fan.

Sometimes, objects were tailored based on the strengths of the player opening them. Maybe this had something to do with the traditional fan dance studied by Artisans?

Taking an effort to flick it open, Urban inspected it more closely. It was black, with a white picture of a landscape. The only thing unusual about it was its size. It was much larger than a normal fan, as big as her torso. A strange ridging crossed it.

The fan flashed green for a moment, but then the color faded away instantaneously. Urban was still fiddling with it when the ground vibrated. Sand trickled off her boots and fell onto the dune.

In the distance, Clay attacked the Scorpions' Camo with a chain. The other Dragons were nowhere to be seen. What had caused the disruption?

The fan flashed green again, and Urban stared at it, perplexed.

The dune trembled–this time, more violently. A shadow fell over her and dread crept up her spine.

From behind the sand hill rose giant chitin legs and razored claws. A stinger swayed dangerously in the air.

Urban froze. She thought for sure the scorpion had gone the opposite direction.

The fan pulsed green. Faster. Its light grew stronger with each approaching step of the insect. By the time the scorpion was close enough to strike, the fan sparked with electricity.

Urban held the fan up, not entirely sure how she was supposed to use it, but knowing intuitively it was meant to protect her.

The scorpion charged, black razored claws clicking.

Urban waved the fan out in front of her and was surprised to see the creature slide to a halt, sending sand flying. Hot particles smacked her face.

Urban squinted, willing the grit out of her eyes. She sensed an attack coming and sidestepped right as the sand next to her exploded. The stinger quickly retracted from where she had been standing.

Urban went on the offensive. She charged, slicing at one of its spindly legs with the fan. A line of electricity from the fan lit up the creature's leg in green.

The insect let out a high-pitched screech, scuttling back and snapping its pinchers furiously. The scent of burning flesh filled her nostrils.

The scorpion charged Urban, and she held out the fan again. The creature ground to a stop, stinger swaying uncertainly as Urban slowly backed away.

Something crashed onto the ground next to her. For a second, Urban thought it was the stinger again, but then she heard the grunts and coughing.

Vance and an invisible force rolled next to her.

Urban stood paralyzed in terror. *Is he going to try and kill me now?*

The Scorpion captain swung a fist down, and Hickory shimmered into view. Withdrawing a wooden club, Vance began bludgeoning the fallen Camo. Hickory zeroed out after two hits to his helmet. Urban winced as the ground opened up and swallowed him away to the med bay.

A ball of fire shot directly overhead, barely missing her and propelling her to action. She sprinted frantically away.

Willow was climbing up the dune, followed by several Scorpions hot on her trail. One of them lugged a giant grenade launcher. Urban dropped to the ground just in time before another round of fireballs blasted above her.

Sensing an opportunity, the scorpion rushed forward and stung one of the Scorpions' players, whose damage counter instantly dropped.

Before the scorpion could do even more damage, the Scorpion with the grenade launcher blew the creature up. Mangled insect parts and armored legs rained down all around them.

Urban had assumed the scorpion was a bot, but that smell . . . She scooted herself up and away from the smoking, hairy leg bits.

The Scorpions players closed in around the remaining Dragons. Urban, Clay, and Willow formed a tight circle with their backs to each other.

"Three versus five. We can do this," Clay encouraged.

Willow suddenly dropped to the ground and began shaking uncontrollably. An arrow pulsing with electricity lodged in her shoulder. Her damage counter zeroed out and she disappeared below the stadium. Urban's heart plummeted within her.

"Okay, make that two against five," Clay amended. He and Urban adjusted their stance.

Urban held out her fan protectively in front of her. The green bolts had all but disappeared.

Vance strode toward the two remaining Dragons, leisurely twirling his scythe. "I would say good game, but that would imply a real challenge." He motioned at a player who loaded a crossbow, then flipped a switch until it hummed with electricity.

The arrow went flying. Urban's body tensed.

It was Clay who yelled, then fell to the ground, arrow lodged in his thigh. His body lay trembling in the sand until he was taken away.

Urban's mouth was dry. She wondered how much a shot like that would hurt with her protective suit.

Vance eyed her for a moment before giving a barely perceptible nod to their Inceptor. Urban glanced in his direction and noticed he held a package. Only, something looked different about it. It wasn't the standard size and coloring of the other packages in the games. It almost looked . . . fake.

The package vanished into a cloud of black mist. The Inceptor subtly flicked his wrist in Urban's direction, and a weird, cold sensation slid over her.

It was as if a giant boa constrictor were releasing her from its grip.

With horror, she realized what it was.

Glancing down, she saw that her suit hung loosely about her, deactivated. *No. No. No!* she inwardly screamed. *This can't be happening again!*

She desperately searched the stadium for an indication that

someone, anyone had witnessed what was going on. Surely the game wardens and judges would see that her suit had gone offline.

But nothing happened.

"Help!" she tried to scream, but her voice was muffled. She looked around in confusion.

Vance laughed as he tossed up a silver ball and caught it. "Funny what a muffler can do. Silences a player and freezes their suit's connection." He cocked his head. "Not that you have anything to say."

He motioned with his scythe at the player with the crossbow.

Urban reached for her familiar stun shield as the Inceptor reloaded the crossbow, but her fingers only grabbed at thin air.

Vance's eyes flashed. "Game over, Urban."

THE CROSSBOW AIMED FOR URBAN'S HEART.

I never got to fix things with my family.

Fear spiked through her veins, but more than that, regret.

The crossbow powered up, sizzling with electricity.

A roar shattered the air.

Urban collapsed to the ground covering her ears. The Scorpions all clutched their heads–even the Aqua on the team, who was usually impervious to loud noises.

If that wasn't their Aqua . . . who's making that sound?

The answer arrived in the form of beating wings. The creature soaring toward them had the wings, tail, and talons of a dragon, but its body and head were that of a lion.

Urban had never seen an obstacle like this before. She'd heard of mythical creatures occasionally showing up in the Games, but they were usually glorified robots with fur. Occasionally, the game wardens would actually go to the trouble of splicing different animals' DNA to form a whole new hybrid creature. But those were so costly and rare, they only appeared in the Games every decade or so.

Urban doubted whatever she was looking at was real, but that still didn't ease her fears.

The Scorpions ran for cover.

Only Vance remained calm, motionless. “A Gamelyon.” His face hardened, then he turned in search of the Inceptor. “Do it now!” he ordered. “Finish her!”

The Gamelyon swooped down with another roar.

The player with the crossbow raised it to Urban again, and with shaky hands took aim. Before he could pull the trigger, flames engulfed him as the Gamelyon blasted him with a fiery breath.

The player zeroed out and disappeared. The Gamelyon swooped back up and over them.

Muttering a few choice words, Vance drew out several knives. He locked eyes with Urban, then charged.

Her mind raced a million miles a second. *How do I defend against a knife attack? There’s a small chance if I take him to the ground, I can trap him.*

When Vance was almost close enough to strike, she stooped down and threw sand in his eyes, before shooting past him. Coming up behind him, she kicked at his knee, staggering him to the ground, all while trying to keep tabs on the knives.

Something leathery and hot pulled her against Vance’s body. She shuddered. It took her a second to realize he was trapping her against him with his wings.

Then they were suddenly weightless, off the ground.

How is he flying if his wings are around me?

A deafening roar directly next to her answered.

With a lurching movement, she was disentangled from Vance. They were only a few meters above the ground and separated. Each in one giant claw of the Gamelyon.

Roaring, the Gamelyon bit down on Vance’s mid-section. Even with the protective suit, Vance let out a scream and immediately zeroed out. The Gamelyon dropped him and he fell, clutching his side, onto the sand, where the tiles flipped over and took him to safety.

Fear and desperation gripped Urban. She beat against the

claws gripping her and was surprised when they let go.

She fell to the sand, then rolled to a stop.

The Gamelyon turned mid-air and eyed her with glowing yellow eyes, plumes of smoke coming from its nostrils.

Urban turned and ran. She heard another player zeroing out behind her as the Gamelyon attacked.

She hadn't gotten far when a shadow hovered in the sand over her. She tried to outrun it, lungs burning, side cramping. The creature easily kept pace with her.

Out of the corner of her eye, she spotted something black and sharp. The stinger from the scorpion. Urban ran to pick it up, turning in one motion to face the Gamelyon.

The creature landed on the ground and crept toward her, a predator stalking wounded prey.

Its head was taller than her own. Up close, it smelled of wet animal and charred wood. Its shaggy mane was covered in flecks of sand.

Is it real?

If it was a bot, would it sense her suit was deactivated? Maybe there was hope yet.

She caught a glimpse of the Gamelyon's teeth, white and sharp near the tips and yellow near the gums. If this were a bot, they had really outdone themselves.

Please be a bot. Please, oh please.

The creature roared again, spittle flying in Urban's face. It whipped around, revealing blood pooling out of a large wound one of the Scorpions had inflicted.

Blood. Not a bot.

Trembling, Urban sliced the air with the stinger, trying to keep the creature away.

The Gamelyon growled. With a casual swipe of its talon, it sent the stinger flying out of her hands and to the ground out of reach.

Urban stared into the massive creature's eyes.

Of all the ways to die . . .

THE GAMELYON STALKED NEARER AS URBAN stood, immobilized by its round, golden eyes.

The creature stared, and its head cocked to one side, almost like Baozi did sometimes. Its lip uncurled, teeth no longer bared.

It stared at her, as if waiting.

When it moved again, Urban flinched, but it didn't prowl or pounce, as she expected. Instead, it padded closer until its hot breath caressed her cheeks.

Urban froze as the Gamelyon nuzzled her gently.

Almost in shock that the creature hadn't attacked, she noticed something. A sound. It was deep and throaty, familiar and soothing.

Suddenly, Urban realized the creature was purring.

The Gamelyon nuzzled her again, and with shaking fingers, she reached slowly toward it.

The creature's enormous golden eyes watched her, and then it nudged forward, meeting the palm of her hand and pressing up against it.

Urban sucked in a breath.

Tentatively, she stroked the smooth, short fur of its forehead. The Gamelyon closed its eyes, and the deep purr sounded again.

Then its knees slowly folded as it knelt on the sand. It bent its head to her.

Her eyes widened. Did it want her to climb on?

The Gamelyon stared at her, golden eyes unblinking.

She hesitated only a moment. She had some sort of connection with this odd beast.

Gingerly, she climbed onto its broad, muscled back. Near the shoulder blades, the fur changed to hot black scales. Urban was grateful for the protection of her thick suit, even if it was deactivated.

Its muscles rippling, the Gamelyon stood slowly and began walking.

When the disbelief of what was happening wore off, Urban was jolted into remembering she was still in the Games. The winning package was a few meters off, at the top of the closest dune. Hoping the creature would obey a command from her, she guided it to the right.

The Gamelyon followed her gentle prodding and strode up the dune, straight toward the pulsing package. When they were directly beside the package, Urban snatched it up.

Their movement changed. Unfurling its giant scaled wings, the Gamelyon ran down the dune, gaining speed. Urban quickly stuck the package between her chest and the creature and used both hands to hang onto the mane. Flapping its wings, the Gamelyon leaped into the air.

Urban's stomach lurched as they shot upward. She clung all the more tightly to the mane.

Gradually, they stopped climbing upward and Urban dared to look down.

They soared over the silent dunes, where the giant scorpion's remains were scattered in the sand, along with several other weapons and a few remaining packages.

The Gamelyon let out a seemingly triumphant roar that thrummed through Urban, and she thrust the winning package up in the sky for all to see.

A sound like thunder crashed around her as the noise cancellation lifted. The stadium beneath her returned to synthetic turf and the blinding desert light faded away to the darkened arena. Strobe lights flashed the Dragons' colors, and virtual, glowing confetti rained down. The place exploded with sound.

"Amazing! Never before have we seen anything like it!" The announcer was yelling to be heard over the screaming fans.

Urban wasn't sure how long they went on like this–powerful, untouchable, invincible. The feeling was as foreign as the hot scales of the Gamelyon beneath her.

The moment ended as the Gamelyon circled back to the stadium floor. The Dragons' team, those not in the medbay, stood clapping and cheering, heads cranked up to watch her approach.

The Gamelyon landed smoothly and Urban dismounted, legs nearly buckling as she hit the ground.

Orion caught her. He had an odd expression on his face. Was it respect? Bewilderment? It almost looked like he was seeing her for the first time. The team crowded in around them. A babbling stream of questions came at once. So many, Urban couldn't comprehend them.

A tile next to them flipped over and a man emerged. "Congratulations on your victory." He strode toward them. "I'm the head developer and game warden. I believe you have something of mine." He gestured at the Gamelyon, who growled and loosed flames toward the man.

The game warden herded the Gamelyon below the stadium. Urban watched it go with mixed emotions, until her team swallowed her in exuberant hugs.

Everything after that was a blur.

Back in the locker room, Urban changed and made sure to grab her stun shield before security escorted them through the back entrance. Throngs of people were already waiting, and the guards had to clear the way past virtual signs, vid drones, and Flyers hovering above. Urban scrambled into a vehicle, and it was silent for a few blissful minutes until they reached the hotel, where they quickly packed and checked out. Then they were off to the city's center.

After that, it was another round of crowds, security, and noise as they made their way to the landing.

Finally, they were all aboard their Hypersonic X8, the happy chatter of the team not quite drowned out by the engine's rumble. The windows showed a peaceful, starlit, inky sky above and glowing fluorescent lights below.

Eventually the team quieted, and Urban leaned her cushioned chair back, exhausted, but sleep evaded her. Her heart beat wildly in her chest, like that of the wild Gamelyon. She checked her updates and found her sosh had skyrocketed. She gasped. It was at 96–higher than almost everyone she knew.

"Attention passengers," a robotic voice said. "Our aircraft has had a slight malfunction. We will be landing in New California in the next few minutes for maintenance purposes. We hope to be back on our way to the Asian Federation soon and apologize for the delay."

There were several groans.

Urban frowned. *What kind of a delay is serious enough to force us to land? I've never heard of such a thing.* She sent a quick group ping to Coral, Ash, Everest, and Trig.

[Urban: We're forced to land in New California. Will you all be there?]

[Everest: I don't like it. I'm six hours behind you, but will get there as soon as I can.]

[Trig: Sorry. Am already halfway to New Beijing.]

Outside her window, the scene changed from a floor of gray clouds to sparkling black ocean.

Soon, they were flying low enough to the ground to see

ghostly illuminated pools of the residences below. With a bump, they landed. Now awake and alert, Urban joined the others as they exited the aircraft and went to wait at a cafe inside a mostly empty building.

An hour later, the team was still grounded. Willow found the nearest hotel and requested rides to it. They weren't the standard bulletproof luxury edition vehicles they were used to. Instead, cyber pickups ten years out of warranty answered the call.

Caribbean music blared out rolled-down windows. Color spilled beneath the body of the vehicles and onto the tires and road.

"Could it be any tackier?" Olive eyed the vehicles with disdain.

The body of the truck was so far above the ground, Urban had to use handholds to pull herself into it. Inside, she squeezed next to Clay. Ash, Dawn, and Brooke were already there.

"That's enough of that." Brooke turned the music off. Urban checked her retina and found it was 0103 local time, which would be even later back in Texicana.

Everyone fell silent as they either dozed off or engaged in QuanNao. Urban's prioritized messages pulled one up from Everest marked as urgent.

[Everest: The AiE team helping investigate hacking of the suit has an update.]

Urban sat up in her seat.

[Everest: It zeroes in on Dawn, the Giver GP lead from your team.]

Urban froze. Her gaze swept over her sleeping teammates until she spotted Dawn. Her never-blinking, toad-like eyes were shut for once.

[Urban: Are you sure? That's so opposite of the Giver characteristics.]

[Everest: Inceptors can read you and they're masterful weavers of words. But they can only manipulate on a small scale. Givers can change people's minds entirely and can do it from afar.]

Urban thought back to how Dawn had gotten Urban's suit and had Willow put the B team in the games. If those were her easily visible endeavors, what had she manipulated from afar?

More pings arrived.

[Everest: Givers instinctively understand people, what drives them, what lengths they would go to in order to achieve their goals, their greatest fears–everything. With that knowledge they are expert manipulators.]

[Urban: But what about their empathy trait?]

[Everest: Empathy is not the same as sympathy.]

Their vehicle pulled up to a building called Motel New Port and the team disembarked. Urban sent a final ping to Everest before joining them.

[Urban: Can you ping this evidence to Willow or the campus authorities?]

As the team checked in, Urban kept her distance from Dawn, though she seemed uninterested in Urban, anyway, per usual.

As they were bringing their luggage in, Olive approached Urban and pulled her aside near the entrance.

"I need to talk to you." Olive glanced around and lowered her voice. "How did you manage to tame the Gamelyon?"

"What?" Urban looked up at the Inceptor in confusion, then quickly tried to mask her reaction.

"The Gamelyon," Olive repeated. "I need to know how you got the Gamelyon to obey you."

"I don't know," Urban admitted honestly. "I just climbed on."

Olive studied Urban, her shrewd gray eyes searching for something before she leaned in closer. "The Gamelyon isn't a standard prop. Each arena or stadium has only one, and it serves a very special purpose. It's a warning mechanism that alerts–"

Suddenly, Olive jerked straight, her head cocked to one side.

A moment later, Urban noticed a slight buzzing noise permeating the air.

"Watch out!" Olive yanked Urban away from the door. A moment later, the doors burst open with a bang.

Urban's heart beat erratically as people came charging in, filling the entryway.

"Where's Ash?" Willow barked. "He was supposed to alert us to this sort of thing."

"He's getting the last of the suitcases," Brooke replied.

Willow's voice hardened. "Supers, help everyone get to safety." She rounded on their guards. "Clear a path."

Brooke pushed Urban and Olive to safety, then turned and activated a blue pulsing weapon.

There were so many people. Urban lost sight of Olive. Warnings about the dangers of mobs filled her mind and made her chest constrict.

"I leave you for five seconds and you need rescuing again."

"Ash!"

"C'mon," he said.

Urban quickly grabbed his waist and stepped on his feet, and he launched into the air. They climbed as high as they could before reaching the ceiling.

Beneath them, the stampede of people came to where they'd been standing. A girl stopped to stare up at them and was knocked down, but managed to crawl to the wall and out of danger.

Urban quickly surveyed the ground for the rest of her team. Everyone had fled except Brooke, who was pushed back by the sheer number of people.

"That's three times now," Ash commented.

"What?"

"Three times I've saved you now." He huffed. "I deserve a promotion from bag boy, if I do say so myself."

Below them, the swarm of people kept growing until the entire lobby was filled. They stood around, agitated like wildebeest trapped in a cage.

That's when Urban noticed blood-red eyes on her. He stood still amidst the frothing crowd, watching.

Despite how much he'd aged, Urban recognized him from *Popo's* memories.

It was the Deadly Fifth.

URBAN'S MIND RACED THROUGH EVERYTHING she'd ever read or seen about the fifth member of the Deadly Five. *Popo*'s memory from the tatt temple was vivid. The hooded figure who had touched a Natural and caused her to die. The body convulsing on the ground. His cold eyes watching without remorse.

As she rapidly sorted through her repository of memories, someone pointed upward at her.

Dawn.

Why isn't she with the rest of the team?

The girl's glittering red eyes were a perfect match to the Deadly Fifth standing next to her. Urban's heart stopped.

There was a definite resemblance in those toad-like eyes.

The Deadly Fifth kept his focus upward and was pointing.

Dawn's father is the Deadly Fifth. A wave of terror crashed into her.

The mob, writhing like a snake, stilled to look where he directed.

A whistling sound filled the air, and a moment later, a heavy rope shot past her and Ash. *A . . . lasso?*

The rope fell back to the ground.

"Uh oh." Ash swerved out of the way of another rope.

Urban eyed the exit door. "Ash, can we get out?"

"It will be tricky." Ash dived out of the way again. Suddenly, he dropped downward so fast, Urban nearly slipped out of his grip. A rope held fast around his foot.

Ash flapped harder, but some of the crowd had joined in, reeling him down like a fish.

Urban quickly pulled out her stun shield, flicked it on, and severed the rope.

"I think that door is our best option." Ash panted heavily. "Can you climb onto my back?"

Urban nodded and carefully made her way around him.

"You good?" Ash asked once Urban was in position.

"Go," she urged.

Ash dove straight down, and at the last second, he put his arms out, slammed the door open, and shot through.

Someone caught Ash's foot before they could gain height and yanked him down. Urban tumbled off his back. Gravel sliced into her, but she ignored it as she sprang to her feet.

"Run!" Ash shouted.

Urban didn't want to leave him, but there was no time. Ash was being dragged away by the crowd. "Go!" he yelled at her.

Urban focused her attention on her immediate surroundings. There was a slight parting in the crowd to her right. She held up her stun shield and charged forward, weapon swinging.

The crowd moved back in surprise as Urban crashed through.

Then she was free of the mob and running. The humid air clung to her clothes and sweat slipped down her back. Pain registered in her leg, but she kept going.

Shouting and rapid blasts erupted behind her.

Urban ran faster.

She pushed her sore muscles to their limit, sides heaving, lungs burning. This wasn't another of Willow's practice sessions.

Heavy footsteps followed close behind. Supers were gaining

ground with every step. Panic spurred her on, knowing one of them could be the Deadly Fifth. If he thought she was the hybrid, he wouldn't know she was a Natural. If he touched her without his XR gloves, she'd be done.

Straining, Urban pushed her legs faster, nearly tripping as she raced over the uneven pavement. The stench of trash filled her burning nostrils. Her senses were heightened, focused on survival.

She swerved down a different alley and kept running, legs turning to jelly, chest aching.

The Supers drew nearer.

The closest one huffed too close behind her and sent Urban running back out onto the main road just as a vehicle swerved in front of her.

Trapped.

Urban skidded to a stop. Her brain tried to come up with an escape plan, but there was nowhere to go and she couldn't run anymore.

The door to the vehicle popped open.

"Get in," a familiar voice ordered.

"Coral!" Urban bolted into the car. The door shut and locked quickly behind her.

She sank against the seat, gasping for breath.

Outside, hands banged against the glass and bodies pressed up against it, but to no avail, as the vehicle immediately took off, leaving the Supers behind.

"The Deadly Fifth," Urban panted. "He was here. He must think–" She tried to slow her breathing. "–must think I'm the hybrid." She began shaking uncontrollably.

Coral put a hand on her arm. "You're okay now."

Urban leaned further back in her seat and closed her eyes. She couldn't stop shaking. "What about Ash? The rest of the Dragons?"

"I already called law enforcement," Coral informed her.

"They should be there soon."

Urban opened her eyes. "Where are we going?"

"To my private Hyperloop," Coral replied. "We can get you back home that way."

"Where's that?"

Something flickered across Coral's face. "That's the part you're not going to like. The only way to get there is through an underwater pod."

Urban groaned and closed her eyes again.

They traveled in silence the rest of the way, not stopping until they reached an underwater dock. After hopping out, Coral scanned her tatt and they made their way into a lobby surrounded by windowed walls displaying the ocean beyond.

Coral walked at a clipped pace across the carpeted lobby to a door where, on the other side, a medium-sized pod sat waiting. Coral activated the pod's entryway and climbed in.

Urban took a steadying breath, then followed.

Inside, it was stuffy, and her boots stuck to the plastic floor. Stale air gushed through the vents and fluorescent lights flickered on as Coral booted it up.

"There's a tea dispenser to your right." Coral gestured without turning. "Might help with the nerves."

Urban headed toward it, grateful. After making herself a cup of green tea, she settled into one of the two chairs and took a sip.

"Alright, here goes!" Coral slid into the other seat.

Urban's stomach tightened. Water rushed into the room around them. With a lurch, the pod left the ground and floated with the water. The engines roared and propelled them into the ocean.

Urban held the warm tea tightly. She took another sip, hot, smooth liquid coating her throat and loosening her insides.

Urban's ears popped–they were descending further down. She took several more sips of her tea, trying to keep the panic at bay.

Coral watched out the inky windows.

Urban was curious how Coral had found her, but she found it very hard to think as a wave of sleepiness overtook her.

Urban knew she should probably let Everest and her team know she was alright, but she was so tired.

Just need a quick nap.

Her eyelids drooped. With her last bit of strength, she looked up and found Coral watching her with a peculiar expression.

Then her eyes closed of their own will.

URBAN AWOKE TO A NIGHTMARE.

Outside the pod windows, a vast water world shimmered to life. Giant rock formations rose up around them, stretching from the blackness below all the way to the bright top of the ocean, like castle spires. Sunlight filtered down through the water.

How long have I been asleep?

Something tugged at the back of her mind, something she should be remembering, but her brain was foggy and thinking took too much effort.

Their pod moved between the rocks, sinking deeper toward the formation's foundation, where fluorescent green moss undulated lazily.

There wasn't a single fish in sight. The ocean seemed deadly silent, the only sound the faint whir of their pod's propellers. As they headed straight for the base of the rocks, Urban braced herself with the arm chair.

Right when they should have made impact, their pod instead glided through, into a dimly lit cave.

"Holo projection?" Urban spoke aloud in wonderment. *This island must be impossible to find by outsiders.*

"Look who's awake," Coral observed. "You were out for several hours."

Urban's brain started to clear. She bolted upright. "I have to ping Everest, my family, and team to let them know I'm alright!" A wave of dizziness hit her and she sank back down.

"Whoa, there." Coral put out a hand. "You'll have plenty of time once we arrive. Right now, we're offline. Too deep in the ocean."

Urban restrained a shudder. "How much longer will we be underwater?"

"Almost there."

The pod dipped down further, navigating the darkness with automated ease. As they turned a bend, the water grew light again.

They were in a large cavern. From the top, sun rays filtered in through gaping holes. The water was a rainbow with brilliant shades of aquamarine, seafoam blue, and teal.

As the pod hovered through one of the light patches, Urban's skin lit up brightly, as if she were on the shore of a beach, not hundreds of meters underwater. "Incredible," she breathed.

"Approaching The Underwater Experimental Lab," announced the AI.

Urban frowned. "I thought you said we were going to your private pod."

"We are. It's at my parents' lab." Coral quickly turned her gaze back out the window.

The pod reached the edge of the cave and entered into a large space with twinkling lights. The circular cave walls encased a large building. Glass windows revealed offices inside, connected by reinforced walkways.

Urban pressed her face closer to the window. "This is incredible."

Several pods like the one they were in zoomed around inside the structure. There were also hammerhead sharks swimming lazily back and forth, sea urchins hiding within the rocks, and black and white stingrays with a haunting bone-like pattern gliding silently overhead. Artificial sunlight shone throughout the space. On the ocean floor, there was a glass-domed walkway surrounded by a coral reef and teeming with smaller but more colorful fish.

"Why are there fish here but not outside?" Urban asked.

"What?" Coral seemed preoccupied. "Oh. There's a transmission signal within a five-mile radius of the lab that wards the marine life off."

"Why?"

Coral shrugged. "Keeps curious Aquas away."

Urban studied her roommate. There was something she wasn't telling her.

Urban felt her adrenaline spiking.

Their pod cruised toward a glass receiver.

With a bump, they settled down in a small ball connected to the main structure by a translucent walkway. Water surrounded them from within and outside the glass dome. Then with a hiss, the water drained away, leaving them in a clear bubble of air.

"Here we are," Coral declared as she unstrapped her seatbelt and hopped up. A glass divider opened automatically at her approach.

The cold walkway smelled mossy and fresh, like a waterfall. With the barrier separating them and the water, it was completely silent, except for Coral's high-tops quickly stepping on the metal-grated floor.

Urban tried to keep up. "Why the rush?"

Coral cast a quick sideways glance at Urban. "No reason."

They reached the end of the walkway, and a blast of bleach-scented air whipped them in the face as the door opened then closed behind them. A labyrinth of hallways and doors spread out in front of them. Each one had a tiny glass window reinforced with metal bars. Above it was a number and a flashing light, either red, yellow, or green.

"What are all these?" Urban asked, indicating one of the rooms.

Coral walked faster. "Offices."

A chill ran down Urban's spine, and not just from the drop in temperature.

Why would offices need reinforced metal windows? Is security a big problem here? Surely not, given how hard it is to find this place.

Her stomach churned. "Coral, what's going on?"

"Hurry."

Urban hesitated. Coral didn't look like she was lying, just nervous. But Urban had never seen her like this before. Urban slowed a little and lagged behind. She examined the rooms they passed more closely. Most of the doors had flashing green lights above them, though there were a few with red. She peered into one of the tiny glass windows.

A room lit too harshly by fluorescent lights exposed a huddled mass in one of the corners. The animal had long furry arms wrapped around itself and a head hung in defeat. As if sensing her, it looked up.

Urban froze.

It was a monkey. Only, something was wrong with the face. It had blistering bumps, bulging stitches, and burn marks.

Urban backed away slowly. She hesitated at a red door, then peered in.

This room was identical to the other one, too bright, and with an animal in it. Only this time, the animal was strapped to a table and had tubes, needles, and blood surrounding its body. Its torso was cut open, revealing its heart, pale lungs, and rigid organs.

Panic rose in Urban's throat. These weren't offices or rooms. These were cells.

What kind of sick experiments were being conducted here?

The Asian Federation would never allow this. This was legal in the Western Federation?

She looked back down the hallway in the direction they'd come. Several lights blinked red. *Everything inside of those must be dead.*

"Ah, there she is."

A brittle voice startled her. Urban whirled around and found Coral standing next to a man in a pristine lab coat. He was too thin, his coat clinging to his lean form. He had sharp eyes, a hawk-like nose, and a smile that sent her nerves skittering.

"Urban, meet Dr. Crane." Coral's voice had an unnatural tightness to it. "I'll be leaving you two to get acquainted."

Stunned, Urban watched her friend go. "Coral, wait!"

Coral kept walking.

What's going on? Urban looked wildly around. Dr. Crane was staring at her like she was a particularly delicate dish to be eaten.

I have to get out of here.

Urban wheeled around to retrace her steps back to the pod.

That's when she saw them.

Her brain stuttered to a stop, temporarily not comprehending. Then everything seemed to fast-forward.

Supers and Aquas with stun clubs and weapons resembling iridescent tridents blocked the entrance.

Urban spun around to race after Coral's retreating figure. "Don't leave me!"

Coral didn't look back. More Aquas and Supers poured in from all sides.

Urban's heart fell.

Coral had led her here on purpose.

She betrayed me.

GUARDS CLAD IN SMART ARMOR AND WITH weapons extended drew near to Urban. She eyed their electric color and tried to remember what she had learned. Blue was for stun and red was for kill. Right?

She hoped so.

If that was the case, the indigo sparks of energy were only meant to stun. They wanted her alive.

What do they want from me? Urban's mind flicked back to the cells of experimented animals she'd gone past. Numbly, she withdrew her own stun shield.

I'm not going to disappear to the bottom of the sea without a fight. She knew with dismay there was no way she could take on all of them.

A stun club flashed toward her, but Urban was able to dodge out of the way. She threw a punch at the Super who'd attacked her, aiming for his jugular. He easily blocked and she retreated.

Get control, Urban told herself. She inhaled a deep breath as two Aquas advanced simultaneously.

Her training took effect. Urban bounced her stun shield off the closest Aqua, and he crumpled to the ground in a sizzling mess of electricity. She caught the Aqua behind her with a back kick. The force of it sent the Aqua sprawling into several guards behind him. She caught her stun shield with one hand as it returned to her.

With a surge, the rest of the guards closed in at once.

Urban spun and twisted out of the way of their weapons. She threw punches and kicks. Her stun shield was a blur of motion, striking guards and dropping them.

But for every guard that went down, there were two more replacements.

Urban's legs were like lead. Her arms burned. Sweat poured down her forehead and stung her eyes.

A hand caught her ankle as she kicked out. She felt gravity reverse itself, and she was flipped onto her back, the wind knocked out of her.

She was so exhausted. All she wanted was to give up–to rest.

Then she thought of the animal in the cell on the surgical table.

With a sharp cry, she rolled away and kicked the guard nearest to her before scrambling to her feet.

Her ensuing attacks grew sloppy and desperate.

Pain shot through her left side.

She looked down where a stun club had grazed her, leaving scorch marks and a tingling numbness. Thankfully, she hadn't received the full electrical shock.

Before she could react, a boot slammed into her sternum, knocking her backward. She landed in the arms of several guards.

Lashing out with both elbows, she managed to drop one of them, but another guard held her tightly.

Urban swung her stun shield backward. It connected to something hard, then the grip around her loosened. She pulled away right as something struck her leg.

Shards of heat shot through her.

A guard swung a fist at her face. Urban tried to block, but her movements were sluggish and the blow clipped her jaw.

She fell to the floor.

So much pain.

Her back was on fire and her body shook from an electric pulse.

Something stunned her again. This time, a full dose of electricity zipped up her spine. Urban screamed as each cell within her body exploded. Tears fell down her cheeks.

She stared up as blurred shapes shouted and moved above her, but she remained–a tomb of quiet agony–frozen.

Another electric stab of pain.

Urban tried to scream, but nothing came out.

The harsh light faded.

Darkness.

Urban dreamed she was back at her jiujitsu gym. Everest was next to her, practicing armbars. His face inches from her own. His familiar scent of jasmine and smoke bringing comfort.

Urban whispered up to him, and Everest smiled and leaned closer, warm chocolate eyes studying her with tenderness.

But then Lillian was suddenly on top of her, choking her. Urban tapped the mat, but her sister didn't yield. "Why didn't you tell me that we're not even sisters!"

As Urban began to see spots, Lillian vanished from the room, leaving Urban sputtering and alone. Only Everest remained, watching her sadly, but then he too disappeared.

Gradually, the gym became less vivid.

Now a new nightmare started, involving Coral betraying her and being trapped in an underwater prison.

Urban tried to go back to the now empty jiujitsu mat. But details of the gym faded and the nightmare sharpened into focus. The searing pain of Coral leaving and the bite of the stun club yanked her back to reality.

She awoke to steel pressed against her face. Blinding light beat down on her. All was completely silent. She was alone in a room that was cold as an ice block and smelled like freezer burn.

Blinking, Urban tried to concentrate on her surroundings, but everything kept swimming in and out of focus. She gradually saw she was in a bare room on a metal cot. The only other amenities were a toilet and sink. A tiny vid recorder blinked in the corner.

Slowly, Urban pushed herself up to a seated position. She took in a sharp breath at the pain in her leg and side. Her left eye was swollen, but without any sort of mirror, she wasn't sure how bad the damage was. Surely, they wouldn't leave her in a cell like this if her injuries were serious. Would they?

Urban tried to steady her breathing as she realized her predicament. She had no idea who her captors were or what they wanted. And why was it so cold?

She tried to adjust her suit's thermal setting in QuanNao, but everything was dark. With horror, she realized she didn't have access to her retina displays anymore.

After a moment, she limped over to the sink.

She was definitely in some sort of experimental lab, not the private island Coral had claimed. And judging by the state of the animals she'd seen in the cells, it was illegal research.

Urban twisted the sink faucet. Cupping her hands, she carefully splashed her swollen eye and wipped away the dried blood.

After cleaning her face, Urban left her hands under the running water for warmth. How long would it take for someone to realize she was missing? Urban thought back to how she arrived–through the hidden caves. There was no way anyone would find her here.

She watched as her hands reddened from the hot water.

I should have listened to my family.

Returning to her cot, she pulled her knees up and hunched

her shoulders to hide from the ever-watching vid recorder.

They were telling the truth and only wanted me to be safe. Will they find out I'm missing?

Her uncle's words from New Year's came back to her: *"They're the only family you've got."*

She'd pushed her family far, far away. For what?

Answers.

And now she was alone with those answers. And even more questions.

Tears streaked down her face. Urban was no more able to stop them than to escape her prison.

She rubbed at her bruised hands, remembering Everest's scarred knuckles. He'd given everything for his family. Why hadn't she been willing to do the same?

Why did I give up so easily?

The Lees weren't perfect, but neither was she.

Too late to do anything now. I'm trapped.

She tried not to think about how far under the ocean she was. The weight of all the water pressed in on the walls, closing in around her. She squeezed her eyes shut until the walls went away.

She tried to comprehend why she was here. They couldn't possibly think she was the missing hybrid. Coral knew the settings in the AI games were changed. She was the one who hacked them. *There has to be some other reason.*

Maybe Coral is secretly a part of SAS and wants my involvement in AiE to end. But then why bring me here to this lab? She's had plenty of other opportunities to kill me.

The same question ran on repeat in her mind. *Why am I here?*

There were several beeps at the door to her cell. A moment later, it slid open.

Time to find out.

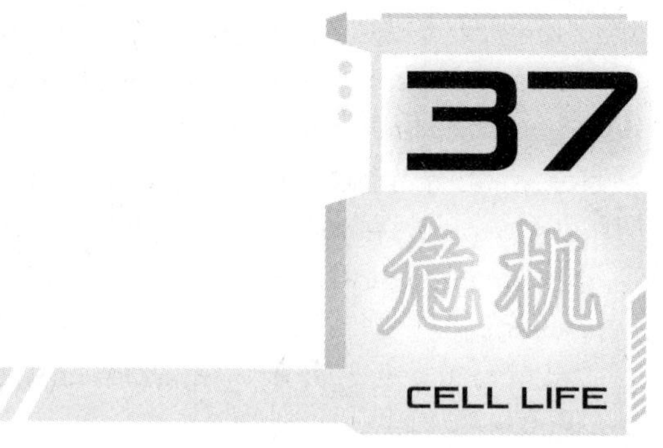

DR. CRANE ENTERED THE ROOM, WEARING THE same lab coat and flanked by security.

Urban drew back. "Who are you? Are you SAS?"

Dr. Crane motioned the guards forward. He let out a short chuckle. "You'd be dead if we were."

The guards withdrew a pair of cuffs and approached Urban.

"What are those?"

"They're harmless, should you cooperate." Dr. Crane's tone was bored. "If you resist, they will administer 50,000 volts of electricity. The alternative is arriving at your destination unconscious."

Warily, Urban extended her arms.

With a click, the cuffs fastened tightly around her wrists and shattered any hopes of escape. Guards escorted her out of the cell.

Urban tried to keep track of where they were going, but eventually gave up. Each fluorescent hallway looked exactly the same.

They crammed into a stuffy elevator and descended to level -2. The doors slid back open, revealing a world saturated in color.

They stepped under a glass walkway with the ocean above.

Coral reef in tangerine, pink, and blue grew around the glass. There were swaying seaweed, floating anemones, even an octopus suctioned to the glass. A clown fish darted in and out of the sea garden. Further above it, larger fish swam together in perfect synchronization.

Urban turned her eyes away from the terrifying beauty of the ocean to focus on the guards. They had the same weapons and uniforms as the ones who'd attacked her earlier.

When was that? Yesterday? Hours ago? Now that she thought about it, she wasn't sure how long she'd been captive.

A briny smell wafted through the tunnel, reminding Urban of the Metropolis Aquarium she'd visited as a child. The thought of New Beijing brought a stab of pain.

I'm so far from home.

At the other end of the walkway, Dr. Crane scanned a keypad with his tatt. A door slid open, revealing a spacious ballroom. After the tunnel surrounded by water, Urban breathed easier.

Long glass lights hung like a curtain from the high, arched ceiling. At the center of the room there were two lavish oak tables. One had medical equipment on it, the type Urban saw at hospitals. The other had a glass-encased model. It displayed a miniature obstacle course.

Gathered around the table were a dozen individuals wearing tailored suits, the latest brands of luxury dresses, and sparkling diamonds. Their perfume and cologne was overpowering.

A shimmering figure in a sparkling dress caught Urban's eye.

Coral.

Urban hardly recognized her former roommate. Gone were her high-top shoes and backward hat. In their place, she wore skeletal white high heels with mini-fans, screws, and bolts, giving her a robotic look. She wore a pencil skirt that accentuated her hips and a high-waisted belt with a silk blouse tucked in. Even her hair was tamed and in perfect silky waves over her shoulder.

Was there anyone she could trust? Even her own family was crumbling from within–because of her.

Realization hit Urban. Coral had an illegal number of enhancements. She was a Camo, but probably also an Artisan and an Inventor. There was no way she was a professional singer and so good at hacking things without those genetics. *I can't believe I didn't catch on to that earlier.*

Who is she really? And who are all these people?

Urban tried scanning them to get their sosh, but her retina display was still disabled.

Then she noticed the figure standing near Coral. Her jaw dropped. She would recognize that light blond hair and athletic stance anywhere.

Orion? What is he doing here?

He caught Urban looking at him. With a smug smirk, he wrapped his arm around Coral's waist, pulled her into him, and whispered something in her ear.

Orion and . . . Coral? They're together? Urban's heart stopped. How many people had betrayed her?

Tears blurred her vision, but Urban blinked them away as a woman approached.

"Ah," the woman said genially. "Our guest has arrived."

Something about the woman gave her pause. She wore a stern suit with a silver cape. Her blond hair was pulled back in a tight ponytail, and her lips were a pale, lifeless color. But it was her deep brown eyes that made Urban's skin crawl.

Inceptor.

With a sudden realization, Urban's eyes darted from the woman, to Orion, then back again. The similarities were clear. The Inceptor running this operation was Orion's mother.

Urban roiled with anger and confusion.

Did Orion know all along I was lying? But then he should know I'm a Natural. If they're the Enhanced prejudiced toward Naturals, why bring me here rather than kill me? Who else other than SAS would do this to me?

"We've so looked forward to meeting you." The Inceptor's voice was rich and smooth, like someone with a high-ranking sosh. "I'm sure you're curious as to why you're here."

A small touch of hysteria almost caused Urban to laugh out loud.

Urban stole a glance at Coral. Her former roommate stood stiffly, eyes refusing to meet hers.

"All will be answered in due time," the Inceptor said. "But before we get to the fun part, we have work to do."

Urban shrank back as Dr. Crane came forward, needle and vial in hand. With a sharp prick, he inserted the needle and withdrew a sample of her blood.

Urban avoided watching, even though those gathered seemed eager to do so.

When the glass vial was full, a technician inserted it into the medical equipment. A hologram appeared, displaying Urban's blood type as O+, along with other stats Urban didn't understand.

The Inceptor pointed at the hologram. "As you can see, her DNA is that of an ordinary Natural. Or is it? We believe this is no ordinary DNA we're looking at. To test our theory, we will be administering the microneedle patch."

The technician stepped forward, a black patch in hand.

Urban's vision swam. It was the same one she had seen in her Genetic Engineering class her first week at PKU. The one in her memories from before being adopted.

Urban took a step back, bumping into a guard's armored chest.

"Don't worry, dear," the Inceptor said reassuringly. "If our theories are in error, the patch will not have an effect on you. If, however, our theories are correct"–her eyes flashed at this–"then we'll have an interesting time."

Urban swallowed. Somehow, she doubted their ideas of interesting aligned.

The guard pushed her forward and the technician put a hand out. "Your arm, please."

Urban didn't move.

The technician sighed and looked meaningfully at one of the guards. Several of them surrounding her pointed their pulsing stun clubs at her neck, should she decide not to cooperate.

"Thank you," the technician said.

Urban wanted to glare, but looked away as a cool, sticky patch adhered to her forearm. As it was pressed into her skin, she felt the slight prick of hundreds of tiny needles embedding in her flesh.

"The microneedles are now combining with her bloodstream and will administer the dose we require," the Inceptor explained tutorially.

Urban felt like she was at her annual doctor's visit. Only, instead of privacy walls, she was on full display for a crowd of onlookers.

It felt violating–wrong.

"Once the patch is administered, her new DNA will be activated."

New DNA?

The Inceptor turned back to the watching guests. "This is the longest part of the process. We'll let our guest return to her quarters to wait for the transformation."

She waved delicate hands toward an adjacent room where the smell of seafood wafted toward them. "In the meantime, might I interest you in some hors d'oeuvres?"

As the group chattered and wandered off, Urban was marched out of the ballroom. Her mind spun furiously all the way back to her cell. Her wrists were uncuffed and a device was strapped to her forearm. The door was locked once more.

Coldness seeped into Urban. The constant blinking light of the vid recorder reminded her of the microneedle patch's constant presence.

She looked at it closely for the first time. A thick metal band wrapped around the patch to hold it in place. Urban tried slipping the patch off of her arm, but it was too tight.

But there was a keypad requiring a scrambling code to release it.

She pressed the keypad and watched as it lit up sixteen glowing dots. Pattern activated. How many combinations could sixteen dots have? She didn't even bother with the math.

It's not like I have anything better to do.

Sitting down on her cot, Urban carefully turned her back to the vid recorder, then strung together several of the dots using her finger.

A glowing line appeared between the ones she'd connected. Then they flashed red and disappeared. Her skin burned.

Urban jerked back.

She examined the band holding the patch in place. For the first time, she noticed the portion of the band jutting out over her arm. The skin underneath that part was smoking and red.

A sick sensation crept into her stomach.

Surely, they wouldn't.

Urban attempted another pattern. Sure enough, the keypad flashed red, then burning pain shot through her arm. Her skin was angry red now.

With each failed attempt they were branding her. Blinding rage made her lightheaded. *When I get out of here . . .*

She looked over her shoulder up at the vid recorder and gave it a death glare.

Just wait.

Urban was dreaming about all the painful things she hoped happened to the Inceptor when a beeping echoed at her cell door. She jolted upright as the base of the door opened. A mini bot rolled in carrying a metal tray of food. It deposited it on the floor before exiting.

Urban moved swiftly to press her face on the cold ground

to watch as the flap opened again and the bot retreated. She caught a glimpse of the endless white walls outside of her cell, but nothing else. The flap wasn't even big enough to squeeze her head through.

With a sigh, she turned to the tray, which contained a bottle of water and three packets of food. Urban opened the largest one and found steamed green beans. The next smaller packet had some orange slices, and the last one, chicken.

Urban sniffed the food. Was it poisoned? Did it contain chemicals that would activate the patch? Was that possible?

But the meal smelled delicious. Normal, even.

Urban considered starving herself. That would show them. But after being in company with the food for a few more minutes, she gave in.

Starvation is a slow way to die. Besides, I'm going to find a way out.

THE DAYS FELL INTO A PREDICTABLE PATTERN. Urban slept until the arrival of breakfast. She'd get up, glare at the vid recorder, wash her face, then carry her tray back to her cot to eat. She took her time with each morsel before swallowing, dragging out the process as much as possible. At least the meals were tolerable–they weren't going to let her starve.

After breakfast was the worst part of the day.

She had a long day of solitude before sleep would come. She'd learned early on that taking naps left her sleepless at night. Now, she kept to a routine that allowed for only one short nap in the afternoon.

The hardest part was the absence of her retina display. Without it, she felt blind, vulnerable, and alone. She was completely cut off from the world and everyone who cared about her. And it allowed her time to think.

Too much time.

After breakfast, when her spirits were lowest, she did a few of her favorite activities. She'd warm up by doing jumping jacks, then work out. She missed the obstacle courses, shooting range, and equipment of Infini-Fit, but made do with exercises using her body weight instead. Pushups, sit-ups, planks, anything that would get her sweating.

She noticed by day ten an increase in her endurance and the number of reps she could do. She began inventing new things to push her limits and to expand targeted areas to include her whole body.

After working out, she typically felt a bit better–like she was accomplishing something rather than rotting in a cell. With the next section of time to kill, she'd brainstorm ways to escape her prison, reanalyze everything involving Coral, the Western Federation, AiE, SAS–anything that might help her know who had kidnapped her and why.

She had made two meager escape attempts. One was by attacking the bot that fed her food, and the other by merely sticking her hand out of the hole in the cell to try and unlock her door. Both had resulted in electric shocks. No one had come by her cell since the microneedle patch had been administered. She hadn't tried again. Yet.

Usually, by the time lunch arrived, her spirits had tanked again and she took a brief nap. Afterward, she'd meditate for a little while, trying not to think about anything. Then it was time for her second workout of the day.

She hadn't wanted anyone watching her to be aware of her capabilities. But they had seen her attack the guards before getting captured. They probably knew anyway. Better to keep in shape and continue training, so by day twenty, she was so bored of her workouts, she caved and added shadow boxing and jiujitsu moves into her afternoon routine.

These new workouts consumed half her afternoon and left her in higher spirits by the time dinner arrived. After dinner, she stretched, worked on balance and yoga, then picked a favorite flick or book and would pretend to rewatch or read it in her mind until she finally drifted off to sleep.

By day thirty-one, even the boxing and jiujitsu routines couldn't help. She yearned, *ached*, for personal interaction.

How long are they going to keep me here? She picked at the microneedle patch on her arm. So far, nothing about it had changed her, at least that she could notice.

She'd explored every inch of her cell. The toilet could be used to do certain arm exercises and was also excellent for jumping up onto for box squats. If she stood on it, she could also reach the vid recorder with her meal tray. She'd managed to smack it down a few times already.

With a satisfactory crunch, it shattered to the floor. She'd enjoyed an hour of blissful privacy before a bot came through the bottom of the door to repair it.

"This is your only warning," the bot had said to her. "Next time, poor behavior will cost you."

But she had still broken the vid recorder on bad days. She'd soon found out this cost her a meal. She was already up to a penalty of four missed meals.

On days when she couldn't stand one more second of the vid recorder watching, she would slide under the metal cot. Most of her body was still visible, but the vid recorder couldn't track her face. It was there she'd let the tears come.

Occasionally, she still tried different codes on the pad. The branding on her arm grew steadily deeper with each failed attempt.

But no matter what she tried, she couldn't find a crack in the system. As her body grew stronger each day, her desire to live shriveled.

I wonder what my family thinks happened. Once, in a rage, she smashed the vid recorder down again and scavenged through it for anything useful. There was nothing.

She screamed in frustration and stomped on the recorder until it broke into tiny parts all over the floor.

Now she wrapped the threadbare blanket around herself and pressed herself into a corner.

What's going on back home? Am I on the news? She could

see the headline now: PKU's top KOL vanishes without a trace. What did Ash, Blossom, and the rest of her team think?

Do they have the Jingcha looking for me? AiE? Is there a warrant out for Coral? What about Everest? Will he try and find me? He has a full-time position with AiE and doesn't have a clue where I went.

She sank her head into her knees.

I hope someone's out there looking for me. I hope they haven't all given up.

Urban lost track of how long she'd been in the corner, but she must have drifted off to sleep, because she awoke to an unusual sound.

With a beeping, the keypad on the door activated and the door retracted with a hiss. Dr. Crane entered.

Urban cautiously stood and saw guards had formed an impenetrable line beyond the doorway.

Urban was so overwhelmed by seeing other people, her mind nearly registered them as friends. They seemed on edge. Their weapons were all pointed at her, but only set to stun. The scientist looked different too. Instead of his white lab coat, he wore a black wet suit.

"It's your big day," Dr. Crane announced, but his eyes darted about.

Urban swallowed. *My last day to escape, and I don't have the faintest idea how to get out.*

Dr. Crane tossed a wetsuit onto her cot. "Change into that."

To Urban's relief, he and the guards left, and she changed into the suit, dread sinking her stomach. *Please don't make me go into the ocean. Please!*

The guards and Dr. Crane returned with the familiar wrist cuffs. This time, Urban didn't bother resisting. To her surprise, they removed the microneedle patch before strapping the cuffs on.

"Come." Dr. Crane motioned her to follow.

As they traveled past the barren white lab rooms, Urban noticed more of the lights flashed red above the cells.

They crammed into the same stuffy elevator, and soon, they were back in the underwater walkway.

I have to escape.

But there were too many guards. Even if she could get away from them, her hands were cuffed and she had no idea which way to go. The odds against her were overwhelming.

There has to be a way out.

As they reached the end of the walkway, instead of heading to the ballroom, like they had previously, they veered right.

Dr. Crane scanned his tatt and a panel opened.

A smaller room filled with people awaited them. Urban was filled with a mixture of deep emotions she didn't recognize. Her isolation had made her hyper-aware of others, yet unsettled and uncertain. Almost shy. She estimated there were about fifty individuals gathered to watch whatever show they'd been promised. The Inceptor stood clothed in an elegant dress resembling a blue wave, laughing in a high-pitched, nasally voice.

Bright light poured in from two glass tanks with a view of the fish and ocean beyond. Currently, both tanks were empty and dry.

The guests were all snacking on dried bits of seaweed and sipping wine. Overwhelmed again by all the people at first, she finally began to pay more specific attention to her surroundings. She saw Coral near the back, half-hidden behind Orion. He had his arm slung around her and was drinking and laughing loudly. Coral, on the other hand, wasn't eating anything, and her eyes kept darting to the tank.

The guards led Urban across pale green carpet toward one of the glass tanks. When her pace slowed, she was shoved forward. Tendrils of fear curled within her as the tank's glass door slid open.

Urban turned wildly and ran straight into a stun club. Two

guards grabbed her and shoved her into the glass cage. The door closed, trapping her inside.

From inside the cage, Urban could barely begin to look out at the crowd of people. When she finally lifted her eyes, she saw Coral again. Her former friend met her eyes and looked quickly away. She gave Orion a quick peck on the cheek and left the room, casting Urban one last look before disappearing.

Urban's heart squeezed.

The Inceptor maneuvered her way onto a small stage. She tapped on her wine glass until the room quieted down. "Now that we're all here, let's commence."

All eyes turned toward the tank.

"Our volunteer will start in this tank, face a series of obstacles, and should she be successful, will finish in the tank over there." She pointed at the other glass cage.

Urban pounded on the glass. "Let me out!"

Though she doubted they could hear, several of the guests looked surprised, even shocked at her actions.

The Inceptor laughed. "Our volunteer is teasing," she reassured everyone.

The Inceptor gave a quick nod at a technician. The glass around Urban began to blur so that she wasn't visible to the guests.

Urban pounded harder. "Someone help me!"

The guests were looking at the other tank, oblivious.

Before the tank completely frosted over, Urban caught a glimpse of the Inceptor lifting her glass in salute. "*Jiayou*, Ms. Lee."

Urban was now invisible in her glass cage.

She slumped to the cold, hard ground. It smelled of formaldehyde.

A gentle trickling sound gradually invaded her consciousness and she looked up. She noticed for the first time the tank was leaking. Salty seawater spread across the floor and toward her.

No, it wasn't leaking.

Urban leaped to her feet.

The panel of glass separating her tank from the ocean was

retracting upward. A small stream of icy water hit her ankles.

They're going to drown me.

It was like her reoccurring nightmare of Lucas, all over again. When he had dragged her to the bottom of their parents' fish tank. She had to kick him in the groin to escape. Now, there was no one to kick except for herself.

I never should have trusted Coral. I never should have trusted anyone.

The cold water climbed up her shins and then thighs.

Urban thought about her family and Everest. They would never know that she had died in some freak science experiment. She pictured Everest's face when he received the news. His kind eyes, the smell of jasmine, his shock of black hair. She'd never run her fingers through that hair again–

Static broke overhead.

Urban's eyes darted around the tank and found a tiny speaker in one of the upper corners. The water gushed around her now, beating against her waist.

More static. "Miss Lee? Can you hear me?"

Urban's skin crawled. One of the panels cleared so that she had a view of the ocean outside, and she spotted the body attached to the voice: Dr. Crane in a wetsuit, flippers, and some sort of scuba tank with a headpiece. Something red blinked on his headpiece. A vid recorder?

Of course, they'd want to record my death.

"Miss Lee, can you hear me?" Dr. Crane waved at her now, scattering a school of fish.

"Yes," Urban said dully. The cold water lapped at her chest. "Can you stop drowning me?" she blurted angrily. She hugged herself, trying to stay warm.

A grating chuckle broke across the speaker system. He ignored her plea. "Here's how this experiment will be conducted. Once you are immersed in the water, you will be guided through a maze." Dr. Crane gestured at the ocean surrounding him. Several yellow lights flashed on, revealing branches of tunnels.

"Follow them to the other glass tank and you win."

Urban looked at the course, fighting panic. "I can't hold my breath for that long."

The scientist swatted at a fish circling around his head. "That's the point. Only a hybrid will survive this test."

So they *did* think she was possibly the hybrid.

He made a motion with his hands and the glass panel began rising faster. "Test subject number three activated."

Urban gasped at the sudden influx of ocean water.

He looked at her. "Let's see if you have some fish genes in you yet."

"You've got the wrong person," Urban pled.

"A specimen with a sense of humor. I like that."

Anger and despair burned together in Urban.

"We have a waiting crowd of guests. We all hope you succeed." Dr. Crane began swimming away, black flippers causing ripples in the snaking seaweed below.

"Wait!" Urban called out. The water in the tank was so high she had to paddle to stay afloat. "I'll drown!"

The scientist kept swimming. "That would be disappointing," came his response.

"No! Stop!" Salty water seeped into her lungs. She coughed it up and concentrated on keeping her head above water.

There has to be another way to beat this test. How long can I hold my breath? She closed her eyes. *Not long enough.*

Eyes still shut, she floated on her back to give her legs and arms a break, and slowed her breathing and closed her eyes.

Think.

The dulled roar of rushing water filled around her. Her eyes flashed open.

The glass ceiling was even closer, and a shaft of fear stabbed at her.

If I knew the way through the maze, maybe I could survive.

She looked out at the cold blue ocean beyond the cage.

The obstacle course was a series of identical tunnels illuminated by lights. Some curved and wrapped in unpredictable patterns, others seemed to be straight, but then dead-ended or branched into different directions. There didn't appear to be a clear path to the other tank at all.

But what's to stop me from swimming straight to the tank? Why should I stick to the artificial glowing paths?

Urban decided to try. Diving down, she swam through the first part of the tunnel, through the yellow barrier lights. But as the course turned right, she turned left.

Instantly, a jolt of pain went through her entire body as she hit what felt like an invisible barrier. Before she ran out of air, she swam quickly back up.

So that's not an option. I have to figure out the shortest way through the maze. That's my only chance.

Urban treaded water while studying the maze again.

She slowed her breathing, holding it for five seconds, then ten, then fifteen. After thirty seconds, she bumped her head against the top of the glass ceiling.

Panic threatened to make her lose concentration. She wanted to hyperventilate, to rapidly suck in the last of the air. With all the self-control she could muster, she held her breath for forty seconds.

If I leave this tank, I'm stuck in the maze. No one's going to be able to come rescue me.

Pressing her mouth up against the ceiling, she inhaled her biggest breath yet–her last.

Then she dove.

URBAN SWAM INTO THE MAZE. THE VAST BLUE ocean stretched in all directions visible beyond the translucent tunnel. Her lungs were overly full of air, her eyes stung from the salt water, and despite her wetsuit, her skin was cold. A school of fish darted away.

Her gaze settled on the fork in the path ahead. She knew the right led to a dead end, but after that, she didn't know which way to go.

She swam to the left, while trying to keep an even pace and slow her need for oxygen. The marine life around her stayed clear of the invisible barrier. They, too, must be unable to cross it.

Urban came to another branch in the maze that split in three directions. She tried not to think about the lack of air while she considered them.

The path in the middle had a sign that glowed "this way," above it, while the other two said, "incorrect".

Urban swam straight ahead. *Strange. What's the point of a maze if the answer is obvious? Or maybe that's to throw me off. Reverse psychology.*

Her lungs ached. *No time to second-guess.*

She swam until she came to another fork in the tunnel where, again, the path was clearly marked.

Urban swam blindly, air running out, bumping into the barrier in her haste. A jolt of pain shot up her arms. She nearly gasped but stopped the influx of water just in time.

The maze split again, and, glancing at the illuminated signs, she swam right.

Her lungs were collapsing in on themselves. Pain radiated from her chest. Her movements seemed sluggish and her senses dulled.

Panicking, she forced herself to swim faster.

I can hold my breath for one minute and twenty seconds. I don't have much time.

Urban searched the base of the tunnel for anything that might help her. But there was no escaping the water coffin.

Pain.

It seared through her lungs, compelling every fiber in her being to breathe. She no longer thought of anything but the need for air–it overrode her ability to think.

She closed her eyes.

I have to take a breath.

She opened her mouth knowing the last of her air–and hope–was gone.

Cold ocean, tasting of salt and fish, surged into Urban's lungs. In that split second, she anticipated with despair the pain, the choking sensation that would inevitably follow.

It didn't come.

Urban involuntarily swallowed the water, and to her surprise her lungs stopped burning. Cautiously, she gulped more water. She didn't cough or choke.

She could breathe.

Baffled, she experimented several more times. Then elation filled her. "I'm alive!" she rejoiced in a chorus of muted bubbles.

Urban spun in a circle. Everything seemed more vivid and

in focus. Giant tuna floated above her, fins glittering silver and yellow in the light. The coral reef below burst with rich marine life.

She saw Dr. Crane floating nearby, but when he motioned at her to continue, she ignored him.

How can I see perfectly underwater? That must have been why the signs were telling me which way to go. Without the Aqua enhancement, I wouldn't be able to read them.

Enhancement.

She examined her hands and skin. Nothing looked different. *But I'm Enhanced. I have to be.*

I'm the one they were searching for after all. I'm the hybrid.

Urban remembered the grotesque monkeys in their cells. *I have to get out of here.*

She swam in the opposite direction of the tank at the other end of the maze, gliding through the water like the fish swimming next to her. After searching in vain for an escape, she bobbed in the middle of the tunnel, considering her options.

She could go forward and end up in the glass cage exactly where they wanted her. Or she could keep exploring the maze to see if there was a way out into the ocean. Those were her only two options.

Outside of the barrier, Dr. Crane was frantically gesturing.

A flash of movement caught her eye.

Further below, in the darker parts of the water, several Aquas herded something toward the maze. *It looks like a . . . whale?*

Urban gasped.

It wasn't a whale.

The biggest shark she had ever seen swam lazily forward, ignoring the spears and hooks of the surrounding Aquas.

"Stupid Megalodon," Dr. Crane's voice roared in her com link. "Someone get that thing into position!"

Megalodon.

The word was familiar. Urban had heard it in her genetic

enhancement class. The Megalodon was a type of shark said to be the size of a whale. But wasn't it extinct? How had they managed to bring it back? Fear stung her like a jellyfish.

The Megalodon thrashed its huge tail, scattering several of the Aquas in its wake, then charged one of them. The creature retreated only after being stabbed by multiple spears.

The Aquas managed to coax it toward the maze. The lights around that section blinked off and they prodded the shark in. Then the lights flashed back on, encapsulating it in the tunnel with Urban.

No.

Above her, Dr. Crane waved wildly, then pointed to the end of the maze as the Megalodon noticed her.

Urban swam quickly toward the other end of the maze and then stopped to look back. *They wouldn't kill the hybrid. Would they?*

The shark was only one turn away.

I'm not sticking around to find out.

The shark bore down on Urban, but a sudden flash of light appeared between them.

BOOM!

The entire tunnel vibrated from the force of the Megalodon slamming against an invisible barrier. The massive shark continued pummeling its head against it.

Urban shuddered. It looked like there was nothing but a few lights separating her from razored teeth the size of hoverboards.

The lights at the bottom of the tunnel stopped blinking.

This time, when the shark crashed into the barrier, its jaw slipped under, sharp teeth gnawing on the invisible force.

Urban swiftly swam away. When she glanced back, the barrier was completely gone and the shark swam toward her again.

She threw up her arms to protect herself.

Right before the shark reached her, another blinking barrier of lights appeared and the shark crashed into it, also.

BOOM!

Urban continued swimming like this, with the shark forcing her onward until she reached the end of the maze. She entered the tank and watched, trembling, as the panel rose, separating her from the Megalodon.

Relief flooded her, but then she turned. In front of her, the room was exactly as Urban had left it. The thick carpet was still a sickly green, the lights too bright, and the guests all chatted, laughed, and sipped wine as if they hadn't witnessed her ordeal.

Only Urban had changed–transformed. Everything was happening too quickly. It was startling, unreal, and made her feel numb inside.

Suddenly, a patron pointed excitedly at her. They all crowded around the tank, staring in wonder.

Urban started to hyperventilate. She needed to get away. She needed to escape.

The Inceptor made smooth hand gestures and spoke, but it was impossible to decipher her words from underwater.

Urban swam to a corner and in desolation curled up in the fetal position. The water around her slowly depleted and the Inceptor's voice became audible.

"–unlike any other DNA in the world. It's revolutionary. Now people can become Enhanced later in life. This will completely alter the course of history."

Urban wasn't sure how long she sat there. Wet, cold, and trapped. When she finally looked up again, the guests were all gone and she was alone in her glass cage. Her body ached. She felt feverish and her body trembled involuntarily.

What's happening to me?

Tears streamed down her face as the last of the seawater drained away.

I'm the hybrid. The thought brought no relief, only a constricting in her chest.

What will they do with me?

URBAN WASN'T SURE HOW MUCH TIME HAD passed when a hissing sound penetrated her consciousness. The glass walls around her lifted. The guests were gone, replaced instead by security officers.

Standing, Urban balled her fists.

I'm not going back with them.

With a guttural cry, she lunged at the guard closest to her and threw him off-balance. Spinning, she sent a back kick toward another. She bobbed and weaved out of the way of stun clubs, dancing just out of the flashing orbs' sting.

An amber mist rained down from the ceiling, cold and wet against her skin.

Her heart skipped a beat when she noticed that the guards all wore masks.

She lashed out at several more, getting a few good kicks in before an overwhelming sense of weariness overtook her.

Her mind and movement grew slow.

It was hard to remain standing, as if the ground kept tilting to one side.

Rough hands grabbed her as a guard shoved her to the floor and cuffed her hands. Everything turned slowly black.

When Urban awoke, she was lying on the cement floor in her cell.

Her body ached and she'd never felt so exhausted in her life. She managed to push herself into a sitting position.

A tray of food sat inches from her face. Her lungs were raw and full of fluid, as if she'd recently recovered from pneumonia. She was surprised her asthma hadn't kicked in. To top it off, she had a throbbing headache.

With curious trepidation, she explored her skin. Nothing felt different. And yet, she had the sense her DNA had been dramatically altered. Her body felt unfamiliar and it was unsettling.

I'm an Aqua now, she thought to herself.

She knew Aquas were all expert swimmers. Lucas could breathe and see vividly underwater. But how?

Her stomach growled.

She was suddenly aware that all the changes in her body had left her with a ravenous appetite. She'd also exerted herself physically in a different way than she'd ever done. It seemed her captors had anticipated this and her normal portion of food had doubled in size. Urban hungrily consumed beef noodles with broccoli and gulped down a protein shake.

"Miss Lee, it is now nap time." A robotic voice startled her.

She paced up and down her cell, ignoring the command. *It's time to find a way out.*

A light amber mist poured down from the ceiling.

No!

She barely had time to get to her cot before she passed out again.

Urban awoke to a sharp pain in her arm. An IV stuck out of her.

"Make sure she gets a double dose of protein infusion," someone was saying. "And up the painkillers."

Urban tried moving, but straps kept her firmly secured on a cold table. Medical equipment beeped nearby, and the place smelled of antiseptic and blood. Dr. Crane, another man in a lab coat, and several medbots hovered around her. One of them checked a needle attached to clear tubes pumping blood from her arm. Urban grew queasy at the sight.

Next to her, projected 3D models of a human body spun slowly. Urban realized with a start that they were of her. Her lungs looked different. She tried to remember her biology classes and what her internal organs were supposed to look like. Certainly not that.

She tried sitting up, but restraints bit into her.

A middle-aged man in a lab coat looked over from one of the 3D models. "Ah. The patient has awoken." His thin, cracked lips split into a wisp of a smile, dark eyes glittering. Something about the way his eyes kept blinking was familiar.

"How are you feeling?"

Urban moistened her lips. "What's–what's happening?"

"We need your DNA, the *hybrid's* DNA, to complete our genomics work."

Urban had a million questions, but her mind was dulled with fear. "How did–how did you know?"

The man moved closer until he was standing directly next to the bedside.

"Because, I designed you."

A second went by, then two, then three. Urban's eyes widened. He was older than the vid Coral had shown her, and clean-shaven now . . . but the resemblance was undeniable. "You're not–" She stopped, then started again. "*You're* Dr. Rai? My father?"

"If you mean, did I contribute my Y gene to experiment number 203, which was *you,* then yes."

Urban frowned "But then . . . who did I meet in Texicana?" Even as she said the words, she realized her mistake. The man she'd met didn't have a twitch to his eyes like Dr. Rai did from the vid–like the man standing before her. *How did I miss that detail?*

"Ah. The plant Coral set up? I see you fell for that as well." Dr. Rai picked up a vial and flicked it. "She's pretty brilliant, managing to find an actor who not only resembled me, but was able to persuade you to give up a blood sample. That was all a way for us to get you to the Western Federation and check your DNA. Had to be sure you were the right one before bringing you here."

Coral again. And now this.

"But what about everything I was told?" Urban's mind ached as much as her body. "Did a colleague put me up for adoption? He said I failed as the hybrid. Was everything an act?"

Dr. Rai inserted a syringe into the vial. "Mostly true, actually."

Lillian. Still not sisters.

Dr. Rai continued. "The only part falsified was that it was actually always known you were the hybrid, but I had to wait until the time was right to be reunited. I was, indeed, on the run for my life."

"So now you're going to imprison your daughter?" Tears surfaced but she blinked them away.

"Daughter." He said the word slowly as if testing it out.

A spark of hope warmed Urban's chest.

"Of course, you are my flesh and blood." Dr. Rai's eyes drifted over to the 3D models, and his face held something indecipherable.

The hope in Urban's chest flickered.

"But there are wrongs to right. The entire state of the world rests on the work we're conducting in this lab. Naturals around the globe are depending on this. On you." His eyes turned back to her. "Can you not understand?"

Urban tasted bile. She wanted to help Naturals, but even if she might be the hybrid, she had never considered being experimented on against her will. Never had she felt so trapped, degraded, powerless–and used.

Dr. Rai continued. “Our experiments would only last a few more years, and then you’d have a global impact–”

“Years?” Urban interrupted. “A few more *years*?”

“Well, yes. This sort of work takes time.”

“Let me go.” Urban’s voice hitched. “Please.”

“I’m sorry, but that’s the one thing I cannot do.”

In desperation, Urban tried to lunge at Dr. Rai and he stepped back in surprise. Restraints cut into her skin, but she ignored them, thrashing and twisting.

“Let me go!” To her dismay, she began to weep. “Please. There has to be a different way. Please.”

“I’m sorry,” Dr. Rai said. “Sometimes what we create must be sacrificed for the greater good.” He motioned at a medbot.

The bot removed the IV, then wheeled Urban, shaking, back to her cell. After lowering her to the ground, still tied up, it left the room with the gurney. When the door closed, Urban’s restraints unlocked and fell to the ground.

Choking on her sobs, she rubbed at her arms. Every bone in her body ached, each muscle felt stretched and torn. And her heart felt like it would never beat again.

A tray of food awaited her, but she pushed it away and crawled under her cot.

Through her tears, she stared up at the metal cot, then blinked. Instead of solid stainless steel above her, there was a crude painting of Federation Mandarin characters inked in black.

Weiji. Crisis.

Urban’s brow wrinkled. Where had she seen it before?

Her eyes widened.

Coral.

When they’d first met, her former roommate explained she had the character *crisis* tattooed on her forearm. The word was made up of two characters: dangerous and opportunity. *"For every crisis, there is both danger and opportunity,"* Coral had explained. *"It's all a matter of perspective."*

What was the character *weiji* doing here, under her cot? Surely it wasn't a coincidence that Coral had the same thing tattooed on her? Was it possible she had done this?

But when, and why?

"Dangerous opportunity," she repeated to herself. She traced the characters with her fingers.

Could it be that there's an opportunity in all this somewhere?

Was the message to communicate hope?

Urban snorted.

Coral betrayed me.

But she couldn't escape the feeling it was from Coral. That Coral had meant for her to see it, and maybe there was a deeper meaning behind it.

But what?

DANGEROUS OPPORTUNITY. SO, WHAT'S THE opportunity here?

Other than transforming into a constantly sleeping and eating version of Lucas, she couldn't think of anything.

Urban gazed idly at her wall while nibbling around a chicken bone.

She stopped mid-bite and examined her hands.

I'm an Aqua now. An Aqua!

She looked up at the blinking vid recorder, then her gaze shifted down at the chicken bone on her tray. She turned it over in her fingers.

I have an idea that just might work . . .

She spent a few minutes visually mapping out her plan and executing it in her mind until she was confident it would work. Energy tingled within her as she considered her timing. It would be best to escape at night, when there were fewer people wandering the halls. But without her retina display, she had no idea what time it was.

She would have to go now, before they came to experiment on her again.

She cast a nervous glance at the vid recorder. Then she sprang up and sprinted to the toilet and climbed on top. She dashed the camera to the ground and began stomping on it.

Instantly, mist sprayed down.

Here we go.

Grabbing the thin blanket from her cot, Urban stuffed it into the bottom of the sink and turned on the water.

Taking a deep breath, she raced back to her tray of food and tucked the chicken bone in a fold of her suit before sprinting back to the flooded sink.

Mist completely filled the room, clinging to her like early morning dew. But Urban didn't breathe it in. Instead, she immersed her face in the sink, keeping alert to any change as she breathed in the water.

Soon, the gas stopped raining down. Urban waited a moment before lifting her head. The air was clear. Urban unplugged the sink, threw her wet blanket under the cot, and sprawled out on top.

Not a moment too soon. The door beeped, and a bot hovered in and whirred toward the smashed vid recorder.

Urban closed her eyes, pretending to be asleep.

She lay motionless while the bot cleaned up the broken pieces. Finally, it left, but as it did, footsteps approached.

Her heart raced.

The door unlocked, and with a hiss, opened. Urban peeked through her lashes and saw four people step into the room. An armed guard, Dr. Crane, and what seemed to be two business people.

"We plan on treating her with bat DNA this afternoon," someone explained. Urban's skin crawled. It was the Inceptor.

Their voices began to fade down the hallway, and Urban saw she was left alone with Dr. Crane and the armed guard.

She remained limp as the doctor and guard lifted her onto a gurney. As they strapped her in, Urban inflated her chest and abdomen. With a swipe of a tatt, the straps holding her locked.

"I'm going to sweep the room and make sure it's secure," the guard said. "One of the surveillance guys said the vid recorder went down again."

"We're pressed for time today," Dr. Crane said with irritation. "I'll meet you there."

Urban's gurney rolled out of the room and down the hall. After they turned, her pulse quickened, but she kept her eyes shut. She could almost feel the large, glass vid recorder staring down at her.

"Dr. Crane bringing in the patient for further testing."

There was a metallic click, then the sound of a heavy wall sliding away, and the gurney moved again. With a thud, the wall closed behind them.

Urban opened her eyes.

Bright fluorescent lights gleamed harshly. Next to her gurney, the doctor strolled at a leisurely pace.

Urban's fingers tightened around the sharp chicken bone. She was grateful she hadn't been searched. Exhaling a breath, she used the extra space and wiggled her hand loose.

She tightened her hand around the bone.

In one swift movement, Urban went for the doctor's hand.

SHE USED WHAT LITTLE BIT OF FLEXIBILITY THE gurney allowed her to drive the bone into his wrist. Dr. Crane gave a high-pitched yell and jerked back.

He lifted his head and bellowed, "Security!"

Cradling his injured hand, he began to run, and gas poured down from the ceiling.

Clenching her teeth, Urban stretched her hands until she was able to unbuckle her waist strap and slide her legs free, but her upper body was stuck.

As the gas sank closer, Urban took in a long, deep breath and held it.

One minute and twenty seconds–starting now.

A low, metallic grind echoed through the hall. The security checkpoint reopened and she saw a masked security officer racing toward her.

She rocked back and forth with as much force as she could muster, attempting to tip the gurney over. Finally, she crashed to the side, stopping centimeters from the ground, the safety belts cutting into her arms.

Heavy, booted steps drew closer as Urban managed to get to her knees. Her chest burned with the urge to breathe.

She swung the gurney still strapped to her back at the approaching guard. With a grunt, he staggered and landed next to her. At the same moment, Urban kicked off his mask.

At the other end of the hall stood a reception center with several benches made of coral reef, an aquarium with jellyfish, a snack dispenser, and a marble fountain.

Encumbered by the gurney, she nonetheless rushed toward the fountain and dropped her head in the water, instantly sucking in deep gulps of water before holding her breath and standing again.

I have to get this thing off my back.

The dispenser. Urban charged at it full speed, lowering the gurney the best she could straight at the machine.

Glass shattered as the gurney crashed into the dispenser.

Several power bars and a bag of seaweed lodged in the front of the gurney. Urban dropped next to a chunk of glass protruding from the machine and began using it to saw away at the safety belt.

It was agonizingly slow.

The thud of security boots echoed closer.

Come on. Come on!

She worked faster. Sawing furiously at the restraints.

Snap.

The device broke off. Quickly, Urban reached for the last strap across her chest and managed to wiggle out of it. The gurney fell away.

A shout from the other end of the hall made her look up. Security officers wearing gas masks swarmed the lobby. Urban sprinted toward the exit but several guards already blocked it.

Urban aimed a kick at the first one. In nearly the same motion, she ripped the mask off the next and ran as she placed the mask on her own face and inhaled.

The last guard dove at her, swinging a fist.

Urban ducked out of the way just in time. His meaty hand smacked the wall with a crack. He pulled his fist back and crumbled plaster fell to the ground.

The security officer came at Urban from the front, hands thrusting out to grab her neck.

Urban slipped out of reach and dropped low. She grabbed the officer around his midsection, sweeping him to the ground with a trip and shoulder flip.

The officer tried to throw a jab at Urban, but she dodged. *All it will take is one well-aimed punch from him and I'm done.*

Urban blocked with her forearm and hands, struggling to back up and get to her feet. She tried to pass his legs, but the officer mirrored her movements. Scooting forward, he attempted to trap his legs around her, all while throwing punches.

Urban kept her head tight and close to her body, protecting against his blows. Finally, she was able to stand and quickly grabbed his ankles.

In her periphery, she saw another security officer sprint toward them.

The officer in front of her tried to kick out of Urban's hold, but she swiftly adjusted her stance and straddled his side, holding him to the ground by his neck, while using her body weight to pin his chest. Grimly, she was grateful for all the side control and guard passes Orion had made her practice.

Urban slid into mount, flattening to spread her weight over the officer's body. Bucking, the officer tried to dislodge her.

She yanked the officer's gas mask off and threw it out of reach. He clawed at his neck as she sprang to her feet and backed away.

Facing the exit once more, she noticed there was another guard blocking it.

Urban stopped.

Not a guard.

Familiar blond hair and amber eyes stared her down.

No, it can't be.

Before her, guarding the exit, stood Orion.

A SMIRK PLAYED AT THE CORNER OF ORION'S lips. "Well done."

Urban's blood turned to ice. She breathed heavily as she assessed her options. *I can't beat him in any sort of combat.* She took a quick look around for something to use to defend herself.

"Do you really think you can get past me?" Orion asked. "You're too easy to read, Urban. Really, the hard part was pretending like I believed all your lies."

Urban tried to swallow the anger and fear rising in her throat.

"I will give you credit for surprising me on the hybrid front," Orion remarked. "I didn't see that one coming until the Gamelyon was released to protect you."

Olive had mentioned the Gamelyon as well. *What does that mean? Who is Orion working for?*

"You should already know who I work for by now."

Urban's skin crawled as Orion seemed to read her every thought. She'd thought she'd been doing well hiding her emotions from Inceptors, but now she realized how wrong she'd been.

"The World Enhancement Organization has a vested interested in the development of Enhancements," Orion said.

"But not everyone is in agreement on what should happen if the hybrid were ever found. Some of us have taken matters into our own hands and formed a sub group of the WEO. We won't let their political games and bureaucratic red tape slow us down from changing the world."

Orion drew close to her. "You know, Coral was convinced you were the hybrid from the start. I must admit, even I doubted her. You seemed too"–Orion scrutinized her–"unimpressive. Coral claimed she never changed the mode in the PKU arena to test out her theory, and that your hybrid DNA is actually what destroyed it. But I had already learned you were a Natural by reading you, and thought that was the reason it broke."

Urban's breath stilled. Her hybrid DNA really had crashed the AI all along. Urban felt so stupid for ever trusting Coral.

"Coral's the best triple agent we have. I should have believed her earlier. And *you* should never have believed her. You really thought someone just found Rai Reed and sent you his address?" Orion threw his head back and laughed. "That was all her doing–"

Pop!

Orion's body seized and sparked before dropping stiffly to the floor.

"He always talked too much."

Urban spun and watched a masked figure shimmer into view, stun gun still extended.

Coral.

Instinctively, Urban backed away.

Coral holstered her weapon and extended her hands in a gesture of peace. "I'm going to get you out of here. The security vids are all disabled for the next minute. After that, I can't help you."

Urban stared at Coral, heart thumping wildly in her chest. *Help me? What game is she playing at now?*

"Look, I know you don't trust me, but I'm your only chance

of escape. You'll need these." She extended what looked like a pair of mechanical flippers.

Urban made no move to get them.

Sighing, Coral placed them on the floor, then turned toward the exit. The scanner flashed red as she tried opening the door, and a disembodied robotic voice rang out.

"Unauthorized exit restricted."

Coral went to the control panel.

Hesitantly, Urban made a move toward the flippers. *Is Coral really trying to get me out of here? Why now? And what other option do I have but to accept her help?*

One of the vid recorders near the exit started blinking.

"Uh, is that supposed to be coming back online?" Urban spoke for the first time.

Coral looked up from her work. Without missing a beat, she lifted one of her flamethrowing arms and aimed. Fire engulfed the vid recorder until it sparked and dripped metal before Coral returned to her work.

A moment later, the door beeped green and hissed.

"Go!" Coral urged.

But Urban didn't move. "Was everything a lie? Were we"–her voice faltered–"ever friends?"

Coral's mouth twisted. Her voice dropped. "I didn't have a choice." She glanced up, her eyes begging Urban to understand.

Urban only stared at her, trying not to think of what she had endured the last few weeks.

"I can't afford friends." Coral's jaw tightened and she looked away. "I'm sorry."

Urban wanted to speak, but words evaded her.

Coral whipped her head around. "They're coming. Run!"

A dozen security officers rounded the corner right as Coral vanished.

Urban spun and sprinted away.

Vast blue ocean stretched before her as she escaped through

the nano-glass tunnel. Despite her new Aqua abilities, the sight made her chest tighten.

Urban sprinted into an empty pod room and smashed her fist on the keypad. An error message popped up.

[Cannot open pod until main channel is sealed.]

Urban hurriedly selected that option and a glass doorway descended. At the other end of the walkway, guards surged toward her.

"Come on, come on," Urban hissed in frustration as the door slowly closed.

The deep blue of the sea surrounded her on all other sides. An occasional fish swam by, unbothered by the commotion of her life. Soon, she'd be out there with them.

She swallowed. *What if my Aqua abilities aren't fully developed? What if I can only breathe underwater for a short time?*

The glass door was now only a small space away from closing, but the guards were already halfway across the tunnel. Would the door stop closing if it sensed movement?

"Hurry!" Urban coaxed the door under her breath.

The guards were only a few meters away as the door finally shut with a sucking sound. A second later, the guards crashed into the air-tight barrier. Their shouting echoed through the circular chamber as if Urban were inside a fish bowl.

Ignoring them, Urban faced the pod entrance and took a deep breath. "Here it goes." She slipped on the flippers, then opened the panel separating her from the ocean.

Cold water flooded in around her so fast it pushed her up against the pod's wall. She swirled around the room as the tsunami-like flood toyed with her.

Once the pod was full of water, the movement settled down and Urban managed to get her bearings. Hesitantly, she took a breath of the briny water. It tasted like rotting seaweed, but she could breathe.

She activated a switch on the flippers and they began automatically propelling her out without her having to do any work.

Below her, a bright coral reef glowed next to a tunnel. Several people in it gawked up at her. Above her stretched the gray concrete and thick-paned nano-glass windows of the facility. Some of the windows had lights on and she could see desks, labs, meeting rooms, and a few bunkers inside.

Only one side of the ring was not man-made. There, the entrance to the cave yawned open, and Urban swam that direction, fish darting away as she neared them.

What sounded like a fog horn blared behind her. The artificial blue lighting shifted to red. Inside the building, people began running toward the other pods and climbed into the waiting submarines.

A grating sound filled the water as a large doorway opened and something flashed silver. Urban caught a glimpse of giant fins and razored teeth.

Terror seized her.

Megalodon.

Dr. Crane says they need me for several more years. They won't kill me.

The huge shark freed itself and swam straight for her.

I think.

The Megalodon's power and grace were almost mesmerizing. Urban swam furiously away, adding her own kicks and strokes to the automated flippers.

It couldn't possibly fit in the cave. She just had to reach it.

Her legs and arms burned. She was close to the cave, but she sensed the Megalodon behind her. Casting a quick glance over her shoulder, she felt her heart stop.

The shark was closing in.

Urban swam like a whirlwind, arms a windmill of activity and legs kicking until they felt ready to fall off. Her eyes stayed fixed on the cave, not daring to look back again.

She reached the entrance, and within seconds, the wall

shook from the force of the Megalodon hitting it. The impact of its raw power spun Urban in a somersault, deeper into the cave. For once, Urban was grateful for the Megalodon's huge size. Otherwise, it would have easily followed her in.

She drew in a few steadying breaths. Her heart felt like it was being squeezed by all eight arms of an octopus. As she continued swimming, the pulsing red cavern fell further behind, and it grew harder for Urban to see. She tried not to think about what else might be swimming with her in the darkness.

Eventually, the blackness was so thick, Urban despaired of ever finding her way out.

Then, up ahead, spears of bright light filtered down from holes in the cave. Relieved, Urban swam up toward them, ears popping from the change in pressure.

Blurred trees and a patch of light blue sky became visible before her head broke the surface. The stillness of the water was instantly shattered by a cacophony of chirping, croaks, and the hum of insects. The air was humid and warm and smelled of damp earth and soured fruit.

Urban pulled herself up onto a shelf of rock and onto land. She peered back down into the water to see if her pursuers were close, but it was too dark.

After catching her breath, she stood and removed her flippers. Her bare feet made suction noises in the black mud as she climbed over roots, through wild underbrush, and under vibrant green foliage.

It didn't take her long to reach the edge of the jungle.

The mud turned into hot, dry sand under Urban. The sun beat down harshly, reflecting off of the ocean, blinding and stretching for kilometers in all directions. She jogged around the land and quickly discovered she was on a tiny island.

There were no other people. No way to call for help. Nowhere to go.

I'm trapped. Again.

URBAN COLLAPSED ON THE SAND UNDER A palm tree. She tried accessing QuanNao for the hundredth time, but without success. Strangely enough, though, her offline inventory flickered to life.

Her favorite stored memories, tools, and items appeared. Urban sorted through them for a map or anything useful.

A scroll caught her eye and she frowned. Opening it without her XR suit and while offline proved difficult, but she managed to unravel it using voice commands.

It was the NFT of the scroll her great-grandmother had painted. The pond with goldfish swimming in unity was even more vivid than she'd remembered. The way the colors contrasted and blended all at once. The peace it held. All of it telling a story about family.

It was the work of a true master, and yet, Mother had said it reminded her of Urban's style.

It felt like home.

My great-grandmother was an Artisan. So was my mother. I may not belong by blood to the Lees, but that doesn't mean I'm not one of them.

I have to find my way back.

Urban contemplated wading into the ocean and swimming away, but where could she go? Even though she could swim and breathe underwater, it would take days, if not weeks, to get anywhere, and she'd need water and food. She wondered if her body could convert the salt water into a consumable liquid.

There were too many unknowns out in the ocean. Not to mention, she was exhausted from her recent swim and had no intention of facing the Megalodon again.

She grabbed hold of a vine and used it to pull herself up into a tree to hide until she could come up with a plan. She scurried up as far as the tree would allow. At this height, she could barely see the jungle floor.

A crunching noise made Urban tense.

Several seconds later, three figures in diving suits crashed through the foliage below. They lugged heavy scuba tanks, tridents, and had face masks slung around their necks. The one leading the way was an Aqua without any gear.

As their voices grew louder, Urban's grip on the tree tightened.

One of the divers, with radiant green hair, threw her air tank onto the sand. "She could be anywhere. There's an entire sea to search."

"But there's nowhere for her to go," the Aqua said. "The closest land is three thousand kilometers away. She couldn't reach it . . ."

They continued on out of earshot.

Urban tried to recreate a mental map of the world in her head. Unfortunately, she'd never taken much time to memorize the particulars of the Pacific Ocean.

I could be anywhere.

Her throat was raw from thirst. She had to find water.

Snap.

Below, a Super with a pulsing stun club pointed his weapon in different directions. It pulsed faster as he pointed it nearer her vicinity. He halted when the weapon pointed at the tree, maintaining a steady stream of light.

Urban shrank back as he looked up into the branches.

"I think I found her," he called.

Urban peered down at the Super. He was attempting to scale the tree, but due to his size, kept breaking the branches he grabbed ahold of. After falling back for a third time, he resigned himself to patrolling around the tree's base.

Urban crept silently down, doing her best to blend in with the growing shadows. When she was directly above the Super, she paused.

Taking in a silent breath, she vaulted off the tree and landed hard on the Super.

They tumbled into the thickets, roots and branches cutting into them, before rolling to a stop. The stun club was nowhere to be seen, but the Super wrestled Urban, managing to pin her down.

Urban's juijitsu training kicked in.

Bucking her hips upward, she managed to flip him on his side. Quickly, she moved to trap his arm. He fought wildly, but couldn't escape. Using her free arm, Urban put him in a triangle choke.

Pulse pounding wildly in her ears, she forced herself to count to fifteen. The Super's body jerked and then fell limp.

Slowly, Urban released her hold on him. He didn't move. *That should keep him out of my way for a little while.* She searched him and found a canteen of water, which she quickly drained.

The island would be overrun soon. The ocean was her only option. She collected the stun club off the ground and continued toward the water. When she reached the shoreline, she stopped short. Dozens of guards patrolled the sand.

Her heart pounded.

Boots crashed behind her.

It's my only option.

She quickly surveyed the beach again. If she ran really fast, she might be able to get past the guards.

One . . .

Two . . .

She inhaled a deep breath.

Three!

She sprinted across the warm beach, sand flying up behind her.

There was a shout. To her right, more guards streamed out from the jungle. They swarmed around her on all sides but one–the water.

Urban ran faster and reached the ocean's shallows.

In the distance, an odd rippling in the water caught her eye. Something was rising out of it. In shock, Urban came to an abrupt halt as Aquas marched out of the sea, blocking her way.

She spun around, frantically looking for an escape. Guards approached from all sides, stun clubs held extended and ready.

It was like a nightmare that never changed.

Almost free–always trapped.

THE GUARDS WERE ARMED HEAVILY WITH weapons and tech. The rising Aquas had nets and tridents.

Urban looked down at her stun club. It wasn't made for water. Would she electrocute herself if she used it?

Despite the Aquas, Urban splashed her way deeper into the water.

"Stop where you are, Lee Urban," a voice commanded.

Some of the guards followed her into the salty sea spray, then paused to throw their stun clubs to the shore and draw out knives instead. The guards on shore withdrew stun guns.

"Lee Urban, you are to stop." The voice belonged to a Super aiming a stun gun at her.

Urban raised her stun club and pointed the tip. A guard in the water shouted and several tried to slosh their way back to shore.

"No!" someone yelled.

Urban held fast. "Shoot me, and this weapon will fall into the water and kill us all."

The guards hesitated, but didn't fire. The Aquas in the ocean, however, continued blocking the way, tridents held at the ready.

"I suggest you move." Urban eyed the nearest guard. When he didn't budge, she let the weapon slip through her fingers, but caught it before it hit the water.

The Aqua slowly backed away. The others parted so that she could pass.

Urban was able to continue deeper into the sea, lifting the stun club above her head as the water lapped at her chest.

Out of reach of the last Aqua, the water brushed against her neck.

She took a few more steps before the sandy floor under her dropped sharply away. Urban used one of her hands to propel herself back up onto the shelf while the other held the weapon precariously overhead. Before her stretched endless, sparkling blue ocean.

This is it.

Her breath quickened. Deactivating the weapon, she flung it far away, and then dove down.

Instantly, the Aquas charged.

Underwater, everything was muffled–otherworldly quiet. Guards came toward her, but it all felt like slow motion. Eventually, she noticed the hum of boat motors in the distance.

Urban swam down the sharp drop-off. The water took on a cobalt-blue hue and grew colder the further she swam.

A shadow on the ocean floor caught her eye.

Three Aquas swam above, trailing her, their glowing tridents strapped to their backs as they glided forward with mechanical flippers. Other guards followed, but their heavy scuba tanks and gear slowed them down.

Urban wished she'd thought to grab her own flippers. She swam harder, weaving her way through dead coral and under hanging rock shelves.

Her chest heaved violently with exertion. But at least she could breathe.

Spotting a small, dark cave, Urban swam into it, too exhausted to go on.

She pressed her back against its slimy wall as the Aquas swam into view. They slowed, heads whipping back and forth. One of them turned to the other two, communicating something.

Urban was completely still.

Two of the Aquas swam away, but the other swiveled in a slow circle and stopped when he spotted the cave. He kicked his way toward it.

Urban pushed further back into the darkness.

As the Aqua reached the cave, he pulled out a device. Fluorescent light flooded the space, exposing every porous hole and crack, exposing Urban.

She made a determined break for it, but the Aqua aimed his trident at her. She froze.

The other Aquas returned and a force field of pulsing tridents confronted her.

I was so close.

There was a strange pop, like that of a bomb being detonated underwater.

Inky blackness filled the cave and crept toward her. Then a gurgled noise like a shout through scuba gear filled the space. She tried retreating, but bumped up against the back of the cave.

Dark liquid swirled forward–encasing her.

A STRONG HAND REACHED OUT AND GRASPED Urban. She struggled, but the grip didn't loosen.

As she was dragged out of the cave, the cloud of blackness began to thin, and she caught a glimpse of the Aqua. There was something oddly familiar about the way he swam.

The Aqua stopped under an overhanging cliff, hidden from the surface. He touched down on the base of the ocean floor, released his grip, and faced her.

Wearing a fluorescent underwater suit and a trendy bow tie, the Aqua had a face mask that obscured his identity. He tapped on his tatt, then reached for Urban's arm and inserted a device into her own tatt. A moment later, her retina display flashed a dull blue.

[Rebooting.]

"There we go," a familiar voice murmured.

Urban stared in shock. "Lucas?"

"Astute observations, per usual." Lucas flipped floating hair out of his face. "You owe me. Big time."

"How did you find me?"

"Funny thing, I got an emergency ping from your tracking device. Shortly after which, your location disappeared. But I know all about losing a tracking device. Knew you had to be in the water nearby. And fortunately for you, I happened to be in the neighborhood."

Urban was a swirling mass of confusion and disbelief. "Was that *you* who set off that bomb?"

"No, it was one of your freakish attackers sabotaging themselves." Lucas peeked out from under the alcove. "And it's called an ink bomb. Now that you've decided to reveal your hidden enhancements, I suggest you carry one, too."

"I never hid my enhanc–"

"Save your story for later." Lucas waved her off. He pointed. "How about we worry more about that oversized sea slug swimming toward us instead?"

Urban turned her head upward to where he was pointing. A boat was stopped above them and a Super in scuba gear was swimming toward them. Several other Aquas now jumped off the boat, pulsing tridents pointed and ready.

"And our parents say I'm trouble," Lucas muttered. He threw her a glance. "Alright, stick close."

As the Super and Aquas drew closer, Lucas unstrapped what looked like a miniature harpoon from his smart suit. He trained it on the approaching group of Aquas and the Super.

With a click, it fired and shot through the water. The arrow exploded before hitting the attackers, thick wire netting expanding and trapping them. They tried to claw and punch their way out, but the wires held fast.

Lucas activated a setting via his tatt, and the net dragged the struggling Aquas and Super downward.

"Alright, time to get back to my parties." Several propellers popped out of Lucas's Aqua boots. He grabbed Urban's hand, and with a cloud of bubbles, they shot through the water.

"Don't think this makes us cool," Lucas said.

Urban lifted her voice. "Why did you come?"

Lucas glanced at her. "Just cause I'm mad at you doesn't

mean I'm going to ignore an emergency ping. Those guys looked like they were going to kill you. Which even I'll admit, is slightly uncalled for."

And yet, you tried to drown me when I was little. Sometimes–most times–Lucas totally baffled Urban.

The ocean floor dropped lower as they traveled further from the island. The light blues and corals changed to a dark blue and an empty expanse. The rays of sunlight grew dimmer.

Eventually, an island came into view. At least, Urban thought it was an island. She squinted, trying to comprehend what she was looking at.

Chintzy lights flashed and a distant thumping beat throbbed through the ocean. Dark shapes floated or twerked in odd patterns near the island.

Not an island, but a ship.

Urban suddenly realized the dark shapes were actually Aquas gathered under floating strobe lights, letting loose their best underwater dance moves.

Based on some of the gyrations, Urban had the feeling a lot of the Aquas were inebriated.

"Welcome to my temporary home, the *Pleasure Cruise.*" Lucas gestured grandly at the ship. "Anything and everything you could ever want in one place."

"Studying abroad, huh?" Urban called out over the roar of a pulsing beat. She reached for one of the twinkling fish floating around them like glowing fairies, but it drifted out of reach.

"I *am* abroad and I *am* studying." Lucas stared. "Studying how to live my best life, that is."

"If Mother and Father found out this is what you're doing with their money . . ."

"But how would they? The company is brilliant. Contact with the outside world is restricted. They have fake classes, report cards, even pictures of me in a staged classroom, all to reassure helicopter parents."

Unexpectedly, the longing Urban had felt for so many days, so many weeks, surged within her. *Oh, Lucas, life is about more than just parties and pranks.*

In dismay, she shook her head.

"Meanwhile, I'm learning skills that are actually valuable," Lucas continued, "like how to play sea urchin pong, the most effective way to pick up girls, and where to purchase all the best illegal underwater gear. You can thank the *Pleasure Cruise* for providing the netting and squid ink that saved your sorry rear."

Urban remained silent.

Lucas slowed his propellers as they approached an underwater resting pod connected to the boat. They climbed out of the water and into a small, circular glass lounge. He selected a setting on the wall display, and the view of the ocean around them faded as the glass clouded over.

"Now, down to business."

Urban blinked in surprise.

"I don't want to hear whatever lame reason you have that ended you up in the middle of the ocean. I do, however, want you to keep your identity secret. For both our sakes."

He ordered a drink and then settled into a chair. "First, you need a fake ID. Can't have the most well-known KOL spotted onboard."

Urban looked at him. "But that won't trick the AI. You know it only obscures my identity in the real world, right? The second this party ship's control tower knows I'm onboard, it will be public data."

"Ah, but that's what's so special about this ship." Lucas grinned. "There is no AI facial tracking."

Urban frowned. "But isn't that–"

"Illegal?" Lucas waved her concern away. "In the Federations, yes. In the middle of the Pacific? No. Why do you think these cruises are in such high demand?"

Urban was still trying to get her mind adjusted to everything that had just happened. The old sharp banter seemed surreal, but it came back easily.

"I assumed everyone wanted to play hooky, like you."

Lucas snorted. "Everything done aboard this ship is completely anonymous. No hiding from the *Jingcha*, no sosh infringements–anything is possible."

She eyed him. "Do you get paid commission or something? I feel like I'm listening to an ad right now."

"I wish."

A bot delivered a bamboo tray with coconut drinks and a food platter with an odd device next to it.

Urban bypassed the drink, but had to force herself not to consume all the party delicacies at once. "So, I can just wear a face scrambler and I'm good to go?"

"It's that easy." Lucas took a sip of his drink, then gestured at the device on the tray. "Speaking of which, I ordered you one already."

Urban picked up the finger-sized strip and examined it. She placed it gingerly on her temple and then activated it in QuanNao. She couldn't feel a difference, but a few seconds later, Lucas chuckled.

"That's a good look on you. Definitely one for the dating profiles." He snapped with his retina display and pinged it to her.

Ignoring his comment, Urban opened the file. The image showed her looking up at him in a candid moment, her jaw hanging slightly loose, giving her the IQ of a jellyfish. Worse still was her new scrambled face.

Her skin color was the same, and so were her eyes, but that's where the similarities ended. With the scrambler, she had projected puffy lips with at least a dozen piercings, heavy eye-liner, a giant, rather unfortunate nose, two perfect circles of splotched bright red on her cheeks, and her eyelashes . . . were something else. Giant glowing things that fanned all the way to her forehead like blue butterfly wings. She looked like someone trying way too hard to look good and failing spectacularly.

So typical of her brother. "Real mature, Lucas."

"I'd invite you to dinner, but, well . . . I wouldn't be caught dead with you." He couldn't wipe the smug grin off his face. "The ship's heading back soon. Should get to the Asian Fed in the next two weeks."

Lucas put his drink down and stood.

"Thank you." Urban's words made Lucas pause at the exit. But he didn't turn back or respond beyond a nod. He strode out of the pod, leaving Urban alone in the lounge.

What must it be like to have no greater worry in the world except what to wear to a party? Sometimes, it was hard to believe she and Lucas were raised by the same parents. But Urban had to admit that today, she was thankful for his wild ways. He had saved her when she was completely out of options. Even if he didn't understand what she was tangled in, he'd proved himself a supportive brother. She never would have imagined it. Never.

Uncertain where to go or what to do, Urban turned to QuanNao. Her system was fully rebooted and she had over three thousand missed pings, vid-calls, and updates. Almost breathless, she ordered her system to prioritize them.

There were several dozen from the Dragons, Ash, and Everest. She opened Everest's messages first.

[Everest: Hey checking in with you again. I'm starting to get worried. Ping me when you get a chance.]

Urban scrolled down through several more worried pings, then stopped on a vid.

Everest looked drastically more haggard in this video. "Talked to your family today. They said you've gone missing. I'm not sure when you'll get this message." He swallowed, his eyes intense. "But I'm coming for you. No matter what."

Warmth spread through Urban's chest.

She instantly tried to ping him back, but only received an auto response.

[Unable to send. All outside contact restricted until the next port is reached.]

This was what Lucas meant when he'd said contact with the outside world was limited.

Her heart ached. She wanted contact with Everest, with her family. She continued sorting through her other messages.

She went completely still. A message from Olive. Their conversation before they were attacked by the mob came to her mind. Olive had been trying to tell Urban something.

She opened the message and began reading.

[OLIVE: WANTED TO TELL YOU THE GAMELYON doesn't release for just any player. It's a signal devised by the World Enhancement Organization. Among many traps devised to alert us of the hybrid's existence, the Gamelyon only activates when it senses hybrid DNA present. I'm a member of WEO and it's been searching for you for years. Agents even hacked several tatts of deceased individuals in search of you.]

The network backdoor was Olive, or WEO, who had been one step ahead of them at the tatt temple. Did she not know about Orion, or Dr. Rai, or the underwater research lab? If the World Enhancement Org was the one hacking the tatt temple, they should have found her and Dr. Rai already. Urban's thoughts grew clearer. Orion did say he was part of a rogue group of WEO, so maybe Olive didn't know what he was up to.

[Olive: Dawn also figured out who you were. She hacked your suit, but, using reverse psychology, made herself look like the victim and framed me. She knew I discovered her affiliation with SAS and wanted me out of the picture so she could more easily manipulate Willow and get you into the Games and killed. If my theories are correct, she's working with Vance.]

I knew Dawn was up to something. But what about Coral?

She's a member of WEO too. How does Olive not know about her?

[Olive: The World Enhancement Organization wants to protect and help you. Please let us know if you'd be willing to meet.]

The broader WEO must have no idea what Orion and Coral were involved in.

There were several more pings after Olive's initial message, all worried about Urban's disappearance.

Can I really trust the World Enhancement Org to have my best interests at heart?

Urban sighed as she scrolled through her other messages.

Croix was threatening to cancel her contract if she didn't respond in the next two weeks. That was three weeks ago. Several top news reporters requested interviews. Auntie complained about Urban's dismal lack of communication. And then . . .

. . . a thread with over fifty pings from Mother alone. Urban's heart twisted as she scrolled through them, each more desperate than the last.

"She really does care about you," Lillian had said.

Suddenly, physical and mental exhaustion hit her like a blast. Tears began to fall. *I need to see them again, soon. Fix things with them.*

But right now, she needed sleep. Urban left the lounge and came upon what looked like a luxury hotel. There were soft red carpets, elegant arched stairways, and classic music drifting softly from an Artisan playing a grand piano on a stage. The only difference was, one of the walls was made entirely of nano glass and displayed the ocean, fish, and Aquas outside.

"Excuse me," Urban said to a concierge bot behind a large marble desk. "I'm new to the ship. Where might I find a pod to sleep?"

The bot scanned her face. "Ms. Gasair, Minnie?" it confirmed.

She started. “Um, yes.”

“I have your reservation here. Your room number is 250.” *Lucas really outdid himself–even managed to get me an insulting number.*

The bot scanned her tatt. “You now have access to your room, along with all of our elite member perks. Would you like a tour?”

“No thanks.” Urban turned and followed her retina display to her room.

She went through a dark but busy corridor with strobe lights that made her head throb. Aquas pushed past her on all sides, laughing and swaying. Their faces were framed in glow-in-the-dark paint and their clothing reflected the neon lighting. The contents of their fuchsia drinks slipped over the tops of their glasses and splattered the floors. One of them bumped into Urban and dumped half of a bright red drink all over her.

“Whoops,” the Aqua slurred.

Urban kept walking, wanting to get to her room. She went by a boarding kennel for pets, with rare turtles, an ostrich, flying squirrels, and a variety of Enhanced dogs.

Turning left at the spa, she climbed a set of stairs to the upper deck and passed a water park where the booming beat of a concert reverberated in her bones. Urban squeezed her way through the jumping crowd and emerged in quieter hallways.

Finally, she arrived at room 250.

With a swipe of her tatt, the door clicked open. The room had a small circular window displaying the black night sky outside. A full moon gleamed brightly overhead and reflected on the gentle waves of the ocean. A slim desk, tasteful love seat, and queen-sized bed with pristine white blankets and fluffy pillows filled the room.

It seemed like paradise after what she’d been through.

Despite the comfortable bed, Urban couldn’t sleep. Her mind kept spinning. The need to contact her family kept nagging at her.

With a groan, she sat back up.

Where would Lucas be at this hour?

Urban left her room and checked several of the bars inside the cruise ship with no luck. She pictured him at her graduation party, swimming in their parent's giant fish tank and flirting with the Aqua girls. Something occurred to her and she found her way toward the bottom of the ship.

She hesitated at the entrance to the ocean. The sight of water, mixed with the thought of Lucas, still brought back memories of him trapping her at the bottom of their fish tank.

But now, she reminded herself, she could breathe in the sea.

Still, her body locked up, not wanting to go further. *I'm an Aqua, I should have no fear of water.*

She forced herself to jump in and swim until she was free of the ship entrance.

It was dark and cold. Floating jellyfish illuminated an underwater bar set among a faux coral reef. A bot bartender with octopus-like arms stood behind the counter, mixing drinks using a variety of vacuum-sealed bottles and tubes. A lone patron sat at the bar. By the way he wagged his fingers at the bot, he was several drinks in. *Of course.*

Urban swam over and took a seat next to her brother.

Lucas turned at her approach and then went back to his drink. "I told you I didn't want to be seen with you."

"There's no one to see us here but that bot," Urban pointed out. "You have nothing to fear."

Urban ordered a virgin piña colada, bracing herself for the backlash she'd get from Lucas for her selection.

But her brother said nothing.

"What's up?" Urban asked.

"Can't a person enjoy a drink and some solitude?" Lucas grumbled.

Urban made no comment.

Lucas suddenly faced her. "I can't believe my whole family is a bunch of liars."

Urban's head jerked back.

"You're an Aqua! Why didn't anyone tell me? Why bother pretending to be a Natural?" He pointed at her with an unsteady hand. "That little ploy could have gotten us killed by SAS, you know that?"

Urban swallowed. "No one lied to you. I really was a Natural. But now–"

Lucas scoffed. "You expect me to believe you suddenly can breathe underwater?"

She tried another tactic. "Lucas, why do you think I was trying to escape that island?"

"I have no idea, and I don't care."

Urban was getting exasperated. But she had to know. "Have you been in contact with our parents at all?"

"You think I'm vid requesting Mom and Dad on this pleasure cruise?" Lucas snorted.

Her voice trembled. "Lucas, I was kidnapped. *Kidnapped!*"

Lucas's eyes narrowed. "By whom?"

Urban didn't want to think about that underwater research lab ever again. The betrayal, the pain, the fear, all of it was still so raw. She bit back nausea. "By a group of scientists looking for the hybrid."

Lucas rolled his eyes. "Back to the hybrid fairytales. No one but our parents and a few crazies believe in that."

"Lucas, I *am* the hybrid." Urban rolled up the tattered remains of a sleeve. The bright marks on her forearms from where they had poked and prodded her had faded into a sickly bruised green and purple. "They . . . experimented on me. Apparently, I have the ability to become Enhanced after birth. That's why I have Aqua abilities now."

"The hybrid is real?" Lucas stared at her forearms. All traces of sarcasm vanished.

Urban nodded.

He was silent, then his face hardened. "I don't believe it."

"Lucas, listen. Please, let me tell you everything that–" she began.

Lucas pushed away from his seat. "I don't need to hear more attention-getting blather from you!"

Lucas swam away, leaving Urban at the bar with the bot and a crab to keep her company. She looked after him with a sinking heart. She had thought, for a brief moment, that her brother's dislike of her wouldn't be as intense as it had been. He had saved her in the cave, after all.

She kicked the bar, sending the crab scuttling away.

The long days in the cell came back to her again. Her biggest regret had been pushing her family away. She wasn't going to give up on them now that she had this rare second chance.

A long, low horn blared from the ship, and several lights flashed.

"They will be leaving soon, ma'am." The bot behind the counter gestured at the ship. "You'd better climb aboard."

Soon, I'll be back in the Asian Federation.

The thought brought a wave of anxiety.

Everest's words came back to her: *"Real family fights for each other."*

He was right.

No matter their response, I'm not going to give up.

A TOWEL FOLDED INTO THE SHAPE OF A starfish greeted Urban in her room. She collapsed on her bed alongside it.

When she awoke, the sun was setting.

Urban checked the time and gasped. She had slept for nearly twenty hours.

Her stomach cramped with hunger as she scanned the ship's map for food. There was a live performing area, an underwater karaoke bar, a dog-racing stadium, surf simulator, mini golf, gym, tennis, polo . . . She skimmed over the rest of the amenities until she spotted restaurants.

There was a burger joint, a café specializing in Western cuisine, a beach-themed BBQ grill, and . . . dim sum!

After a quick shower, Urban found, to her delight, that her closet was full of clean clothes. Upon closer inspection, her joy was short-lived. There was a clown suit, a skin-tight cat outfit complete with leopard print, tail, and ears, party dresses way too short to even be pajamas, and more jokes from Lucas.

Urban gritted her teeth. By a process of elimination, she wavered between the clown costume and cat outfit, landing on the leopard print onesie.

Using a razor, she managed to hack off the ridiculous tail.

The ears were attached to the main fabric of the hood, and Urban was afraid she'd damage its smart capabilities if she tried to rip them off. Instead, she left the hood draped on her back, not caring if the ears flopped around.

She reactivated her identity scrambler, grateful she wouldn't be recognized like this. The outfit alone was ridiculous. The piercings and outrageous makeup and exaggerated nose of her identity scrambler only amplified the look.

Shaking her head, she made her way to the dim sum restaurant. Several partygoers hooted at her outfit or made obnoxious meowing noises, but Urban ignored them.

She arrived at a small and cozy restaurant smelling of stir-fry. It reminded her of home.

Home.

A fresh round of emotions crashed over her.

"Table for one?" a bot greeted Urban, shaking her out of her thoughts.

"Yes, please."

The bot led her past a group of people wearing sun shirts and hats, and some Aquas in bedazzled swimsuits. Each table was made of lacquered wood and accompanied by bamboo tea chairs, their firm backs keeping the few patrons around seated upright.

The bot guided Urban to a spot with a view of the ocean. Taking her seat, she glanced at the table next to hers. "Lucas?"

Her brother turned and glared at her. "Quit following me."

"I'll sit here," Urban informed the bot as she moved and plopped down next to Lucas.

He groaned.

"The carts will be around shortly." The bot poured her a glass of jasmine tea and then hovered away.

Urban tried to think of something witty to say, but Lucas spoke first.

"I thought more about your story of being the hybrid, and it actually checks out."

Urban looked at him in surprise.

"Then I double-checked Dad's digital will. I'm still the one inheriting his underwater chain and am on the hook for running it–not you. So now that I don't have to worry about you stealing my empire, we can be on speaking terms again."

"Seriously?" Urban's mouth fell open. "That's what you were worried about?"

Lucas shrugged. "Sunzi says, 'The greatest victory is that which requires no battle.' I take that seriously."

"This is your family you're talking about. Not war."

"Sometimes family is war."

If this last year was any indicator . . .

"Anyhow, I still think you're annoying and find your sense of fashion"–Lucas pursed his lips–"lacking. But I wanted to apologize."

Urban almost fell off her chair. "My Aqua ears must not be working. You want to what?"

"I won't say it again."

A bot came by, pushing a hover cart with three levels of foods from which to select. The top level had fried bamboo shoots and pork, thinly sliced potatoes with peppers, and glazed ribs. On the middle row sat soups and steaming breads. Desserts filled the bottom portion of the tray.

Lucas selected a spicy bell peppers and beef dish, sautéed sour cabbage, scallops with garlic sauce, a hot and sour *doufu* soup, scallion pancakes, and then for dessert, crispy green tea balls, juicy coconut cakes, and fresh tropical fruit.

Urban didn't take anything. She watched her brother. "Lucas, what happened when we were kids?"

Lucas gave her a look.

"Why did we stop getting along?" She really wanted to know.

"Funny," Lucas retorted. He caught her expression. "Wait.

You're serious?"

He sobered. "I guess Mother and Father wouldn't have told you . . ." He eyed Urban a moment, appearing to debate something internally.

When he spoke again, his voice was quiet. "Growing up as an only child was boring. I begged Mom and Dad for a sibling for years. Then you and Lillian came, and I was so happy." He seemed embarrassed at the memory. "But Lillian never played with me. I think she was too jaded from the orphanage or something. But you were different. You were friendly and fun and I finally had a sibling like a friend."

Lucas stared out the large sea-facing windows at the hibiscus-colored rays of sun. The light reflected off of the porcelain plates and bowls on the table.

"We were just kids," Lucas continued. "I didn't know much about enhancements or Naturals. Mom and Dad didn't tell me you were a Natural. They were afraid I would tell the wrong people. I had no idea. All I knew was, every time I played with you, I got in trouble."

"What do you mean?" Urban interjected.

"The time I tried to give you a haircut, punished. When we rode Baozi and broke that expensive vase, yelled at. The time I tried to teach you underwater martial arts, grounded for a year."

"Wait." Urban stopped him. "Say that again."

"I was grounded from QuanNao for an entire year! Like seriously, what parent does that? Despite the fact that you were the one who kicked me in the–"

"No, not that," Urban interrupted him. "What were you trying to do in the tank?"

"Show you some Aqua moves and get you to spar with me." It was Lucas's turn to look confused.

Urban stared at him for a long moment, realization dawning. "You were trying to . . . play with me?"

"What else would I be doing?" Lucas asked, baffled.

"I thought you were trying to drown me."

"Are you insane?"

"Lucas, I couldn't breathe! I thought I was going to drown. Why do you think I was afraid of water for ages?"

"Well, that explains a lot. Like why I was grounded for a whole year. Have I mentioned that I was grounded for an entire year from QuanNao?"

Urban rolled her eyes.

"So, yeah, it seemed every time I played with you, I got punished. Until I finally realized it wasn't worth it. Plus, you got really bitter after the whole underwater expedition. Which, in hindsight, makes sense, now that I know you almost drowned and all." Lucas slurped some soup. "Also, I . . . I was jealous."

"Jealous?" Urban gaped at him. "Of what? My total lack of enhancements?"

"All the attention you got from Mom and Dad."

Urban sat in stunned silence.

"Before you and Lillian joined the family, I had Mom and Dad to myself. Then you both arrived, and, though I wanted a sibling, you both were pretty demanding. You especially needed their help learning to adapt to an Enhanced world. They bought new tech. Hired tutors. Put me in a boarding school so they wouldn't have to worry about me and could devote all their time to you. I went from being an only child to being . . . invisible." He looked away.

It took a moment before Urban could find her voice. "Lucas, I'm sorry. I guess I never thought about what it must have been like for you."

"No one did. Anyway, it doesn't matter now," he said abruptly. "We're grown up and I don't need them."

Urban thought back over memories from her childhood with this missing piece of the puzzle. All her interactions with Lucas now made sense. His extravagant pranks, parties, and tendencies toward trouble; all desperate attempts to get someone's–anyone's–attention.

But no matter what he did, their parents were always focused elsewhere. It had seemed to her they always placated him, but he was more invisible than Urban had felt for most of her life.

They were silent as the food tray came back around. After selecting a few dishes herself this time, Urban spoke. "They love you, Lucas," she said softly. "You know that, right?"

A sense of déjà vu flashed through Urban.

Lillian had said the same thing to her over the holidays. Only, Urban hadn't believed her sister at the time. How odd to be echoing those words now and actually mean them.

Lucas blinked a few times. "Look, tea balls, my favorite." He snatched one up and plopped it in his mouth.

They remained silent for the rest of the meal, but it was a companionable silence. Urban's mind continued replaying the version of events from her childhood, but through Lucas's eyes.

It was nearly dark out when they finished. The table was still covered in half-eaten dishes, but they were stuffed.

"Want to go for a swim?" Lucas asked.

Urban only hesitated a second before answering. "Sure."

Back in the water, Lucas sank to the bottom of the ocean floor and Urban followed.

Lucas was prodding at a sea urchin when a reminder ping flashed in the corner of Urban's retina display. She uttered a cry.

"What?" Lucas asked.

"It's my midterm project," Urban explained. "I'm so behind in all my classes. I just got a reminder that it's due today. I'm definitely going to fail. But," she admitted, "it wasn't something on my mind the last few weeks."

Does it really matter?

She thought of Dr. Yukio. Her mentor was sure to be disappointed in her. She would be expelled from the Artisan Leadership Program just as quickly as she'd entered it. But maybe being kidnapped was a valid excuse? She smiled wanly to herself. It humored her to worry about a class assignment as opposed to being trapped in an evil scientist's lair.

"What's the project?" Lucas asked.

"It's for my Mixed Media Art class. I have to make something that shows new perspectives. And I have to make it out of water." She shook her head. "After everything that's gone on, I'm not sure it even matters now."

Lucas stopped her. "When exactly is it due?"

Urban checked the time. "In two hours."

He pursed his lips. "I think I can help."

"Really?" Urban was both grateful and skeptical. "We don't even have access to the outside world."

"They make exceptions for school updates and reports. I'll be right back," Lucas told her. "In the meantime, collect as many colorful shells and loose debris as you can."

After Lucas swam away, Urban moved across the sea floor, picking up brightly colored shells, dead bits of coral, even a few fish scales. By the time Lucas reappeared, her hands were full.

"Here." Lucas extended a glass tube.

"A large shot glass?"

"Yup. Now, put what you collected in it."

Urban arched an eyebrow, but did as she was told.

Her brother popped a glass orb in.

"Is that an ice cube maker for drinks?"

Lucas grinned. "For someone who doesn't drink, you're 2 and 0."

"I swear, if we're making some sort of weird alcoholic beverage right now–"

Lucas waved her away. He pulled out what looked like a miniature bamboo mat and lined the inside of the shot glass with it. "Tada!" He handed it proudly to her.

Urban took it skeptically. "And how does this help me?"

Lucas grinned. "Hold it up to the light and look through."

Urban peered through the darkened tunnel of the shot glass and up through the bottom of it. The glass ball kept all the sea debris in place, preventing it from falling into her eye. The light filtered through the thin seashells and scales, creating a prism of colors.

"Now twist it," Lucas instructed.

Slowly, Urban spun the glass, eyes still focused on the inside. As the shells floating in the seawater moved with gravity, the multicolored patterns changed.

"It's a kaleidoscope." Urban laughed. "This is awesome!"

Lucas smirked. "You mean, *I'm* awesome." He stayed there a moment more, watching. "Well, I have parties to get to and more fascinating people to meet."

Urban lowered the kaleidoscope. "Thank you, Lucas."

Lucas smiled, and for the first time, it reached to his eyes.

"You've rescued me twice now."

"What is family for?" Lucas's smile turned into a grin. "Couldn't have you stealing the family fortune with a ransom."

Urban found herself grinning back.

"Say, now that you're an Aqua, you going to give up seafood?"

"Not a chance."

Lucas feigned horror. "But fish are friends!"

Urban made a face at him, but inside she felt like she was freed from a long-time burden.

Lucas leaned forward and covered the side of his mouth in an exaggerated whisper. "Pro tip, don't let anyone catch you eating seafood. It's highly offensive among the Aqua community."

"I'll keep that in mind."

"See ya, sis." With an underwater somersault, Lucas swam away.

Urban's heart soared. *Lucas and I were able to work through our differences. Surely, I can make things right with the rest of my family.*

Hope ballooned in her chest.

An ocean current trailed Urban's hair behind her. She lifted a hand and rubbed it against her neck, wondering at the texture of it. Nothing felt like it had changed, and yet, everything had. Her body, once so familiar, was unalterably different.

I'm an Aqua–not a Natural. I finally got my wish to be Enhanced.

But the thought brought her no comfort. Rather, it made her insides roil like the waves above. Her recent elation faded.

I was used. Experimented on. Just like it was when I was a baby. Experiment 203. Named by my so-called father.

She breathed deeply, the tears choking her throat.

But if I can be Enhanced, that means there's hope. The world doesn't have to be divided by Enhanced or Natural. If we can spread my DNA to others, they could choose what they want to be. The divide wouldn't be so sharp.

Urban thought about the Naturals she'd met. The stoop-shouldered and hopeless people at the AI training facilities. They could have a future beyond the confining walls of the factories.

In the distance, the ship cast warm light. A few Aquas swam nearby, their laughter chortling through the water. Suddenly, there were squeals of excitement.

Urban looked where they were pointing. A giant, dark shape moved methodically through the water. A low, sing-song cry floated through the ocean.

A whale.

Urban watched breathlessly as the tremendous creature approached. It kept its distance from the boat, but Urban was so near that it slowly swam directly overhead, casting her in its shadow. Urban stared in awe at its beauty. A magnificent tail and flippers propelled it forward. The sun shone again through the water as the whale passed.

Dr. Yukio's three stages of art and life came back to mind: *"First, it seems unsurmountable, then it becomes challenging, and finally, it is complete."*

She lifted the kaleidoscope to her eyes. Brilliant shades of color danced with every twist of her wrist–a new pattern of beauty forming before her each time.

It's only a matter of perspective. She brought the kaleidoscope down.

Urban swam back toward the ship. *It's time for change.*

But first, she had a project to turn in.

ACKNOWLEDGMENTS

IT TAKES A METROPOLIS TO RAISE A KID–ER, I mean–a book. And *Hybrid* was no exception. So now, a few mentions of gratitude are in order.

First, I want to thank the Flyers. For the readers who soared with me through not just *Enhanced,* but stuck with me in *Hybrid* as well! It means a lot to me and I hope you enjoyed flying to new destinations as much as I did. And if you're craving Chinese food after reading *Hybrid*, well, you're in good company.

Next, thanks to the Givers of this book: KidLitNet for showing me the ropes, my local Austin Mastermind for your support, and my marketing mastermind for encouraging me and allowing me to bounce crazy ideas off of you guys.

Artisans, thank you for your creative help! Caleb for all of our calls where I went round and round over broken parts of the story and you helped me think through them. Thank you, Nova, Hilary, and Ellen, for reading terrible rough drafts and giving me the feedback I needed and the encouragement to keep going. Thank you, Bekah, Rebecca, Katie, Karyne, and Janine, for your feedback on various drafts.

Brynne, you've been Super when it came to all things jiujitsu. Thank you, Kathleen, Harrison, Christian, and Dr. Robinson, for putting on your Inventor hats and helping with all the tech and science. Thanks to all my incredible beta readers! Each of you Enhanced the story of *Hybrid*.

Of course, this book wouldn't be what it is without the fabulous help of the Camos! Enclave and Oasis, no one sees all the work you all do behind the scenes, but you really made *Hybrid* the best story it could be. Thanks, Steve, for believing in this story; Lisa, for your editing magic; Lindsay, for your organizational expertise; Trissina, for teaching me the ropes (and answering countless questions); Avily and Katie, for your edits and making my story shine; and Jamie, for helping me with all the marketing things.

Of course, I owe a huge thank you to the Inceptors! AKA my family who can read me so well and always know how to encourage me along the roller coaster of publishing. A special thank you to my husband for all the times you've taken our baby so that I could get away and write or work on edits. I absolutely wouldn't have been able to write this book in a timely fashion without you, *Baobei!*

And finally, to the ultimate Giver of life and master of stories. Thank you for everything.

ABOUT THE AUTHOR

CANDACE KADE LIKES TO SPEND HER TIME dreaming up stories involving tech, psychology, culture, and/or swords. She's a certified Krav Maga assistant instructor and loves writing action-packed martial art scenes. A third culture kid, she considers Chengdu and Austin to be her homes. When she's not exploring new countries, she enjoys hiking in national parks, moving, teaching her husband Mandarin, and keeping a baby human alive. She can be bribed with boba tea, fluffy puppies, and breakfast tacos.

IF YOU ENJOY

THE HYBRID SERIES

YOU MIGHT LIKE THESE NOVELS: